FINAL SACRIFICE

Suddenly Dion saw his master's intent—but only a split second before Sagan saw it, too. Neither had time to react. Lunging forward, Platus impaled himself upon the bloodsword's flaming blade.

Dion sprang to his feet, his fear riven by the same blade that had pierced his master. A cry in his throat, he reached for the windowsill.

A hand caught hold of him by the back of his neck; a flash of pain shot through his head. . . .

"Listen to me, kid, and listen good!" Tusk shoved Dion's head back into the dirt. "A man just gave up his life for you. Are you gonna make that mean something?"

Dion struggled, but it was a struggle against fate, against the forces of destiny. . . .

Also published by Bantam Books

THE DARKSWORD TRILOGY
by Margaret Weis & Tracy Hickman
Forging the Darksword
Doom of the Darksword
Triumph of the Darksword

Darksword Adventures

ROSE OF THE PROPHET TRILOGY
by Margaret Weis & Tracy Hickman
Will of the Wanderer
Paladin of the Night
The Prophet of Akhran

THE DEATH GATE CYCLE
by Margaret Weis & Tracy Hickman
Dragon Wing

STAR OF THE GUARDIANS

Volume One

THE LOST KING

BY

MARGARET WEIS

BANTAM BOOKS
NEW YORK • TORONTO • LONDON • SYDNEY • AUCKLAND

THE LOST KING

A BANTAM BOOK   0 553 40274 9

First Publication in Great Britain

PRINTING HISTORY
Bantam edition published 1991

Bantam Books are published by Transworld Publishers Ltd.,
61–63 Uxbridge Road, Ealing, London W5 5SA,
in Australia by Transworld Publishers (Australia) Pty. Ltd.,
15–23 Helles Avenue, Moorebank, NSW 2170, and in New
Zealand by Transworld Publishers (N.Z.) Ltd., Cnr. Moselle
and Waipareira Avenues, Henderson, Auckland.

Made and printed in Great Britain by
BPCC Hazell Books
Aylesbury, Bucks, England
Member of BPCC Ltd.

In memory of my agent and friend,
Ray Puechner

You always had faith in Maigrey and in me.
I think you'd be proud of both of us. We miss you.

And as we are to have the best of guardians for our city, must they not be those who have most the character of guardians?

Yes.

And to this end they ought to be wise and efficient, and to have a special care of the State?

True. . . .

Then there must be a selection. Let us note among the guardians those who in their whole life show the greatest eagerness to do what is for the good of their country, and the greatest repugnance to do what is against her interests. . . .

And they will be watched at every age, in order that we may see whether they preserve their resolution, and never, under the influence either of force or enchantment, forget or cast off their sense of duty to the State.

Plato, *The Republic*

And as we are to have the best of guardians for our city, must they not be those who have most the character of guardians?

Yes.

And to this end they ought to be wise and efficient, and to have a special care of the State?

True.

Then there must be a selection. Let us note among the guardians those who in their whole life show the greatest eagerness to do what is for the good of their country, and the greatest repugnance to do what is against her interests.

And they will be watched at every age, in order that we may see whether they preserve their resolution, and never, under the influence either of force or enchantment, forget or cast off their sense of duty to the State.

—Plato, *The Republic*

Introduction

If Fantasy is a romance of our dreams, then Galactic Fantasy is a romance of our future.

It has always seemed to me that the heart of any truly good and memorable story is the romance of its characters and their environment. It's a viewpoint which Margaret and I both share and which has always and continues still to bring us together telling tale after tale. The emotions and perspectives of the story's characters are shared by us as we read. It is their thoughts which concern us; their fulfillment that we long for; and their pain that we share. Galactic Fantasy is about people of the stars—but it is also about people we feel we could know.

Galactic Fantasy is certainly not science-fiction. Sci-fi often deals with the romance of plastic and chrysteel; our love and worship of technology. The Gods of Science, rising from the crucible of the industrial age, sought to bring its own order into romance and, somehow, dehumanized us. Now, in the closing decade of the twentieth century, we find that our century of technology has nearly overwhelmed us with capability, but has done little to increase our wisdom in using it—we are still children with the tools of giants. Inevitably, technology has failed mankind as a god.

I believe that man will reach the stars. When he does, the 'science' of how our spaceship gets from place to place will ultimately be less important than how we, as people, act when we get there. Galactic Fantasy explores how we deal with our own fears, ambitions and passions as we soar among the heavens—not the technicalities of getting there.

Both Margaret and I are patrons of Galactic Fantasy; so much so that each of us is writing our own series in this genre. I've rolled up my sleeves and parked myself in front of my Macintosh to spin my own yarn in the time between books with Margaret. But don't wait for me. Here is a story which is about all of us in another, future time. It's a story which Margaret has wanted to tell for years—I am delighted now that she has the chance to tell it.

Tracy Raye Hickman

THE LOST KING

Book I

Rebel Angel

. . . *his face*
Deep scars of thunder had intrenched, and care
Sat on his faded cheek, but under brows
Of dauntless courage, and considerate pride
Waiting revenge. . . .

John Milton, *Paradise Lost*

Chapter ◆━◑◉◖━◆ One

"I shall be as secret as the grave."
                    Miguel de Cervantes, *Don Quixote*

The man in the white coat watched a bright line of blips scitter across his portable monitor's screen in irregular bursts and pulses.

"Finally!" he muttered, mopping his sweating brow with the starched sleeve of his coat. He glanced around distractedly, having been so intent upon his work that he had forgotten, momentarily, where he was. "You"—he motioned to a guard, faceless in a gleaming, feather-crested helmet, who stood at rigid attention in the doorway—"inform his lordship that the subject is ready."

"Yes, Dr. Giesk."

The centurion turned immediately. He did not run down the glistening corridors of the deserted university building in search of his supreme commander. Running would have been a serious breach of discipline. The soldier certainly marched double-quick time, however, while two of his comrades, left behind standing duty in the doorway, exchanged relieved glances beneath the visors of their crested, Romanesque helmets. The Roman touch was a whim of their lord, a fancy. The uniforms were designed to dazzle, to intimidate, to look well on the vids. Going into battle, they would have worn the standard plastisteel armor. This wasn't battle, however. This was a torturing—formal, ceremonial. And their lord had been growing impatient.

Heavy, measured footsteps could be heard advancing down the corridor. The centurions snapped to attention, their already stiff bodies achieving a state of rigidity normally approached successfully only by rigor mortis. The clenched fists of their right hands thudded against their armor-plated

chests—over their hearts—in salute as a tall man entered the·
room that had been, only a few days before, a chemistry lab.

"Ah, Dr. Giesk. I was beginning to think you might fail me."

The deep baritone voice was emotionless, almost pleasant
and conversational. But Dr. Giesk shuddered. *Failure* was a
word the Warlord never spoke twice to any man. The doctor
could not remove his hands from the controls of his delicate
equipment, but he managed to give the Warlord a beseeching
look.

"The subject proved unusually resistant," Giesk quavered.
"Three days, my lord! I realize he was a Guardian, but none of
the others held out that long. I can't understand—"

"Of course you can't understand."

The Warlord's voice was dispassionate, but Giesk could have
sworn he heard the man sigh. Stepping around overturned
desks, his boots crunching broken glass beakers and tubes, the
Warlord approached a steel table that had been hastily
wheeled into the lab—now deemed "interrogation chamber."
Upon that table lay a human. Small white dots of a plastic-like
substance had been placed upon the man's head and chest.
Thin beams of light ran from the dots to the doctor's machine,
holding their victim in their grasp like the delicate legs of a
spider. The man's naked body twitched and jerked spasmodically. Traces of blood stained his mouth, nose, and chest. No
blood marred the floor or the gleaming steel of the table. The
centurions had made certain all was clean. Their lord demanded things be neat.

The Warlord stared down impassively at the man on the
table. The lord's stern face was visible only from the nose down
beneath his gleaming crested helmet that, like those of his
guards, had been copied from the early Romans. The face
might have been made of the same metal as the helmet, for it
registered no emotion of any type—no elation, no triumph, no
pity. The Warlord laid a gauntleted hand upon the quivering
chest of the man with as little regard as he would have laid that
same hand upon the man's coffin. Yet, when the Warlord
spoke, his voice was soft, tinged with a sadness and, it seemed,
regret.

"Who is there left now who understands, Stavros?"

The gloved fingers touched a jewel the man wore around his
neck. Hanging from a silver chain, the jewel was extraordi-
narily beautiful. Giesk had been eyeing it greedily during the
last three days, and the doctor could not refrain from casting a

jealous glance at the Warlord when he fingered it. Carved into the shape of an eight-pointed star, the gleaming jewel was the only object worn by the naked man, and it had been left around his neck by the Warlord's express command.

"Who knows of the training, the discipline, Stavros? Who remembers?"

Again, Giesk thought he heard the Warlord sigh.

"And you. One of my best."

The man on the table moaned. His head moved feverishly from side to side. The Warlord watched a moment in silence, then bent close to speak softly into the man's ear.

"I saved your life once, Stavros. Do you remember? It was at the Royal Academy. On a dare, you had climbed that ridiculous thirty-foot statue of the king. You were what—nine? I was fifteen and she . . ." the Warlord paused, "she would have been six. Yes, it was soon after she came to the Academy. Only six. All eyes and hair, wild and lonely as a catamount." His voice softened further, almost to a whisper. The man on the table began to shiver uncontrollably.

"Frozen with fear, Stavros, you hung onto the statue's arm. It would not bear my weight, and so it was she who crawled out to you, carrying the rope that would save your life. Can you see her, reaching out her hand to you? Can you see me, holding the ropes, holding the lives of both of you in my hands?"

The man's body convulsed.

"Fascinating," murmured Giesk with professional interest, monitoring his instruments. "I haven't been able to elicit a response that strong in three days."

The Warlord moved his hand up to the man's head, the gauntleted fingers stroking back the graying hair almost caressingly. "Stavros," commanded the Warlord, his helmeted visage bending over the man. "Stavros, can you hear me?"

With what appeared to be a violent effort, the man wrenched his head back and forth. He wasn't, it seemed, negating the fact that he could hear the voice from his past. He was negating the horror.

"That was the night we discovered, she and I, that we were mind-linked. None of you could understand. I could not understand myself, then, and thought bitterly it was a cruel joke played upon me by the Creator, who seemed to have played cruel jokes upon me from my birth."

It occurred to Giesk that he was hearing the story of the

Warlord's childhood. The subject of many rumors among the men under the Warlord's command, his past had become legend. Giesk foresaw nights of numerous rounds of free drinks in the officer's club, all present calling on him to repeat what he was hearing this day in this strange situation.

"The bastard son of a High Priest, a man whose inability to control his passions caused him to break his vow of chastity. I was his penance—a daily reminder to him of his sin. He accepted it, never shirked it, but from that day I was left in his care to the day of his death he never spoke. By the king's command, I was sent to the Academy. You hated me, didn't you, Stavros? Hated me because I was smarter, stronger, better than all the rest of you. You hated me, and feared me, and respected me."

The man on the table made a gasping sound. Giesk, monitoring his instruments, saw the need for haste but hesitated to interrupt the Warlord, who seemed to have forgotten the presence of anyone else in the room except the naked man.

"But as much as you hated me, you loved her. Barbarian child of a barbarian king, she came to the Academy—the first female student ever admitted, and that only because she'd been thrown out of the girl's Academy. Rescuing you, saving your life, Stavros—it was then that she and I discovered that we could speak to each other without words—our minds, our hearts, our souls were one." The Warlord fell silent, perhaps walking the paths of the past.

Were those paths dark and twisted? wondered the doctor. Or did they run straight and true, leading those two children inexorably to their fate?

"My lord," ventured Giesk, "his heartbeat grows increasingly erratic—"

The past slammed down its iron gate of no return.

"Stavros," said the Warlord, "you have held out long against the torture—as you were taught. Our masters would have been proud of you. None of the others were able to withstand half so much, as you must surely know since it was they who betrayed you. But resistance is useless now, my old friend. You have no will of your own. You must do whatever I ask. And I am going to ask you only one question. One question. You will answer. And then I will release you from this torment. Do you understand?"

The man on the table made a slight moaning sound. A froth of blood appeared on his ashen lips.

"Be quick, my lord!" cried Dr. Giesk, "or you will lose him!"

The Warlord brought his face so near to that of his victim that his breath touched the man's skin, displacing the bubbles of blood and saliva on the gaping mouth.

"Where is the boy?"

The man shivered, fighting with himself. But it was useless. The Warlord regarded him intently. The gauntleted hand moved to rest upon the cold white forehead.

"Stavros?"

In a wild, tortured shriek, the man screamed out words that made no sense to Giesk. He glanced at the Warlord uncertainly.

The Warlord slowly rose and straightened. "Well done, Dr. Giesk. You may now terminate."

Giesk closed his eyes a moment in intense relief. His shirt, beneath his lab coat, was wringing wet with sweat.

"Yes, my lord. Thank you, my lord."

Giesk reached out, flipped a switch. The light beams attached to the man's body flared to a brightness that made all in the room avert their eyes. The limbs strapped to the table jerked. The man gave one last, hollow cry. The body stiffened and then, horribly, relaxed. The lights blinked out, and it was all over.

The Warlord had remained to watch the end. He stood beside the body, his hands clasped behind his back beneath the long, flowing red cloak that hung from golden clasps upon his shoulders—clasps carved in the shape of a phoenix. His lips—a thin, dark line beneath the visor of his helm—parted to speak the dead man's eulogy.

"Three days, yet at the end you broke."

Turning on his booted heel, the Warlord nearly collided with Dr. Giesk, who was coming to remove his monitoring instruments from the corpse. Dr. Giesk shrank back, the Warlord swept around him. The centurions sprang to attention. Giesk once more approached the body, his hand outstretched.

Pausing in the doorway, slightly turning his head, the Warlord remarked, "Don't touch it, Giesk."

The doctor snatched back his hand. "But, my lord," he protested, his eyes on the jewel that no longer gleamed, but seemed as devoid of life as the still, cold chest on which it rested, "the gem's value is measured in planets! Surely, you can't mean to—"

"The starjewel is buried with its possessor," said the Warlord. "The curse of God on any who steal it."

A patriotic member of the Republic, Giesk had no fear of the wrath of some mythical eternal being. The doctor did, however, have a healthy fear of the wrath of the Warlord. Giesk began peeling plastic off the corpse's gray skin.

The Warlord, with a smile that was only a deepening of the dark slit of his lips beneath the helm, left the room, detailing a centurion to stay behind.

"You had better hurry, Giesk," the Warlord remarked from the hallway. "We leave within the hour."

The doctor was packing his equipment away with the practiced ease of a man who had done this sort of thing often.

"Five minutes, my lord, not longer," Dr. Giesk promised, slamming lids, locking latches, and coiling power cords most industriously.

There was no reply. The Warlord was already halfway down the corridor. He walked swiftly, as he tended to do when thinking, his pace dictated by the rapidity of his thought. Almost running behind him, his guard of honor was hard-pressed to keep up.

"Prepare the shuttle to lift off, Lieutenant." The Warlord spoke into a communications linkage inside his helmet. "And patch me through to Admiral Aks."

"Yes, my lord," a voice crackled in response, and within seconds another voice sounded in the Warlord's ear.

"Aks, here, my lord."

"We will not rejoin the fleet. Determine the location of a planet known as Syrac Seven and plot a course for it. I want the ship ready to leave within the hour."

"Yes, my lord."

"One thing more."

The Warlord paused reflectively, both in thought and in his strides. Stopping before a window, he glanced down the empty hall where only days before students from this planet's solar system had been hurrying to classes, discussing the problems of the ages in solemn, youthful voices. The university had been closed by the Warlord's command when he had arrived to take Stavros prisoner. The half-million students and other members of the faculty had been ordered to leave.

Where did they go? the Warlord wondered idly, his gaze

flicking over the ancient brick buildings. Six white columns—remnants of a bygone era—gleamed in the system's white-yellow sun. Were the students crowded into one of the small cities on this planet or had they taken this opportunity to return to their homes? Had this been an unexpected holiday or a major annoyance? The Warlord inspected the new, modern buildings with their sleek, windowless design. His gaze went to the smooth, well-kept lawns, the flower beds cultivated in letters that stood for an abbreviation of the university's name.

What was the name? He couldn't remember. Not that it mattered.

I wonder, he thought, resuming his walk just as the centurions behind him had managed to catch their collective breath, if Stavros had been a good professor.

"Admiral Aks," he spoke into the commlink, "I want every object within a one-hundred-kilometer radius of where I am standing destroyed."

"My lord?" The admiral's tone indicated he did not believe he had heard correctly.

"Destroyed," the Warlord repeated slowly and distinctly. "I trust we are not experiencing a communications malfunction, Admiral Aks?"

"N-no, my lord." Aks ventured a protest. "The university is extremely popular, my lord. This will create a most unpleasant incident in the solar system."

"Then it will give our diplomats something to do besides shuttling from one pleasure spa to another. Inform the ruler of this world—"

"Governor, my lord."

"Governor, then! Inform him that no one, not even the so-called intelligentsia, is above the law. These people knew what Stavros was, yet they harbored him. I will show them, as I have shown others, what happens to those who shelter the Guardians. If the governor has any complaints, he may send them to the Congress through the official channels."

"As you command, my lord." The Admiral's voice crackled and went out.

··◄■ ■►··

Dr. Giesk was the last to board the shuttle, arriving in a flurry of white lab coat, clanking instruments, trailing wires, and fluttering necktie. The hatch slammed shut behind him, the airlock sealed. Fancifully designed and painted to resemble a phoenix, the red and gold shuttlecraft tucked its landing gear neatly up into its sleek body and lifted off-planet swiftly, spiraling up into the sky.

Out on the fringes of the solar system, waiting to receive its commander, was the Warlord's flagship. When it had been determined that the shuttle had broken free of the planet's gravitational pull and was safely away, a beam of laser light shot from a lascannon to the surface of the planet below. The bombardment lasted only seconds, then ceased. The Warlord arrived aboard his ship to find the course to Syrac Seven already plotted. The flagship, *Phoenix*, sailed into the chartered paths of hyperspace and vanished from sight.

On the planet below, searing flames reduced to ash the university and the beautiful countryside surrounding it, creating a ghastly, gigantic funeral pyre for one corpse.

Chapter ❖❖❖ Two

Adieu, adieu, adieu! remember me.
William Shakespeare, *Hamlet*, Act I, Scene IV

The dock foreman snarled impatiently when a shadow fell across his clipboard. The shadow was not caused by clouds obscuring the sun—a rare occurrence on the desertlike Syrac Seven. The shadow was caused by a human body coming to stand between the dock foreman and the sun. And thus the foreman snarled. He was a harassed and busy man. If the day had been a year long on Syrac Seven—as it was, by report, on Syrac Nine—he would not have had time enough to get everything done.

Syrac Seven was at the cross-routes of one of the most heavily traveled shipping lanes in the galaxy. Huge space freighters were either in orbit waiting to dock, on land waiting to be loaded, on land waiting to be unloaded, or on land awaiting permission to get off. Their captains, ever conscious that time is money, were invariably furious over delays—real and imagined. Their crews were always undisciplined—what could you expect of merchant seamen?—and picked fights with the foreman's longshoremen, And, as if the foreman needed any more trouble, the Syracusian government sent officials by on a regular basis to throw everything into confusion.

One such personage had been around that morning, accusing the dock foreman of turning a blind eye to the theft of computer parts shipments en route to underdeveloped planets; planets who were trying desperately to take their places in the Republic, and who had been assured that computers were the answer—provided the planet had electricity, of course. The dock foreman recalled with pleasure his conversation with the government official in which he'd described in graphic terms just what the official could do with his computers. And it hadn't involved plugging them in—at least not where one would normally plug one in.

"Now why would anyone on this blasted rock steal computer parts?" the dock foreman bellowed, raising his head to glare at the person whose shadow fell across his clipboard.

"They wouldn't," stated this person, although he appeared considerably astonished at being thus addressed. "There's no market on this planet for stolen computer parts."

The dock foreman regarded the stranger with more interest and less irritation.

"You can see it. I can see it. Why can't the friggin' government see it?" The dock foreman shoved a large finger into the stranger's chest. "Drugs, landcruisers, spacecraft parts—those get stolen so fast that all you'll find left is the smell. But computer parts?" He snorted.

A captain of one of the lumbering, elephantine freighters leaned over a railing and yelled that he was six days behind schedule and what was the dock foreman going to do about it.

The dock foreman yelled back that his men were working as fast as they could, remarking that he (the captain) would wait his turn like everyone else. The dock foreman then added what he (the captain) could do if he didn't feel like waiting.

The captain issue a threat.

The dock foreman made an obscene gesture.

The captain stomped over the metal deck in a rage, and the dock foreman turned back to discover that the shadow remained across his clipboard. Apparently this stranger hadn't dropped by to commiserate about the government.

"You still here?" the dock foreman growled.

"Yes, I am still here," the man said in a mild voice.

"Why?" the dock foreman snapped, eyeing the stranger irritably.

The man might have been considered tall, but he was thin-boned and stooped and his height—which must have been beyond the ordinary—was considerably reduced. Long wispy hair straggled over his shoulders and hung down his back. Probably in his late forties, he was dressed in faded blue jeans and a blue denim work shirt and appeared at first glance to be a down-and-outer looking for work. But those soft, delicate hands had never done manual labor, the dock foreman noted shrewdly. And there was something about the faded blue eyes—set in a pale, careworn face—which suggested that the stranger's quick appraisal of the computer parts theft had not been casual. This man was accustomed to giving serious, respectful consideration to all matters, and the dock foreman appreciated being taken seriously for once.

"Well, what do you want?" he found himself asking grudgingly.

"I am looking for a man I was told worked here," the man said, speaking almost shyly, as if he weren't used to talking to strange people. His voice matched his hands—refined, delicate, with an off-planet accent. "His name is Mendaharin Tusca."

"You're in the wrong place, mister!" The dock foreman laughed. "I ain't got anyone working here with a silly-ass name like Men Da Ha Rin Toosca!"

The stranger seemed to wilt. A flicker of desperation kindled the faded eyes.

"Wait, please do not go! This is quite urgent. Would there be anyone with a name similar to that?"

The dock foreman, who had started to walk away, turned back. "Well, there's a guy works for me calls himself Tusk. That's close, I guess. You can see him. He's right over there. Black-skinned human." He jerked his thumb in the direction of a group of men and aliens who were loading crates onto a skid. "That him?"

"I do not know." The man sounded embarrassed. "It might be him. You see, I've never met him before. Could I talk to, uh . . . Tusk . . . for just a few moments? The matter is serious, or I would not take him away from his work."

The dock foreman scowled, then sighed and shook his head, wondering why he was even wasting his time with this bum, much less calling off one of his men to come chat with him. The stranger stood looking at him apologetically, implying he understood and appreciated the dock foreman's problems and would do his best not to add to them.

"Hey, Tusk!" The foreman's breath exploded in a rumbling roar that bounced over the noise of the forklifts and cranes and the wind that swept across the flat surface of the docks.

The black-skinned human straightened up from cinching a rope around a crate. Staring across the sun-baked cement, his eyes squinting in the bright light, he looked to see who was calling.

The dock foreman made a motion with his arm.

The man called Tusk gave the alien standing next to him a pat on its bony back, then pointed at the foreman. The alien nodded one of its heads, and Tusk sauntered toward the stranger with lazy, easy strides. He was dressed in the working clothes of the dock which—in the heat of Syrac Seven—was practically nothing, and his ebony skin glistened with sweat in the bright sunlight. About average height for a human, Tusk was muscular and well built. His short hair was tightly curled and, when he turned his head, a glint of silver caught the light, sparkling from his left earlobe.

As the young man approached them, the dock foreman glanced curiously at the stranger. Tusk was a rough-looking character—one who easily held his own in the occasional brawls that broke out among the dock workers and the sailors. The ordinary citizenry of Syrac Seven generally crossed over and walked on the other side of the street to avoid the likes of Tusk, and the dock foreman wondered if this gentle stranger wouldn't suddenly remember that he had an appointment elsewhere.

The dock foreman was surprised. The stranger's face underwent a subtle change, but it did not register fear or nervousness. It reflected only the quiet sorrow of the faded blue eyes.

"Yeah?" Tusk slouched, hands on his hips, in front of the foreman.

"Visitor." The foreman jerked his head.

Tusk glared at the stranger.

"You're not from the collection agency, are you? Look, man, you guys can't hassle me at my place of employment! That's the law—"

"N-no," the stranger stammered, obviously taken aback. "I am not from a . . . um . . . collection agency." The blue eyes went from Tusk to the foreman and back to Tusk again. "Is there someplace private where we can talk?"

The foreman waved his hand at a nearby empty warehouse.

Why am I being such a nice guy? he wondered. I've been standing in the sun too long. It's affecting my brain.

He watched as the two walked away, heading for the warehouse, and tried for the life of him to figure out what was going on. The sadness on the stranger's face, the flicker of desperation in his eyes, fell across the foreman's thoughts like the shadow that had fallen across his clipboard. The foreman didn't sympathize with others; his own problems were a full-time occupation. But it occurred to him that life was really tough sometimes.

A bellow from the catwalk above broke into the foreman's

musing. Looking up, he saw that the ship's captain had returned.

"Ah, blow it out your porthole," the dock foreman muttered dispiritedly. Casting a final glance at Tusk and the stranger, he turned and walked away.

··◁■ ■▷··

Trudging along beside the stranger, studying him suspiciously, Tusk saw the sadness, but not the desperation. Not yet. The man walked with his eyes averted, his head bowed. The long blond hair was blown back from his face by the wind and it was easy to see from his expression that whatever the strange's thoughts were, they weren't happy.

And whatever this has to do with me can't be good, Tusk concluded, feeling his stomach muscles tense and a tiny shiver prickle the back of his neck.

The two men entered the warehouse. Cool shadows washed over them; the noise of the dock was swallowed by the silence of the huge, empty building. Grimly, Tusk turned to confront the stranger.

"We're here. So talk."

The man did not reply, but gazed intently into the shadows, his head cocked as though he were listening.

"If you're looking for rats, you've come to the right place," Tusk said. "That's all you'll find here."

To Tusk's surprise, the stranger smiled wanly. "I am not looking for rats." He unsnapped the collar of his blue work shirt.

Sunlight streamed through an open doorway. Beckoning Tusk to step into the shadows, his blue eyes on the door, the stranger drew forth an object that hung from his neck on a silver chain and had been hidden by the shirt. No light touched it, yet the jewel—carved in the shape of an eight-pointed star—burned with a radiance that might have come from the flames of a thousand suns.

Tusk stared at it, his hand moving reflexively to touch the small silver object he wore in his earlobe. It, too, was an eight-pointed star. Sighing, he shook his head.

"Damn!"

"You recognize it?"

"Hell, yes, I recognize it. What do you want?"

"Pardon me." The man's voice was gentle but earnest. "I

must know for certain. What is your real name? From where do you come?"

"Mendaharin Tusca. I'm from the planet Zanzi where my late father was a member of the Senate. Highly respected, my father. Unlike his son. He was once a Guardian, whereas I'm a—"

"Hush!" The stranger grasped Tusk's swarthy arm with a strength the young man found impressive. "That word should not be spoken!"

Glaring at the stranger, Tusk jerked free of his grip. "What? Guardian? Why? Because it tends to lead to nasty consequences?"

The man lowered his eyes. "I heard about your father. I am sorry."

"Yeah, well, he asked for it." Tusk glanced out to where the dock foreman was involved in a heated altercation with a ship's captain. "Look, man. I need this job. Don't get me fired. What do you want? Make it quick!"

The man smiled again at this. "You won't be needing this job, Mendaharin Tusca. My name is Platus. Platus Morianna. How much did your father tell you?"

Tusk frowned. Like the dock foreman, he found himself drawn by this man into doing things he wasn't accustomed to doing. Things like talking about his father . . . or even thinking about him.

"Not much. He was in pretty bad shape at the end."

"I understand," Platus said with a sigh.

"Do you? Well, I wish you'd explain it to me!" Tusk rounded on the man and had the satisfaction of seeing him fall back a pace. "By the time I reached home, the Warlord's men had already taken him away. They brought him back a day later—or what was left of him. Name of the Creator!" Tusk swore, his fist clenched. "I wish I'd been there when they came for him!"

"Be thankful you weren't! There was nothing you could have done."

"At least I'd have given them a fight. I had to sit . . . sit there and watch him die!" Angrily, Tusk turned his head from the stranger's sympathetic gaze.

"I know, and I am truly sorry." Platus reached out a hesitant hand that Tusk ignored. "I realize this is painful, but I must know what your father said to you about— That is, I received a message from him—"

"I followed his death promise, if that's what you mean."

"And that was?"

"To use this planet as my base. Check in, every few weeks no matter where I was, to see if there were any messages. Messages! Who from? Who to? What about? I never knew. And for the last five years I've either lived on this hell-blasted planet or, when my line of work took me off it, I've left word how I could be reached. Which hasn't been exactly safe, since I'm a wanted man."

"Yes. I know." Again the wan smile. "I've known, these last five years. You see, I am the one from whom you've been waiting to hear. But now, Tusk, you must vanish. Disappear completely. Obliterate all trace of your ever having been here before you leave."

"Leave? Look, man. I haven't said I was going anywhere!" Tusk pointed out, crossing his arms across his chest.

"No, you haven't." Platus ran a fine-boned hand through his long hair. "I apologize. My mind— I cannot think. I cannot function. Bear with me, Tusca, please."

The blue eyes fixed on Tusk with a pleading look, and the young man saw the desperation. He turned, seemed about to walk off; exasperated, he turned back. Platus reached out his hand. Tusk inched away. "Go on," he said.

"For your protection as well as mine, I cannot tell you why you are doing what I am going to ask you to do. I can only ask you to do it. If you agree, it will fulfill the death promise. You need never come back to this planet again. In fact, it would be better if you did not."

Tusk waited without speaking, his face impassive.

Drawing a deep breath, Platus continued. "I need you to take a young man, my ward, off this planet. Immediately. You must leave tonight, if possible."

"It isn't. I damaged my spaceplane landing on Rinos in the middle of a civil war. I'm not working out here on the dock for the exercise. I need money for parts—"

"That can be supplied!" The desperation was creeping from the eyes into the refined voice. "If you have the parts, how long?"

"A few hours, I guess." Tusk shrugged, squinting out at Syrac's sun. "Working all night, I could leave by morning."

Platus was silent, his face drawn and pale. Tusk kept his expression hard, although he couldn't help but feel sorry for this guy, who was obviously in deep trouble.

Trouble that's being passed right along to me, Tusk realized gloomily.

"I guess that will have to do. But I will bring the boy to you tonight. He will be safer with you than with me."

"Uh-huh. Danger just follows you guys around, doesn't it? A fact I pointed out to my father when he tried to hang that jewel around my neck."

"But you are a mercenary, or so I understand," Platus remarked, the slight smile returning at the young man's vehemence. "You seek out danger—"

"And get paid for it! Well paid. Look, Platos, or whatever your name is, let's get one thing straight." Tusk jabbed a finger warningly. "I'm doing this for one reason only—to get rid of a ghost that's been hounding me. You see, I was a disappointment to my father. Why? I joined the Galactic Democratic Republic's Naval Air Corps. The old man blew up. Accused me of siding with the enemy. As if there was an enemy anymore! Or there wouldn't be if guys like him didn't keep waving around a bloodstained crown. The revolution was seventeen years ago! It's all over now. Or it should be.

"Like I said"—Tusk drew an angry breath—"the old man couldn't forgive me for that. And then they murdered him. Then *I* murdered him, I guess. No, wait a minute"—this as Platus attempted to interrupt—"I don't want to go into it. Let's just say that I'm not doing this for your precious jewel or the Guardians or your dead king or any of the rest of that romantic crap. I'm doing this because maybe it'll square me with him. You understand?"

"Yes," Platus answered.

"Yeah, well. Just so you don't expect too much from me. There's a bar in town called the Screamin' Meemie. We'll meet there—"

"No!" Platus shook his head. "Too open. Too many people."

Tusk could have cheerfully throttled this bastard. He shoved his itching hands into the pockets of his khaki shorts. "Well, how about here? The docks'll be empty. The night man stays down near the ships. No one comes after hours."

Platus cast a considering look around the warehouse. "Very well."

"Good. Now where am I supposed to take this kid?"

The man's blue eyes widened. A slow flush spread over his pale face. "I . . . really do not . . . know." Platus sounded helpless. "I never thought— You see, I did not expect things to take such a drastic turn this suddenly. I thought at least I would have time to—to make arrangements. But I haven't. I was caught unprepared." He ran his hand through his hair again, combing it back with trembling fingers. "Why did they give this to me? Of all of them, I was most unsuitable!"

Tusk sat down on a crate, staring at Platus in blank astonishment.

"Man! No wonder there was a revolution. You're just like my father. Idealistic. Impractical. I'm a fighter! What the devil am I supposed to do with a kid?"

Platus sighed. "I do not know." He twisted his thin hands in distraction. "I do not know."

"Hell! I'll think about it. Wait here. I gotta go take care of business."

Figuring he might do something he'd be sorry for—like slug this fool in the mouth—Tusk loped off in search of the dock foreman.

Alone, Platus stood in the shadows of the warehouse, watching the sun sink lower in the sky. He felt time creeping up on him, its hands reaching for his neck.

"The young man is right," Platus murmured. "We were idealistic, impractical. Some of us, at least. I was, I know. I wanted only to be left alone with my music, my books. Why couldn't they understand? I wasn't a warrior. I wasn't like my father. Maigrey took after him. She was most suited for this responsibility. But that was impossible. At the end, I was the only one left.

"I could send the boy to her." Platus began gnawing on the knuckles of one hand. "I know she is still alive. But if I know that, then so does he! So I cannot send the boy to her!" Platus clutched his head. His thoughts were running in circles, like a mouse on a wheel. "She was the one who told me to do this. And then she left me! Left me alone to bear the burden!" He sighed wearily and wiped chill sweat from his forehead. "She fled to protect us. She could have put us all in deadly peril. Yet the peril has come anyway, and now who is left?"

Platus called the roll of that famed elite corps. Maigrey—vanished. Danha Tusca—dead. Anatole Stavros—dead.

Derek Sagan—

Softly, unconsciously, Platus began to sing in a tenor that was thin and reedy yet perfectly in tune. "*Libra me, Domine, de morte aeterna in die illa tremenda—*' Deliver me, O Lord, from everlasting death on that dread day." Abruptly, he cut himself off. "That music's in my head! I mustn't keep singing it aloud, though. Dion will recognize it, suspect—"

"Hey, man, I could hear you clear outside! Jeez, what a weird song." It was Tusk. "Gave me the creeps, echoing around in here like that. What was it, anyway?"

"A requiem. A mass for the dead."

"Jeez, you're a creepy guy!" Tusk felt a shiver crawl over him and hurried on to business. The sooner he was rid of this character, the better. "Listen, I had an idea. How old is the kid?"

"Seventeen."

"Hot damn! What about a military school? I got a friend who runs one. He owes me a favor. I could get the kid in easy."

"A military school," Platus repeated, swallowing hard. "What irony! What bitter irony—"

"Look—" Tusk's dark eyes narrowed.

"I know!" Platus wiped his hand across his mouth. "Time grows short." The blue eyes looked intently into the young man's face. "Very well. I trust you, Mendaharin Tusca."

"Trust *me*? I'm a deserter! A thief—"

"Why did you leave the service?" Platus interrupted.

"Let's say I didn't like what it paid."

"Didn't like what it paid, or didn't like what you had to do to earn that pay? You have a great deal of your father in you, Tusca. More than you will admit. Danha Tusca was a man of honor and courage and—what is more important—compassion. I turn the boy over to you. The boy . . . and much more, perhaps," Platus added, but only to himself.

"Yeah? Whatever." Tusk was obviously anxious to end the conversation. "I'll meet you here—"

"Remember—tell no one of your plans. Let as few see you or know what you are doing as possible. We will be waiting. Tonight. 1800." Pulling an old leather pouch out of a torn pocket of his blue jeans, Platus handed it to the mercenary. "Here. That should take care of everything, I believe."

Tusk took the pouch, hefted it, heard the chink of coin, and stood balancing it in his hand irresolutely as Platus began to walk rapidly for the warehouse door.

"Say, wait a minute," Tusk called out. "My father said that if you guys ever did need me, things would be pretty bad. Desperate, in fact. I got a feeling that describes the situation?"

Platus stopped and glanced around. "It does."

Tusk sauntered up to him. "One question."

"I do not promise to answer."

"Who's after the kid? I mean, it's obvious. You're getting him off Syrac Seven 'cause he's hot. And it might help if I knew who it is we're running from."

"Yes, it would." Platus smiled his sad smile. "I planned to tell you tonight. A Warlord wants the boy."

"A Warlord! You guys don't make small enemies. I figured as much, though. It's all tied in with my father somehow, isn't it?"

Platus did not reply.

Tusk tried again. "All the Warlords, or one in particular?"

"There is one who is most dangerous. You know who he is, I do not think I need speak his name. But avoid them all."

"Okay. Now. Why do the Warlords want the kid? What could a seventeen-year-old—"

Platus's face went ashen. "Ask no more! For your own protection! Just . . . take the boy where you will and leave him! I wish I could believe Someone will be watching over him, but my faith died long ago. Now I must go and prepare him for his journey. Good-bye, Mendaharin Tusca."

Platus fled, almost running.

"Hey, you!" Tusk yelled angrily after the man. "Quit calling me by that name!"

◦◦═▶◦◦

Standing in the shadows of the warehouse long after Platus had gone, Tusk stared after him, pondering everything he'd said—and what he hadn't. All the Warlords chasing one pimply-faced kid. Which meant, of course, that Congress wanted the teenager. Which meant—what? Nothing that made sense to Tusk. Scowling, the mercenary's hand went to the silver ornament in his earlobe, the ornament that matched the shape of the jewel Platus wore around his neck.

Swearing bitterly, Tusk kicked an empty wooden crate with such force that it split apart.

"You're still here, ain't you, Danha Tusca?" he shouted into the empty, echoing darkness. "Dead and buried, you're still reaching out, still trying to run my goddam life!"

Chapter ·✦✦✦· Three

Tears were for Hekabe, friend, and for Ilion's women,
Spun into the dark Web on the day of their birth,
But for you our hopes were great . . .

Plato

Twilight came to the docks earlier than to the rest of the town. The huge freighters swallowed up the sun, casting their shadows over the dockyards. The afterglow of sunset lit the sky, the docks became intense patches of extremely bright light alternated by pools of sharp-edged darkness. Every few hundred meters, a security lamp shed its harsh white radiance over the ugly gunmetal-gray paint of the ships' hulls; some of the more recent arrivals were still splotched black with the so-called space barnacles that would take work crews days to remove. Outside the circle of light, the shadows were thicker by contrast.

The dock crews had gone home for the day, the sailors—those who had shore leave—were in the bars, and the docks were relatively quiet. The footsteps of the watchman making his rounds rapped against the cement, his voice occasionally called out a greeting or a question to one of the guards on board the freighters. The wind that shrieked incessantly on Syrac Seven during the day was nothing but a teasing breeze by night. Faint sounds of raucous laughter drifted from the bars along the wharf. Those unfortunates burdened with guard duty glanced longingly in that direction and muttered beneath their breaths.

"I hope that Platus fellow didn't get himself lost!" Tusk looked impatiently, for the sixth time, at the glowing digits of his watch. Dressed in a dark fatigue suit, the mercenary was little more than a shadow himself in the early night. He had taken up a position just inside the warehouse door, being careful to keep out of a circle of light cast by a lamp above the entrance. Every now and then he poked his head around the huge corrugated iron wall, keeping vigil, being certain of seeing before he was seen.

The watchman rarely came this direction. He was more concerned about the freighters and the goods that stood on the docks than an empty warehouse. Still, he might take it into his head to glance this way, and Tusk was worried about the middle-aged tenor and the kid. The mercenary supposed they'd have sense enough to keep to the shadows, but the more he thought about the refined voice, the desperate eyes, the trembling fingers— Tusk shook his head, gritted his teeth, and made ready to leap out and grab them at first sight.

Tusk leapt all right, but it wasn't out. It was up. A touch on his shoulder nearly sent him straight into the rafters of the warehouse. His lasgun was in his hand in a split second, his body twisting, elbow ready, to debilitate his assailant with a blow to the gut. A deft block countered his elbow jab, and a firm hand closed over his, relieving him of his weapon.

"It is Platus," said a voice as Tusk's body tensed and he prepared to fight for his life. "Forgive me. It was not that I did not trust you, but I had to make certain you were not followed. Here is your weapon."

Tusk's heart slid from his throat back down to his chest. His breathing began to return to near normal. Snatching back his lasgun, he jammed the weapon in its holster. He was shaking all over.

Platus's hand patted his shoulder "Excellent reflex time. I almost could not disarm you. Of course, it has been a long while since I—"

"Where's the kid?" Tusk growled. He wasn't in the mood for a discussion of his reflex time.

"Dion. Come forward. I want you to meet Mendaharin Tusca. He will be taking you on . . . on your journey."

A young man, barely visible in the shadows, stepped into a circle of light that streamed from a lamp outside the warehouse door. The harsh light illuminated the boy's face and body with an eerie, otherworldly glow that seemed, by a trick of the eye, to come from some enchanted source within him rather than from any mundane source without. Expecting a typical teenager—gangly, awkward, maybe a little sullen—Tusk experienced a shock almost as great as when Platus touched him from the darkness.

The boy was tall and walked with head held high, his well-muscled body moved with an athlete's grace. His skin was fair, his eyes were a deep, clear blue. Red-golden hair—blazing like Syrac's sun—sprang from a peak on the boy's forehead, and fell to his shoulders, framing the finely chiseled face in a wild, glistening mane.

The boy's gaze met Tusk's with unwavering steadiness. Tusk noted the strong chin, the proud stance, the slightly parted lips. If the kid was frightened by this strange and sudden journey into the night, he was keeping that fear to himself. Tusk let out his breath in an unheard whistle.

He'd been scoffing at this whole business. After all, what possible interest could the Congress have in a scrawny seventeen-year-old kid? This Platus was paranoid, jumping at shadows. Now, after seeing this boy, Tusk was beginning to revise his opinion. There was something unusual about this young man; something fascinating and compelling, something dangerous. It was the eyes, he decided. They were too thoughtful, too grave, too knowing for seventeen.

Who the devil was this kid? He didn't belong to Platus, that was certain.

"I've lived as long as I have because I've followed my gut feelings," Tusk said to himself. "And now I've got a gut feeling I should bid everyone good night, sweet dreams, and get the hell out of here."

But just as he was starting to speak those words, Platus moved to stand beside the boy. The light beamed off the glittering jewel he wore around his neck and, for a brief instant, it shone like a small star in the darkness of the warehouse. Tusk's hand moved to tug at his earlobe, then stopped halfway. Growling, he glanced about in the darkness.

"All right, Father, back off!"

"What?" Platus glanced about in alarm. "To whom are you talking?"

"The kid. I said, 'Better keep out of the light.'"

Catching hold of the boy's sleeve, Tusk pulled him into the shadows. He could feel the boy's body tense like a cat's, coiled, ready to spring.

"So, Dion," Tusk continued, feeling jittery. "You got a last name?"

It seemed a natural enough question, but the boy went stiff and rigid as if he'd been stabbed. Dion turned to confront

Platus. The blue eyes caught the light, glittered cold and clear as the starjewel. Platus shook his head. The expression on his face was faintly apologetic, faintly stern, wholly uncomfortable. Dion smiled a thin, bitter smile and turned his back on them, folding his arms across his chest.

What the hell was that all about? Tusk wondered irritably, liking this less and less.

"Right, skip it. Most places I go, I don't use a last name either. Everyone calls me Tusk." He held out his hand.

The boy turned, his face a struggle, seeking self-control. He achieved it, after a moment; his handshake was strong and firm. Tusk saw a brief, strained smile and a flicker of warmth in the eyes—gratitude, he knew, for not asking any more questions.

After the introduction, the three stood staring at one another in the dark shadows of the warehouse.

Tusk fidgeted. It was an awkward moment. Should he leave the two alone for a last good-bye, or would it be easier on everyone to just get the kid out of here? He had a decided preference for the latter. He'd left XJ in charge of the repairs while he came to pick up the kid and, though Tusk knew the computer could do a better job than he could of rewiring the complex electrical circuitry that had been damaged in the battle on Rinos, he still felt better keeping an eye on things.

The silence was deafening. Tusk could hear it roar in his ears, and he started to say something that would probably be wrong but would at least get everyone moving when Platus stepped up to Dion. Reaching out, the man laid his hands on the boy's shoulders, holding him at arm's length.

"You have given me so much. And I have given you so very little in return. I cannot even give you a name, and you may never understand why. But, oh, Dion, I have loved you!" Platus drew the boy near.

Dion's lips tightened, his blue eyes flashed, and he seemed about to break free of the man's hold. Suddenly the boy crumbled. His head sank down, his shoulders slumped. Platus gathered Dion into his arms, embracing him tightly. The young man threw his arms around Platus and buried his face in the man's shoulder with a sob.

Tusk, watching, turned away. It wasn't the sight of the boy's tears that brought the sudden, bitter taste to his mouth. It was the sight of Platus's face—a pale mask in the reflected light.

On that face, Tusk saw death.

The mercenary had seen that look before. He had known those who had a premonition or whatever it was that they were going to die. And they'd gone into battle . . . and they'd died.

Tusk felt an urgent need to get off this planet. He touched the boy on the shoulder.

"Uh, kid. We better get moving. I still got a lot of work to do on the plane before morning."

"Yes. He's right, Dion. You must go."

Platus ran his hand lovingly through the boy's mane of red-gold hair, then pushed Dion away from him. Leaning down, he picked up a large duffel bag and silently handed it to the young man. Tusk walked over to the warehouse door, pretending to check around outside. In reality he was giving the kid time to wipe his eyes, blow his nose, and pull himself together.

"Here are your clothes, some books—your favorites, plus a few you will need to continue your studies. I've included several lesson plans so that you can keep on as if I were—" Platus's voice sank, nearly failing him. "Your syntharp and your music is in there as well," he added with a tremendous effort of will.

"I'll continue my work. And I'll let you know where I am, how I'm doing." Dion must have seen the look on Platus's face, too, though probably he didn't understand it. "You'll be all right?" the boy continued, speaking firmly, as if his words could make it so. "You'll let me know when I can come home?"

"Yes."

Tusk heard the lie in the older man's tone, he heard the love, the anguish. Turning from the doorway, the mercenary walked over and took hold of Dion's arm.

"C'mon, kid. Back to the plane. We got a lot to do before sunrise."

··◁■ ■▷··

"So this is the passenger," a synthesized voice commented tinnily as Tusk and Dion lowered themselves through the hatch into Tusk's spaceplane. Ignoring the ladder, Tusk dropped lightly onto the deck below. Dion was forced to climb slowly and awkwardly down the narrow steel rungs.

"C'mon, for'ard," Tusk said, motioning. "I'll show you where to stow your gear. Watch out," he cautioned, pointing to a maze of tubing and steel beams and gauges overhead. "Low clearance."

Crouching, trying to get a close look at the complicated instruments he'd read about only in his books, Dion took a step forward and stumbled headlong over a toolbox.

"Sorry," Tusk muttered, moving hurriedly to pick it up.

He juggled the box uncertainly for a moment, glancing around for a place to stash it. Every square centimeter already had something in it or on it. Long coils of electrical wire lurked like snakes in the corners. A pile of clean clothes had been dumped in the center of the small circular chamber that was the spaceplane's living area. Tusk shrugged and set the box back down where it had been before. Dion stepped over it, this time watching carefully where he put his feet.

Pulp mags, their lurid covers spread out like the wings of exotic birds, roosted everywhere—on the deck, piled in a hammock, their pages fluttering in the soft whoosh of cool air blowing from the vents.

Following Dion's gaze, Tusk picked up a mag whose cover portrayed in graphic detail an alien love ritual and flipped through it. "Interesting articles in this issue," the mercenary said, grinning, "on sociology. You interested in sociology?" he asked, holding the mag out to the kid. "You could take a look at it while I work."

Dion made no move to touch it, but stood regarding Tusk with cool, unblinking blue eyes.

"Guess not," Tusk muttered, tossing the mag back onto the deck. "Uh, I'll try to make you as comfortable as possible." The mercenary was starting to grow warm about the ears and neck. "These fighters"—he gestured around him—"weren't really meant to be lived in, at least not for more than a few weeks at a time. Know anything about spaceplanes?"

The boy didn't answer.

Tusk drew a deep breath. "This is what's known as a long-range fighter. It's called a Scimitar—that's from the way the bow's shaped, like the blade of one of those fancy swords the guys in baggy pants were always using back in the old days. This type of fighter's generally based off a mothership, but they carry enough fuel to survive on their own for up to a month if they have to. Not like short-range fighters, which are faster, but have to refuel oftener. The Navy uses these for convoy detail and scouting, mostly. Guarding the uranium shipments, that sort of thing."

As Tusk talked, he began quickly and efficiently stringing up another hammock next to his. "The Scimitar normally carries a two-man crew."

Glancing at Dion, Tusk had the uneasy feeling that he was not being heard so much as absorbed. "Uh . . . what was I— Oh, yeah. Two-man crew. Pilot and gunner. Gunner sits up top in the bubble during a fight." Tusk gestured with his thumb. "XJ and I generally prefer to handle this bird ourselves. XJ figured out how to reroute the gun controls through its systems if we need to. But the guns can still operate independently. Better that way, in fact. Leaves the computer free to take care of emergencies. Sometimes I hire on a gunner. Maybe I'll teach you, kid."

Tusk was babbling and he knew it. He turned away from the scrutiny of those eyes. The kid gave him the willies!

"Stow your gear under there." The mercenary pointed to a row of metal storage units covered with cushions, apparently serving double duty as a couch. "There's the galley, the head, a shower." Tusk began stuffing the mags, one by one, into the trash liquidator. "There's a vid machine in the cockpit and—"

"Me," said the voice they had heard when they had come on board. "I'm also located in the cockpit, and I expect to be introduced!"

"Give the kid a break, will you?" Tusk glared down another ladder that led below the deck on which they were standing. "We had a long walk from the warehouse. Go ahead and unpack, kid. Underneath where you're sitting is—"

"I don't have to put up with this," the voice snapped.

Everything went dark.

"Damn!" Tusk stood up and cracked his head smartly on an overhead pipe. It was dark as hyperspace and so quiet he could hear the boy breathing. Too quiet. "Turn the air back on!"

"Not until I get some respect," the voice answered. "And that's sealed shut, too," it added smugly as Tusk made a move toward the hatch.

"All right! We're coming for'ard. But not until you turn on the lights, you son of a—"

The lights flared, nearly blinding them. Life-support began its comforting, purring hum. Heaving a long-suffering sigh, Tusk motioned Dion to follow him—warning the boy about the same overhead pipe—and slid expertly down another, shorter ladder. Dion came after him, descending one rung at a time, unable to slither down it like Tusk.

The boy looked around for the source of the voice, but the cockpit was empty except for a fascinating array of dials, controls, and flashing lights.

"Dion, XJ-27," Tusk said, pointing to what looked like a large blue box perched on the side of a control panel. The box's blinking lights, buttons, and audio grid gave it the facial expression of a startled monkey. "XJ-27, meet Dion."

"Kid got a last name?" the computer asked.

Tusk glanced sharply at Dion, saw the blood drain from the boy's face.

"No. And leave it at that, okay?"

"Hah!, I will not! What if the kid croaks and we have to notify next of kin?"

Tusk sucked in his breath.

"Sit down, kid," the computer ordered hastily, before Tusk could explode. "Punch in your vital stats for my records. Follow the instructions on the screen. I won't be here. I got work to do. I don't suppose you know, offhand, how many respirations you take per minute?"

"I don't. I'm sorry."

They were the first words Dion had spoken since he and Tusk had left the warehouse. The boy stood behind a chair, staring at the computer.

"That figures!" XJ's lights flashed irritably. "How'm I supposed to reprogram life-support if you stupid humans don't know—"

"Uh, I'm going to go finish that welding, XJ," Tusk said, climbing back up the ladder. "Fix yourself whatever you want to eat, kid, if you're hungry. If you're sleepy, lie down, take a nap. Watch a vid, read a mag—"

Dion heard the man continuing to talk his way up the ladder, onto the living deck, up the other ladder, and outside the hatch. And then it was quiet.

Slowly, the boy sat down before the computer screen. A keyboard slid out of nowhere, appearing at his fingertips. Words flashed on the screen, scrolling past Dion's eyes.

NAME. LAST NAME FIRST. FIRST NAME LAST:

MOTHER'S FULL NAME:

FATHER'S FULL NAME:

DATE OF BIRTH:

PLANET OF ORIGIN:

Dion stared at the screen, his fingers resting, unmoving, on the keys.

Name. Last name first. First name last.

···◁■ ▷···

Tusk tightened the loose bolt, his jet wrench whirring it into place, practically fusing it to the metal. He thought briefly of what it would take to get the bolt off again, then put it out of his mind. At least it was on, that's all that mattered for the time being. Lying in the darkness beneath his fighter, Tusk yawned and considered stealing a short nap under the belly of the plane, where XJ couldn't see him.

"Ouch!" A mild electrical jolt tingled through Tusk's body. "What the— Ouch! Stop that!"

Sliding out from beneath the spaceplane, he blinked in the bright beam of light being aimed at him. XJ fired another tiny probe, hitting Tusk in the knee.

"I'm out, damn it!" Glaring at the holes burned into his pants, Tusk made an angry swipe at the computer's remote unit. It bobbed nonchalantly out of his reach. "What is it? The circuitry ready to test?"

"Forget the circuitry," the computer replied. "The kid's gone."

"Kid?" Tusk's mind, intent upon his damaged deflector shields, couldn't recall for an instant what kid was gone or why he should be worried if one was. Then he remembered and swore earnestly and with feeling.

"Colorful, but does nothing to alleviate the situation," XJ commented. "And may I point out that the use of foul language is the typical response of the uneducated and unimaginative human, who has a limited vocabulary—"

"You were supposed to be looking after him!"

"Who the hell died and made me his mother?" The computer beeped in indignation. "I had that blasted circuitry you fried to reroute! Besides, I was watching him—sort of. One minute the kid's sitting at the keyboard and the next he flies into a rage and storms out. Right when I got life-support reprogrammed, too. I— What in the—"

A brilliant flare of light, blazing like a comet, streaked across the night sky.

Only there were no comets due in this solar system for the next hundred years.

"Name of the Creator!" Tusk breathed, staring up at the

fiery arcs of blue-white flame. "The Warlord!" The mercenary broke into a run, dashing around to the front of the spaceplane.

"Where are you going?" XJ demanded, floating after him.

"The kid."

The remote's lights blinked wildly. "Now your brain's fried as well as your circuits! We're deserters! We got a hot spaceplane! We'll be doing good to get off this rock ourselves!"

"Not without the kid." Tusk clambered up the ladder and dropped down through the hatch of the spaceplane, XJ whirring angrily behind.

"Forget the kid! We got the money. And not much at that, mind you. Barely enough for the parts and the fuel. I had to—"

"It isn't the money." Flinging clothes around the cabin, Tusk found the pants he'd been wearing that afternoon and, after a rapid search of his pockets, came up with the battered leather pouch. He opened it feverishly.

"There's no money left in there," the remote said, its tiny arms wiggling. "I already checked."

"I know there's no money left!" Tusk shook his fist at the computer. "And I've told you to keep your metal hands out of my pants!" He found a scrap of paper, pulled it out, and read it. Stuffing the paper into his shirt pocket, he grabbed his lasgun and started back up the ladder.

"I've caught you trying to hold out on me before! This is an equal partnership, remember that!" The remote bobbed along after Tusk as he pulled himself up through the hatch and dropped over the side of the spaceplane onto the ground. "You never should have accepted this job without consulting me. It's a breach of our contract. I'll see you in court!

"And what do you mean it isn't the money?" XJ yelled. "Since when has it ever been anything else?"

But Tusk had disappeared into the night.

XJ-27 went out as far as the remote's limited range allowed it to go.

"Maybe his brain'll kick in." XJ peered into the darkness, waited several minutes for Tusk to return. But, probing as far as its sensors ranged, the computer picked up no trace of the mercenary.

Gleeping to itself irritably, XJ returned to the spaceplane, where it relieved its frustration by tying all of Tusk's clean underwear into knots.

Chapter ❖❖❖ Four

Benedictus qui venit in nomine Domini.

Requiem Mass

Blessed is he who comes in the name of the Lord.

Though Dion had been to town rarely, he reached the outskirts of the small port city without getting himself lost. Platus taught that all of life is a great chain, the nature of which can be known from only a single link. Thus he had trained Dion to be observant of everything around him, no matter how small or insignificant. Recognizing the various landmarks he had unconsciously imprinted upon his mind, the boy was able to retrace his steps with ease. He jogged through the empty streets, pausing occasionally to get his bearings, and soon reached the city limits. Once outside the town, he was in the broad, flat plains and he relaxed. Dion had explored this land since boyhood and knew every tree and bush.

The young man increased his speed, running over the sun-baked terrain at a smooth, easy pace. He was enjoying the exercise, letting it slowly unwind the coiled spring of his emotions. One of Syrac's two moons had risen and shone brightly in the sky, lighting his way. There was no clearly marked trail through the outback, but the land was flat, with only a few scrubby bushes, stunted trees, and ravines to avoid. Within an hour, he came within sight of the isolated dwelling where he and Platus lived.

Light shone from one of the windows. That was not unusual. Platus often stayed up reading until late into the night. He heard music—a boy soprano's clear voice cut achingly through Dion's heart.

"Dona eis requiem." Grant them rest.

Dion increased his speed. He glanced behind him, but only

out of instinct, not because he was truly afraid of being followed. The mercenary had his money, that was probably all he cared about.

Nearing his home, Dion noticed the blazing blue-white flash of light streak across the sky. It intrigued him but didn't even cause him to break stride. Never having seen one of the Warlord's massive ships before, Dion had no idea what it was, and assumed it must be an unusually large meteor. At any other time, such a phenomenon would have fascinated him. He and Platus would have marked where it landed and gone out the next day in search of it. But tonight Dion had no interest in the heavens. Platus had some explaining to do.

The boy's earliest memories were of this small house and the quiet, gentle man who had been not only father and mother to Dion, but teacher as well. The two had lived a secluded life, shunning contact with the outside world. Dion had not missed the world particularly. He'd been around children his own age a few times and thought them silly and stupid. The boy was perfectly content with his life—or would have been but for one thing.

He had no idea who he was or, still more important, *why* he was.

"You must be patient, Dion," Platus told him, time and again, in the mild voice that grew strained and tense whenever the boy brought up the subject. "There are reasons for what I do, though I cannot explain them. When and if the time comes for you to know, then it will be revealed to you."

"And if that time never comes?" Dion asked impatiently.

"Then you will not know and you must accept it. What does it matter, anyway, who your parents were? It is who *you* are that is important in this life."

Maybe that answer had been good enough for Dion once. But not now. Not when he was being sent off who knew where. Seeing the lights of his home gleaming softly in the distance, Dion couldn't believe that Platus had actually expected him to go meekly away with that crazy mercenary and his uncouth computer. It just didn't make sense! Platus never did anything on impulse. He always planned everything. Why, only the first of this week, he and Dion had gone over what they intended to study in the upcoming months. They'd laid out the garden, even argued as usual over whether to put in radishes, which the boy loved and Platus detested. And, as usual, the radishes had won.

Then, two days ago, Platus had been called to town to receive an interplanetary space transmission. He refused to let Dion accompany him, though it was the first time the boy had known his master to receive such a message. When Platus returned, his face was ashen, he had aged years. He would not discuss the matter but was silent and withdrawn. That afternoon, he told Dion to begin packing—the boy was leaving Syrac Seven.

Dion was now so close to the house he could begin to pick out the details of the simple dwelling. Suddenly the boy stopped running, a curse on his lips that would have done Tusk proud. Of course! Platus was in danger!

"That's why I'm being sent off!" he said aloud. "I've been a fool, thinking only of myself! I saw it in his face when he said good-bye. Only I was wallowing so deep in self-pity I couldn't get my head out of the muck long enough to think."

The boy started running again, fear lending impetus to his stride. Why his gentle master, who revered life so highly he wouldn't even use mousetraps, would be in danger was beyond Dion's comprehension. But then he began to consider. How much did he know about Platus? Nothing—as little as he knew about himself. The man hadn't an enemy in the world. He didn't have any friends in this world, either.

In this world. The space transmission. It wasn't an enemy in *this* world. It was coming from somewhere beyond.

Dion glanced up into the heavens and stumbled, nearly falling. He'd never seen a real space shuttle before. He'd seen only photographs in textbooks that were more than twenty years old. He was seeing one now, he knew, and it was bigger and more beautiful than anything he could have imagined.

The moonlight glinted off a beaked prow painted red and gold and resembling the mythical phoenix. Decorated with images of fire and feathers, its sleek wings extended out from its body. Traces of flame flared in the air, its engines having just been shut down. The shuttle was gliding to a soft, air-cushioned landing—a landing that would take it within a kilometer of Dion's house.

An oppressive sense of uneasiness that grew stronger the nearer the shuttlecraft crept toward the ground swept over Dion. Mingled with this unease was an overwhelming curiosity. Slowly, the young man moved forward, keeping instinctively to the shadows of a huge spike-cactus.

The boy longed to rush ahead and confront this mystery directly, but Platus's training made him stop and carefully consider his next action. No, it was far better to keep hidden, at least for the time being. Should his help be required, an element of surprise was always good. And besides, Dion told himself grimly, his excitement starting to mount, it would give him a better chance of learning something about his master . . . and perhaps about himself.

A gully—the remnant of a dried-up creek bed—ran beneath the house. Dion scrambled down the bank, treading silently over the flat, rock-strewn ground. The gully led him into his own backyard. He'd lost sight of the shuttlecraft; the gully's sides were steep. But he could see the craft's lights shining, bathing the land for miles around in a garish red and orange glow.

Dion kept to the ditch until he judged he must be almost parallel to the garden. It would be easy to pad through the soft, newly tilled soil without anyone hearing him. Catching hold of the weedy bushes and tree roots that stuck out from the dirt sides, he pulled himself up the bank and peered cautiously over the lip of the gully.

He could now see the front half of the shuttlecraft clearly. The back part was being blocked by the house, standing between him and the craft. Watching, he saw a hatch open. Bright white light streamed out, broken by silhouetted figures of men. These parted, and one taller than the rest—wearing a feather-crested helmet and a long, flowing cloak—emerged from the lighted hatchway and walked down the gangplank that extended from the hatch to the ground.

Although he couldn't see the figure clearly, Dion could see light gleaming off the man's helmet. The man was moving toward the house. He was apparently alone. No one was with him. This man was coming to see Platus. A meeting. Platus was meeting with this man! That was the reason Dion had been sent away. Like a child told to leave the room so that the grown-ups could talk!

Anger burned away Dion's uneasiness. I'll find out what's going on, and then I'll—I'll— Well, I'm not certain what I'll do but I'll do something!

The man emerged from the dark shadow cast by the shuttle's wing. The bright running lights of the spacecraft illuminated him. Curious, Dion studied the man approaching the house, wondering who he was. The boy caught his breath at the magnificence of the sight. The man's armor reflected the red and golden light. He himself might have been rising out of the flames like the phoenix. He was tall; Dion had never seen a man quite so tall or so muscular. His helmet was burnished gold, as was his breastplate—all done in the style the boy recognized as being copied from the days of ancient Rome. A red plume ornamented the helm, the feathers glistened in the light. The red matched the flame red of his cloak, the cloth sparkling here and there with golden trim. The boy couldn't see the man's face—it was lost in shadow. The man walked with long, swift strides, moving so rapidly his cape floated out behind him in the still evening air. There was intense, serious purpose in every line of his body.

The man drew nearer to the house, and was lost to Dion's view. This was the boy's chance, for the house would prevent the man from seeing him. Crawling up over the edge of the bank, Dion dashed through the garden, heedlessly trampling the neat rows of newly planted seeds, dodging the stakes that carefully labeled each one.

A light shone in the window of the living room. The night was warm, the window was open, the bamboo shades raised. Dion crept close. A twinge of guilt pricked his conscience at the thought of spying on Platus, but he swiftly rationalized it. His master might be in danger, after all. Dion could help best by remaining hidden.

Sneaking silently across a lawn carpeted with smooth prairie grass, the boy reached the house and crouched below the window. He listened but couldn't hear anything. Cautiously he rose halfway and peered over the windowsill.

What he saw made him gasp in astonishment. He clapped his hand over his mouth, fearing he might be heard.

Platus stood alone in the room. His back was to Dion; he faced the front door. But this wasn't a Platus Dion knew. This wasn't his teacher, the poet, the musician. The long blond hair fell over shoulders encased in shining silver armor—armor that appeared old-fashioned and outmoded. Armor that dated back before the revolution, armor that was marked with the emblem of the late king.

But it wasn't the sight of the armor that made Dion gasp—although the sudden, confusing knowledge that Platus had perhaps been a member of the murdered king's own elite guard made the boy's mind reel in confusion. What took Dion's breath was the sight of a silver scabbard lying on a table before him, lying within easy reach of his gentle master's hand.

Three knocks fell heavily upon the door.

Fear convulsed Dion. He didn't know why, he didn't know what he feared. Perhaps it was the sight of Platus, dressed so strangely, so unlike himself. Perhaps it was the sound of those knocks, falling upon the door like the three dread notes representing the hammer-blows of Fate that opened Verdi's opera, *La Forza del Destino*.

The forces of destiny. Dion, for the first time, felt their power. If he could have been granted any gift in the universe, he would have frozen that moment and lived this one single instant into forever. But he could no more stop this minute, those forces, than he could stop the sun in its orbit. What would follow was as inevitable as the coming of night after a bright and beautiful day.

"Enter," Platus said, and Dion saw the door flung open.

Flashing golden armor, and the great bulk of the man from the shuttle was framed in the doorway. The man's eyes beneath the shadow of his helmet widened in astonishment no less than the boy's at the sight before him.

The two men stood regarding each other, one from the doorway, one from the center of the room. The boy watched from his hiding place at the window. No one spoke; not an indrawn breath broke the silence.

Then Platus smiled slightly. Taking off his glasses, he wiped them—a habitual movement that made Dion's throat hurt with unshed tears. "You come upon me like Lucifer, Derek . . . his face, deep scars of thunder had intrenched . . . ? Do you remember your Milton?"

"Still the poet," the man in the doorway commented in a deep baritone that was passionless, grave, and quiet. Removing his helmet, he placed it under his left arm in military fashion, then—ducking his head—he walked through the doorway and stepped into the simple living room. Dion could see him quite clearly; the light of a lamp shone directly on his face.

The man called Derek appeared older without the helmet. Though he had the muscular build of a young man, Dion guessed that he was in his late forties, about the same age as Platus. It was the face that aged him. It might have been carved of granite, each stroke of the sculptor's blade bearing downward in grim, stern resolve. Black hair, damp from perspiration, was worn long and was tied at the back of his neck with a leather thong. His skin color was the rich, even bronze of those who live in space and must depend on artificial suns for their health. The eyes that glanced about the room were dark and narrow, cold and forbidding as a grave.

Dion shivered in the warm darkness.

"I remember my Milton, poet. I'll finish the line: '. . . waiting revenge.' You were warned of my arrival. Stavros, of course. I thought I had shut down his transmission in time."

"You did. You were as efficient as always, Sagan. It was only a simple, mathematical sequence sent out by a friend of his when Stavros knew it was too late to escape. Easily overlooked by your monitoring devices, yet it told me . . . all."

Sagan glanced about the room, taking in the shelves and shelves of books; the few, fine paintings hanging on the wall; the simply, homely luxuries. Dion saw them, too, with new eyes, eyes blurred by tears. How precious they seemed suddenly. When the man reached down and picked up a small lap harp—Platus's harp—with his gauntleted hand, the boy would have given anything for the strength to rush inside and snatch it from him. But Dion barely had strength enough to hang on to the windowsill. He could still give no reason for his fear, but it was very real and it was eating him alive.

"It has been a long time, poet," Sagan said, returning the harp carefully and respectfully to its place. "I have sought you many years."

He walked across the room toward the window and Dion's chest almost burst from the suffocating fear that he'd been seen. But the man turned his back to Dion, to face Platus. A magnificent phoenix, embroidered in gold, had been stitched on the man's cloak. "The boy is gone."

"Yes, I sent him away."

"Why didn't you go with him?"

Platus shrugged, the silver armor glistened in the light. He turned to face his visitor and Dion saw a marvelous jewel, hanging from a silver chain around his master's neck.

"I am easy to find, Sagan. You have me on file, everything from my blood type to my hand print to the pattern of my brain waves. Witness how easily you traced me to this house, once you knew the name of the planet on which I lived! How much longer could I hide from you, Derek? Yet, the boy. That is different. He is anonymous—"

"Anonymous!" Sagan sneered. "Bah! Whatever else that family of his may have been, they were never anonymous. Surely, he must have all the traits! Unless . . ." The man stared at Platus in disbelief. "He doesn't know!"

"No. He knows nothing, not even his real name."

"Creator!" Sagan breathed. His face darkened and it seemed to the boy that the man was not swearing but calling upon God in reverence. "And I can imagine how you have raised him, you weak, sniveling worm!" The narrow-eyed gaze swept the room. "Poetry! Music!" His booted foot shoved contemptuously at the harp. It fell over, its strings quivering in a discordant cry. "Why she left him in your care, I will never understand!"

Sagan pondered silently for a moment. "This makes it difficult, Platus, I admit. Difficult, but not impossible. Stavros did you no favor. Your death would have been quite easy and painless—a simple execution as proscribed by the law of the Galactic Democratic Republic for those royalists once known as the Guardians. Now, of course, it will be different. I must find the boy, and you will tell me where he has gone. Stavros held out only three days against me, Platus. Three days. And he was far stronger than you."

Dion gripped the windowsill with hands that were white and slowly losing all feeling. He wanted to scream, yell, rush inside. But he could do nothing. Fear had stolen his voice, his reason, his strength. None of the words the two men spoke made sense to him. It would only be later that he would recall them.

"I must say, Platus"—Derek Sagan regarded the slender man with a cool, grave expression of contempt—"that I am amazed to find you still alive. Surely you knew what you faced at my hands?"

"You are right, Sagan. I—I am not strong." Platus drew a deep breath. "Nonetheless, I am of the Blood Royal. You will not take me alive."

Reaching out his hand, Platus grasped hold of the silver scabbard that lay upon the table, lifted it unsteadily and appeared—to Dion—to remove the scabbard's handle. Five needles projected from a short, stubby hilt. Platus, somewhat clumsily and with a wince of pain, pressed his palm over the needles, driving them into his skin. "I will fight . . . for my life."

Sagan stared at him a moment, completely confounded. Then he began to laugh—rich, deep laughter that sprang from some dark well deep inside.

Platus stood before him, unmoving, holding the sword's hilt awkwardly in his hand.

"So, pacifist," Sagan said, when his laughter had subsided, "you have found something worth fighting for at last. Put the bloodsword down, fool!" He made a contemptuous gesture. "It is of no use against this armor."

"I know better than that, Derek," Platus answered with quiet dignity. "Though I was not a swordsman, my sister was. One of the best, in fact, as you well know, for you were her teacher. Forged by the High Priests, guided by my mental powers, its blade will cut through your armor as if it were so much feeble flesh. You want to take me? You must fight me."

"This is ridiculous, pacifist!" Sagan's lips twitched in a smile.

It *was* almost funny, the gentle Platus holding at bay a man who wore his own sword with the casual ease of long familiarity, a man whose bare, muscular arms were seamed with the scars of his battles. Dion felt wild laughter of his own surge up inside him and he buried his face in his hands, choked it down, then again lifted his head.

The smile on Sagan's face had vanished, the dark eyes grown narrower still. Moving slowly, he raised his hand. "Give me the weapon, Platus. You can't fight me. You can't win. You know that. This is a waste . . ." Continuing to talk in a hypnotic monotone, the man took a step toward Platus, his gloved hand reaching for the bloodsword. "You are an avowed pacifist, poet. You believe in peaceful means to settle contentions between men. Life is sacred, so you have often said. Hand me the sword. Then tell me where to find the boy."

It seemed the man's spell was working, if spell it was. Platus's sword arm began to droop, his body trembled. Sagan drew another step closer.

There was a blur of movement. Dion heard a wild cry and saw flame burst from the sword's hilt, swinging in a deadly arc.

The blow would have cut Sagan in two if the warrior had not saved himself by an experienced, reflexive dive backward. Leaping after his enemy, Platus pressed his advantage, attacking with such violence that Sagan—unable to take time to draw his own sword—was forced to block one savage blow with his left forearm. The fiery blade of the bloodsword cut through the metal bracer Sagan wore, cut painfully into his wrist. He kicked Platus in the leg, knocking his feet out from under him, throwing him off balance.

Recovering himself, Platus was up, slashing out again. Sagan flung his helm to the floor and drew his own sword—a weapon similar in design to the one Platus held. Blood streamed down the man's left hand, pulsing from his wound. He appeared to ignore it.

Sagan held his sword in a defensive attitude, prepared to block his opponent's jabs and swipes, seemingly looking for an opportunity to disarm or wound him. Platus continued to attack, but it was obvious he was rapidly weakening.

This man would take his master prisoner. Dion would come out of hiding and reveal himself and then there would be no reason for this Sagan to hurt Platus. The boy tensed, ready to pull himself up through the open window, when he saw Platus's lips part in a smile, a strange smile in such a hopeless situation—a smile of triumph.

And suddenly Dion saw his master's intent. He saw it only a split second before Sagan saw it, too. Neither had time to react. Lunging forward, Platus impaled himself up the blood-sword's flaming blade.

With a bitter oath, Sagan instantly shut off the sword. The blade disappeared, but it was too late. Blood spurted from the silver armor. Platus sank to the floor. Dion sprang to his feet, his fear riven by the same blade that had pierced his master. A cry in his throat, he reached for the windowsill.

A hand caught hold of him by the back of his neck; a flash of pain shot through his head . . .

··◆■ ■▶··

Derek Sagan heard a noise outside the window, a muffled thud. But he couldn't turn his attention from the dying man long enough to investigate. Kneeling, he lifted the bleeding body in his arms.

"Platus," he said urgently, turning the head, forcing the fast-dimming eyes to look into his. "You fool! Killing yourself is a mortal sin! You've doomed your soul to endless torment!"

Platus smiled wearily. "I don't . . . believe in your god . . . Derek. It is fitting this way, after all." He gasped for breath. "My blood is on your hands . . . as was the blood of my king."

"Tell me where to find the boy!" Sagan urged.

With his last strength, Platus raised his hand, the fingers closed over the jewel that hung around his neck. "The boy is safe!"

Sagan, in his rage and frustration, shook the dying man. "You have damned yourself eternally! I alone still have the power of the High Priests to intercede with God! I can—"

The eyes fixed in the head, gazing unseeing at the ceiling of the small house. The body, encased in silver armor, shuddered and was still. The hand holding the jewel went limp.

Cursing, the Warlord dumped the lifeless corpse to the floor and stood up, staring in fury at the wretched husk at his feet. His men would search the house, as a matter of course, but Sagan knew Platus well enough to know that they would find nothing. No trace of the boy, nothing to tell what he looked like, no clue as to where he had gone.

Reaching down, the Warlord picked up the hilt of the sword, now as lifeless as the body. Once again the Guardians had defeated him. Once again they had been just one step ahead of him!

"Why, Creator? You have given them to me, as I prayed. Yet still you thwart me! What is the reason?" He waited a moment for the answer to his prayer. None was forthcoming and he irritably thrust the bloodsword back into its silver scabbard.

He spoke into the commlink in his helmet, calling his men. Remembering the noise he had heard outside, he took a step toward the window to investigate when suddenly he stopped, his attention arrested.

A sound had caught his ear. It was not a sound from his ship, it was not a sound from outside the dwelling. Indeed, it was not a sound that emanated from this world, and he heard it not with his physical ear but with the ear of his soul. A voice! A well-remembered voice . . . a voice that had not spoken in seventeen years.

Sagan closed his eyes, shutting out his surroundings, withdrawing deep into himself as he had been taught as a child until he was aware of nothing around him or even within him. His soul left his body, floating into the night, and there it listened, free from the noise of heartbeat and rushing blood.

And he heard the sound, falling upon his burning spirit like cool mist. A cry of grief and sorrow—the cry of a sister mourning the death of a brother.

The answer to Sagan's prayer. God's plan became clear to him. "Forgive me for my doubts, Creator. I understand!"

"My lord."

This voice was coporeal and it grabbed hold of Sagan and snatched him back to the world, forcing him to meld the two separate halves of his being together again. Opening his eyes, the Warlord stared without recognition at the centurion standing before him.

"My lord, forgive me for disturbing you, but the men have been deployed and I'm reporting to you as ordered—"

"Yes, Captain. You have done well." Sagan glanced around the house, remembering. "I heard a sound outside the window. Have your men investigate."

"Yes, my lord." The captain made a motion and two centurions standing inside the door departed with alacrity, two others moving to take their places. "Further orders, my lord?"

"Secure the town immediately. Ground all spacecraft of every type. No one is to leave the planet. Any spacecraft that attempt to flee are to be captured, not shot down. Send interrogators into the city. Begin a systematic roundup of the town's population. I want to know everything, no matter how insignificant, about this man"—the Warlord shoved the body with the toe of his boot—"and a boy who lived here with him. The dead man's name was Platus Morianna, though according to our reports he used the alias Platus Moran. Search the house. Bring me anything that looks like it might belong to a teenager—anything! A picture of a girl, a model spacecraft, his computer files. When you've finished, burn the house."

"Yes, my lord. And the body?"

"He was an atheist and he died by his own hand. May God have mercy on his soul." Sagan bent down on one knee. "*Requiem aeternam dona eis, Domine.*"[1] Closing the staring eyes, he lifted the limp hand and placed it over the starjewel, whose bright light was fading into darkness. "Leave the body in the house. Burn it over him."

"Very good, my lord." The captain gestured again, and the two centurions, followed by two more, entered the house and began to literally take it apart. Speaking into his helmet's commlink, the captain relayed his orders, and soon hoverjeeps loaded with men could be seen leaving the shuttlecraft, sweeping over the plains, heading for the small port city.

[1] Rest eternal grant them, O Lord.—Requiem Mass

A centurion poked his head through the open window.

"Captain, the grass is so trampled out here, we can't make out any definite tracks. Footprints all over—here and in the garden. There're animal tracks, too. Wolves, looks like."

The captain glanced inquiringly at the Warlord, who shrugged, no longer interested. "The tracks could have been made days ago. This late at night, most likely it was the animal I heard."

Stepping over the body, he walked across the living room and out the door. Behind him, he heard the thud of books hitting the floor, wood splintering, the jangling twang of a broken harp string. The Warlord's gaze went to the stars burning in the heavens, stars that to poets might be sparkling gems but to him were pins upon a huge galactic map.

Mentally taking up one of those pins, he twirled it in the fingers of his mind.

"At long last, my lady. At long last!"

Chapter ❖ Five

Freedom's just another word for nothin' left to lose.
                    Kris Kristofferson, "Me and Bobbie McGee"

"Hey, kid, damn it! Can you hear me?"

A hand was over his mouth. A heavy weight was smashing down on his chest, and burning pain seared his soul. Dion opened his eyes. He didn't recognize the face of the mercenary inches away from his. Or if he did, it didn't matter. Dion's muscles leapt, he struggled desperately to free himself. He had to get inside the house! He had to get to Platus!

"Shit, kid, that's a Warlord in there!" hissed the voice, not an inch from his ear.

The pressure on his chest increased, the hand tightened over his mouth. Dion glared furiously at the black face. Lit by the red and golden lights of the shuttlecraft, it might have been a demon's face gazing at him from the fires of hell. Beads of sweat stood on Tusk's forehead; the shuttle's lights were tiny pinpoints of flame in his dark eyes.

"Listen to me, kid, and listen good!" Tusk shoved Dion's head back into the dirt. "A man just gave up his life for you. Are you gonna make that mean something?"

Dion struggled, but it was a struggle against fate, against the forces of destiny, and, after a moment, he ceased. Closing his eyes, he relaxed and nodded.

"Good," Tusk muttered. Watching the boy warily, he let loose his hand from Dion's mouth and lifted his knee from the young man's chest. "We're in the bottom of some sort of ditch in back of your house," Tusk breathed into Dion's ear. "The Warlord's still inside. Any second this place is going to be lousy with marines. We've got to make ourselves real scarce, real fast! You understand?"

Dion nodded again, his hand reaching to rub his head.

"C'mon, kid!" Tusk grunted, hauling him to his feet. "I didn't hit you that hard. Keep low."

Dion stood up cautiously, glancing around to get his bearings. They were in the bottom of the deep ravine in back of the house, safely concealed for the time being. But they wouldn't be hidden long; he could hear voices coming from the house. One voice he recognized, the voice of the man who had killed Platus. Dion made a move toward the embankment.

"Wrong way, kid!" Tusk's hand closed over the boy's arm.

Dion's lips pressed together; his eyes burned with the ache in his heart. Jerking his arm out of Tusk's grasp, the boy turned and began to run down the dry creek bed, running as hard and fast as he could, running away from the house, away from the red and golden lights, away from the blood, spilling down silver armor. . . .

Caught flat-footed by Dion's sudden movement, the mercenary scrambled to keep up with the boy. "Kid's a goddam jackrabbit!" Tusk stopped once to risk a look back over his shoulder, but he could see nothing except the lip of the embankment and the flaring lights of the shuttlecraft.

"Just a matter of time, though. Hey, kid!" He panted, catching up with Dion. "This ditch . . . take us . . . all the way . . . into town?"

Dion shook his head, his only answer. Tears blown back by the rushing wind in his face made dirt streaks across his cheeks. He gestured abruptly and obscurely, never slowing his pace over the uneven ground. Tusk had no idea what the boy meant. The mercenary could only hope the kid knew where he was going. Putting his head down, Tusk concentrated on keeping his legs pumping, his breath coming.

··◗■ ■◖··

"Down!" Tusk grabbed hold of Dion and pulled the boy into the shadow of a sand-blasted sign that welcomed travelers to the port city, advised them of the town's population, and issued invitations to buy real estate.

Hoverjeeps roared past, their air blasts sending up choking clouds of sand that rolled around the boy and the mercenary.

"What is it?" Dion asked, coughing. "What does it mean?"

"The Warlord's army." Tusk squinched his eyes shut against the stinging sand. "He's declared martial law, gonna take over the town. Ten to one he's lookin' for you, kid." The dust settled. He gazed thoughtfully after the jeeps that were speeding toward the lights of the port city.

"What are you smiling about, then?" Dion cast the mercenary a bitter glance. "This means I'm finished—"

"This means you've got a chance," Tusk corrected, his smile broadening into a grin. "C'mon. You'll see."

Back in familiar territory once more, Tusk led Dion into the outskirts of the town, the two keeping to back alleys and side streets. Rounding a corner, they nearly walked into a hover-jeepload of marines being deployed at one of the major intersections. Sirens wailed, red lights flashed.

Pulling Dion back into an alley, Tusk whispered, "Watch!"

A local police squad car pulled to a screeching stop only centimeters from the hoverjeep.

"Just what the hell do you think you're doing?" the cop demanded, climbing out of the squad car and confronting one of the marines.

"Warlord Derek Sagan has declared martial law over this planet. This city is now under our control." The centurion held out his hand. "I'll need to see your identification."

"Identification?" the cop repeated in disbelief. He yelled over his shoulder, "Charley, call for some backup! Look, you!" The cop returned his attention to the marine and drew his service revolver, an old projectile weapon. Syrac Seven had entered the space age, but had not gone to extremes. "I think you're the ones better fork over some I.D. Stop that right there! Keep your hands where I can see 'em. Those're real fancy clothes you're wearin'. I'd hate to blast a hole right through the heart."

A gesture brought the centurion's men to back him up.

"I am certain, officer, that you recognize the insignia of Warlord Sagan."

"Warlord again. You mean *Citizen General* Sagan, don't you?" The policeman, seeing himself outnumbered, retreated behind the open door of his squad car, but kept his gun trained on the soldiers, his partner covering him. "We got rid of lords seventeen years ago. And if he *is* here, he can just clear out. We run our own affairs on Syrac Seven. Now drop those weapons."

"The cooperation of the police has been requested." The centurion was well trained; he was keeping his patience. "Contact your superior—"

"Dispatch reports these guys are all over town!" the cop's

partner yelled. "They've started a fight in one of the bars by the docks!"

Two more police cars, sirens wailing, came roaring around the corner. The centurions looked to their lieutenant, who was speaking into the commlink in his helmet.

Catching hold of Dion's arm, Tusk winked and pulled him down the alley. "See what I mean? Keep walking, nobody's gonna notice us." He was trying hard to ignore the pain of a stitch in his side.

"Will there be a fight?" Dion asked.

They left the altercation behind them. Pausing to catch his breath, Tusk leaned against a graffiti-covered brick wall, keeping well out of the light of a nearby street lamp.

"Hell, no. In an hour, the police'll find out that there really *is* a Warlord on this planet! Then the cops'll be crawling around, licking his boots. But we got that hour. Tired?"

"No."

The boy's face, reflecting the nearby light, was white. The long red-golden hair, damp with perspiration, clung to his brow and his cheeks. Gray smudges beneath the lids darkened the blue eyes. But the eyes themselves glittered hard as glare ice.

"Well, I'm about done for!" Tusk mopped sweat from his face. "And we still gotta get our balls out of this sand trap. You play golf, kid?"

"Shouldn't we be going?" Dion said coldly.

"Just a sec." Bending over, hands on his knees, Tusk tried to ease the pain in his side. With a groan, he straightened. "It's not very far. And I'm not as young as I used to be—"

"How old are you? Twenty?" Dion snapped, his gaze flitting up and down the dark alley.

"Twenty-six. Black skin doesn't age like that pasty white stuff of yours. But I thought . . . I was in shape!" Tusk finally caught his breath. "Don't tell XJ. He'll blame it on the jump-juice. Look, when we get to the RV parking lot where the plane's stashed, we'll go in the back way. Climb the fence. The Warlord probably won't have men there yet, but that'll be one of the first places they'll search. With luck, we'll be long gone by then."

Dion nodded and started to walk in the direction Tusk indicated, when the mercenary caught hold of him.

"I sort of came in on the tail end of things with . . . uh . . . your master and the Warlord. I don't suppose you heard anything about why a Warlord as powerful as Derek Sagan wants you bad enough to . . . uh"—Tusk was about to say *kill a man* but the sight of Dion's rigid face made him change his mind—"disrupt a planet."

Dion stared straight ahead. "Let go of me."

"I'm sorry." Tusk backed off. "I understand. I guess it doesn't matter. Just one of those little pieces of information I can live for a real long time without knowing."

Out of the corner of his eye, he saw one of the red and golden hoverjeeps pull to a stop at the end of the street. "At least I hope so!" he amended.

•◁▭ ▭▷•

"XJ? You got the circuitry fixed?"

Tusk slid down the ladder into the body of the spaceplane. Dion followed quickly, but almost not quickly enough. The hatch was shutting while he still had his hand on the rim and he just managed to snatch back his fingers in time to keep them from being smashed to a pulp. Engines fired. A tremor shook the plane, causing Dion to slip on the ladder, and land heavily on the deck.

Tusk was already in the cockpit; Dion saw the top of his curly-haired head disappear down the ladder and then everything went dark.

"All systems shutting down for launch," the computer announced. Dion stood crouched on the deck, afraid to move. Red emergency lights flickered on, casting an eerie glow, making everything in the plane seem strange, less real than a dream. The boy groped his way forward, and had reached the ladder leading into the cockpit when a black shape suddenly loomed up in front of him.

"Kid? Oh, there you are."

Grabbing hold of him by the shirt collar, Tusk yanked the boy down the ladder, literally tossing him into a chair.

"Sit and keep quiet!"

Bruised and shaken, more tired than he would admit, Dion sat, nursing a cut on his hand inflicted by a sharp metal edge on the ladder. Leaning over in front of the boy, Tusk hit a button. Sturdy plastic arms swung up from below the chair and clamped firmly over Dion's thighs and upper body. The boy nearly jumped out of his skin, but realized after a moment that the arms were only fastening him securely. He was not being made a prisoner.

In the seat beside him, Tusk was busy flipping switches and checking readings.

"Scared?" he asked, taking time to glance at his passenger and noting the clenched jaw muscles, the hands curled over the armrests of the chair.

"No." Dion forced himself to relax.

"Had any brains, you would be," XJ remarked.

"I asked you about the circuitry," Tusk said to the computer. "Or has your audio gone bad?"

"I heard you."

"Well, why didn't you answer?"

"Ignorance is bliss."

"Look, dammit, can we launch, or is something going to short out?"

"Tusk," XJ said, "have you ever reflected on the fact that life is an endless series of questions? Why are we born? Where are we bound? Can we launch, or is something going to short out?"

Tusk muttered beneath his breath.

"No swearing!" the computer snapped. "You know how it irritates me. Here, you better listen to this. At least it will give you something constructive to swear about if you must resort to such—"

Words trailing off, the computer's voice was replaced by an official-sounding human.

"General Grounding Order. Repeat. General Grounding Order. Corasian vessels have been sighted near this quadrant. The forces of the Galactic Democratic Republic have placed the planet Syrac Seven under martial law by order of Warlord Derek Sagan until the current emergency situation is alleviated. Until such time as this report of enemy alien craft can be confirmed, all spacecraft are hereby grounded for their own protection—"

"Corasians?" Dion shouted over the drone of the official voice. "Who are they?"

"A bunch of weird alien life-forms who live in the galaxy next door," Tusk answered. "Real nasty types. Scary bastards. And one hasn't been seen in this galaxy in eighteen years. Just an excuse, kid. The Warlord always used it when we needed to put some planet's government back on the straight and narrow. Frightens the whatever out of the populace."

"In case your government should require your services," the official voice continued, "all pilots of private spacecraft are hereby ordered to report immediately to the nearest command post with identification papers—"

"Yeah, yeah!" Tusk flicked a switch. "We see the picture. Shut that twerp off, XJ, and let's get out of here before they get organized. You got a fix on the Warlord's flagship?"

"Yes." Coordinates flashed across the computer screen. "You think you can avoid something that big?"

Scowling, Tusk read the coordinates, made adjustments accordingly, and barked instructions to the computer, who barked right back. Both were absorbed in their work, leaving Dion unnoticed, for which the boy was grateful.

Sitting back in his chair, he had time to think about what had happened, and almost instantly he regretted it. Memory returned, beating at him with dark wings. Closing his eyes, he heard the voices, the conversation. He saw the swords flash, silver and golden, he saw the flow of dark blood, Platus's body sag to the floor.

Anger stirred in Dion. How could you do this to me? he demanded of Platus silently, tears stinging his eyelids. How could you die? How could you leave me like this, not knowing? Why? Why? His fists clenched. Bitter bile flooded his mouth, he thought he might be sick.

Pride made him swallow the hot liquid and choke back the tears sliding down his throat. His fingernails dug into the palms of his hands, and he opened his eyes. He would forget everything, concentrate on the danger they were facing. Tusk's words came back to him. *A man just gave up his life for you. You gonna make that mean something?*

It was suddenly very important to Dion to escape.

"Will they try to stop us?" He tried to speak casually.

"I don't think they'll line up and give us a rousing huzzah as we leave. You ready, XJ?"

"Beginning system check."

"What will they do to us? Shoot us down?" Dion persisted.

"Well, now, that depends," Tusk said, glancing at the boy. "That's why I asked you if you had any clue what the Warlord wants with you. Might make a big difference."

"How?"

"Obvious, kid. If he wants you dead they'll shoot us down. If he doesn't, they'll try to capture us alive. I really hope, kid," Tusk added fervently, "that you got some sort of sentimental value!"

"System check complete," XJ reported.

"And?"

"Ignorance is—"

"Oh, stow it! Start launch sequence. You all set, kid?"

The deck began to vibrate beneath Dion's feet. Then everything was vibrating—the chair, his teeth. . . . Blood spilling over silver armor. . . . The garden trampled, its neat, orderly rows destroyed. What would grow, now, without care and nurturing? Left on its own . . .

"And go!"

The breath expelled itself from Dion's body; the force of lift-off pushed him back into the seat, pulled his skin tight across his bones, forced his lips into an unnatural grimace. Looking at himself in the reflection in the steelglass opposite, he saw his face grinning like a skull. For an instant he couldn't breathe and he began to panic, fearing suffocation.

The frightening sensation was over in an instant. The lights of the city fell away from him with dizzying swiftness. Everything was falling away from him, too fast . . . too fast . . .

The garden, the house . . .

Falling out from under him.

The city, the world . . .

He wanted to reach out, grab hold, hang on. But there was nothing to hold on to. He was caught, held, immobilized in fate's grasp . . . in the Scimitar's seat . . . by the strong, uncaring grip of the security arms.

And then all life was gone. He stared into black, vast space, its stars shining bright and cold as the star Platus wore around his neck. . . .

"Damnation!" Tusk swore.

A screen on the instrument panel had come to life, even as everything around the boy had seemed to die.

"I knew Sagan made improvements since we left, XJ, but— Damn!" Tusk swore again. "How the hell did he get his ships deployed this fast?"

"What do you mean? What's wrong?" Dion sounded strange to himself, as if his own voice had been left down below with the rest of his life.

"Warlord's got the blockade going already. Blasted place is crawling with planes!"

"Told you so!" XJ said in gloomy satisfaction.

"No you didn't, so don't start—"

"I have it on file!" the computer returned smugly. "Scimitar closing, Mach thirty—"

"I see it."

"Where's the gun turret?" Dion asked eagerly. "I can shoot!"

It was a lie, but he wanted to kill something, anything. He wanted to end the hurt, the anger, the fear. Blow it up in a fiery ball that would take him, too.

The computer's lights flashed wildly.

"Calm down, XJ!" Tusk ordered. "Thanks for the offer, kid, but . . . uh . . . that gun's kinda complicated equipment and . . . well . . . to be honest, I'd rather face ten of those characters out there than have one amateur sitting above me with an itchy trigger finger. I mean, you shoot your foot up there and we're nothing but a gleam in someone's eye—and that only for about ten seconds."

"Besides," XJ added, "not even Tusk is dumb enough to try to fight his way out of this one. Are you?"

From the irresolute expression on Tusk's face, Dion thought that the question might be debatable, but the mercenary glanced at the computer screen and grunted.

"Ten seconds and he'll be in range . . . and so will we," the computer reported.

A slow smile spread over Tusk's lips. "The drunken pilot!"

The computer's lights flickered in derision. "That old trick? What is this—a nostalgia trip?"

"We got nothing to lose. I've flown blockade duty, so have you. No matter how sharp they look there's bound to be the normal amount of confusion."

"I want to go on record that I am opposed—"

"Go on record as any damn thing you like, just do what you're supposed to. There must be a Lane around here—"

"There is. Come to this heading—"

A series of number appeared on the computer screen.

"What—"

"Keep your mouth shut, kid," Tusk said, his slender fingers flying over buttons. XJ hummed to itself industriously.

"Military channel?" Tusk asked, glancing up to see the other Scimitar closing fast.

"Open. This is the latest code update. Cost us a bundle. It better be right—"

The commlink crackled, announcing that the other pilot was about to contact them.

"Halt and iden—" Tusk began, a split second ahead of the other Scimitar pilot.

"Halt and—"

"—tify your shelf." Tusk slurred.

"—identify yourself," echoed the pilot, sounding slightly confused. "I repeat, Scimitar. Identify yourself."

"I asked you first," Tusk roared belligerently.

"What's your number, Scimitar? I can't read your markings—"

"I can't see yoursh either." Tusk belched. "They're all kinda fuzzy."

"Give the password."

"Yeah, you'd like that, wouldn't you?" Tusk sneered. "Sell that for a couple thousand gold eagles on the smuggler's market."

"Who's your commanding officer, mister?"

"A sonuvabitch. Whose yours?"

"Excuse me, sir—" XJ cut in.

"Stay out of this!" Tusk smacked the computer on the side of its box.

"You enjoyed that!" XJ stated accusingly in an undertone. "Excuse me, sir!" The computer turned up its audio so that it could be heard clearly by the other pilot. "Scimitar out there! Don't shoot!"

"Who are you?"

"Shipboard computer, sir. I hereby report my pilot unfit for duty."

"You filthy—" Tusk mumbled obscenities.

"I tried to alert the deck crew before we took off," XJ continued in injured tones, shouting to be heard over Tusk's swearing. "But they refused to listen to a mere computer. This isn't the first time this has happened. He sucks up the jump-juice before every flight, and frankly I'm getting sick and tired—"

"Who's his commanding officer?"

"I have no idea because one night in a drunken fit—"

"Name, rank, and charge-card number," Tusk leered into the commlink. "That's all yer gettin' outta me!"

"—he erased the name from my memory banks," XJ continued loudly.

"I'll have to report this. Stand by."

"I've had about enough!" Tusk was yelling angrily. "You're not gonna take me alive!"

"He won't shoot, will he?" the pilot asked nervously.

"No, sir. I have the guns under my control," XJ replied.

"I'm reporting this. Wait—"

Dion strained his ears. In the background, he could hear the pilot talking. "I've got a Scimitar here, long-range, out of position. Pilot appears to be inebriated. Yes, sir. Computer confirms. No, I can't read the numbers. Covered by carbon scoring." The voice faded, then returned. "Yes, sir."

While this conversation was ongoing, a series of numbers flashed on XJ's screen. Looking at them intently, Tusk flicked his hands over his control panel and nodded just as the pilot's voice crackled back.

"I have been ordered to escort you to the docking bay where a tractor beam will be locked on and you—"

"No, Commander, you idiot!" XJ screeched in such real-sounding panic that Dion's heart lurched into his throat. "Not that button!"

A brilliant flare of color seared the boy's eyes. His entire body turned inside out—skin peeled back, living organs laid bare, bones exposed.

He felt one last horrible moment of sickening fear. . . .

··◈ ➡··

"You okay, kid?"

Dion opened his eyes to see Tusk's face hanging over him. The boy was lying stretched out in one of the hammocks.

"I'm all right," he mumbled. His head ached and he put his hand to it. "What happened? Were we hit?"

"Naw, just the Jump. Does that to people sometimes. Sorry I couldn't warn you, but I didn't dare risk giving us away. Feels like you're being turned inside out, doesn't it?"

Dion started to nod, but that only made his head hurt worse.

"Don't worry. You'll get over it. Each Jump gets a little easier."

"Where are we?"

"A long way from home, kid. The Lanes. Know what those are?"

Memories of lessons with Platus returned. The early morning breeze blowing through the open windows carried the spicy smell of sage and wildflowers. The wind flipped the pages of the books, ruffled the young pupil's red-golden hair, stirred the thin blond hair of his teacher.

Dion closed his eyes, averting his head.

"Not feelin' so good, huh? Better get some sleep, kid. I'm gonna take a shower."

A warm, firm hand closed over the boy's, giving it an

awkward squeeze. Then the hand was gone. Boots scraped across the metal deck. Dion heard Tusk pull open one of the storage containers and begin to rummage around in it. Burning tears crept from beneath the boy's eyelids. Rolling over, he muffled his face in his pillow.

"Damn you, Platus!" he cried. He bit into the fabric, trying to stop the sob that welled up in his throat. "Damn you!"

Across the small cabin, Tusk exploded in a barrage of obscenity. "My shorts! They're all tied in fuckin' knots! XJ! You . . ."

Darkness closed over Dion, and he wept.

Chapter ❖ Six

But the age of chivalry is gone. That of sophisters, economists, and calculators, has succeeded . . .

Edmund Burke, *Reflections on the Revolution in France*

The Warlord's shuttle landed on *Phoenix* without ceremony—no lines of troops drawn up to salute him, no drums, bells, or whistles as was practiced on other ships of other Warlords in the galaxy. Four of his Honor Guard preceded him from the ship, lining up at the door two on either side, clenched fists over their hearts. After he had passed, they fell smartly into step behind him, following him as he crossed the deck of the landing dock. No one else in the dock or in any of the corridors of the ship into which the Warlord walked appeared to take the least notice of the fact that their commanding officer—military lord of one entire sector of the galaxy—was walking past.

Derek Sagan had no patience with waste. Men concerned with other duties stopping their work, snapping to attention, and saluting every time he came into view was a waste of time and energy not to be tolerated. It was a show of false respect. He'd know men salute an officer to his face and shoot him in the back at the first opportunity.

Sagan did not demand respect of his men. He commanded it by example. Discipline on his ship was severe, but he was hardest on himself. His word was law and when that law was broken his judgment was swift and often harsh—as it had been against the university he'd discovered harboring Stavros. Those under his command feared him as they feared God. (Perhaps more. The Creator, after all, was a nebulous being spoken of by priests who were no longer around. Derek Sagan was flesh and blood and in close proximity.) His men feared him, yet the most honored and valued position that could be held in this ship was to be selected as one of his own personal guard.

Sagan strode rapidly through the corridors, appearing to take little interest in his surroundings. Yet everyone knew that the eyes hidden by the shadow of his helm saw everything, noted every detail of shipboard operation from a scrap of food bar wrapper littering the metal deck to a malfunction light flashing its warning on a control panel. Men walked past him with studiously averted eyes, jaw muscles clenched, their bodies unconsciously straightening to achieve the stalwart posture of their Warlord. Sagan was proud of his ship and his men and he liked to see that pride reflected in both. Both—it seemed—went out of their way to please him.

A gesture from his gloved hand brought one of the guard forward. "Where is the admiral? He was informed of my arrival?"

"Yes, my lord. He is on the bridge. He thought he should remain there until the planet was secure."

"My compliments to the admiral, and request him and Captain Nada to meet me in the committee room with their reports."

"Yes, my lord."

The centurion fell back a pace behind the Warlord, relaying the message via the communications linkage in his helmet. Sagan continued walking. His boots rang on the metal deck, the red cape that denoted his high rank swelled out behind him.

The Warlord was essentially a guest on *Phoenix*, Admiral Aks's flagship. Aks was in command of the fleet, Captain Nada in command of the ship. Thus Sagan's polite usage of the word *request*. Everyone on board *Phoenix* knew the true meaning of the word, however. Both the admiral and the ship's captain were awaiting Sagan when he entered the committee room.

Sagan's official rank in the Republic was actually Citizen General. His title was Marshal. There were numerous marshals scattered throughout the galaxy. Following the establishment of the democracy, the President had placed these commanders in charge of maintaining law and order—sort of an interplanetary police force. However, during the years of governmental confusion that naturally followed the revolution, several of the marshals began acquiring more and more power. (As Derek Sagan was once heard to observe, "If it's lying around loose, someone will pick it up.") The news media began referring to these generals as "Warlords."

The appellation was meant to be derogatory. Derek Sagan took it as a compliment. Even after the political situation stabilized and the Congress and President had gained control, Sagan continued, despite howls from the liberal press, to refer to himself as "Warlord." His men addressed him as "my lord." It sounded more suitable. Derek Sagan was, after all, of noble—if slightly unorthodox—birth.

"No interruptions," the Warlord informed his guards, who took their accustomed places outside the door.

The committee room was huge, one of the largest aboard ship. Several hundred crewmen could stand within its round walls and not feel the least cramped. It was empty of all furnishings; no viewport broke the vast sweep of black walls. The only object in the room was a large vidscreen located at one end.

"My apologies for bringing you here, Admiral, Captain," Sagan said as the door slid shut behind him. "I know this has been a long and tiring day for both of you. I must contact the President, however, and I want to hear your reports first. Then you may return to your duties or your rest, whichever I have taken you from."

Numerous small lights located in the ceiling could illuminate the room as brightly as day when necessary. The committee room was in relative darkness now, the need for conserving energy always uppermost in every captain's mind. Small pools of light shone at intervals, therefore, leaving the rest of the room in deep shadow. The admiral and Captain Nada stood in one pool of light in the center of the vast circular floor. Sagan stepped from bright light into darkness, where he was lost for several seconds, the sounds of his footsteps the only indication of his presence. Both the admiral and captain knew they were under his scrutiny. The admiral was relaxed. Captain Nada was not. Sweat beaded on the captain's lip and he swallowed several times. Nada was unhappily aware that his report was not a good one.

"Captain, proceed." The voice resounded from the darkness.

"Yes, my lord." Nada cleared his throat. "The planet Syrac Seven is completely secure, my lord. Martial law is in effect. Reports of the sighting of an enemy invasion force have been transmitted to the heads of each of the governments of the planet and all have given us their complete support."

"Yes, yes, Captain," Sagan responded with a touch of impatience. "What of the blockade?"

Nada heard an unusual tenseness in the Warlord's voice and the captain wondered what had happened down below. It was known that one of the Guardians had been located and executed on Syrac Seven, but Guardians had been executed before without the need for sending the entire civilian population of a planet into a state of panic. And now Sagan talking of contacting the President! It didn't make the captain's news any easier to deliver, particularly when he knew nothing about what was transpiring.

Nada glanced at his admiral, but Aks remained staring straight ahead, leaving his captain without support. There was little love lost between these two. Aks was an old friend of Sagan's, devotedly loyal to his lord. Nada was a staunch democrat.

"The blockade was successful, my lord, with . . . um . . . one exception."

Nada paused, struggling to keep command of his voice. The Warlord had not moved, but the captain knew his lordship was displeased, knew it by the very fact that Sagan had not moved, that not a finger twitched, not a fold of cape stirred.

"Several pilots attempted to fight, my lord. As you ordered, we did not return fire but surrounded them and each was forced to land. They were arrested and are being held as you requested on the planet's surface for interrogation. First reports indicate that most of them are ordinary criminals, my lord, wanted for a variety of offenses."

"The one exception, Captain Nada."

"One of our pilots reported contact with a long-range Scimitar—"

"Long-range!" Sagan broke in. "Why were those deployed?"

"They weren't, my lord, and that made our man suspicious. Upon being requested to identify himself, the long-range pilot was discovered to be intoxicated and was further reported unfit for duty by his shipboard computer. The plane's markings were obscured by heavy carbon scoring and so could not be identified through usual channels. Our pilot informed the pilot of the Scimitar that he would be escorted back to base when—"

The Warlord, hands behind his back beneath his cape, stepped into a pool of light. "—when the Scimitar, having maneuvered itself into position during the conversation, found an open Lane and made the Jump."

"Why, yes, my lord!" Nada stared at his lordship in amazement. "That's exactly what happened."

"I assume the standard data on the plane was recorded?"

"Yes, my lord."

"Have photographs relayed to Syrac Seven and show them to the inhabitants of the city closest to where the Guardian lived—"

"Begging your lordship's pardon," Nada said, somewhat stiffly, "but that has already been done. The plane was identified by the owner of an RV lot where it had been parked. It belonged to a young man known only as Tusk. The Scimitar was one of ours—stolen, of course. The young man apparently lived in the plane. He was a dock worker, but the lot owner was under the impression that this was only a temporary job. The young man dressed like a mercenary and would often disappear for several months at a time, always returning to the planet with money."

"Had he said anything about leaving?"

"No, my lord, apparently not. According to the lot owner, this Tusk had rented the lot for several months and spoke of spending the time making necessary repairs to his plane. The lot owner stated that he was extremely surprised when Tusk appeared yesterday afternoon, paid his overdue rent in gold, and said he would be leaving the next morning before dawn. The landlord was suspicious and stated that he had considered reporting the matter to the police."

"Suspicious of what?"

"The gold, my lord. He had never seen coinage like it and he thought they might be counterfeit."

"He didn't report it?"

"No, my lord. He knew the police had more important matters to worry about."

"In other words, he found out the coins were genuine."

"Precisely, my lord."

Nada began to gain confidence. If it had not seemed too impossible, the captain could have sworn he thought he saw Sagan's tight-lipped mouth relax in a smile, just visible beneath the helmet.

"Do you have a description of this young man?"

"Yes, my lord. He is human, black-skinned, age approximately twenty-six, and he wears—"

"A silver earring in the shape of a star in his left earlobe."
Derek Sagan spoke softly, almost to himself.

"My God, my lord!"

Captain Nada looked stunned. He had heard rumors of the
Warlord's extrahuman mental abilities, but he had never seen
them displayed and truly believed they were no more than
rumor. But this . . . this was—

"Put out a report at once, Captain. To all sectors. The black
human known as Tusk—full name Mendaharin Tusca—
originally wanted for desertion from the Navy of the Galactic
Democratic Republic, is now wanted for questioning by the
Revolutionary Congress. Tusca is to be captured alive. Make
that understood—especially to those trigger-happy bounty
hunters. As a deserter, there must be a reward already offered
for him. Find out what it is and quadruple it. But no bounty
will be paid if he's brought in dead or in any condition that
renders him useless to us. The same applies to the passenger
he's carrying."

"Passenger?" Nada raised his eyebrows, then caught the
Warlord's cold-eyed stare. "Yes, my lord. Is—is there a
description of the passenger as well?"

"A boy, about seventeen," Sagan said in low tones, one hand
tapping restlessly against his thigh. "He might possibly have—
No, belay that. Don't put out any description at all on the
passenger." He raised the gloved hand. "I want it emphasized.
Taken alive!"

"Yes, my lord."

"Thank you, Captain. You are dismissed."

"Yes, my lord. Thank you, my lord."

Bowing, fist over his heart, Captain Nada left the committee
room. When the door had closed behind him, Sagan yanked off
the war helmet and ran his hand through his long, damp hair.

"The captain takes you for a phenomenon," Admiral Aks
remarked, the first words he had spoken since the Warlord
entered the room. "I must admit that I, too, am impressed—"

"Bah!" Sagan shrugged, then winced and began to tug
irritably at the tight bandages that had been hastily wrapped
around his left forearm. The movement brought the hem of his
red robe into the full light, and Aks noticed that the usually
glittering gold border was soaked in blood.

"The Guardian resisted," Aks said, his gaze on the stain and
on his lordship's wound.

"The fool impaled himself on my sword!" Sagan said with an

impatient gesture that brought another grimace of pain. "I'm getting too old for this, Aks."

"Nonsense, my lord." At age sixty, the admiral was older than his Warlord by twelve years and considered the subject of old age an indelicate one, if not positively insulting. "You've had no rest for twenty-four hours. You're tired, that's all."

"Twenty-four hours. The day was, Aks, when twenty-four hours without sleep was nothing to me. But those times are gone . . . like so much else." He fell silent, the tanned face dark and brooding.

Aks shifted uncomfortably. His lordship invariably fell into these dark moods after an encounter with one of the Guardians. The slightest infraction brought a snarl of anger. Men walked on tiptoe in his presence. Aks hoped devoutly that all this would end soon.

"And so you believe the boy is traveling with this . . . Mendaharin Tusca?" Aks brought the conversation back to official business.

"Of course!" Sagan flexed the muscles in his shoulders and upper arms. "Nada thinks I'm exhibiting my mystical powers but it's a matter of simple deduction. A dock worker suddenly pays his landlord off in golden coins of a type never seen before on this planet. Not only that, but the mercenary escapes Syrac Seven at the earliest opportunity. He has the boy, you may be certain."

"That is understandable, my lord. But how did you recognize the somewhat unusual method he used to effect his escape?"

"The drunken pilot? I taught that little trick to his father."

Aks coughed uncomfortably. The conversation had gone full circle, it seemed. Back to the Guardians again.

"Didn't you make the connection, Aks? Tusk. Who else but Mendaharin Tusca—"

"The son of Danha Tusca!"

The Warlord's mouth twisted into a bitter smile that had a trace of pride about it. "He taught his son well. One of my old squadron. But then, they were the best. . . ."

The faint sound of bells could be heard ringing throughout the ship, keeping the time as they had for centuries. Impatiently, Sagan shook his head. "This is getting us nowhere and I must contact the President within the hour, while the Cabinet's still in session. Admiral, I want you to make preparations to transfer your flag to *Eagle*."

"My lord?" Aks looked startled.

"Relax, Aks, I'm taking this ship and breaking off from the fleet. Have Nada set a course for Sector X-24."

"That's in General Ghia's sector, my lord."

"I am aware of that, Admiral. That's my I want you to remain behind to handle this. It will involve skilled diplomacy. Ghia will be angry no matter what you say, but he'll get over it. I'll clear it through the President. You will tell Ghia that I am on special assignment, sent to bring a political prisoner of the highest importance to justice. You need say nothing more than that. Ghia's no fool. He knows of my 'obsession,' of my 'bloodthirsty lust for revenge,' as the press puts it."

Aks regarded his lord with admiration. "So you have found her."

"Yes, Aks, I have found her," Derek Sagan said quietly. "And now, I believe you have a great deal of work with which to occupy yourself?"

"Yes, my lord." Admiral Aks bowed and, taking the not too subtle hint, left the committee room.

Alone, Sagan walked slowly to a control panel beneath the huge screen. Removing his glove, he started to place his hand on the grid that would scan his DNA and verify his identity, allowing him to open the direct access channel to the Cabinet Room. But Sagan paused, considering what he would say. Not that words would much matter. He knew how the President would react. Still, the Warlord would have his arguments on record.

Abruptly he placed his hand upon the grid.

The screen began to glow faintly.

"Identification verified," came a synthesized female voice. "Derek Sagan, marshal of Sector M-16. Do you desire access to the President?"

"I do," Saga replied. "Priority One."

"One moment while your request is forwarded."

The screen's glow continued to brighten. Removing his hand, Sagan again ran it through his hair. He was not attempting to smarten his appearance before his commander. Far from it. The cool air felt good on his scalp. He rotated his arm, attempting to loosen the tight muscles bunched up in the back of his shoulders. Exercise in the gym, a hot bath, and a rubdown. He wished he'd been able to relax first, but the Cabinet was in session only once a day and he'd cut the timing close as it was.

The blank screen came to life with a suddenness that never failed to catch Sagan by surprise. Thirty humans and aliens seated at a long oval table had their attention more or less focused on a screen of their own.

"You stand now before the duly appointed members of the Cabinet of the Galactic Democratic Republic, Citizen General Derek Sagan," the female voice said. "You may proceed."

Sagan glanced along the length of the table, scanning the thirty faces that stared back at him. Some he recognized, others he did not. That wasn't unusual. He hadn't been in contact with the cabinet for months and there was bound to have been changes. The President liked fresh blood. Sagan's gaze went to the thirty-first face—a face he knew well. The President of the Republic. Wasn't Robes's about due to run for reelection? Sagan did some hasty mental calculation. That could have an effect on his actions.

"Greetings, Citizen General."

"Mr. President."

Robes sat in the center of the group gathered around the table. His hands were clasped casually in front of him; his friendly, open face was smiling. Blond and tan, Robes appeared frank, honest, ingenuous. Sagan was among those who knew the cold, calculating genius beneath the actor's mask.

"You must have important news for us, Derek," the President said, his words enhanced by the charming smile that had won him so many elections. "Please, don't keep us in suspense!"

Sagan cringed. As President, this man had the right to call him by his given name, but this familiarity had always irritated the Warlord and he found it grew more irritating as time passed. What were you, Robes, before I put you into power? A political science professor at a small university.

"I hereby inform the cabinet members and you, Mr. President, that the Guardian Platus Morianna is dead."

There was a murmur of disapproval from around the table. Robes's expression changed with facile ease from charmed to disappointed. Only Sagan saw the flicker of danger in the eyes.

"I am distressed to hear this, Derek," the President said with a slight shrug of the shoulders beneath his expensive, tailored business suit. "You are, of course, aware that this man was wanted for public trial—"

"I was aware of that!" Sagan snapped. He was tired, his

control slipping. "Mr. President. As in the case of the Guardian Stavros, I deemed this death necessary."

There, let them chew on that, he thought, watching with grim satisfaction the quick range of emotions pass over the President's face. Robes removed disappointment and tried on anger, but immediately discarded it—one was rarely angry with a general who controlled one-twentieth of your military forces. The President settled upon mildly threatening.

"I trust you will make the reasons known in your full report, Citizen General—a report which we will expect to be receiving from you immediately. Have you other news?"

"Not at this time, Mr. President."

Robes's bright blue eyes narrowed, regarding Sagan intently. "Very well, Citizen General. Thank you."

"Mr. President."

The screen went dark, but Sagan remained standing before it, waiting with as much patience as he ever waited for anything. He knew it wouldn't be long. Robes was noted for quick, decisive action.

Within moments—just as long as it would take to clear a room of thirty people—the screen came back to life.

"Sagan. Thank you for waiting."

The Warlord made no response. The President was alone, the room empty. "Activate scrambler."

That was to be expected, considering the delicate nature of the discussion. Reaching down, Sagan depressed a button. The annoying buzzing in his ears told him that their conversation could now be held in strictest security. The words spoken by each man were being transmitted in coded audio impulses that could be understood by only these two alone. Although it was highly unlikely that anyone could be monitoring their conversation from the tight security of the sealed Cabinet Room or from the equally tight security aboard *Phoenix*, this conversation was far too dangerous to take even the tiniest fraction of a chance.

"Continue," the President said. Now that they were alone, he did not bother to control the eagerness of his expression. "Was he the one you suspected? Did he have the boy? Is the boy with you?"

"I regret to report that the boy escaped, Mr. President. However"—Derek raised his bandaged hand, seeing the look of eagerness tighten to anger—"I know who has him. I have a description of the craft in which they fled. The alert has gone out to all sectors. But, more important, I have now another, surer means to locate the boy. I have no doubt that he will soon be within our grasp."

"I am glad that *you* have no doubts, Derek," Robes said in a low voice. "As for leaving this in the hands of reckless bounty hunters—"

"If I may be permitted to continue, sir, I will elaborate."

Frowning, the President tapped a manicured fingernail on the table. He had no choice but to listen, and both he and his Warlord knew it. Sagan also knew he would be made to pay for this insubordination at some later date, but he would worry about that later.

"I have discovered the whereabouts of Lady Maigrey Morianna."

The Presidential fingernail paused, the emotions on Robes's face were unreadable as he absorbed this unforeseen information, rapidly assimilating in his mind what it might mean to him.

"Indeed? I had no idea she was still alive."

"I knew."

It was a flat answer, carefully delivered. But the President was quick to catch it.

"Yes," he said thoughtfully, "you must have known. She was . . . rather special to you once, wasn't she, Derek?"

Sagan disdainfully declined to answer such an impertinent question. His face dispassionate, he regarded the President with the cool gaze of one who waits patiently for a colleague to have his little joke and then get on with the business at hand.

"No, no, my friend. I was not referring to *that*!" Robes said with a sly smile. "I refer to the fact that you two were . . . what did they call it?" He made a graceful gesture with his hand. "Mental . . . mental. . . ."

"Mind-linked, sir."

"Yes, mind-linked. That was it. Quite a fascinating phenomenon. It occurred, as I recall, only between those of the Blood Royal, and infrequently at that. But tell me, Derek, if the woman was not dead, how is it that she has escaped you all these years? The mind-link is not affected by distance."

"No, sir." Sagan discovered he had to steel himself to discuss the matter. He had not supposed it would be this difficult. "The mind-link is not affected by distance or by anything else in this universe except—"

He checked his words. "But I will not take up your time

with medical and parapsychological details, Mr. President. Suffice it to say that seventeen years ago, the mind-link between Lady Morianna and myself was severed. It has now been reforged. She can no longer hide from me. I know where she is."

"Then you must apprehend her at once, Derek," the President said, placing his hands palms down upon the table.

"She is on a planet located somewhere in Sector X-24, sir. General Ghia's sector. I will need some time to search out the planet—"

"I will make the necessary arrangements with Ghia." The President made a decisive gesture. His next words came hesitantly; he was considering each carefully. "I assume that since you are aware of her, she is also aware of you—"

"Yes, sir. But there is nothing to fear. She will not escape me."

"I remind you, Derek, that her brother escaped you— through death."

"I am aware of that, sir. You forget, my lord, I know this woman. She is a Guardian. The last of the Guardians. As long as the boy lives, her vow to protect him will bind her to this life."

"You know this to be true? You are in contact?"

"No, Mr. President." Sagan was beginning to lose patience. His body ached, he needed rest, and there was still work to be done to prepare for his journey. Yet he had to put up with this. "The mind-link is still very fragile. I sense her presence in this universe, as she senses mine. It grows hourly, but she is fighting against it. Only by direct and constant contact will I be able to break down her strong mental barriers. We have time, however. Should she try to take her life, there is one who will stop her."

"And who is that?"

"God, Mr. President."

Sagan had the weary satisfaction of seeing Peter Robes shift uncomfortably in his chair. The President adjusted the cuffs of his shirtsleeves, straightened his tie, and cleared his throat. To an avowed atheist, as were all good democrats, this bold reference to a god who didn't exist was embarrassing.

The President abruptly changed the subject.

"You stated that Lady Maigrey will be of help to you in finding the boy. I fail to understand how, if she is sworn to protect him."

"She is a visionary, sir. She can visualize events as they are transpiring. Once the mind-link is reforged, I will 'persuade' her to contact the boy."

"She is not a woman who can be easily persuaded, if I remember her correctly."

"There are ways. You forget, I know her. I know her well," Sagan repeated. The words left a bitter taste in his mouth, as though he had drunk tainted water.

Perhaps the President heard this, even through the scrambler. Or perhaps he saw the grim, dark expression on the already grim face, shadowed by a weariness that came from struggling not so much with outer conflict as with inner.

"I congratulate you, Derek," Robes said, his hands coming together on the tabletop, fingertips meeting. "It seems that at last, after all these years, our long search is ended. It will be a splendid day when we can bring this royalist to public trial and remind the populace of the injustices they suffered under the monarchy. Her execution should end once and for all this talk of—"

"May I offer my advice, sir?" Sagan broke in.

"Since when have you ever felt the need to ask permission, Derek?" Robes said acidly, irritated at having his flow of thought stopped.

"Allow me to kill her swiftly and quietly when I am finished with her. She is of the Blood Royal, bred to exert a power over the minds and hearts of others. I warn you, if you give her access to the public, she will turn your trial into a royalist forum and make herself a martyr."

The President's face flushed in anger. The hands on the table slowly clenched. "I have put up with a great deal from you today, Derek. I have allowed you to interrupt me. I have endured references to a religion now known by all to be weak-minded superstition and the practicing of such by *all*"— he emphasized the word—"considered a traitorous act. I tolerate this in you, Derek, because of my gratitude for the help you have given me in the past and because you are one of the best of my military commanders. But you are only one, Derek. You are one . . . and I am many. Remember that. And never tell me again how I am to run my government."

"Yes, Mr. President."

"When you have gleaned the necessary information from this woman, she is to be brought to the Congress, fit to stand trial. At such time, you will deliver the boy as well. I don't suppose you have any advice for me concerning *him?*"

"No, Mr. President."

"Very well. Thank you, Citizen General." The President raised his right hand, palm outward in a salute. "The People."

Sagan raised his right hand. The screen was dimming rapidly. The scrambler carried his last words, but not the image of the curled lip or the flare of contempt in the man's eyes.

"The People."

Chapter ··❦··❦·· Seven

Whereto answering, the sea,
Delaying not, hurrying not,
Whisper'd me through the night, and very plainly before
   daybreak,
Lisp'd to me the low and delicious word death . . .
   Walt Whitman, "Out of the Cradle Endlessly Rocking"

Oha-Lau was one of two planets belonging to a small star located in Sector X-24 on the very fringes of the galaxy. The star was noted on the great interstellar space maps by the configuration of QWW31648XX, this indicating its position in the galaxy, the number of planets with some type of life forms, the type of the life forms, and so forth. In point of fact, this number told anyone who knew how to interpret it that this was a star of very little importance. Of its two planets, only one contained life, and it had nothing that would benefit the galaxy at large. The planet's climate was tropical, the land overrun with flora and fauna so varied that botanists had given up categorizing it once they discovered most of it was inedible. (Some of it, in fact, had eaten the botanists.)

The natives of the planet of QWW31648XX, were human and, so scientists believed, had arrived on the planet centuries before during the second Dark Ages, one of Earth's early colonization periods. That they had come here by accident was almost certain, for why should anyone come on purpose? It was presumed that, sick and tired of wandering among the stars, they had landed their craft here and obliterated all traces of the repressive civilization they had been fleeing.

In essence—as Sagan told Captain Nada, who did not understand the literary reference—the sailors threw the breadfruit trees overboard and went native. They named their planet Oha-Lau, which means "Forgotten." It is presumed the name did not apply so much to those early travelers themselves as to their attitude toward where they'd originated.

Safe from the ravages of galactic progress, the descendants of those early immigrants led a peaceful existence. They lived in harmony with the lush tropical environment, hunted strange beasts with spears and bows, and dwelt in huts made of woven grass. They danced and feasted and sought, always, to appease the glittering lights in the night sky. For there was a legend, ancient as the dimmest memory of their ancestors, that out of the glittering lights would come doom for the people of Oha-Lau.

Therefore, when anyone—man or alien, scientist, soldier, or smuggler—landed on Oha-Lau in his fire-tailed bird, the natives treated him with respect, fulfilled his every wish, and hustled him off their planet as speedily as possible. There were few extraterrestrial visitors to Oha-Lau, but on occasion the outside universe did make its presence known. The scientists, of course, spent time on Oha-Lau when its intelligent life-forms were first discovered. Every type of -ologist known to man arrived, confounding the innocent natives with their light-blinking boxes and questions that seemed to mostly concern the coming of age of young women. A military patrol landed once, but promptly left upon ascertaining that these people weren't interested in fighting each other, much less anybody else. And no planet, no matter how insignificant, is ever below the notice of—as they deemed themselves—interplanetary entrepreneurs.

Oha-Lau did possess one thing of value—to the jewelers if not to the scientists or the military. This was moonrith—a semiprecious gem, much prized in the galaxy for its soft, translucent beauty. Any daring, enterprising businessman who happened to find his way to Oha-Lau generally left with enough moonrith to grant him three months of high living. Those who entertained ideas of returning with mining machines and geologists were invariably disappointed, however, for the natives maintained stolidly that they had no idea where the moonrith could be located. The entrepreneur who entered the jungle in search of it never returned.

The small green planet might have continued to circle its unassuming sun forever ignorant of the troubles and turmoil of the worlds beyond. But Oha-Lau was doomed, and its doom came out of the stars as legend foretold.

Doom fell, literally, on Oha-Lau in the form of a spaceplane—a small fighter, to be exact—that crash-landed among the thick foliage near one of the principle villages. The natives were accustomed to spaceplanes landing on their planet, but not to one smashing into the trees, cutting a wide swath of destruction through the vegetation. In vain they waited for something or someone to come out of the wounded bird, but it sat still and silent.

No one dared approach it. The natives had all seen these strange birds shoot flame from their tails and roar into the night sky, and everyone feared this might do the same without warning. But, finally, curiosity got the better of them. The crippled bird appeared to be near death; it was making the most pathetic beeping sound, and some of the young warriors approached it, spears ready.

The bird was, indeed, dead (or it was after a spear jab killed the object that was beeping). Its pilot was not, however. She was unconscious, suffering from severe dehydration and starvation—a victim of space narcosis, though the natives did not know this. The computer system had saved her life, guiding the craft on controls she had set when she realized she was losing her grip on consciousness.

There was one person in the tribe who cautioned against helping this stranger from the stars, one wise and cynical being who reminded them of the legend and protested taking the woman into their midst. But the gentle people ignored the old man and brought their doom upon themselves.

The warriors lifted the pilot from the spaceplane and carried her to the hut of the tribal healer. He had no idea what was the matter with the young woman, but thought the symptoms appeared similar to those experienced by his people who lost their way in the jungle and were later found, half-crazed and wandering. He treated the young pilot accordingly with herbs and potions and soothing music and—either because of his medicine or in spite of it—the pilot made a complete and rapid recovery.

And thus was the beginning of the end. The natives did not notice, when they buried the bird, the black carbon streaks down the sides of the spaceplane. They saw the wrecked deflector shields but had no idea what they meant. They could not know, in their innocence, that their guest had been involved in some terrible conflict and had barely escaped with her life. They could not know that she was going to bring that conflict to them.

··⟨■ ■⟩··

If the young pilot had foreseen the grief and destruction she would inadvertently bring down upon the innocent people she would grow to love, she would have fled to an even more remote part of the galaxy. But her spaceplane was at the bottom of a bog. She herself was wounded in mind and body. Oha-Lau was a sanctuary of peace and beauty, kindness, compassion, smiles, and laughter. She had almost forgotten such things existed. So she stayed on Oha-Lau and let it heal—so she supposed—the deep gash in her soul.

The natives, usually so eager to be rid of visitors, made an exception in the case of the young pilot. She did not ask stupid questions about virgins. She didn't want to know where to find moonrith. She lived among them, yet apart. She learned their language, respected their ways, and, unconsciously, began to exert her influence upon them.

They didn't know why, except that she had, as the old man said, ancient eyes. Certainly the eyes of the twenty-four-year-old woman had seen more grief and suffering and horror than most see in a lifetime. But behind the shadow of pain and sorrow was a wisdom and power that came from centuries of genetic research. She had been born and bred to shape men and events, and she could no more deny this part of her nature than she could deny the sea-gray eyes that came from her barbarian father or the pale, sea-foam color hair that was the gift of her unhappy mother.

The downed pilot began her quiet rule by solving small problems and settling minor disputes. Impressed with her skill and tact, the elders sought her out for advice, particularly on the handling of other-world guests. She had as great a reluctance to encourage these unwelcome visitors to Oha-Lau as did the natives. Her regal presence caused even the most arrogant smuggler to regard her with awe and, without quite knowing how, within a few years, the downed pilot had become the beloved ruler of the people of Oha-Lau.

The woman was content. Her past, with its bitter memories, began to fade away for her as she hoped desperately it would do for others. Everyone must believe her to be dead. She tried to convince herself of that, although she knew in her soul that this was impossible. One man, at least, was aware that she lived. But if she was very, very careful, she might remain hidden from him and be able to rest on this lovely, peaceful planet forever. Like the natives, she avoided looking up into the stars at night.

··◁▪ ▪▷··

Doom did not fall swiftly.

The woman had a gift of vision—"longsight" the natives called it. She could see in her mind a fearsome beast approaching camp and send the warriors to kill it before it could harm anyone. She could see unwelcome visitors approaching their planet as well, and these often found an "honor guard" waiting for them upon their arrival. What the natives did not know, of course, was the true power of the woman or her gift. With it, she could see to the ends of the universe. It could reveal, if she chose to use it, the events transpiring in the galaxy. She did not choose to use her gift, however, having made up her mind to shun the worlds above. But the gift was not one she had complete control over, and sometimes the visions came to her unbidden.

This happened the first time seventeen years after she had arrived on the planet. One evening, while walking with her attendants to her simple hut, she frightened them all by crying out in anger and fear for no reason whatsoever—no reason, at least, that they could see. She covered her face with her hands, but she could not blot out the sight that was transpiring before her mind's eye.

"Stavros!" she cried through her tears, forced to watch as the dear friend and companion of her childhood died in unspeakable agony.

And she knew, as he died, that he had revealed the secret.

··◁▪ ▪▷··

Doom was poised, ready to fall.

Her people watched her in concern after that. The woman was preoccupied, given to pacing the smooth grassy stretches of the garden they had made for her. Muttering strange names, her hands twisting together, she walked back and forth, back and forth. Then she would begin to weep and, shaking her head, run to her hut and hide like a child in the darkness.

Hide from what? Her people grew terrified. Was there some dread beast in the jungle coming to attack them? Something more awful than anything they had ever previously encountered?

The woman tried to reassure them. "It has nothing to do with you," she told them.

But this time they were more gifted with foresight than she.

··◁▮ ▮▷··

Doom fell.

A heartbroken scream shattered the tropical night—a scream of such fury and hatred, such loss and grief, that the people, after a moment of frozen fear, rushed to their ruler's hut in terror, expecting to find her murdered, torn apart by some savage creature. Instead, they found the woman, shaking with sobs, crouched on her knees beside her cot. Her attendants sought to comfort her, but she would not be comforted. Seventeen years of peace and beauty and safety had ended.

Her piercing cry had awakened everyone in the village, filling those who heard it with vague, unknown terror. But the woman's cry had gone far beyond the village. It echoed beyond the green planet into the stars, carrying its message of grief and anguish out into the galaxy. And so it was that, even as the sword pierced her brother's body, his killer heard that cry and knew, deep in his soul, who it was that mourned. Her hatred and sorrow and pain touched him as nothing had touched him in seventeen years. And he knew, if not where she was, how to find her. The mind-link between these two, broken seventeen years ago, was reforged.

The fate of Oha-Lau was sealed. For the first time in the planet's history, one man now began to actively search for it. And that made it only a matter of time before his attention was drawn to the speck of green, sparkling like a tiny jewel on the fingertips of the great galactic arm.

··◁▮ ▮▷··

Maigrey sat cross-legged on a rattan mat inside her hut. Her eyes were closed. She leaned back wearily against the sturdy, living walls formed by the mothering tree—so called because this tree, with its strong trunk and sheltering branches, could be uprooted from its home, replanted in new ground, take root again, and flourish. Plant many mothering trees together, side by side, and the trunks would fuse, forming walls, the leafy branches intertwining to create a roof so thick that only minimal thatching was added to protect the dweller from the heavy jungle rains.

Once Maigrey had loved the thought of living within a living tree. It spoke to her of the reverence and respect these people held for life. She was touched and amused by the name—the mothering tree. Often, when she had awakened in the night, tormented by some dreadful dream she could never remember, she lay upon her bed, cowering in nameless fear, only to hear the whispered lullaby of the leaves of the mothering tree. Though she had never known her own mother, never heard her own mother's voice, she thought she knew the words of that lullaby, words that came only in fragments and could never be recalled, words spoken in a language she only vaguely remembered. Comforted, she would fall into sweet, dreamless sleep.

Dreamless sleep. Maigrey squeezed her eyes tightly shut against the sun's bright glare that shone through the open doorway and filtered down among the leaves of the tree. Dreamless sleep.

"Heavenly Creator, is this too much to ask?" she muttered, pressing her hands against her burning forehead. "No!" She stared defiantly up into the branches tangled above her head. "It is *not* too much and I *will* have it." She glared at the inoffensive leaves, which trembled in the jungle's slight breeze, yet seemed to be trembling at her tone of bitter anger. "I know Your law! I will argue my case before Your Heavenly Tribunal! 'See!' I will cry. 'See what You have made me endure! And I have borne it all—the pain, the suffering—without complaint. I kept my vow. I did,'" she repeated angrily. "'Did You keep Yours?' Ha!"

That vicious "Ha!" startled an old man entering the hut. Cringing, he made as if to back away, but Maigrey—seeing him—rose hastily to her feet.

"Please, Healer, please come in. I am sorry if I offended you. I wasn't talking to you. I . . . was talking . . . to myself . . ."

Nodding and shrugging, the old man hobbled into the hut. He was a very old man, this ancient healer. So old that the children of the companions of his youth were now dying of old age.

"I am meant to see the end," he used to say, and he always said it in the tone of voice of one who is cursed.

Shuffling across the dirt floor of the hut, he eyed Maigrey

with a shrewd, eager gaze in which there was a gleam of hope. The woman spread a fresh mat upon the floor of her hut, knowing that the old man would appreciate the gesture of respect. He did so, lowering himself onto the mat awkwardly and slowly with a great show of infirmity. Maigrey knew this bone-creaking *was* show—the day the tiger wandered into the village the spry old man outran most of the young warriors. But the shaking legs and snapping bones gained him many advantages—the best place by the campfire, the choicest bits from the dinner pots, nubile young women to aid his feeble steps.

Kneeling down on her own mat facing him, Maigrey smiled at the old man nervously. "Have you brought it today?"

The old man glowered at her, as if wondering why she should ask such a fool question, though he had been three days before without bringing it. Of course he had brought it. He made a major production of fumbling at the knot of a ragged scrip hanging from a rope tied around his shriveled middle. Maigrey's hands twitched to snatch it from him, but she dared not anger him and could only sit and wait in impatience that the old eyes were quick to note.

He drew it forth slowly and tossed it onto the mat between them. "I have brought what you requested, Sea-Eyes," he said in a quavering voice that was probably as phony as his creaking legs.

"Will it work as they say?" Oddly she made no move to touch it now that it lay within her reach.

"Yes, yes!" The old man waved a gnarled hand at the pouch. "Boil the bark in water until the green foam rises. Drink it, then—"

"Slowly? Swiftly?" Maigrey stared at the pouch in fascination.

"Oh, slowly. The taste is said to be quite exquisite and you might as well enjoy it going down."

"And then?"

"You will begin to feel very tired."

"No pain?"

"None. Lay yourself down. It would be of help to your women," the old man hinted, "if you were to dress yourself in the burial gown beforehand."

"I understand," Maigrey said, swallowing a sudden wild burst of laughter that welled up from her knotted stomach.

Reaching out with a firm and steady hand, she lifted the pouch and opened it casually, sniffing at the contents as if she were buying spices in the market. The smell was pleasant, even enticing. The old man watched her without expression.

"Will your death stop the grandfathers?" he asked suddenly.

"I—I don't know," Maigrey faltered, unable to meet his eyes. "I hope so."

"We will hold the funeral many days," the old man promised pathetically, spreading his hands. "Many days we will celebrate and beat the drums. Surely they will hear and go away?"

Maigrey had a sudden vision of her corpse, lying for days in the jungle heat. "Yes," she murmured. "Yes, they will hear and they will leave." Rising to her feet, she was about to offer the old man food and drink, as was customary.

Her eyes opened wide. The words caught in her throat; she nearly strangled.

The old man, watching her closely, saw her pale face become paler still, her eyes stare in disbelief. His back to the door, he turned his head quickly to see what had terrified his ruler.

It was a spirit.

The old man had never seen a spirit, but he wasn't particularly surprised by this one's appearance in his camp. At the old man's time of life, nothing much surprised him anymore. He might have been frightened if the spirit had appeared hostile. It didn't. It just looked tired, as though it hadn't slept in a long, long time. It made no threatening move or gesture, but stood in the doorway, staring inside with a wistful expression.

And it suddenly occurred to the old man that no one had greeted the spirit or asked it to enter.

The old man gathered himself together and rose to his feet.

"Welcome, spirit," he said with a bow that sounded—from the cracking bones—as if he'd been snapped in two. As near as he could recall, a spirit had to be invited inside a dwelling or it couldn't pass beyond the threshold. He glanced at Maigrey. It was her dwelling, after all. She said nothing, simply stared at the spirit, the bag of lovepoison clutched tightly in her hand.

Edging over to the woman, the old man gave her a poke with his finger. "Ask it in!"

"Platus!" Maigrey whispered.

The old man looked back at the spirit, thinking that perhaps this was some sort of invitation, spoken in the strange language that the woman spoke to herself sometimes. But apparently it wasn't. The spirit remained standing in the door, regarding the woman with sad eyes.

Maigrey turned her back on the spirit.

"No, no!" screeched the old man, appalled. He'd never visited with a spirit before, and, by the gods, he wasn't going to lose this one. "Come in, honored spirit," he said, shoving his own fresh mat across the floor with his foot. "I am not the owner of this lodge"—a rebuking look at Maigrey—"but I am the elder of the village"—a proud lifting of the head—"and as such I invite you to be our guest."

The spirit looked from Maigrey to the old man and back to Maigrey again with some astonishment.

"I don't know," Maigrey said in a helpless tone. "I don't know why he can see you, Platus. Unless Whoever sent you needs a witness."

"He needs no witness, sister," Platus said in the mild voice Maigrey remembered so well, though she had not heard it in seventeen years. "He is all-seeing, all-knowing. And all-forgiving, as I have reason to know."

The old man had no idea what was being said, since the two spoke in an unfamiliar language. He saw the spirit still standing in the entrance to the hut and poked Maigrey again.

"Come in," she said dully, with a halfhearted, despairing gesture. She pressed the knuckles of the hand that held the bag into her mouth, but it did no good. She began to cry.

The spirit entered and came to stand beside the woman. Its hands reached out to comfort her, but there is no comfort the dead can offer the living. It must be a new spirit, the old man thought, not to know that.

The spirit was kin to the woman, the old man realized: slender build, pale hair, the features were similar though the mold from which they had been cast seemed to have been made stronger when it formed the woman. This was a family matter, then. The old man knew he must leave. He did so, but not before he had spoken his mind.

"I mistrust you are from the grandfathers, spirit," he said. "Perhaps you have been sent to lead your kin to her rest. I hope she will not keep you waiting long." The old man cast a meaningful glance at the bag Maigrey held in her hand. "Tell the grandfathers they do not need to come. The funeral will be a fine one, very fine." He repeated this several times, bobbing in the entrance of the hut. Then, finally, he was gone.

The evening air, fragrant with the perfume of growing

things, drifted into the hut. It was the wind's gentle touch that Maigrey felt on her shoulders, not the hands of the spirit. But the fingers grazed her soul, if not her flesh. Raising her head and moving away from the spirit, she stared straight ahead defiantly, blinking the tears from her eyes.

"It's good to see you, Platus. How have you been?" she started to ask casually, then broke off with a hysterical giggle that ended in a sob. God! What a stupid question!

"I meant, where are . . . *were* you living? What have you . . . *were* you doing . . . all this time?" she stammered. Rubbing the heel of her hand in her eyes, she dragged it across her nose, sniffing.

"Still the same as when you were young," Platus said, smiling sadly, fondly. "Never a handkerchief. What was the name of that captain friend of yours who used to carry a spare for you in his uniform—"

"Don't start, brother!" Maigrey whispered, her eyes on the ground at her feet. "I can't bear it. Not now."

"I lived on a planet named Syrac Seven. Stavros, Danha, and I chose it because it was on a major trade route with good channels of communication and there are large portions of it that remain undeveloped. It was easy for me to lose myself there—with him," he added in wistful tones. "Danha and Stavros left me, and went their separate ways. You know, I suppose, what happened?"

Maigrey glanced at him unhappily. "I know about Stavros," she said, a catch in her throat. "But . . . not Danha, too?"

"Five years ago. And others before. One by one, Maigrey, Sagan tracked them down, broke them, forced them to betray their fellows. And so the end came, inexorably."

"And so it will come to me. I've made my decision."

"Your decision is the wrong one. You know it, Maigrey. Seventeen years ago you fought for your life—"

"Did I?" she demanded, turning suddenly to confront him. "Did I? Or did I betray us? Seventeen years ago, did I betray my king?"

"Maigrey"—Platus appeared confused—"I don't understand! What do you mean, did you betray us? Of course, you didn't! You led the fight against Sagan!"

"Perhaps that was all part of his plan! Don't you see? I must have known!" Maigrey cried, twisting the leather bag in her hands. "He must have told me in advance! He told me everything! I knew him, better than anyone! We were mind-linked! How could I *not* have known?"

"Maigrey, this is . . . irrational! Because of you, we escaped him! Don't you remember?"

"No, I don't remember!" Her clenched fists pressed her forehead. "I remember only fragments of what happened that night! The doctors said I might never remember."

"Maigrey, I can tell you what happened—"

She shook her head impatiently. "I *know* what happened! I've been *told* what happened! In the hospital, when I was recovering, I saw them look at me. I saw them thinking, 'Why you? Why did you survive when so many others died?' Don't you see, Platus?" She stared at him, beseeching him to understand. "He let me live! There had to be some reason! That's why I ran away. I didn't want to hear him say, 'Let us congratulate ourselves, my lady. Our plan worked. None of them suspect.'"

"No! No, I don't believe it, Maigrey. You were wild, willful. But you were always honorable. A true daughter of our father. My God," Platus continued in a low voice, "don't you remember that time our father made us watch when he tortured that man? The one who had betrayed a friend—"

"And Sagan *was* my friend! No matter what choice I made, I ended up betraying somebody!" Her laughter cracked and she gritted her teeth, fighting not to lose control. "But that is all past. The mind-link is reforged. He is coming to seize me and you say that he should find me alive? You know the danger. He will use me to locate the boy."

"No, sister. You will use him."

Maigrey looked at her brother, puzzled. He did not explain, and she shook her head. "Riddles! You haven't changed," she muttered, regarding Platus with the same impatience and frustration she had felt around him seventeen years ago.

When his spirit had first appeared to her in the hut, she saw him as she had known him earlier—the older brother, the scholarly genius, whose sensitive, expressive face no amount of armor or military training could mold into the hard, cold face of a warrior. The spirit seemed to age, though, when he spoke of his past, and Maigrey saw Platus as he must have looked when he died—a man in his late forties with the mild face and vacant eyes of one who had taken to gazing far away in search of a reality that is close at hand.

You will use him. Suddenly, she understood.

"Oh, no!" she protested.

"I am sorry, Maigrey," Platus answered, the thin, shimmering shoulders slumping in defeat. "I failed. You see, the boy has no idea of . . . of anything."

Maigrey regarded him silently, impassively. "Nothing?"

Platus shook his head. "I hoped they'd forget about him. I hoped they would never find out. I love Dion, Maigrey. I love him as I have loved nothing in this life! All I wanted was that Dion be—" Platus drew a soft breath—"ordinary."

If a spirit could have wept, this one would have. But tears are a comfort the dead are denied.

"You still don't understand, do you, brother?" Maigrey said, wearily dragging her sweat-damp hair back from her face. Walking to the door of the hut, she stood there, letting the evening breeze dry her fevered skin. Her gaze went to the stars, burning coldly above. She hadn't looked at them for a long, long time and now her heart ached with memories. "We are born to be what we are. We can't escape it. The boy can't escape it!" Turning to face her brother, she asked impatiently, "Surely he must have wondered. Didn't he ever question? Around other people, didn't he—"

"He was never around other people. I raised him . . . isolated, alone. We didn't need other people. We had our studies, our music. He was happy, Maigrey. He truly was! And so was I. These last seventeen years of peace were the blessing of my life."

"Yes, I can imagine," Maigrey answered, looking around at her own peaceful surroundings. The two stood silently, their thoughts on the boy—one recalling pleasant memories, one trying desperately to recall any memories at all.

"Who does . . . he look like, Platus?"

"He takes after his father's side. Anyone who knew the Starfires will recognize him instantly—the cobalt blue eyes, the red-golden hair that gave them their name."

"What is there of . . . Semele?" This question was so low, the spirit could not have heard it spoken had he not heard it first in his heart.

"Her spirit. The boy has strength, resolve, firmness of purpose. In that, he is *not* like his father."

"Thank the Creator," Maigrey muttered.

"Thank Him? For what?" Platus retorted. "I did everything possible to protect the boy, to save him . . . but it was all wrong, it seems. Even my death was meaningless, since it revealed you to our enemy. Now Dion is out there alone, with no knowledge of who he is, no understanding. You must find him, Maigrey. You must try to warn him, to . . . to tell him. To . . . to do something!"

"But if I find him, Sagan finds him! And how long do you think Derek will let me live after that?"

"'Two must walk the paths of darkness to reach the light . . .'" Platus murmured.

"Don't ever speak that, brother . . . ever! I fulfilled their damned prophecy! I walked the paths of darkness! For seventeen years, I've walked them! How could you understand? You were always weak, Platus. You wanted to save the boy, you say. Save him from what? Himself? From being one of us? Ordinary! Yes, you fought all your life to be ordinary! And that's the reason you've been doomed to living death! Because in life you refused to accept what you were!"

"And I would do it all over again," Platus returned with quiet dignity. "I came because I thought you could help, Maigrey. I hoped time had changed you. But now I wonder if I did right. When you find Dion, sister, look at him, look at him closely. You will see a gentle, sensitive, caring young man. Hold that image of him in your heart, because it will not be there long. You and Sagan, between you, will corrupt him." The spirit's face became anguished, his voice broke with the tears he could not shed. "May the Creator grant that my spirit finds rest before I see that happen!"

The incorporeal body began to fade.

"Platus!" Maigrey stretched forth her hand as though she could grasp the ephemeral being and hold it fast. "I'm sorry! Don't leave me. I'm frightened! I can't face this alone!"

"Who is it that you fear, sister? 'Know your enemy.' Wasn't that what our commander always told us? Do you know the enemy, Maigrey? The true enemy?"

The voice died away on the fragrant winds; the presence of the spirit died in Maigrey's heart. But the words remained, rankling, like a barbed arrow that could not be removed without drawing life's blood with it.

Know your enemy. . . . Who is it that you fear?

Slowly, the leather pouch slipped from Maigrey's hand and fell, unnoticed, to the floor. Her gaze was focused on a metal trunk that stood—had stood for seventeen years—at the foot of her cot.

Seventeen years ago, she had hauled it from her damaged plane. She had never, until now, opened it.

Kneeling down, she fumbled at the crude lock. The combination was easy to remember—the anniversary of her birth, the anniversary of her mother's death. The hinges had rusted in the damp tropical climate; they screeched shrilly as she prized the lid open. Only two objects were inside the trunk. One was a worn, green, canvas flight bag. The other, a shapeless bundle of stained cloth. Her hand went to the cloth bundle, her fingers gently touching the reddish brown splotches. She started to draw back the cloth, uncover the object wrapped in the blood-splattered shroud.

Maigrey hesitated, then dropped the bundle and picked up the flight bag. She held it in her lap, running her hand over the rough fabric, her fingers toying with the rusted buckles. Undoing the straps with a trembling hand, Maigrey lifted the flap and dumped the contents of the bag onto the dirt floor.

There wasn't much—just what she had been able to lay hold of in the darkness the night she'd escaped. She hadn't been thinking clearly. They'd given her drugs, but that hadn't eased the pain. Nothing short of death itself could have eased that pain!

A bar of hospital soap, still in its wrapper. A small bottle of shampoo, a washrag, and a towel. Odd, how the mind will run on little things, the small wheels keeping the larger turning. She had packed as if going on weekend leave. A hairbrush, strands of pale hair caught in it. A small rosewood box. Maigrey's hand lingered on this box; the smooth wood always seemed alive to her touch.

But, like the bloodstained bundle, she did not pick up the box either. Her hand went instead to another object. She raised it up and, for the first time in seventeen years, Maigrey looked at herself in a mirror.

The face was older, more solemn than the face of the twenty-four-year-old young woman who—in a half-drugged, wholly despairing state—had thrown these random articles into a flight bag. Long, pale hair fell from a center part down around her face, cascaded over her shoulders. The pain returned, burning, throbbing.

Raising her hand, Maigrey touched the terrible, disfiguring scar—a jagged slash of white that ran from her right temple down her cheek, brushed past the corner of her lip, and ended at the chin

A voice came to her, repeating the phrase. This time, it wasn't her brother's. It was her commander's.

Know your enemy.

"I do, Sagan," Maigrey said, her hand tracing the scar, flinching with pain as though the fingers were the blade of the sword that inflicted it.

She lay down wearily on the floor of the hut, her head pillowed on the flight bag. Reaching out, she touched the face in the mirror.

"I know my enemy. And I fear her more than death!"

Chapter ❖ Eight

> History—a distillation of rumor.
> Thomas Carlyle, *The French Revolution*

Tusk awoke with a start. Rolling out of his chair, he cracked his shin on something and groped about in the darkness, cursing fluently beneath his breath.

"Lights!" he hissed, massaging his bruised leg.

The lights on the bridge flashed on with a brightness and suddenness that caused Tusk to move his hand from his leg to his eyes. "Damn!" he swore. "Turn 'em down!"

The lights dimmed. "Too much jump-juice," XJ commented.

"Shut up. I did not. Now be quiet. Listen—"

The computer was silent.

Blinking his eyes, Tusk leaned forward, waiting for the sound that had awakened him from his nap.

"I don't—"

"Shhhh!" Tusk gave the computer a thump that caused it to whir in irritation. "There it is!" he said, cocking his head. His brow furrowed. "What the deuce is it? I've heard this ship make a lot of weird noises before, but I can't place that. Maybe it's the coupling on the—"

A sound vaguely reminiscent of an asthmatic, laughing monkey came from the computer.

"What's so funny?" Tusk growled. "If it *is* the coupling you won't be laughing long because—"

"You're juiced. It's a syntharp."

"Sinwhat?"

"Harp. Syntharp. Definition: 'An electronic musical instrument with beams of light spanning an open, triangular frame. When the light beams are broken by the passage of the fingers across them—'"

87

"I know *what* it is," Tusk snapped, rubbing his injured leg again. "Just *why* the hell is it?"

"Kid's got it. Go take a look. I was going to wake you, anyway. We're coming to the end of the Lane in twenty-nine minutes and fifteen seconds. I need to know what course to set."

"Harp," Tusk repeated gloomily. Limping across the deck, he caught hold of the ladder and cautiously and quietly pulled himself up far enough so that he could see through the hatch to the living quarters above.

It was dark, and Tusk could barely make out the kid, lying propped up in his hammock, the glowing instrument in his hands. Dion's blue eyes, glinting in light reflected from the syntharp's "strings," stared out into a pain-filled landscape with a fierce, rapt intensity that made the boy appear spellbound. His music ached with the pain of his vision, and made Tusk feel suddenly very much alone. Bitter memories came to mind: his father's hand grasping his in agony, refusing the easeful drugs until Danha had heard his son swear to fulfill his dying request . . . the last, shuddering gasps for breath.

Mad at the boy and mad at himself for being mad, Tusk swung back down the ladder, landing on the deck with a thud.

"Hush," XJ said. "You'll disturb the kid."

"Hell!" Tusk snorted, returning to his seat. "I could blow the rivets out of this mother and the kid'd never miss a note. He's off in some other universe, which is where he's going as soon as we can find someplace to unload him."

Muttering to himself, Tusk glanced at the half-full bottle sitting snugly in its compartment within arm's reach of his chair. XJ saw the look. The lights on the bridge flickered.

"All right, lay off. I'm going to work," Tusk muttered, adding a few other colorful phrases beneath his breath. "Course change." Sitting forward, he began punching up star charts on the computer screen and stared at them, bleary-eyed. "God, I'm half-asleep! Must be that blasted music. Give me our location. How close are we to Dagot?" Tusk rubbed his eyes and studied the coordinates. "That's good. Real good. Look up the name of that city on Dagot where old Sykes has his military academy, will you? We'll deposit the kid there. Sykes owes me his life. He'll take good care of him."

Tusk leaned back comfortably in his seat and reached for the bottle. The harp music had changed. Still sad, it was peaceful now. Death was not the end. There was a greater good. Tusk heard the prayer spoken over his father's body during the funeral—a funeral that had been held in secret in the middle of the night by a priest who had himself been in fear of his life.

The clamp that held the bottle in place during flight refused to unlock.

"Hey, let go!" Tusk commanded the computer. He glared at XJ. "Say, didn't I give you a course change? Let's see those lights flash. Let's hear that disk whir—"

"I like the kid," XJ said.

"Son of the Creator!" Tusk swore in profound astonishment. "That's impossible. You're not programmed to like anyone."

"Liking is an emotional state, therefore it is supposedly an attribute of so-called intelligent life-forms. But you underestimate me. I like the boy for logical, unemotional reasons based solely on his future worth."

"Hah! A kid who doesn't even know his own name, and you're talking future worth? Besides, from what I've seen, people who hang around him don't *have* a future!"

Tusk gave the bottle another, surreptitious tug, just to see if the computer had forgotten. It hadn't.

"I've been thinking about this," he continued, hoping to distract XJ, "and there's a lot about this kid that doesn't add up. At first, I figured he was the son of some Guardian, trying to escape the Warlord. But *I'm* the son of a Guardian. They tortured and murdered my father and you don't see Lord Sagan taking any wild personal interest in me, do you?"

"Not up until now," returned the computer in ominous tones.

Tusk grunted, scowling, and propped his feet up on the control panel.

"Then I decided the kid must be Sagan's son. I discarded that, though. I've seen custody fights over kids before and they get pretty messy sometimes, but we're talking swords and fancy armor here, not to mention the disruption of an entire planet."

"Not to mention the rumors floating around the service to the effect that Lord Sagan doesn't like women."

"He's not discriminatory. He doesn't like men either. He doesn't like anyone, in fact. And quit interrupting me. Where was I? Oh, yeah. I tell you, XJ, this kid is special to someone or maybe a whole bunch of someones. And I don't even like to think who they might be. The sooner we get rid of him, the better. For all of us. The kid included."

"I find that very interesting," XJ mused. "It never ceases to amaze me how you humans come up with intelligent ideas following the most chaotic thought processes. Kid special to someone. We know who at least one someone is. I'll search my files and see if there's anything that ties together the boy and the Warlord. Despite what you say, Sagan's human, after all. Although much superior to most, I might add. Still, in a moment of weakness, he might have made a tiny little mistake. How old is the boy? Seventeen? Born the year of the revolution. That's interesting."

"Is it? Check on the couple of hundred million other kids born that year while you're at it," Tusk commented, yawning.

XJ ignored him, its lights flashing in a subdued, studious manner.

"Hey! What about the course change?" Tusk asked, thumping the computer's terminal.

"The boy could be worth his weight in golden eagles," XJ snapped. "And you want to hand him over to that pompous ass Sykes? I suggest we make no decisions without having more data. I'll bring us out of the Jump. Why don't you find us a nice little war where we can pick up some quick cash and relax while we decide what to do next?"

"Military academy!" Tusk reiterated, glaring at the computer. Realizing that XJ was ignoring him—and that the computer wouldn't release the bottle—Tusk flopped himself back into his chair, activated the vid screen, and inserted a new *Mercenary Mag* disk he'd picked up on Syrac Seven.

"Classified," he ordered.

"Personals? Spaceplanes? Weapons?" the mag inquired.

"Conflicts," Tusk said. He noticed that the harp music had stopped. Dion must have fallen asleep. Tusk hoped the kid had made peace with the demons who hounded a man after the death of someone he loved . . . and hated.

"Blood feuds, corporate wars, interplanetary wars, intra-planet wars, interstellar wars—"

"No blood feuds, mag. Those guys get carried away, never know when to quit. Closest I ever got to being blown to cosmic dust was in a blood feud. And no religious wars. Those bastards are sore losers, sacrifice you on the spot if you retreat. Fortunately"—Tusk adjusted himself more comfortably in his chair—"there're enough planetary wars to go around. Give us that list, will you?"

The mag complied. Tusk scanned the list, frowning. That

one was too risky, he decided. Like siblings who have learned to argue quietly lest it bring down the wrath of their parents, conflicting groups were constantly mindful of the watchful eye of the Warlords. There had been following the revolution, an increase in the demand for mercenaries.

The revolution had been well planned. The night the king met his death in the Glitter Palace, certain hand-picked rebel officers in the Royal Armed Forces had stepped in to take command, either killing or imprisoning those superiors loyal to the king. The takeover occurred simultaneously in every major system, on every planet, in every unit. But an operation that big can't go unnoticed. Many commanders had known something was up and—so it was rumored—had tried desperately to convince their king of the danger. Amodius Starfire had refused to heed their warnings. A devoutly religious man, he believed that he ruled by divine right, that the Creator would never allow the monarchy to fall.

Many soldiers in the Royal Armed Forces died in the coup that night, but it was discovered the next day—the day that became known among the revolutionaries as Coffin Run because of the huge numbers of orders for coffins—that many more royalists had escaped. At first the Revolutionary Congress had ordered these soldiers hunted down and destroyed. This grisly quest took up time, money, and manpower, and eventually the Congress—concerned with holding elections, placing their candidates in office, and a myriad other functions—ordered that the search for those still misguidedly loyal to a dead king be called off.

For many of these men and women, soldiering was the only trade they knew, and they began to sell their services to the highest bidder. And there were always plenty of bidders. Although the Commonwealth preached peace and brotherhood among the nations (and maintained, every election cycle, that this goal was near fulfillment), the truth was that there were just as many or possibly more conflicts under the new regime as there had been under the old one.

The citizen generals were supposed to keep peace with their sectors, but they protested to the Congress that they wasted time and money putting out minor flare-ups. The Congress, in response, established intervention guidelines. Cities, states, corporations, and planets were allowed their bickerings and squabbles as long as they posed no threat to the sector or the galaxy at large. Mercenaries could find work in almost any of these conflicts. Those soldiers of fortune who, like Tusk, were hot carefully avoided any conflict that might attract undue attention.

The Warlords knew that the Congress was never likely to bring peace to the quarreling systems. The Congress itself rarely agreed on anything, although their press releases would have people believe otherwise. There'd been no major system wars, but that was due to the generals, not to the Congress or the President. And now the generals were eyeing each other askance—or so rumor had it. Rumor also had it that one or two major systems were considering pulling their money and support out of the Republic. Secession. Civil war. Tusk immediately crossed these off his mental list. Step over the Warlords' unseen boundaries and reprisal would be swift and deadly.

"Nope." Tusk scanned the rows of code names and numbers that every mercenary could easily translate. "Too small. No money. And that one's too big. Four planets and a moon? Nuclear bombs? Couldn't pay me enough." He continued to read to the end of the column, thinking that the military academy might win out by default. Then he whistled. There it was.

"Here's something, XJ." Tusk read off the coordinates to the computer. "Vangelis."

"Planetary war, right?"

"Intraplanet. Nothing likely to involve the big boys."

"Money?"

"You bet. Guess who's in charge? John Dixter."

"General Dixter? Excellent. Well, have you made up your mind? Do I plot a course for Vangelis or Dagot?"

"Dixter'd be a good man for the kid to know. He taught me a lot. We could always take Dion to Dagot later. It's the middle of the semester, anyway," he added for the computer's benefit.

Blinking in triumph, XJ placed the spaceplane on a new heading and returned to its studies.

Tusk sat back in his chair. Now that they were out of Jump, he could watch the stars. He considered ordering XJ to make the Jump again—there was a Lane to Vangelis from this location, he was certain. But, after consideration, Tusk rejected the idea. Never wise to Jump into a war zone. Approach cautiously, monitor the transmissions. Vangelis wasn't that far. Traveling close to light speed, the trip would probably take them a week or so.

"I've got a lot to teach the kid, anyway," Tusk reflected.

"Wouldn't do to land him cold in the middle of a war. Not that he's gonna start shooting or anything," the mercenary added hastily, going cold at the thought. "Still, he should know how to use a lasgun. Maybe I'll give him some lessons on flying." Tusk grinned. This might be fun. There was nothing more boring than space flight. He and XJ got on each other's nerves. It would be good to have someone else to talk to. Someone human.

Tusk yawned again and stretched. He had another bottle hidden in his locker. "I'm going to lie down," he said, heaving himself out of his chair. But before he could reach the ladder, XJ-27 began to flash and whir in as much excitement as the computer was programmed to exhibit.

"Tusk"—it spoke in a subdued voice, pitched low, apparently, so as not to wake the sleeping boy—"sit down in front of the vid screen. You're not going to believe what I'm about to show you!"

"Do I really want to know?"

"Why do humans fear knowledge?" XJ demanded irritably.

"Because we've seen what can happen when we get too smart. We built computers, for one thing," Tusk said, pleased. He rarely put one over on XJ, and he considered that he'd scored a point. He thought longingly of the bottle. "Is this gonna take long? I don't think I can stay awake."

"Oh, you'll stay awake all right."

Not liking XJ's tone, Tusk sat back down and cleared the mag off the computer screen. At first the screen was blank, then column after column of extremely fine print scrolled into view.

Tusk groaned. "Come off it, will you? What is this?" He peered at it closely. "Why, it's a blasted government document! You expect me to read that? Condense it!"

With a vicious bleep, XJ killed the image on the screen. There was a momentary pause, then several short paragraphs appeared.

"That's better." Tusk settled back. "Hey, where'd you get this stuff?" He sat forward suddenly. "It's marked classified!"

"I was tied into Lord Sagan's central computer for updated mechanical data before we . . . er . . . departed his service, and while I was there I did some browsing around on my own. Picked up a few things that interested me, mostly about the revolution. Never know when that sort of stuff can come in handy."

"Yeah? For what?"

"Blackmail, for one," XJ said smugly.

Tusk said something beneath his breath.

"What was that?" XJ demanded.

"I said when you decide to blackmail Derek Sagan, let me know so I can watch him rip your electronic guts out with his bare hands. Now go on, before I fall asleep."

"This data you will find particularly interesting. Much about what truly happened that night in the Glitter Palace was kept secret for fear of adverse public reaction. When Robes siezed control, he moved quickly to present his side of the story to the general populace. One of the first orders of business, therefore, was to secure all palace records. Much was destroyed, or at least so the people believe. I'll bet the press'd be real interested to know how much Warlord Sagan retains in his files."

"Uh-huh. And you found it all, right?"

"No, of course not! The Warlord's got it locked up so tight that even he probably can't remember how to access it. But there were a few things lying around that he apparently didn't consider important. Like this. It's just a file that a data record computer—"

"A what?"

"Data record computer. Lots of big corporations and all the government offices have them. In this instance, small cameras and tiny microphones located in all the rooms of the Glitter Palace fed information to this central computer. It analyzed all the data it received and noted down events by date and time. The information recorded is pretty cryptic. It wasn't meant to go into detail, after all. It was designed for use by historians and those in charge of budgets. But you can read between the lines. I've deleted what's not appropriate."

Tusk grunted. He could hear the boy stir in his hammock and he suddenly realized how truly tired he was. Rubbing his eyes again, he blinked at the screen. "'1800 hours. Colonel Derek Sagan, Golden Squadron, arrives at Palace. 1809 hours. Colonel Derek Sagan, Golden Squadron, requests audience with King Amodius Starfire. 1830 hours. King Amodius Starfire denies Colonel Sagan.' Hey, hold that a moment." Tusk's interest quickened. "That's odd, isn't it? Why would Sagan request an audience with the man he was going to betray and murder?"

"I wondered that myself. Keep reading."

"'1831 hours. Cook removes one side of beef from freezing

chamber. 1832. Cook requests following: one sack potatoes, two sacks flour, two sacks sugar—' What the hell is this?"

"Sorry. Slipped by me. Supply list. I told you, this computer recorded everything, including information on running the household."

"'Salt, mousetraps . . .' Would you get rid of this? Thanks. Here we go. '1900 hours. Changing of the guard. Arrival of the Guardians. Guest list—'"

"They were coming to attend the banquet in honor of their victory over the Corasians," XJ said.

"Yeah. Hey, don't roll that by so fast. There's my father's name. You know, he never talked to anyone about what happened that night. Not that I ever asked him. I was a stupid, blaster-happy kid. What did I care about the old man and his war stories? Now I wish I had. It might have helped me understand why they did . . . what they did to him."

"The Guardians were all in attendance," XJ told him. "That was why the rebels chose that night to attack."

"'2200 hours. Enemy forces launch assault against Glitter Palace. 2229 hours. Enemy forces invade palace.'" Tusk shook his head. "Read between the lines, you said. This is spooky. Think about this machine, calmly recording all this while hundreds of people fought for their lives."

"The battle was hopeless from the beginning," XJ said. "Robes had everything under control. His plan was brilliant. The only ones who could have possibly hoped to stop the revolution were the Guardians. They alone had the influence with the people to prevent the coup from succeeding—or at least make it pretty tough. And here they were, locked in a banquet chamber—weaponless as befitted a ceremony of state. All but one of them, of course. *He* had his weapon—"

"'2230 hours. Death of Aladais Arocus Amodius Starfire. 2230.15 hours. General chaos.' This machine had a gift for understatement, didn't it? How many of the Guardians died that night?"

"Hundreds. The true count was never known, of course. Robes put out orders to find any who escaped and bring them to trial—the last of the supporters of the tyrannical monarchy. The most famous of all those who escaped alive were the members of the Golden Squadron. That included your father—"

"I sometimes think he wished he hadn't. He was a changed man when he came back. I was only nine, but I remember.

That's when things started going wrong between us. Damn it!"
Tusk slammed his hand down on the arm of the chair. "I didn't
understand! Why didn't he take the time to tell me, to explain?
But no. He was so blasted proud—"

"All right, all right. You can spend the night kicking
yourself. We're coming up on what I want you to read. Where
was I? Oh, yeah. The Golden Squadron. You know the old
story that went around about them. How they had supposedly
agreed to go along with their commander, Derek Sagan, and
lead the revolt, but they betrayed him at the last moment.
Because of that, he's been making this notorious 'hunt' for
them for the past seventeen years—royalists, enemies of the
people, and all that."

"That was why he murdered my father."

"But why torture him?"

Tusk stood up. "This is stupid. I don't want to read any
more—"

"Listen to me!" XJ insisted. "If this search for the Guardians
was politically motivated, as the Congress keeps insisting,
then why take your father off and torture him? Why not a
public trial and execution? No, they're after something . . .
or someone."

"And you think we've found him? A seventeen-year-old kid?
Why?"

"Read on!" XJ was triumphant. "I have the answer."

Tusk lowered himself back into the chair. "I'll give you five
minutes, then I'm gone. This better be good. Let's see, 2230
hours, death of Aladais Arocus Amodius Starfire and so
on . . . '2230.30 hours. Child born to Princess Semele Starfire. Son.'"

Tusk flexed his hands. His fingers had gone numb with cold,
though there were beads of sweat on his upper lip. "Did you
turn down the heat again?"

"Put on a sweater." XJ's screen went blank for a moment.
"We're conserving fuel. It costs, you know. Enough of the data
computer. Look at this."

"A genealogy!" Tusk wiped his hand over his mouth. "First
supply lists, now begats and begots."

"Shut up and read."

"Okay, so the lady had impressive relatives. So what?"

"Lady Semele Starfire. A direct descendant of the Royal
Family—on both sides. Father and mother were cousins. And

she was the king's sister-in-law. Her husband was the younger brother. Now look at this."

"A death list. Oh, wonderful. We're going from bad to worse."

"All those in the Glitter Palace whose deaths were recorded during that night," XJ said. "I'll bet this is one of the only accurate lists to have survived. You'll note the names of Guardians. This is, of course, how Sagan knew who was alive and who wasn't. One of his staff members must have made this list before the palace was destroyed. Scan down. There you go. 'Semele Starfire.'"

"Poor woman. I can imagine—"

"Keep reading!"

"All right!" Tusk snarled. "There, I'm finished. So what?"

"What about her baby?"

"What about the baby?"

"It wasn't listed."

"So." Tusk heaved himself out of the chair. "It's too friggin' cold in here. Something's wrong with the life-support systems—"

"Tusk—"

"Look, you could easily miss a dead baby in all that confusion. I'm going to bed. You trash this stuff and work on life-support—"

"The computer listed dead servants, janitors. Here's the cook and her helpers. It wouldn't miss a baby, Tusk," XJ continued relentlessly. "Especially a direct descendant of the Royal Family. *Especially* a child who was, at that moment, heir to the throne!"

The computer hummed to itself in satisfaction.

Snorting, Tusk slammed his hand down on the controls, erasing the screen. "Not a word to the kid, understand?"

"Sure." The computer began shutting itself down for the night.

Tusk climbed the ladder slowly. His legs felt heavy, his feet were numb. Probably from the cold. Pulling himself up into his living quarters, he started to activate the lights, then remembered. The kid was asleep. Fumbling around in the dark, Tusk found his locker, opened it, and retrieved the bottle. He swung himself into his hammock, lay back and swallowed a mouthful of the intoxicant known as jump-juice because its effects were supposedly similar to those experienced making the Jump to hyperspace. Tusk sighed as the soothing liquid slid down his throat, leaving a warm glow behind.

The plane was night-silent, the only sounds being the comforting whir and whoosh of life-support, the steady drone of the engines, and the occasional clicks or muffled bleeps as the computer continued its job of running the Scimitar. In the hammock next to him, Tusk heard the boy talking to himself in his sleep. A jarring, discordant note sounding from the syntharp made Tusk start.

"Kid's fallen asleep with the damn thing in his hand," Tusk muttered. Groaning, he fought his way out of the hammock and stumbled through the semidarkness to the kid's berth. Hidden beneath a blanket, the instrument was revealed by its bright beams of light. Carefully and quietly, Tusk removed the harp from the boy's sleep-limp hand and propped it up against a locker.

Lying back down, the mercenary took another pull from the bottle.

Heir to the throne. The kid might be the rightful ruler of the whole blasted galaxy.

Fervently and with feeling, Tusk said, "Bullshit!"

"I heard that!" XJ snapped. "And if you think it's cold in here now, just wait until morning!"

Sighing, Tusk grabbed a blanket, drew it over his head, and, cradling the bottle in his arms, closed his eyes and fell asleep.

Chapter ❦ Nine

Who, or why, or which, or what . . .
Edward Lear, "The Akond of Swat"

Tusk woke, shivering. Calling down imprecations on the computer's metal head, he pulled on his winter fatigues, including his leather flight jacket. The kid's hammock was empty and he could hear voices from below. He reached the ladder just in time to hear the kid say, "That doesn't prove anything."

"Damn!" Tusk said, sliding down the ladder. "I thought I told you not to tell the kid."

"Why not?" Dion's blue eyes turned on Tusk, their expression cold and suspicious.

Tusk sighed. "Look, kid," he said, fumbling for words beneath that intense, penetrating gaze, "it's all speculation. Circumstantial evidence—"

"And I'm a word processor!" XJ flashed. "Circumstantial evidence. We caught the kid standing over the body, the smoking gun in his hand!"

"And the body's probably mine!" Tusk snapped. "You yourself said it didn't prove anything. I wasn't going to tell you, kid, until we had a little more to go on, that's all. And you promised not to tell him either!" he shouted at XJ.

"I am not programmed to recognize a promise. Honor is merely a word in my spell checker. And I say we have plenty of information to go on! Look, this kid's mentor was a Guardian. I found his name right here—Platus Morianna. Platus's sister was also a Guardian, Maigrey Morianna. They were both in Sagan's squadron, both survived the holocaust that night. The Warlord, Derek Sagan, comes to this planet and he kills—"

"XJ," Tusk warned, seeing Dion flinch.

99

"Er, disrupts a planet to try to find you, kid. Your master, this Platus, dies to keep your whereabouts secret. The Guardians swore an oath to guard and defend the Royal Family with their lives. It all makes sense. Didn't this Platus ever tell you anything about himself, about the Guardians?"

"About the Guardians, yes," Dion answered. "I learned their history. How they are all members of the Blood Royal, those people specifically bred to be genetically superior to others and therefore to have the ability to be good rulers. The idea came from the ancient philosopher Plato. He spoke about it in the *Republic*: 'Then there must be a selection. Let us note among the guardians those who in their whole life show the greatest eagerness to do what is for the good of their country—'"

"Uh, right. Plato," Tusk interrupted hastily. "Look, I'm going to go pay a visit to the head. Why don't you find something for breakfast, kid, and you"—he glared at the computer—"turn on the heat!"

"I'm conservation-minded," XJ said.

Tusk, with a muttered comment, clambered back up the ladder.

"You know," Dion said, looking after him, "he'd be one, too, wouldn't he? A Guardian. A member of the Blood Royal. Genetically superior—"

"—to earthworms," XJ scoffed. "He's royal, all right. A royal pain."

"But his father—"

"Just goes to show you, kid. Even science is fallible. Hungry? Grab a couple of those frozen food trays and pop them in the nuker."

Tusk came back to find food cooked and waiting for him. Dion, sitting in the co-pilot's chair, was eating his meal slowly, but he was eating—a fact that Tusk noted with relief. The kid had gone all day yesterday without a mouthful. Because of that, Tusk never mentioned that he wasn't accustomed to starting his mornings with spaghetti and clam sauce. He'd have to remember to tell the kid that the trays marked *B* were for breakfast.

"So, what else did your . . . er . . . mentor tell you?" Tusk asked, thinking that the spaghetti didn't taste half-bad. "About himself, I mean, not Plato's *Republic*."

"Nothing," Dion answered, shoving the spaghetti around with a plastic fork. "I didn't even know he had a sister. He never mentioned her, he never mentioned friends, anyone.

You, Tusk"—the blue eyes nailed him—"were the first person I've ever known him to talk to."

"Hey, come on, kid," Tusk said, trying not to look worried. The more he heard about this, the less he liked it. "I mean . . . you must've gone to the grocery store, the hardware store, somewhere."

"No, we didn't. We grew our own food or ordered what we needed over the computer. Supplies were delivered by helicopter."

"You never went to school, to the vids even?"

"No. I studied at home. And I've never heard of vids. What are they?"

"They're . . . Well, never mind." Tusk scowled. This Platus had been scared, scared as hell. "So your mentor never talked to anyone. What about you? Kids your own age?"

"I met some once, not too long ago. A group of scouts got lost, hiking through the outback."

"And?" Tusk prompted.

"And what? I didn't like them," Dion said shortly, his eyes on his plate.

"Uh-huh," Tusk said, munching garlic bread and exchanging glances with the computer's electronic eye. He noticed that XJ was being unusually quiet and that the computer was surreptitiously recording every word the boy said. "So, why didn't you like them?"

"Look, what does it matter?" Dion tossed his half-empty plate to one side on the control panel and stared out the viewport at the stars, his arms folded tightly across his chest. "I didn't like them, that's all."

"Just trying to be sociable, kid," Tusk said easily. "We're going to be spending a lot of time cooped up together and there's not much to do around here except sleep or talk. So, these kids," he continued, seeing the boy's stiff shoulders begin to relax, "what did they think of you?"

Dion shrugged. "They seemed . . . awed, I guess."

Tusk closed his eyes. Awed. Yes, that was the word. He could understand, he could imagine. It explained the feeling he got every time he looked at the kid. There was something about Dion that made you want to step back away from him, to think twice about touching him. It was the blue eyes, Tusk decided. That intense, brilliant blue gaze that stared not at you but clean through you. Tusk tossed his food tray in the trash liquidator. From the taste in his mouth, he might have been chewing the plastic plate.

Dion sighed suddenly, and ran his hand through the mane of red-golden hair, brushing it back from his face with his fingers. The brilliant red-gold color was the only warm spot in the cabin. Huddling deeper into his down-lined flight jacket, Tusk shot the computer a vicious glance.

"I can see what you're leading up to," Dion said suddenly. "Platus told me we led the lives of solitary scholars, unspoiled by contact with those who wouldn't understand us. But we were really leading the lives of fugitives, weren't we? We were hiding."

"It looks that way, kid. And with good reason, apparently. I mean, after what happened and all."

"It fits." Dion stared out into the ever-changing star patterns. "I knew I wasn't any relation to him. He always told me the truth about everything and so I rarely asked him anything about myself. It seemed to cause him pain and I never— He was so good to me, I—"

Dion's voice faltered. Shaking his head, he forced back his emotions, and when he spoke, his tone was steady. "But one time, about a year ago, I pressed him. I don't know what made me do it. I felt angry and tight inside and I didn't care if I hurt him. I *wanted* to hurt him, in fact!" His hand clenched. "I didn't know myself. I felt like some kind of monster—"

"Puberty," XJ remarked knowingly.

"That's what Platus said." Dion almost smiled. "Afterward, I apologized. He apologized, too, for losing his patience."

"What did he say about you?"

"When we were arguing, he lost his temper and told me never to bring up the subject of who I was again. You see this necklace I wear—this ring?"

Dion pulled it out from beneath the collar of his shirt. Tusk leaned over and looked at it. It was an unusual one. He didn't think he'd ever seen anything like it. A circlet made of tongues of carved flame opals, it burned with a bright red and orange and purple fire. Tusk felt relieved; he'd half-expected to see the royal crest or something.

"I've worn it ever since I can remember. Platus told me that there'd been many times when he was tempted to rip this off and throw it away. Something this insignificant shouldn't signify what a man is or what he becomes. A man's past isn't important. What is important is who a man is now and what he plans to become in the future."

"So, what are your plans?" Tusk asked, thinking he could have argued with good old Platus over that one.

Dion gave a brief, bitter laugh. "Plans! I have no idea who I am, where I come from, why I was born. All I know is that a man I loved and honored and respected gave his life for me. What can I give back?"

He swiveled in the seat, turned to stare directly at Tusk. "Someone expects me to give something, that's obvious." Dion paused. When he spoke next, his voice had an odd quality—a coolness about it that startled the mercenary. "There's one person who knows who I am—Derek Sagan."

The mercenary choked. "Sure," he said when he could talk. "He'd probably be real glad to tell you, too! Right before he stood you up against the wall and shot you."

"Incorrect data," XJ informed him. "They don't do that now, not with vaporization chambers and other, more efficient—"

"Oh, dry up!"

"Do you think he'd do that?" Dion asked casually, staring down at the instruments and idly running his hands over them.

Tusk grunted. "I take it you never heard news reports, never talked about politics?"

"I'd never heard of a Warlord until . . . until—" Dion frowned and changed the subject. "I studied government, but it was all abstract. Platus said he was inadequate to teach anything else. Oh, I knew there were other planets out there and that something governed them, but it never mattered much what. It all seemed so far away, so far removed from us."

Tusk cleared his throat. "Government. Well, you see, kid—" The mercenary scratched his head. "The monarchy was around for a century or so. Each planet was ruled by a member of the Blood Royal and all the Blood Royal swore allegiance to the king—also a member of the Blood Royal. It was a good system, I guess, for a while—"

"Benevolent monarchy." Dion nodded wisely. "The best form of government, according to—"

"Yeah, yeah"—Tusk waved a hand—"benevolent whatever. Anyway, what it comes down to, I guess, is that if the king's good everything's fine, but if he isn't you're in a hell of a mess."

"And this Starfire wasn't a good king?"

Tusk squirmed. Hell, they might be talking about the kid's uncle! "Uh, he was okay, I guess—"

"He was weak, wishy-washy," XJ cut in. "Dumped everything in the lap of the God. 'If the Creator wills it'—that sort of philosophy. Without the Guardians to cover for him, Starfire wouldn't have lasted as long as he did."

"So there was a revolt," Tusk said, taking over the lesson. "A guy named Peter Robes—a professor of political science at some university—got together with Derek Sagan and some of the other high-level malcontents in the armed forces and staged a coup. Now the galaxy's run by—ostensibly—a democratically elected Congress. It's got some fancy name, but everyone calls it just that—the Congress. When they call it anything polite, that is. The Congress is so divided that the President, Robes, is the real power. You see, following the overthrow of the king and the Royal Family, Robes divided the galactic empire up into one million sectors. Each sector elects two members to sit on the Congress. Each has an equal vote in how the government's run."

"Democracy," Dion said. "A democratic form of rule."

"Yeah, that's what they promised. And I guess that's what it looks like, on the surface. As time went by and the Congress couldn't get much done, what with half the members running for reelection and the other half arguing among themselves, Robes began to acquire more and more power just so that someone could get something done.

"Now some people want the Congress abolished and all power consolidated in the hands of the President. Others want the President abolished and everything put in the hands of the Congress. And you know what some others want?" Tusk propped his feet up on the control panel, his gaze fixed on the tangle of wires above his head.

"What?"

"They want the good old days. They want a king. They're starting to think they made a mistake. Life was pretty great, back then, when they didn't have to think about who to vote for, didn't have to make all these decisions. There's a lot more royalists around than you might think, kid. And their numbers're growing. If the true heir was to turn up . . ."

"The Congress would kill him," Dion said, fiddling with a dial.

"Or the President, or both at once. I know I would, if I were in their shoes!"

"I wouldn't," XJ struck in. "And, hey, kid, don't mess with the equipment. No, I wouldn't bump off the true heir. Not as long as the true heir minded his manners, of course. Think about it—what would be more impressive than the true heir appearing on prime time, putting his arm around Peter Robes's padded shoulders and swearing that there's nothing like the good old democratic system, after all. Get out and vote for the candidate of your choice. Throw in a few remarks about how the king was a money-grubbing, power-hungry elitist and how the Republic's made for life, liberty, and the—"

"Whose life?" Tusk demanded. "Certainly not the heir's if one of the Warlords steps in and wipes out the Congress."

"Are there any powerful enough to do that?" Dion asked.

"Sagan, for one. At least that's the rumor."

"Mrrft!" XJ made a noise that the boy was later to learn was the computer's approximation of a snort. "No way."

"Well, maybe not yet," Tusk amended. Sneakily, he shed the leather flight jacket, hoping the computer wouldn't notice. XJ had apparently become so interested in the conversation it hadn't realized that Tusk had readjusted the thermostat.

"So what do I do? Rot in some military school?" Dion put his finger on a button, then suddenly snatched it back. "Ouch!"

"Told you not to touch those, kid," the computer said. "Small electrical charge. Won't hurt you. This time."

"Uh, well, you see, kid, we've decided not to take you to the military school, after all—" Tusk began.

"You could be worth your weight in gold," XJ remarked.

"Oh, so that's it!" Dion said, flushing angrily. "You can sell me to the highest bidder—"

"That's not it!" Tusk snapped. "I promised, remember? And I may not be good for much else, but I keep promises." He gave the computer a swift kick beneath the console. "I promised that Platus of yours that I'd take care of you. We ought to try to find out for certain—if we can—who you are and . . . and—" Tusk's eyes brightened. He sat forward excitedly in his chair. "And, by the Creator, I know someone who might be able to help us!"

"Who?" Dion asked sullenly, sucking his injured fingers.

"Someone who was on Minas Tares the night of the revolution! John Dixter. He's fighting a war on Vangelis. We're already on course for the planet, aren't we, XJ?"

The computer muttered something unintelligible.

"You really think he can help?" Dion was still regarding the mercenary suspiciously.

"Sure!" Tusk said with more confidence than he felt. "Dixter was a general in the Royal Army. Barely escaped the revolution with his life and now he earns his living by selling his military expertise to those who can afford him. And that's not just anyone. He's good, kid. Real good. Fair and honest, too. Besides, you'll probably see some combat. And what's military school compared to the real thing?"

"I guess you're right." Dion relaxed. Sighing, he shook out the mane of red-gold hair. "I'm sorry, Tusk. I shouldn't have jumped to conclusions—"

"Think nothing of it, kid. Now, XJ and I got a lot of work to do around here. Why don't you go up and . . . uh . . . play some more of that harp stuff for us?"

"You like it?" Dion appeared pleased.

"You bet!"

Stuffing his plastic dish into the trash liquidator, Dion climbed the ladder that led back up into the living quarters of the Scimitar. Within moments, the weird music of the light strings reverberated through the small cabin.

"Liar!" XJ said.

"Shut up," Tusk muttered, gritting his teeth.

Chapter ❧❧ Ten

One flesh; to lose thee were to lose myself.

John Milton, *Paradise Lost*

"My lord, we have landed."

"Yes. Thank you, Captain."

The information was unnecessary. The Warlord's shuttle did not touch down with such smoothness that landings went unnoticed. This landing had been a particularly rough one, the shuttle having been forced to blast away a large portion of jungle growth to create a clear area in which to set down the craft. Despite that, branches splintered, trees cracked, vines slithered past the steelglass windows before the shuttle came to a bumpy, bone-jolting stop.

Why the Warlord had chosen to land in this overgrown jungle when there was a large smooth area near a principal village was a mystery to the shuttlecraft's commander. He had obeyed orders, however, and hoped that Sagan would take into account the difficulties of setting down by night in heavily wooded terrain when it came time for the commander's next review.

The captain of the centurions left the bridge and hastened to post himself at the hatchway to await orders. He was considerably startled to find no one there. Following landing, the Warlord was invariably on his feet, standing by the hatch, waiting with obvious impatience for pressure seals to release, the hatch to slide open, the ramp to slide out. But now he was not there. He was nowhere to be seen.

His uneasiness increasing, the captain waited a few nerve-racking moments to see if the Warlord would make his appearance. When he did not, the captain made his way to Sagan's quarters aboard the shuttlecraft. It was the officer's duty, after all, to inform his superior that they had arrived on-planet, in case the Warlord had not noticed that vine-looped tree trunks now replaced the stars outside his viewport.

The Honor Guard stood alert and rigid outside the entrance to Sagan's quarters, and if the centurions had been exchanging wondering glances between themselves before their captain's arrival, they immediately assumed a formal impassivity in the presence of the commander of the ring of steel they formed around their lord. The captain could not forbear casting them a questioning look. One raised an eyebrow and his left shoulder. They didn't know what was going on either. The captain entered the compartment.

The Warlord sat by himself in moonlit darkness. The moonlight glistened off the moisture-slick boles of the trees and their huge, dripping wet leaves outside Sagan's viewport, shone brilliantly on the silver scabbard of a sword—one of the legendary bloodswords—lying across the Warlord's knees. His hand rested on the hilt. Seen by moonlight, the Warlord's face was a series of deep cleft marks scored into rock, all slanting downward. The eyes were abstracted, staring intently at nothing, and the captain realized that the Warlord's body may have been in this compartment but his soul was not.

The captain was at a loss. He had been given strict orders to attend the Warlord the moment they arrived on the planet. He could do nothing but obey, although it was quite obvious to him that his liege lord had gone into one of his mystical trances. The captain knew that speech sometimes roused the Warlord. Sometimes not. Having no idea what to do if it didn't work, the captain decided to speak.

"My lord, we have landed," he said in the tone one uses to waken a fast sleeper.

"Yes. Thank you, Captain." Sagan spoke quietly, without turning his gaze on his officer.

The captain felt hot blood rush to his cheeks.

"I'm sorry, my lord, I didn't know— I thought you were—"

"We'll leave now, Captain."

Sword in hand, Sagan rose to his feet. He was clad in the Romanesque military style he fancied. A golden phoenix decorated a breastplate made of null-gravity steel. Lightweight, comfortable, it could withstand the blast of a laser. Projectiles—including those fired by gas-guns—bounced off harmlessly. The only weapon that could penetrate it was reputedly the bloodsword, and then only one wielded by a person whose mind was powerful enough to fully control it.

If the Warlord had been going into battle, he would have worn full armor made of this material. He expected no danger on this mission, apparently, for he was clad in a short tunic protected by heavy leather strips, ornately decorated with inlaid silver and gold. Leather sandals that laced to the knee completed his costume. The Warlord had no adjutant. At his gesture, one of the centurions brought forward the red cape and draped it around the man's bare, well-muscled shoulders. A golden chain, attached to two phoenix pins—one on either shoulder—held the cape securely in place. The Honor Guard reverently lifted the Warlord's golden helmet with the blood-red feather crest and stood holding it patiently until his lord should request it.

The captain was somewhat confused. He had been told they were landing on this planet to apprehend a prisoner. From his ceremonial dress, Lord Sagan might have been going to an audience with the defunct king.

"Have the quarters adjacent to mine prepared to receive a guest, Captain," the Warlord instructed, carefully attaching the bloodsword to a belt girded about his waist.

The captain blinked. "My lord," he said hesitantly, "I was told we were transporting a dangerous political prisoner. I have made ready the hold—"

"She will be a prisoner, Captain. She is dangerous. You will remember that. She is also the daughter of a planetary king, Morianna—one of the most feared warriors of his time. Her mother was a princess of the Leiah system. Of course, I realize, Captain, that in our present society this noble lineage is worth less than the cost of the microchip on which it is recorded. Nevertheless, you will accord her the same respect you accord me."

"Yes, my lord."

The captain heard something that sounded like a sigh. His face as grim as if he were facing an army of ten thousand foes, the Warlord covered his face with his golden helmet and started for the hatch.

··◁▥ ▥▷··

Accompanied by his Honor Guard, the Warlord moved through the thick vegetation resolutely. The way seemed impenetrable. The guards' weapons sliced through twisted, slimy vines as big around as a man's leg, chopped down giant elephant-ear plants, and hacked the limbs off trees that seemed—by acts of eerie intelligence—to be determined to block their path.

It was hot work in the steaming, humid jungle air, and after only a few yards had been cleared, the men were panting, wiping sweat from their faces, and wondering how much farther was their destination. A short distance from the shuttle, however, the Warlord came upon a cleared path. He did not arrive at it by accident. He had obviously been expecting to find it, and chose his direction and began walking along it without hesitation.

The Honor Guard followed close and with more caution than their lord. His life, after all, was in their hands, and the centurions knew this planet to be inhabited by natives—so it was reported—who were fearful of them and hostile to their intent. And although these natives were purportedly only a step removed from the stone age in terms of weaponry, a spear through the gut kills just as surely as a laser blast. Sensing devices were useless. The life-form readings they would pick up in this jungle environment would be too numerous to count, more confusing than helpful. Their lord preferred depending on God-given senses—saying that a man was safer to rely on instincts bred over thousands of years of survival rather than a machine that, no matter how sophisticated, had never walked in fear of its life.

An army of thousands could have been hiding in that moonlit mass of plant life and the centurions could never have seen it. They could hear rustlings and growls, snufflings and furtive slitherings among the undergrowth and in the branches above their heads. Animals going about their nightly business, said their lord.

The centurions did not relax their vigilance, but followed closely behind their lord, who was forging his way ahead without pause. Occasionally, the path split into two separate trails, heading in diverging directions. Occasionally, another path left the one on which they walked, wending its way into another part of the jungle. Sagan never hesitated when it came to a choice, but went to the right or to the left as whatever was guiding him dictated.

What *was* guiding him? His guards had no idea. The magnetic force that both drew him and repelled him was invisible to them, though its effects on him were not. He had drawn his helmet over his head; his face was hidden. He walked purposefully, determinedly, never wavering. Opposite magnetic fields attracting. Yet every step seemed an effort. The cords of his neck were taut, the muscles of his shoulders twitched and bunched as though he were pushing against something that was pushing back. Like magnetic fields repelling.

His tension communicated itself to his men, who—after a half-hour of watching him fight this internal battle—would have welcomed a flight of arrows. Suddenly one guard touched his captain's arm, pointing ahead in silent communication. Through the breaks in the jungle's growth, a light could be seen. It was a bright light, yet pale and eerie, with a bluish cast to it, almost as if the moon had fallen from the sky and landed on the ground before them.

The Warlord headed straight for the light, and no man among his guard had any doubt that this was their destination. The light grew brighter, illuminating the jungle with a stark, white glow that sucked all color—and thereby seemingly all life—out of any object it touched. The centurions' own flesh appeared corpselike, luminescent, transparent. Trees seemed carved of white marble; metal glistened like ice.

In contrast to the light, the darkness around them became complete, impenetrable. To step into the shadows was to step into black depths that were not the purient, sterile voids of space but a smothering, unfathomable miasma.

The Warlord's footsteps slowed. His breathing was heavy and measured, as one who makes a conscious effort to draw every breath. With a gesture, he brought his guards up around him. The jungle ended. With the next step, they would walk out into an area open and unprotected.

Here was the source of the light.

The centurions, each and every one, were men proven and tested in battle. Each had performed some act of heroism, daring, and courage that had brought him to the attention of the Warlord. They sacrificed everything to serve him—country, home, family. Sagan allowed no loves, no other loyalties that might distract or interfere with their duties. They led grueling, Spartan lives, for their commander denied himself comforts and they lived as he did. Outwardly they were cold and hard and emotionless as their lord. Midas, it was said, had a touch that turned all to gold. Sagan, it seemed, turned all he touched to iron.

Yet more than one centurion, staring at the sight before him, saw it through a sheen of tears.

They gazed on the Hall of Moonrith, one of the wonders of the universe. And the universe did not even know it existed.

Moonrith, the semiprecious gem, was thought to be so-called because of its moonlike whiteness. In reality, moonrith gained its name through the gem's ability—unnoticed by those who imprisoned it in metal settings—to diffuse and radiate moonlight.

Standing in a large, open area of the jungle, on the top of a small hill that rose up out of the vegetation, was a large, natural formation of moonrith. The natives held it to be a sacred place and had done it honor by smoothing the rough edges of the stone, rounding and shaping the pillars nature had carved with tools of wind and rain.

By day, the building—formed out of a huge slab of rock supported by as many as sixty irregularly shaped, crude pillarlike columns—was nothing more than a geological curiosity. On a moonlit night, the beauty of the Hall of Moonrith pierced the heart.

The stone absorbed the moonlight, diffused it, radiated it forth. The templelike structure glowed with a white luminescence that shone from within the stone. The hill leading up to it had been terraced, carved into steps. At the foot of these, some meters back, stood the trees of the jungle—whispering guardians, who worshiped at a distance.

The Warlord, after a long look, turned to see the reaction of his men and, immediately, faces softened by the miraculous loveliness hardened. Eyes blinked back tears, sighs of awe were swiftly checked. He saw that they had been touched, however. Even as he, who had thought himself immune to beauty, had been touched. Sagan's face grew grimmer still.

He should have come alone.

Turning his back upon his guard, the Warlord climbed the stairs that had been delved into the hillside. His red cape—drenched black by the eerie light—billowed out behind him. His men, ashamed, hurried after him, attempting to keep their eyes on their lord but finding their gaze drawn irresistibly to the glowing temple.

The centurions hastened up the stairs and reached the pillars that formed a colonnade around a vast, rectangular hall. Above them, the moonrith ceiling shed a silvery light, bright enough that each man could see clearly the lines fate had etched upon his palm, the scars of battle and of death man had etched upon his flesh.

"Wait here," the Warlord commanded. Leaving them, he passed in between the glowing columns and entered the hall.

At the far end stood a woman. She was dressed in white; the folds of her long gown hung in smooth, flowing lines, broken only by a silver belt around her waist. Pale fine hair, the color of moonlight, was worn loose, falling over her shoulders in a glistening stream. Her back was to them; she did not seem to notice them but stared up into the night. Thin clouds, gliding before the moon, dappled the dark sky with silver.

The virgin goddess of the silver orb, discovered alone in her temple. Sagan, glancing back, thought it likely his men might fall down and worship her.

She was good. Very good. And how well she knew him. She had played into his myth. Diana to his Mars.

And what was Mars but a bumbling, stupid, bloodthirsty oaf?

Sagan's lips twisted to a bitter smile. Peter Robes, he thought, former professor of political science, this woman will chop you up and feed you to the public with a silver spoon.

The Warlord crossed the floor. His booted footsteps rang on the stone, the hollow sound echoing gratingly through the quiet, peaceful air.

Paler, colder than the moonlight, the woman did not move, not even when he came to a halt directly behind her. A slight breeze, whispering through the jungle, stirred the gold-trimmed hem of his robe, reverently lifted wisps of the woman's pale hair.

"Lady Maigrey Morianna," spoke Derek Sagan.

His voice, harsh and discordant, caused a stir among the jungle animals. Infuriated shrieks and cries answered him, wings flapped angrily, trees shook and rustled. His guard started in alarm and drew their weapons. Sagan raised a warning hand, and they relaxed. Gradually, peace and calm returned.

The woman answered softly, without turning her head or looking at him. "I am Lady Maigrey Morianna."

"Then, Lady Maigrey Morianna, by order and decree of the Revolutionary Congress of the Galactic Democratic Republic, I hereby place you under arrest."

She faced him now. Perhaps it had taken her this long to

steel herself. Gray as the sea beneath a leaden sky, her eyes confronted him. Like a prisoner who knows the blow is coming and can't avoid it, Sagan braced himself and absorbed the pain without flinching. It passed swiftly, burned away by an anger whose flames he had fed daily for seventeen years.

"What is the charge against me, my lord?"

"The charges are numerous, my lady—and all punishable by death. The most notable is aiding and abetting the smuggling to safety of an offshoot of a family whose crimes against the people are legion."

"A newborn baby!" Maigrey's face was colorless, pale as the moonlight except for the gray eyes that had darkened as in a storm. "You would have murdered him that night as you murdered his mother. As you murdered my king."

"I did not make war on children! You know the truth of my actions that night—"

Her lashes flickered, her gaze faltered beneath his. Sagan noted this weakness in her defenses, he read the doubt in her mind, but he was too caught up in his own anger, too intent on keeping his own walls manned to take advantage of this lapse on the part of his enemy. It would be a long time before he remembered the crack in the fortress and came to realize its import.

"I had no intention of killing the child. He would have been raised a citizen of the Republic—"

"—taught to believe his parents were criminals! Taught to be ashamed of what he is! Taught to denounce his own heritage—"

"At least it would have been the truth, my lady," Sagan said. "Better than what your brother taught him!"

He saw the scar on her face. The moonlight had masked it, the white line blending with the pallor of her complexion. Now it leapt out. Her heart pulsed in it, blood stained it, and it seemed almost as if the wound had been reopened.

Seeing his gaze fix upon the right side of her face, Maigrey felt the pain again and consciously put her hand to her cheek to cover it. Sagan shifted his eyes to meet hers.

Looking into them intently, Maigrey saw no pity, no remorse, no disgust, no compassion. Nothing.

"I lack time to argue irrelevancies, my lady. We will be off-planet within the hour. I must ask you to surrender your weapon."

A silver scabbard, decorated with an eight-pointed star,

hung from her waist. Wordlessly, she nodded. Her hands moved to unfasten the buckle.

"The people of this planet know nothing about me," she said, inwardly cursing her trembling fingers that fumbled at their task. "They are a primitive race. They live peacefully. They have hurt no one." Slowly, she drew the belt from around her slender waist. Putting the ends together, she folded the leather as was proper, the scabbard resting on top. Maigrey held it out. "Don't vent your anger on them, Sagan!"

It was the first time she had called him by name. He was caught off guard, the point of the bloodsword she held might have slipped beneath his armor and touched flesh.

"It's not anger, my lady," he said evenly, accepting the weapon. "It is justice."

Maigrey saw that it would be useless and undignified to plead. Tears filled her eyes, and she lowered her head, allowing the long hair to slide forward and hide her face.

The Warlord was familiar with this trick and ignored it. "My guards will carry what other possessions you have to the ship."

"There is no need. I have only the sword and this." From a pocket in the loose-fitting white gown, Maigrey produced a rosewood box. "And you will not take this from me."

Sagan knew what the box contained. "No, my lady," he said, after a pause, "that you may keep."

For long moments, he stared at her in silence. She lifted her head, her tears burned dry, and steadily returned his gaze. Though neither moved, a battle raged. Their minds probed and touched in a mental fencing match, seeking out weaknesses, learning once again to respect strengths.

His gaze broke first, but it was not defeat, merely drawing back to consider a new angle of attack. When it came, it was unexpected and effective.

He held her sword across his forearm and presented it back to her. "Give me your word, Lady Maigrey Morianna—your word, as a Guardian—that you will not attempt to escape from custody, and you may wear the bloodsword."

Maigrey stared at him, confounded.

"Well?" he said impatiently.

"You have my word, my lord." She accepted the weapon in its silver scabbard, and stood clutching it awkwardly, fumbling not to drop it or the rosewood box.

"My lady."

Bowing, Lord Derek Sagan turned on his heel and left her,

crossing the stone floor to where his men waited in the shadows of the columns. "Bring her," he instructed as he passed them.

The centurions hurried to obey. A cloud passed over the moon, obscuring it completely. The Hall of Moonrith, bereft of its source of light, was suddenly nothing but crudely carved rock. The centurions were forced to switch on their hand-held nuke lights. Seen by the harsh, sterile beams, the goddess dwindled to a woman in her early forties with a scarred face, holding a sword and a wooden box.

The centurions surrounded her—one at her right, one at her left, two behind her. They did not touch her but waited respectfully for her to proceed. They would give her a few moments to move on her own. If she did not, they would most certainly drag her. Lifting her chin, Maigrey moved resolutely forward, the sound of her slippered footfalls obliterated by the guards' heavy tread.

Ahead of her, the Warlord had disappeared into the darkness.

She would be taken onto a ship of war, a ship populated by hundreds, and every man loyal—ostensibly—to whatever this bloodstained government of the revolution was calling itself. In reality, however, Maigrey knew they were loyal to one lord. One lord who might fight against the heritage within himself but who would never fail to use it.

He had been very clever in returning the sword, playing to her honor. He must know that now, at the end, it was all she had left.

Leaving the Hall of Moonrith, Maigrey heard the dry and broken sobbing of an old man.

Chapter ·◆○○◆· Eleven

Not all the water in the rough, rude sea can wash the balm
   from an anointed king.
           William Shakespeare, *The Tragedy of Richard II*,
                           Act III, Scene 2.

"We're coming into their instrument range. You been
monitoring public transmissions?"

"Yes," XJ answered in a preoccupied tone.

"And?" Tusk pursued, his hand on switches, his eyes on a
reddish planet that during the last four hours had been
growing increasingly larger in the viewscreen.

"Nothing. You sure there's a war down there?"

Tusk grunted. "Corporate battle. They'll be controlling the
official broadcasts. Civilian population probably doesn't even
know the war's going on—outside of the few hundred or so
who get in the way and get hurt, of course. The corporations
try to seize control of mines and factories, maybe lay siege to
a corporate town. That sort of thing. If anyone asks questions,
it's put down to union violence, terrorist bombings, or a new
p.r. campaign. But, if Dixter's running the show, it'll be a clean
fight—on our side, at least."

"I thought you didn't enlist in corporate wars," Dion said,
remembering one of Tusk's lectures on how to enjoy a long and
profitable career as a soldier of fortune.

"I don't usually," Tusk admitted. "Corporations hold grudges
longer than the Warlords. Once they hand over money, they
figure they own you body and soul and you better be ready to
lay down both in their cause. Show a natural reluctance to get
yourself killed, and they take it as a personal affront. Only
blood feuds are worse. Never get involved in a blood feud,
kid."

117

"So why are we here?"

"Because of Dixter. Like I said, if he's in charge, it'll be a fair fight. He doesn't like corporate wars any more than I do. Must be something different about this one," Tusk muttered, frowning intently at the numbers that were flashing in front of him. "What's the problem?"

"Somebody doesn't think we ought to land," XJ said.

"Missiles?"

"Maybe. You got those coordinates Dixter transmitted?"

"Yeah."

"Use 'em. No standard orbit entry. Come in like a ball of fire."

"Which is what we may turn into. Better fasten yourself in good, kid."

Having learned in the past week how to operate the safety restraints on the co-pilot's chair, Dion did as he was told. Despite Tusk's ominous prediction, the boy was looking forward eagerly to the landing. As Tusk had said, space flight was, for the most part, intensely boring. You could be in awe of the grandeur and majesty of flying among the stars only so long. Then, with the natural perversity of human nature, you begin to dream of trees and air that hasn't been circulated through your lungs a thousand times and water that—though it was purified—made you think about the fact that it, too, had been recycled.

The days in flight had actually passed relatively swiftly. Dion had spent long, absorbed hours either with Tusk or XJ studying space flight and learning how to operate the Scimitar. Tusk had been both amazed and discomfited at how rapidly the boy learned.

"Why are you throwin' that stuff at the kid?" Tusk had demanded of XJ one evening shortly after leaving Syrac Seven. A three-dimensional image of one of the Scimitar's main engines was slowly rotating on the computer's screen. "You'll confuse him. He wants to fly the plane, not build it!"

"I asked to see it," Dion had said. "It's all right, isn't it?"

"Sure. But why bother? Most of the systems aboard these craft are designed to repair themselves if anything breaks down. If it's something that can't be fixed internally, then XJ reports it to me and tells me what to do. You'll learn as you go along. No need to study something that doesn't make sense to you now."

"Oh, but it does make sense. Look." Calmly, Dion had

explained the function of the myriad complex parts; the computer responding by magnifying, colorizing, rotating, simulating—whatever was needed.

"How did you do that? How did he do that?" Tusk had rounded on the computer.

"He has the mind of a machine," XJ had answered, with an electronic sigh of rapture.

"No kidding." Tusk had stared at Dion in awe tinged with uneasiness.

"It's nothing, really," Dion had said, flushing red with embarrassment. "I was just passing time. I didn't mean to show off."

"Photographic memory?"

"More than that." XJ was enjoying showing off. "Humans or aliens with the so-called photographic memory can call up images of what they see in their minds—such as a page from a book, a diagram of an engine—but sometimes that's as far as it goes. Ask them to analyze it, explain how it works, relate the meaning of what they've read, and they can't do it. The kid here not only remembers everything he's ever seen but he can tell you how it works or what it means. He has all of Shakespeare memorized. Give Tusk the scene from *Richard II* you were doing for me. The one about the king deposed—"

"Not now, XJ," Dion had mumbled, feeling his cheeks burn.

"A little culture would be—"

"He said not now!" Tusk had thumped the computer.

With a vicious bleep, XJ had killed not only the image on the screen but the lights as well. It had refused to turn even the emergency lights on, and Dion and Tusk had been forced to grope and fumble their way to their hammocks and had spent the rest of the day in bed.

Remembering the incident. Dion shifted uneasily in his chair. He hadn't meant to expose his innermost thoughts to Tusk like that. King deposed. Why had he ever brought that up? The boy was startled to discover how easily the mercenary saw through him, understood what he was thinking. Dion realized that he had underestimated Tusk. The boy had marked the mercenary down as a materialistic, restless adventurer. Quick to act and act intelligently, Dion had to admit, but that was probably due to instinct and training. Limited intellectual capacity.

Dion was forced to revise his opinion. The man was smarter

than the boy had originally thought. Smarter—and therefore more dangerous. Dion set increased guard upon himself.

··◄■ ■►··

The landing on Vangelis was uncomfortable, terrifying (for Dion, though he took care not to admit it), and uneventful. Nobody shot any missiles at them, although the commlink with the planet threatened immediate destruction if they didn't go into standard orbit until their credentials could be properly cleared.

"They gotta keep up their image!" Tusk shouted as the small plane rocketed through the atmosphere.

A fiery orange glow surrounded them, the heat in the cabin increasing markedly, life-support doing its best to compensate for the burning hot temperatures outside. Sweat poured down Dion's face. He gripped the arms of his chair so tightly that his hands and fingers ached for an hour afterward. The jolting caused him to bite down painfully on his tongue.

Once they had entered the atmosphere and were gliding through sunlit wispy clouds, receiving landing instructions from a base somewhere below, Dion was forced to leave his seat hurriedly and race to the head. When he returned, he was extremely pale. Tusk glanced at him but never said a word, for which Dion thanked the man deep in his heart. XJ, fortunately, was too occupied with the landing to comment on the boy's weakness, though Dion thought he heard a synthesized chuckle during a momentary interval in the conversation with ground control.

The plane landed and was towed to a parking place in a spaceport General Dixter had commandeered for his use, according to whoever was manning the control tower. Staring out the viewport as they trundled slowly to their position, Dion saw the strangest and mottliest assortment of flying craft gathered in one place outside of a museum. There were several long-range Scimitars (Tusk wasn't the only one to appreciate and "borrow" one of the Navy's renowned fighters), their markings either cleverly changed or—like Tusk's—completely obliterated.

"That's an old needle-nose!" Tusk said, peering out the port excitedly, in search of old friends. "They used to fly those in the days before the revolution. Yeah, they look real sleek," the mercenary said in response to Dion's admiring gaze, "but the Scimitars are ten times more maneuverable and practical.

Should be. Derek Sagan designed them and—so I've heard—he was the best pilot to ever come out of the Royal Academy."

"Royal Academy? What's that?" Dion asked.

"There's Zebulon Hicks, that S.O.B.!" Tusk sat forward.

"Where?" XJ demanded.

"Isn't that his plane? Turn your scanner about ten more degrees to the left. Now—"

"You're right! And stop swearing."

"How much does he owe us?"

"Sixty-seven Korelian mandats. I'll have to check on the exchange rate, but it's somewhere close to eighty golden eagles."

"The Royal Academy?" Dion persisted patiently. Derek Sagan. The man who'd killed Platus. The man who was after him. The Warlord held a strange fascination for the boy.

"Uh? Oh, that was a special school they used to run for kids of the Blood Royal. There were two of them—one for boys and one for girls, each established on uninhabited planets. The kids were sent there at about eight or nine. Since these kids were going to grow up to be kings or emperors or presidents or whatever else form of government they had back on the home planet, they were given a lot of advanced training in politics and stuff. XJ, is that Reefer?"

"No, your eyes are going."

"It is! I'd swear it! How much cash we got on board?"

"Oh, no, you're not!" The computer's lights flared. "No ante-up for you, mister! You lost one hundred and seventy-two—"

"Tell me more about the Academy," Dion interrupted. "What happened to it?"

Tusk shrugged. Releasing his safety restraints, he got to his feet, stumbling slightly as the plane jolted over the cracks and bumps of the cement runway. "The President did something with it, I guess. Shut it down. Turned it into a retirement village or low-income housing. How should I know?" He staggered toward the ladder. Dion, fumbling at the safety restraints, noticed his body felt unnaturally heavy and clumsy, as if somebody had wrapped weights around his wrists and ankles and stuffed his fingers full of lead.

"You should know more about it than I do, kid," Tusk said, his voice floating down from the living quarters. "Open up, XJ. I'm goin' out to make sure we get leveled off."

"Don't pay any more than six gilders," the computer warned. "I checked. That's the going rate. These crooks'll charge you twenty if they think you're a tourist! Tusk always gets taken," XJ said bitterly to no one in particular. "He won't haggle. I've told him and told him—"

Dion was hurrying after the mercenary. "What do you mean, I should know something about the Academy?"

"That master of yours must have attended that school. My dad went there. All the Guardians did!"

The hatch whirred open. XJ's attention focused on shutting down systems that wouldn't be needed once they were on the ground. Dion, anxious to get outside and breathe fresh air, climbed the ladder, his feet and hands feeling clumsy, as if they'd grown too large during the night.

No, Platus hadn't said anything about a Royal Academy. Just one more thing he'd never mentioned, kept secret. Why? Was it just too painful to talk about, to remember? Or had he been afraid it might give the boy ideas?

———

Emerging from the spaceplane, Dion drew in a lungful of air and immediately began to cough. A couple more breaths and he felt dizzy and light-headed and wondered if there were some sort of deadly chemical in the air that the computer's analysis had missed. He started to go back for his oxygen pack but noticed that Tusk—though he was breathing rapidly and heavily—hadn't keeled over yet and didn't seem to be afraid that he might.

Real sunshine felt good on the boy's skin. Slowly he slid down the ladder that ran along the hull of the spaceplane and came to stand beside Tusk, who was peering beneath the craft, yelling instructions to the man who had towed them and was now preparing to detach his vehicle from theirs.

"What's wrong with the air?" Dion asked, panting.

"Nothin'," Tusk said, glancing at him with a grin. "You're used to the healthy, pure stuff we breathe on board the plane. You'll get used to this in a day or so. Just take things kinda easy for a while. Do too much and you'll pass out cold."

Dion nodded. Tusk disappeared under the plane and the boy—out of curiosity—was about to follow when he felt a touch on his arm. A green tentacle had wrapped around his wrist.

It was the first time the boy, raised in total isolation in a barren desert, had ever met an alien life-form, and his heart rate leapt so that he came near fainting, as Tusk had warned him. The large blob of green regarded him with apparent concern while another tentacle wrapped itself around his other arm and held him upright.

"Xrmt!" Tusk cried, coming out from beneath the plane, or at least that was the approximation of the sound he made.

Another tentacle snaked across and gripped Tusk's hand (the other two still keeping firm hold of Dion) and a fourth tentacle made what seemed to be a pointing gesture while a sound like a buzz saw came from the blob's interior.

"What? Wait. I forgot my translator. No translator!" Tusk shouted, pointing to his chest. The alien understood and released Tusk. The mercenary scaled the ladder, disappeared inside the spaceplane.

Dion tried to call to him, but Tusk was gone before he got the chance. The boy thought about attempting to free himself from the alien's apparently solicitous grip, then wondered if that might not offend it. Dion's initial surprised fear had eased; his mind was running through classifications of alien life, attempting to place this one.

Tusk reappeared, a small black box hanging around his neck. Placing a disk attached to a wire at the base of his skull, the mercenary listened attentively to the alien's buzzings.

"Dixter's looking for me, huh? Yeah, I'll report right away. The kid? Naw, he's all right. First time for him, that's all. He just needs to get his land legs."

The tentacles released Dion gently, and the boy managed a bow and gave the creature a greeting in its own language.

The blob appeared delighted, if tentacle waving indicated delight, and Dion thought it did. The alien buzzed and crackled loudly and excitedly.

"That's the only words I know—" Dion turned to Tusk. "Tell the Jarun that I know only how to greet him, in his language."

Tusk was staring at the boy wide-eyed.

"I never learned to speak it," Dion said in apology, thinking that this was why Tusk was looking at him strangely. "Platus told me it could damage the human vocal cords."

"Uh, right." Tusk cut into the alien's torrent of words that sounded vaguely like a lumber company removing half a forest. He relayed Dion's message. The alien, listening on its own translator, bobbed up and down.

"He understands and says that, anyway, it was a great

pleasure to him to hear the words of the Jarun spoken by an alien race and he hopes you will join him for dinner."

Dion bowed. The alien bobbed, waved several tentacles, said something to Tusk, and went on its way.

"Reefer, huh? I knew I recognized his RV," the mercenary said in satisfaction. "Ante-up game there tonight. Uh, don't mention it to XJ, will you, kid? And say, how did you know that stuff?"

"Know what?" Dion turned his attention to their next-door neighbor—a recreational vehicle that had been converted into a fighter and had evidently seen better days. "About the game? I didn't, until you told me—"

"No, not the game. The Jarun. Who he was and what you said to him. And what do you mean you don't speak his language?"

"I don't. And I've studied the languages and habits of many of the races in the galaxy."

"Just out of curiosity, kid. How many languages do you speak?"

"About eighty, I guess. Only thirty or so fluently, though. The others I have trouble with sometimes. Why? How many do you speak?"

"Two—my native tongue and gruntspeak—what we're talking now. Didn't that master of yours ever hear of translators?"

"Of course. I know how to use one. But Platus said that a person who could communicate directly with another being in his own language was paying him a compliment that would always be remembered and appreciated."

"Well, you've won the Jarun's heart—if it has a heart." Shaking his head, Tusk laid a hand on Dion's shoulder. "Let's go see the general."

Chapter ❦ Twelve

Who is this? and what is here?
And in the lighted palace near
Died the sound of royal cheer;
And they cross'd themselves for fear,
All the knights at Camelot.
> Alfred, Lord Tennyson, "The Lady of Shalott"

The sun's heat radiated off the concrete slab of the spaceport in shimmering waves, creating mirages of pools of blue water in the distance. Back inside the cockpit of the spaceplane, Dion wiped sweat from his face and glanced enviously at Tusk, who had changed into khaki shorts and a mesh weave, sleeveless T-shirt.

"You want to borrow a pair of my shorts, kid?"

"Aren't we going to meet this general of yours?"

"Sure, but Dixter doesn't stand on formality," Tusk assured him.

Dion's opinion of this general was being lowered every moment. He climbed into the crew's quarters to change.

"Hurry up, kid."

Having completed the initial shutdown of all the important systems, Tusk left the remainder of the work to XJ and pulled himself up into the cramped living quarters.

Dion was standing near the metal storage chest where he kept his clothes. He had put on a clean pair of blue jeans and was holding what Tusk supposed was a shirt in his hands. Staring at the fabric intently, Dion was smoothing it with his fingers.

"What'd you find? Moths?" Tusk was in a good humor. "Damn, you've got white skin! Must come with the red hair. You're gonna burn to a crisp on this planet. We'll have to get you some sunblock. Come on— Hey, what's wrong?"

"Nothing," Dion said. He seemed startled and irritated that Tusk had interrupted him. Pulling the shirt over his head, he turned to climb the ladder leading up to the hatch.

Tusk, coming up behind him, took the opportunity to stare intently at the shirt, wondering what about it had attracted the boy's attention.

Actually, it wasn't a shirt so much as tunic. It was loose-fitting, obviously homemade, with a slit opening for the head and raglan sleeves. Some sort of fanciful design had been embroidered on the cloth with shiny silver thread. Beyond the fact that the tunic was handmade—and a clumsy job of sewing at that, thought Tusk, who was accustomed to mending his own clothes on long flights—there was nothing special about it. . . .

The decorative embroidery.

Around the neck, around the hem of the sleeves and the hem of the tunic itself glistened tiny symbols—eight-pointed stars.

Tusk's good mood evaporated.

"Open up, XJ! And say, what about the air cooler? It's hotter than hell's kitchen in here!"

"Do you realize how much fuel we use up running that system? And have you seen the prices on this planet?" the computer demanded. "Besides, the perfect temperature for a human being, nude, with no wind, is eighty-six degrees Fahrenheit. Which is the current interior temperature—"

"Fine. I'll hang around here nude!"

"Nude! You—!" XJ's circuits jammed, it was so outraged that it momentarily lost its voice. "I run a respectable plane! What would people think? Suppose General Dixter dropped in! And do you have any idea what they're charging us for electricity on this planet? It's criminal—"

The hatch whirred open. Dion pulled himself up and out. Tusk—his gaze fixed with a weird sort of fascination on the boy's tunic—followed more slowly. What was it? A sign to someone? Some sort of superstitious protective nonsense? I wonder if lasbeams would bounce off . . .

Tusk grinned at himself. You're headed for the edge. And you're letting the kid and that damn computer drive you there! It's a pretty design. That's all. A pretty design.

The two walked swiftly across the burning hot pavement. Tusk shot a glance at Dion's face, but he might have read more emotion in the concrete beneath his feet. Whatever the kid knew or was thinking, he was keeping it to himself.

I should dump him, leave him here, Tusk decided. He's an eighty-year-old man inside a seventeen-year-old body. And a cold and calculating old man at that. That "stand off, don't touch me" air of his sets my teeth on edge. To say nothing of the fact that he now knows as much or more about that damn spaceplane as I do! Speaks eighty languages, but only thirty fluently! Ha! Why did I let that electronic nightmare of mine talk me into this? I should have followed my instincts and gotten rid of the kid like I planned. I should have—

"Hey!" Dion tugged on the sleeve of Tusk's shirt and pointed. "Isn't that the direction you said the headquarters was?"

"Huh? Oh, yeah. Sorry, guess I wasn't watching where I was going. I got a lot on my mind."

Quit kicking yourself. You didn't have to listen to XJ. Sure, life on board the plane would have been hell for a while, but the computer would've gotten over it eventually. It was your own damn curiosity got you into this. You had to know.

Well, he thought gloomily, now maybe you're gonna find out.

··◁■ ■▷··

General Dixter's headquarters were easily visible once the two got out beyond the jumble of planes parked in the spaceport. Painted the same tan color as the arid, barren land surrounding it, the mobile trailer appeared—by some trick of the eye—to be close to the port. In actuality, it turned out to be about five miles away, as Tusk realized wearily when he and the boy set out walking. A hitched ride from a passing hoverjeep took them to their destination.

Dion looked with disfavor on the hand-painted sign over the door. He couldn't read the lettering but presumed it was regulation military—the language taught to all those who entered the Commonwealth's Armed Forces. Computer devised, the language had been designed primarily to develop manuals that could be read and understood by all races, but it had degenerated into a spoken language that was a crude mixture of military alpha—as it was called—and several major languages in the galaxy. Translators were far better for daily communication and were relied upon heavily, but this unofficial language had gained favor among the troops—particularly the mercenaries, who had modified it to their own sort of cant.

"What does that say?" Dion asked, pointing at the sign.

"Oh, so's there's something you can't understand?" Tusk remarked, still preoccupied with his inner misgivings.

The boy's flashing blue eyes brought the mercenary up short.

"Sorry, kid. Didn't mean to be sarcastic. Just in a bad mood." Tusk felt his face grow warm and was thankful that his dusky skin hid his embarrassed flush. "The sign's written in grunt-speak. Says 'Army Headquarters.' It's no wonder your master never taught this to you. For one thing, it isn't recorded anywhere. For another, it's probably a lot different than what it was years ago. And for third, the Guardians were above this sort of thing. We grunts use it. That's where the name came from."

"Will you teach it to me?"

"I'll try." Tusk was dubious. "Only it really just sort of grows on you—"

"Like a virus?" Dion's voice was cool, but the mercenary—looking at the boy sharply—saw a smile in the blue eyes.

"Yeah." Tusk relaxed and grinned. Sometimes he had to admit he kind of liked this kid. "Yeah, like a virus."

The mercenary climbed up several rickety stairs and shoved open a screen door that had—from the smell—been recently repainted. Strolling inside with easy nonchalance, Tusk turned to say something to Dion and discovered he wasn't there. The boy was holding back, outside the door, his lips stretched taut, his face so pale the mercenary was half-convinced he could see through the translucent skin. It was as if the kid thought his life's fate were going to be decided in the next three minutes.

Catching hold of the sleeve of the boy's tunic, Tusk hauled him inside.

"Hi, Bennett. I'm Tusk, remember? Here to see the general," the mercenary said to a soldier seated at a desk.

Bennett's neatly pressed and immaculate uniform was in marked contrast to what the boy had seen the other mercenaries wearing—everything from loincloths to long, flowing robes, to nothing but scaly skin.

"One moment, sir."

The aide stood up from his desk. After giving Tusk a sharp, appraising glance and letting his eyes flick briefly and curiously over the boy standing tense and tight as a drawn bowstring at the mercenary's side, Bennett vanished into an adjoining room, carefully closing the door behind him.

Tusk strolled over to examine several maps that had been Velcroed onto fuzzy boards and hung on the wall. Though every window in the place was wide open, it was only slightly cooler inside than out, he noted, mopping sweat from his brow. The air-conditioning must have broken down again. An ancient fan standing on top of a file cabinet near the aide's desk whirled its blades industriously. The only apparent effect it was having, however, was to require that every scrap of paper be held down by a weight. The aide returned.

"The general will see you—" Bennett began formally, but his words were run over by the man himself, who came out of his office to meet them.

"Tusk! Where've you been?" Dixter grasped the mercenary's hand and shook it warmly. "I was told you requested our coordinates. But that was days ago! Didn't you Jump?"

"Into a war zone, sir?" Tusk shook his head.

Dixter grinned. "This isn't that much of a war. Still, it pays the bills. Come in. Come in. And your friend, too. How did you make out on Rinos 4? I heard from Ridion that you got caught in that mess—"

Dion—not expecting the general's sudden arrival—had leaned over the desk to examine the aide's computer. His face was averted when Dixter entered the room, and by the time the boy stood up and turned toward him, the general had started back into his office, his hand resting on Tusk's shoulder.

Tusk launched into a doleful account of flying his spaceplane smack into the middle of a civil war. The general was listening sympathetically, his eyes fixed on the mercenary. Dion slipped in behind Tusk and stood with his back to the wall. While the two soldiers discussed the civil war on Rinos—in which, apparently, the general had considered taking part, then rejected as being a no-win situation—the boy studied both his surroundings and the man in charge.

The room in the general's trailer drew his attention first. Not because as a room it was anything extraordinary—it wasn't, being small and boxlike with two windows, a closet, and a large fan. What captured the boy's attention was that the walls were papered from ceiling to floor with antique maps and star charts. Dion had never seen so many maps or imagined that so many maps existed and could be gathered together in one space. Rolls of maps hung from hooks, maps were nailed to the walls or had been stuck up with masking tape. And some of the maps seemed—to Dion's fascinated gaze—to be clinging to the wood of their own volition.

Maps of star systems vied for attention with maps of planets, maps of countries, and—stuck up in a prominent place near the general's desk—a street map of some city. Hundreds more maps stood rolled up in corners or arranged in bundles on the floor. A whirring ceiling fan above the general's desk brought the maps to life. They whispered and fluttered and rustled like wild things.

Platus had never had access to maps like these. Dion's gaze went hungrily to systems whose names he recognized yet had never seen mapped out. He could live in this room for a year and never grow bored, he thought. Wondering idly how many of these worlds the general had visited, Dion turned from the maps to study the man.

John Dixter's tanned face was seamed and lined, gray streaked his hair at his temples and his receding hairline made a high, lined forehead seem even higher. His rugged outdoor life made it difficult to tell his age from his appearance, but Dion guessed him to be in his early fifties. Of medium height, the general's upper body was firm and muscular, with only a hint of softening around the waistline. His brown eyes, caught in a web of fine wrinkles, were clear and sharp and penetrating and seemed accustomed to scanning great distances. His uniform, unlike that of his aide's, was rumpled and creased and looked vaguely as if it had been slept in. (Dion was to discover later that this was precisely the case. When the general was too busy to return to his own quarters, he often slept in the trailer, on a cot stored in the closet.)

Dixter's voice was deep and resonant and when he laughed—which he was doing now at the expense of Tusk—it was hearty, infectious laughter. But though the laughter was genuine, his mirth did not seem to reside within him permanently but only visited from time to time. When the laughter was gone, the man's face was grave and solemn, though with a lingering smile in the brown eyes.

"Tusk," John Dixter said, clapping his hand on the mercenary's shoulder, "I think you were lucky to have escaped alive. Next time, heed my warning."

"Yes, sir," Tusk said ruefully, shaking his head over his misfortune.

"And now, introduce me to your friend. I thought you traveled alon—"

Dixter turned to the boy, his face set into a smile of welcome.

Dion, facing the general, saw the smile slip. The hand the general had raised to extend in greeting halted, the fingers clenched involuntarily. A look of recognition came to the man's eyes. Dion's heart leapt; the boy half-expected Dixter to greet him by name.

Dion started eagerly forward, lips parted to speak, when he saw himself once again a stranger in the general's eyes. Dixter's expression grew cool. Although he did not continue his sentence, he shook hands firmly, politely, and impassively. Turning away from them, the general circled around to take a seat behind his desk. He paused a moment, keeping his back to them, to stare at a map, perhaps giving himself time to regain his composure. When he sat down and faced them, he looked directly at Tusk.

"Please." He gestured at the chairs.

Tusk glanced meaningfully at Dion, and the boy knew he had not mistaken the general's reaction to him. Brief as it was and now well covered, it had been too obvious to miss. Tusk had noticed it, too. The mercenary took a chair opposite the general's desk. Dion sat down but the next moment he was standing up again without even knowing what he was doing.

"Sit, kid," Tusk shot out of the corner of his mouth and Dion subsided back onto the edge of his seat.

"What did you say the young man's name was?" Dixter asked, his eyes on Tusk, speaking of the boy as if he weren't in the room.

"Dion, sir," the mercenary said. "No last name."

John Dixter nodded, not seeming surprised. With an effort that was obvious, he kept his eyes leveled on Tusk.

"Is this young man a friend? Surely you haven't brought him to fight. He's hardly old enough—"

"He's seventeen, sir," Tusk interjected.

"Seventeen." The general coughed. His eyes darted to Dion, then shifted to a map.

"And, no, sir, the kid's not a friend. That is, he is a friend, but that came later." Tusk was nervous and getting confused. "I guess you could say I'm the boy's guard—" He stopped, his tongue frozen to the roof of his mouth.

"Guardian," suggested General Dixter softly.

"No!" Tusk slammed his hand down on the arm of the chair
with such force that he winced in pain. "No, sir," he amended
belatedly. "Chauffeur. That's more like it." Drawing a deep
breath, Tusk glanced at Dion and decided to plunge into the
atmosphere that had suddenly grown chill and dark. "The fact
is, sir, that I brought the kid here to meet you on purpose. I—
We, the kid and I, were hoping you could help us. We left
Syrac Seven about three parsecs ahead of Lord Sagan—"

John Dixter's eyebrows raised. He held up a warning hand
and Tusk fell instantly silent.

"Bennett!" the general called.

The aide appeared in the doorway.

"Drive into town and see if Mr. Marek has arrived. He
should have been in contact with me before this. He may be
having trouble finding transport."

"Yes, sir." Bennett turned to go.

"And lock the outside door when you leave. I don't want to
be disturbed."

"Yes, sir."

The aide left, shutting the door to the office behind him.
Tusk opened his mouth but Dixter frowned and shook his
head. No one said a word until they heard the front door close.
Rising to his feet, the general opened the office door a crack
and peered out. He motioned Tusk to check the windows.

Satisfied that they were alone, Dixter returned to his seat.
"A Warlord, Tusk," he said, shaking his head. "I thought you
had more sense!"

"It wasn't my fault, sir. This kid's . . . uh . . . mentor
needed to get the boy off-planet quick and he came to me."

"By accident? He chose you at random?"

"No." Tusk sighed. "Because of my father."

"I see." Dixter's expression was grave.

"Apparently, the Warlord is after the kid."

"How do you know?"

Briefly, concisely, Tusk related what happened the last night
on Syrac Seven. He told about Dion's return to his home, the
encounter the boy witnessed between Sagan and Platus, the
takeover of the planet by the Warlord's forces.

"We had to pull the drunken pilot routine to get past the
blockade."

"They got a good look at your plane?"

"I'm afraid so, sir. Probably pictures, too."

John Dixter, for the first time since they'd sat down, turned his eyes directly on Dion. Troubled, perplexed, the general stared intently at the young man, his penetrating gaze pinning him to the wall like another map.

"Your mentor, Dion. What was his name?"

"Platus. Platus Morianna."

Dixter's expression didn't change, but he leaned his head on his hand, slowly rubbed his forehead.

"You knew him—Platus," Dion said.

"Yes, I knew him." Dixter placed his hands on the desk, folded them, the fingers clasped tightly. "I knew them all. The Golden Squadron."

"It seems everyone knew him except me!" the boy said bitterly, "and I lived with him all my life!"

"So he never said anything—?"

"No. I didn't know he'd been a Guardian until Tusk told me."

"And you don't know, then, if any of the others are still alive?"

"One is, sir." Tusk inserted.

The unspoken name cast a palpable shadow over the general's face. "Yes," he answered.

"Sagan. You mean Derek Sagan, don't you?" Dion said. "The Warlord who killed my— Who—" Dion bit his lip, swallowed. "But what about the others—like Tusk's father—?"

Dixter lifted a cautionary finger. "Don't mention that aloud, young man. I'm the only one who knows the truth about him . . . that he is the son of a Guardian."

"Not the only one now," the mercenary muttered beneath his breath.

"Stavros," Dion was saying. "The Warlord said something about Stavros—"

"One of them." Dixter kept his hands folded. The knuckles were turning white. "What did he say about Stavros?"

"Only that Sagan thought he had shut the man's transmission down in time. It was Stavros who warned Platus that the Warlord was coming, I think. And the Warlord said something about Stavros holding out three days. . . ." The boy's voice sank.

"He's dead," John Dixter said. "They're all dead now, I suppose." The lines in his face grew deeper and more pronounced. Finally, shaking his head, he unclasped his hands and began to unroll a map that lay on his desk.

"So," he continued more briskly, "how can I help you, Tusk?

I don't know what can I do against the Warlord. I try my best to keep clear of his path. Sit down, boy. You're safe enough for the time being." This to Dion who was jumping up out of his chair again. "Sagan will take no interest in Vangelis. Not as long as the uranium shipments keep going out, and I intend to see that they do. But your time is short. As you say, Tusk, he has pictures of your plane, descriptions of you from the planet's surface. The Warlord is no fool. He's probably discovered your real name, my friend."

"We didn't come for help, sir. Not exactly." Tusk shifted uncomfortably in his seat. Lowering his voice, he glanced out the open window, then sat forward, mistrusting—it seemed— even the sand that blew in. "You see, sir, we've been trying to figure out why Sagan wanted the kid enough to kill for him. And we found a curious piece of information in some files that XJ . . . er . . . appropriated from the Warlord's computer. Nothing more than a history tape, but it recorded all the events of the night of the coup."

Dixter's eyes narrowed, his lips tightened. His hands ceased their task and lay flat and unmoving on top of the map. "Go on."

"There was a child born that night, sir. To a Princess Semele Starfire, wife of the king's younger brother. Seventeen years ago. The kid, here, is seventeen. His master was a Guardian. What we figure is—"

"*Don't!*" Dixter slammed his hands on the desk. The map rolled up with a snap. The word exploded among them like a grenade. Dion—nerves taut and stretched—fell back, grabbing the arms of his chair. Tusk started and stared at the general in astonishment.

Dixter licked his lips. "Don't speculate further, Tusk! Don't ask me for information. I can't tell you anything, I wasn't at the palace that night."

"Damn it!" Dion shot to his feet. Leaning over the desk, he confronted the general. "You know who I am! Or you think you do! Tell me!" His hands clenched to fists. "Tell me!"

Shocked, Tusk tried to grab hold of the boy, but Dion jerked free.

General John Dixter was not, it seemed, to be intimidated by flaring blue eyes. A smile twisted his lips, as if he were reliving old memories. It was almost as if he had been under such angry scrutiny before.

"Platus told you nothing?" Dixter asked.

"Not even my real name!"

"Then, Dion," the general said regretfully, in a tone that left nothing open to argument, "he must have had a good reason."

"You recognize me! I see it in your eyes."

Dixter's face hardened. "Don't try my patience, young man." Emphasis on the word *young* made Dion flush in anger and shame. "What I may know or guess is so minimal that it would only confuse the issue. Besides, to speak of it would be to betray a confidence. A confidence made to me by someone very dear." The general began, once more, to unroll the map. "Someone who was dying."

"Sir," Tusk said, getting to his feet. "I apologize—"

"No," Dion interrupted, suddenly and uncannily calm. "Sir, it is I who apologize. You are right, of course. I'm sorry, I behaved like a child. And I'm sorry to have brought back painful memories."

John Dixter smoothed out the map, holding it in place with an ashtray, two dirty glasses, and a staple gun. "I accept your apology, Dion. Pilot's briefing tonight at 2200, Tusk."

He bent his head, studying the map. The two were obviously dismissed. They left, Tusk careful to shut the door behind them.

When they had gone, Dixter raised his head, the map forgotten. Staring at the chair where the young man had been sitting, the general seemed to see the afterimage of the boy on his retina—as if Dion had been made of flame.

Chapter ·◆◐◯◑◆· Thirteen

So all life is a great chain, the nature of which is known
whenever we are shown a single link of it.
Sir Arthur Conan Doyle, *A Study in Scarlet*

Derek Sagan sat before his computer, his gaze intent upon
the screen. He was alone in his private quarters aboard
Phoenix. Located on a level separate and apart from the rest of
the ship, his chambers could be accessed only by an elevator
whose controls were set to respond to his voice command. All
others, with the exception of Admiral Aks and the Warlord's
own personal guards, had to request the Warlord's permission
to enter.

Fear didn't keep the Warlord isolated, as it did some rulers
in the galaxy. He had fears—all men do—but his fear was
nebulous, internal, buried deep like a piece of shrapnel in an
old wound. He never felt it—the sliver was never debilitating—but he knew it was there and he knew that someday
something would jar it loose and it would do its damage. Sagan
was afraid of nothing and no one over which he could exert
control. His need for privacy, his need to be alone with his
thoughts, his work, and also his prayers and meditations to an
outlawed deity kept him aloof from the men under his
command.

He knew this did him no harm with them. He was of the
Blood Royal, he had been born knowing how to manipulate
people. He never appeared before them unless he was in full
dress armor. Not only did the shining metal look impressive,
but it concealed as well as protected. A face covered by a
helmet never shows fatigue or pain. A gleaming breastplate
hides the slight thickening of the waistline. Sagan could always
appear invincible—at least to the enemy without. As to the
enemy within . . .

136

The Warlord waited patiently for the computer to complete its search. The crisp notes of a Bach partita played in the background, the intricate patterns aligning and altering and realigning themselves in the portion of his mind attuned to them. Bach was one of the few composers he admired, whose music he enjoyed. The mathematical order and precision appealed to him.

"Search complete, sir," came the mechanical voice.

"Reveal."

"Search linking one Mendaharin Tusca of Zanzi to persons known as the Guardians revealed Danha Tusca, former senator of the planet Zanzi, deceased in—"

"Next," ordered Sagan.

"Nothing further on Mendaharin Tusca."

"Match with the name Tusk."

"Searching." A pause. "Search complete."

"Reveal."

"Search of some seventy thousand subjects known as Tusk—"

"Yes, yes."

"—discovered one whose birth date, planet of origin, and DNA match with subject known as Mendaharin Tusca. Military service—"

"Skip that. Match Tusk with Guardian."

"Searching." Almost immediate. "One match. Platus Morianna, Guardian, met subject Tusk on Syrac Seven—"

"I entered that information myself."

The computer was not intimidated by its commandant's growing ire. "Search concluded, sir."

"Very well." Sagan had expected as much, but he felt annoyed all the same. "Next."

"Search linking subject called Tusk, known as Mendaharin Tusca, to second circle—those people closely associated with persons known to be Guardians. Search revealed—"

The computer paused in mid-report; some glitch in the system caused it to hesitate two or three seconds on occasion before continuing to function. The specialists aboard ship blamed it on system overload and advised Sagan at least every other ship's day that the problem had been solved. Tomorrow, he would pay them another visit.

"—one match."

"Indeed?" The Warlord was surprised.

"Subject known as John Dixter. Age fifty-two. Deserter.

Former general in the Royal Army. Youngest man ever promoted to rank of general by personal authority of—"

"Enough." Sagan knew Dixter's history better than the computer. His thoughts went to his prisoner aboard the *Phoenix*. "This is how the poet says journeys end, isn't it, my lady? Computer."

"Sir."

"Current location of John Dixter. Search files on mercenaries and their activities, all sectors. I want that report priority one."

A Bach fugue thundered around him. Sagan picked out the central melody and followed it through the various convulsions and diversions, keeping hold of it in his mind—one silken thread woven into a harmonic tapestry.

"Search complete."

"Reveal."

"Current location of John Dixter is on Vangelis, planet number—"

"I know it. Skip." He knew it very well, but why? Vangelis. It was in his sector, but that didn't mean much. There were hundreds of inhabited planets in his sector and he didn't know the names and numbers of all of them. Vangelis was connected with something, something important. Hastily he searched his memory but couldn't find it.

"A recent war has developed between one Marek, Douglas, Ph.D. Engineering—"

"Skip."

"—and the local planetary government over control of the uranium mines."

"Policy."

"We are operating under the standard policy of nonintervention with the provision that if the uranium shipments are interrupted we have the right to move in and place the planet under martial law."

A mining planet. Why would he be familiar with a mining planet?

"Search. Anything at all involved with Vangelis."

"Working." The answer was a long time coming. The Warlord thought the computer had, in fact, ceased to function and was about to give the specialists their fright for the day when he heard, "Search complete."

"Reveal."

"Vangelis is the site of an experiment being conducted by

Snaga Ohme, classification Red. Further information can be obtained only by your voice command override—"

"End of need."

Sagan stared at the blank screen. Vangelis. Experiment. Snaga Ohme.

Obsessions. That's what they did to you. His obsessive search for the boy, his discovery of Maigrey had driven Ohme's project completely from his mind. And he prided himself on his discipline—physical and mental! Of course, there was no particular reason why he should have kept it in his mind. All was arranged; he assumed it was proceeding as planned. Ohme wasn't particularly trustworthy, but the Adonian was almost as fond of money as he was of himself. Ohme's last report had been satisfactory and there wasn't another report due for another half-cycle. Still, Sagan should have kept informed. He certainly should have known that war on that planet was imminent.

John Dixter. Deserter. Royalist. The night of the coup, Dixter had fought with the Royal Army. He'd been captured and held prisoner, but he'd managed to escape. Most thought the general had slipped through Sagan's fingers. None knew that the Warlord had deliberately opened his hand.

If there was anyone to whom Maigrey might have run after her disappearance, it would have been John Dixter. Sagan kept the man under close watch, but Maigrey never came to him, never contacted him. Dixter turned to mercenary work and was quite successful at it. The Warlord could have closed his fist, crushed the mercenary leader anytime he wanted. But he chose not to. John Dixter was a good commander. He and his mercenaries performed a useful function, kept small fires from flaring into major conflagrations.

And now, John Dixter might be even more useful.

Leaning back in the chair whose shape and contours had been specially molded to fit his body, Sagan played the central theme of his melody and heard the echoes of the expansions.

If Tusca didn't know the identity of his young passenger, surely he must suspect. Platus must have been forced to tell him part of the truth, if not the whole, in order to get him to accept the responsibility. And wasn't it likely that, saddled with this burden, Tusca would turn to a friend? A friend who knew the Guardians, a friend who might be able to answer any unanswered questions?

It was worth a try.

At his signal, the entry door to his room slid aside and one of the Honor Guard appeared, fist over his heart.

"My lord?"

"Pass the word for Admiral Aks."

"Yes, my lord."

The centurion vanished, the door slid shut. Sagan could have summoned the admiral over the ship's commlink, but he preferred to keep this strictly confidential, especially with Maigrey aboard. He intended to spring this on her like a land mine, shatter her with the explosion.

The door slid aside and the guard appeared.

"Admiral Aks, my lord."

The admiral entered.

"That was quick," Sagan commented. He moved his hand over a beam of light and the Bach ceased. The Warlord had never been able to cultivate a taste for fine music in the admiral.

"I was on my way to see you, my lord."

"What about?"

"The Lady Maigrey, sir."

"Lady Maigrey?"

"Yes, but it can wait. What was it you wanted of me, my lord?"

"*That* can wait. What of the lady?"

Aks flushed and appeared slightly embarrassed. "I'm not certain quite how to put this, my lord, but—"

"Just spit it out, Aks, and don't waste my time."

"Yes, my lord. The fact is, my lord, that the lady is . . . er . . . damaging morale."

"Morale?"

This was not unexpected. Sagan was relieved to discover it was nothing more serious. Then he was angry at himself for being relieved. It meant that he was uneasy about her and he should have taken precautions enough to have precluded uneasiness. Yet even as he told himself this he told himself as well that he could never take enough precautions.

"Well, what has she done, Aks? She's not making speeches in the gym, calling the men to king and country?"

"Oh, no, my lord!" Aks looked shocked. "I would never permit such a thing. Your own orders—"

"It was a joke, Admiral."

"Ah, yes, my lord." Aks did not appear to consider the subject one for levity.

"Well, what has she done?"

"She has been walking around the ship, my lord."

"I gave her permission to walk around. She's under guard at all times and permitted to speak to no one."

"Yes, my lord. She doesn't need to speak."

"No, she wouldn't," Sagan muttered, but it was beneath his breath and the admiral didn't hear.

"She has only to appear on deck and everyone quits working. They can't help themselves. I've felt it myself, my lord, and I'm not an imaginative man."

"One of your more endearing qualities, Aks."

"Thank you, my lord."

"It wasn't a compliment. Please continue your report. I was not aware that the lady's beauty was so entrancing."

Aks was accustomed to such verbal barbs. His skin was coated with his own self-worth; he lacked the imagination to feel pain. "No, my lord. That isn't the problem. The men say it's like a ghost walking the corridors. She freezes the blood. No one can talk. No one can work. All the men seem to be able to do is to look at her. That terrible scar—"

Aks could not repress a shudder, and consequently did not see the darkness gather on Sagan's face. He heard it, however, in the answer to his complaint.

"Nonetheless she will continue to be allowed the freedom of the ship. It suits my purposes that she do so. As for the effect she is having on the men, she is fighting me the only way she has at her command. I admit that this is a different kind of enemy from those we usually face, but she is an enemy and the men must react accordingly. I presume that if the Corasians boarded the ship the men would not stop working to stare at them?"

"No, my lord. But—"

"Any work stoppage is a breach of discipline and is to be punished as such. Is that understood, Aks?"

"Yes, my lord."

"I want you to set a course for the planet Vangelis. Routine. I don't want any undue alarm. There's a war going on there, Admiral. Put it out that we're concerned with the uranium shipments getting through. The information's on the computer. Read up on it."

"Yes, my lord." Aks waited for further orders, suspecting

that this wasn't the real reason for the diversion from their normal course.

"I want the description of that Scimitar of Tusca's and the offer of the reward for information concerning it circulated in the area."

"You have reason to believe it's there, my lord?"

"John Dixter's there, Aks. I think it highly likely that we will find not only the Scimitar there but the boy as well. Such are the results of my deductions." The Warlord glanced at the admiral, who was regarding his lord in silence. "Now is the proper moment, Aks, for you to say, 'Gad, Holmes, you're brilliant!'"

"Holmes, my lord? I'm not certain who—"

"A literary allusion, Aks. Don't let it concern you."

The admiral didn't. It had been on his tongue to ask the Warlord why he hadn't used the lady to locate the boy. After all, that was one reason she'd been brought aboard. But Aks had seen Sagan's face upon his return from the planet of Oha-Lau. The admiral did not bring up the subject.

The Warlord leaned back in his chair, fixed his dark-eyed gaze on his admiral.

"Have you ever considered the workings of the universe, Aks?"

The admiral frowned. Aks disapproved of these philosophic ramblings. They invariably led Sagan to a discussion of unlawful topics.

"Our illustrious leader, President Robes," Sagan continued, "would say, no doubt, that it is random chance which seems to be bringing all these people together again. A sociologist would figure up the stats and chart the probabilities and see in it the herd instinct. But I believe it is the will of the Creator, Aks. He is bringing us all together for a purpose."

"Yes, my lord."

By merely agreeing to such a thing the admiral made himself liable to treason. But Aks had seen long ago that the Warlord's path was veering off the smooth, well-traveled road and heading into a dark and dangerous wilderness. The admiral was not a gambler but he knew the wisdom of the saying "Nothing ventured, nothing gained," and a man does not have to have to be imaginative to be ambitious. Aks never thought about chance. He knew nothing about sociologists. He didn't believe in a higher purpose or this mystical god. He did, however, believe in Derek Sagan.

The Warlord made a gesture. The music started—Bach, *The Well-Tempered Clavier*.

Aks knew that he was dismissed.

Chapter ---❧◯❧--- Fourteen

> I love my truck . . .
> Glen Campbell, "I Love My Truck"

The hatch beneath Tusk's hand opened so quickly he nearly fell inside head first.

"Where've you been?" demanded a voice from the darkness.

"Turn on the lights!" Tusk snapped, slithering down the ladder.

Dim lights flickered on in a circle around the center of the spaceplane's interior. Dion followed Tusk, the young man repressing a strong desire to see if he could slide down the ladder, heels on the rungs, as did the pilot. A fine sight he'd look if he failed, tumbling in a heap on the deck.

"Do you know what time it is?" XJ said in a querulous voice. "You've been gambling. I heard about the game—"

"We went to see Dixter," Tusk muttered, struggling to pull a sweat-soaked shirt off over his head, "and then I took the kid around to meet a few people and to show him some of the other planes. Then we went to the briefing." He snapped his lips shut on the word as if he'd like to bite it in two, hurled the shirt in a corner. Tugging on a sandal, trying to yank it off, he hopped about the cabin on one foot.

"Briefing?" XJ perked up. "Let's hear it. What's going on?"

Tusk's answer was a snarl and a sandal flung against the side of the cabin wall.

"My, my, we're in a pet, aren't we? It isn't the money, is it?" XJ was suddenly alarmed. "Not one of those die-now, pay-later plans?"

"You know Dixter better'n that," Tusk grumbled. Sitting on his bunk, he wrestled with the other sandal. "The money's okay. Fact, it's damn good. It's what I got to do to earn it."

"Ah, then—" XJ sighed contentedly.

"Drive a damn TRUC!" Tusk began to swear. "I'm a fighter pilot, not a friggin' Teamster—"

The lights went out. Dion, having been prepared for this, was safely stretched out in his hammock. He heard the other sandal hit the wall.

"If you are quite through with your tantrum," XJ said, peeved, "I would appreciate knowing what is going on. You've left me stuck here for hours. Our only neighbor is an outdated NICAR unit in that beat-up RV next pad over. It talks in numbers, when it talks at all."

"The kid will fill you in." Tusk was fumbling around in the darkness. "Where're the towels? I'm taking a shower."

"Not in here, you're not. All systems shut down except lights and air. Saves money. Go use Dixter's water. The towels are where you always stow them, in the third compartment down, just below the dehydrated fruit. Remember to hang it up on the line outside. I don't want to find a wet towel on the deck in the morning!"

Snarling an obscene rejoinder, Tusk thumped and bumped around the cabin. Dion heard a compartment slide open and hit something. There was a curse. Apparently, Tusk had been standing too close. The lights in the ship just barely flickered on and Dion saw a hunched-over Tusk, rubbing his shin and hauling out a frayed piece of cloth. The abused sandals flapped again on his feet. He wrapped the towel around his naked loins and limped up the ladder and out of the plane, still swearing.

Dion realized in admiration Tusk hadn't repeated himself once in his long string of curses.

"I, personally, am shocked," the computer said. The lights came back on. "Now, then, kid. Tell old uncle XJ all about it. Are you the long-lost prince of our dreams?"

"Yes, I am," Dion said, leaning his head back on his hands.

"You *are*?" The lights flashed in a wild, strobelike effect. "Did Dixter say that?"

"No." Dion shrugged. "But I know from the way he acted. He recognized me. He knew Platus and Stavros and Derek Sagan. And he was at the palace that night. Oh, he says he wasn't, but he's lying. There's a lot he knows that he's not telling." The boy yawned until his jaws cracked. The thin air and the excitement and the long day were getting to him. "It makes sense."

"Well, well." The lights dimmed as XJ recovered from the

shock. "Maybe so, but the general didn't actually *say* anything."

"He didn't need to," Dion countered. He settled himself more comfortably in his hammock, moving slowly so as not to set it swinging. "I know. I am."

"I hate to ask this, because it's admitting the occurrence of an improbable situation, but what does Tusk think?"

"We didn't discuss it." Dion had tried. Tusk had refused. The boy felt a return of his irritation.

XJ hummed to itself, assimilating the information, and decided to change the subject. "So, what's this about Tusk and a TRUC?"

"I'm not sure." Dion yawned again and shifted in his bed. Tired, he felt nervous and keyed up, his muscles jerked, and he couldn't get comfortable. "I understood only a little of the briefing. They all talk in a different language. Tusk explained most of it to me on the way back. Dixter introduced a human named Marek—I think that was it. Apparently he used to own the uranium mines in some country—I can't remember its name. He was a type of corporate feudal lord, it sounds like. The mines've been in his family for generations. Anyway, about two years ago, there was a civil war and the government of this country fell into the hands of an oligarchy. They nationalized the mines and sent Marek into exile. Marek was well liked by his people and the government was careful to treat him nicely. He went peacefully—not wanting to prolong the fighting, which was disrupting the economy—and he might have been willing to stay where they had sent him, which was on a planet somewhere on the fringes of this system. The government gave him a percentage of the income, anything he wanted to keep him happy and away from the mines.

"But then Marek got word that his miners were being mistreated. Production was falling off, profits were dropping. The miners walked off the job. The government sent in troops and there was bloodshed. Marek heard talk that the Warlord would step in if the uranium shipments were halted and place the country and maybe the whole planet under military control—"

"Which means kiss your ass good-bye," XJ interrupted.

"I guess it means kissing the profits good-bye, at least," Dion said, smiling slightly. "And nobody wants that, not

Marek, not the miners, not the government. But nobody's willing to back down."

"I get the picture. They're all holding a gun on each other; meanwhile, the Warlord steps up and shoots them all in the back."

"Yeah, and the government's got the shakiest hand, according to Marek. The oligarchs can't agree on anything. The people are fed up and there's a group all set to move in and take control. Tusk thinks Marek's involved in that, too, but Dixter has drawn the line at helping him overthrow the government. All we're doing, I guess, is making sure the uranium shipments keep going out while Marek tries to regain control of the mines."

"That's why Dixter's lived as long as he has. Mercenary generals like him start overthrowing governments, and we'd find the Congress breathing down our necks. While we still *had* necks," XJ added as an afterthought. "Who's likely to try to stop the uranium?"

Dion yawned again. He was finally relaxing and wished the computer would keep quiet. "According to Marek, there's one or two in the government who think that the Warlord taking over might not be such a bad thing. Sagan would be so grateful, he'd leave them in power—"

"Uh-huh. So grateful he'd put them in the cellular disrupter. Sagan can't stomach a traitor. Kind of funny, when you stop to consider that—depending on how you look at it—he's got a good chance of winning the Traitor of the Century award."

There was no answer.

"How much did Tuck lose?" XJ asked gloomily.

"Twenty-seven gildons," Dion murmured.

··◆·· ··◆··

"How much did you tell XJ I lost?" Tusk asked, leaning over in his chair to whisper to Dion.

"Twenty-seven gildons."

"Good kid!" Tuck whistled in relief. Pulling out his well-worn wallet, he thumbed through a fat stack of plasticene bills and, pulling two out, handed them to the boy. "Here's your cut. I got to admit that system of yours really works. Now if there was just some place aboard the plane where I could hide my stash so that—"

"Attention!" Bennett's crisp voice silenced conversation. There was a scrapping and scrabbling as the mercenaries got to their feet or claws or whatever it was they stood on, each informally saluting General Dixter in his or her or its own way, each with the utmost respect.

Walking across the tarmac, the general motioned for them to be seated, and those that used this form to rest their bodies did so, while others leaned back on gigantic tails, slithered to the ground, or—like the six floating Kandar—bobbed slowly up and down in mid-air.

Due to the intense heat during the day, pilots' briefings were held outdoors, in the relative cool of the Vangelian night. Camp stools were drawn up on the still-warm concrete. Harsh lights illuminated the pilots and their fighters. Force fields surrounded the airstrip. Security was tight.

Dixter nodded in greeting, his brown eyes flicking over each, silently acknowledging and thanking each for his, her, or its presence. The gaze included Dion, and the young man thought he noticed the tired lips widen in a small smile that remained when the general began to speak.

"Knowing how rumors spread around this outfit, I guess you don't need me telling you that Marek deployed his ground forces today. He's taken over the mines. You probably know more about it than I do by now, so I'll skip the details."

Appropriate laughter and nodding of heads. Dixter's smile left, his face returning to business.

"We have nothing to do with the ground end of things," he said.

Dion, remembering the maps on the walls, raised an eyebrow at this. Maybe not, but Dixter was certainly keeping himself well informed. Peeking curiously into mobile field communications, Dion'd seen numerous people monitoring radios and transferring information onto computers. Walking from one to the other, staring at the constantly changing light-maps on the huge screens, Dixter studied them and discussed them in low voices with his officers.

A thought occurred to the boy. If the general was this well equipped with modern technological advancement, why the old paper maps on the walls? Why the obviously loving care given to them? Perhaps, Dion answered himself, because Dixter's entire life is where he's been, not where he's going.

"Repeat!" Dixter's stern voice caught the boy's wandering attention. "This better sink in. The uranium shipments will get through. After me."

The mercenaries obediently chanted the chorus.

"Again. Louder. The uranium shipments will get through."

Everybody said it again, this time laughing.

"Once more, and this time, mean it. Your skins and your hides and your bubbles"—a glance at the bobbing Kandar—"depend on it. If even one TRUC is destroyed, we'll have the Warlord's battle cruisers down on us so fast you'll think bosk snails move at supralight. Repeat—the uranium shipments *will* get through!"

Grinning, everyone shouted it out with enthusiasm.

Dixter smiled and nodded. "Very good. Most of those in power around here don't want the Warlord on Vangelis any more than we do. But you've all heard Marek. He believes that this government might attempt to try to capture the uranium shipments and sell them directly to the Republic, concocting a story for the Warlord guaranteed to put them in a good light and Marek in eternal darkness. There's a lot more riding in that TRUC with you than uranium, Tusk."

"Yeah, like our payroll!" someone sang out from the back.

Everyone laughed and several leaned forward to pound Tusk on the back or shove him playfully. Tusk scowled darkly. He'd spent ten minutes in the general's office, trying to see Dixter to argue, but the general had been too busy.

"Three fighters will go up with each shipment. The TRUC Tusk is babysitting will be the first and the only shipment for the time being. I wish like hell we could send numerous TRUCs at the same time and split up the enemy's attack forces. But what with the strike and then the fighting yesterday, the deliveries are late as it is. The miners have been working day and night to load up just one, and therefore it *has* to get out. There is a piece of good news. The TRUC has been equipped with lascannons—on loan from the Warlord."

Everyone laughed.

"What's the joke?" Dion whispered to a sulking Tusk.

"The Warlord doesn't know he's loaned them."

Dion looked at him blankly.

"Stolen, kid. They're stolen. Like most of the rest of the equipment."

And like yourselves, Dion thought. He glanced about the group of pilots, remembering their varied histories as recited by Tusk during interludes in the card game. Some were deserters from the Galactic Democratic Republic's Armed Forces, who like Tusk had become disillusioned with life in the military. Some had been honorably or dishonorably discharged from the former and, accustomed to fighting and finding other jobs less fulfilling and less lucrative, had kept on doing what they knew best. Others were outlaws, on the run from planets, systems, bounty hunters, the Republic, or a variety of the above.

Each was known to Dixter, who personally interviewed every applicant wanting to join his team. Any human or alien who didn't live up to the general's high standards was paid off and told not to bother to come back. Dixter and his mercenaries soon developed a reputation not only for being expert soldiers but a disciplined and organized fighting force. The general was, therefore, able to carefully select the causes for which he and his people fought. After all, it was a cause that could conceivably cost them their lives.

"Those scheduled for the first run assemble at the location point at 0400. Tusk, report to me immediately following this meeting. The rest of you are dismissed."

Lurching to his feet, knocking over the camp stool on which he'd been sitting, Tusk hurried after Dixter. Dion followed, feeling a growing sense of excitement and exhilaration over the impending mission. The young man brushed aside the stinging gnats of guilt that assailed him whenever he heard, in memory, the gentle voice of Platus argue against warfare and violence. It seemed to Dion that they—Marek and Dixter—were in the right and the oligarchs in the wrong. Marek had tried to settle the dispute peacefully and had failed. Certainly Platus would have understood that. The young man was even mildly disappointed to find that Dixter had no plans to rush in, overthrow the government, and seize power.

Tusk had a head start and Dion, becoming entangled in the dispersing crowd, dashed up on Tusk's heels just as the mercenary was arguing his case.

"I'm a fighter pilot, sir, not a freight hauler. Let me fly escort. I'll be of more use—"

"I've made my decision, Tusk," Dixter said, striding across the tarmac toward the GHQ building. "I'm not asking you to fly the TRUC; you'll have a driver, one of the best in the business."

"Not fly it! Begging your pardon, sir, but then what the hell—"

"You're a skilled gunner, Tusk. You've got to handle the lascannon—"

"Riding shotgun!" Tusk swore.

"What was that?" Dixter paused in mid-stride, glancing at Tusk and raising his eyebrow.

"Nothing, sir."

The lines around the elder man's eyes crinkled, the corner of the lips deepened into the folds of the cheek—a weary smile of understanding. Tusk, his eyes on his shoes, didn't notice and there was no indication of sympathy in Dixter's crisp voice.

"You're the only gunner I've got who's had experience with these new models. Not only that, but you're intelligent and imaginative and not prone to shoot your way out of a problem if there's a more logical solution."

The general wiped his hand over his perspiring face. Even at night, the heat lingered. "I guess you and the rest think I'm a damn fool." He glanced at the other mercenaries heading back to their ships or the bars or the nearest ante-up game. "But I can't emphasize too much the importance of getting this shipment through without causing any more of an incident than we can help. I chose you for one reason, Tusk. I trust you." Dixter laid his hand affectionately on the man's shoulder. "Don't let me down."

The general gave the mercenary a nod that was friendly, yet indicated that the subject was closed and would only be reopened at considerable peril.

Tusk ducked his head. "Yes, sir," he mumbled.

"Now, come to my office. You'll meet your driver."

Dixter withdrew his hand from Tusk's shoulder and turned his attention to Bennett, who had been hovering at his shoulder with a clipboard, papers, and obviously important news. The two walked rapidly on ahead. Dion, slowing his pace to follow at a discreet distance, discovered that Tusk had come to a complete standstill.

"I don't like this," Tusk muttered. "Not one damn bit!"

◄━━ ━━►

Dixter's trailer was crowded, noisy, and hot. People were coming and going constantly, mostly from a large white van that was mobile field communications and carried an assortment of various monitoring and transmitting equipment mounted on the top.

"They're in touch with Marek, picking up his troop reports, probably listening in on the government forces' transmissions," Tusk explained.

Dion nodded, attempting to look wise. His gaze shifted to

another van, parked next to the first. This one was smaller and much newer. Unlike the other van, no one was coming into it or going out of it. It appeared to be operational, however; lights glowed from instruments on the van's roof, where several long, gleaming metal tubes pointed fixedly at the sky.

"What's that one doing?" Dion asked.

Tusk gave him a swift, sharp glance. "Monitoring the fleet."

"The Warlord?"

"Uh-huh."

Dion stared at the van, his fingers tingling, a shiver that was half-pleasurable and half-chilling crawling over his skin.

"C'mon, kid. It's not polite to keep a general waiting."

"Maybe I should stay out here."

Tusk looked at Dion, looked at the van, and, shaking his head, got a firm grip on the young man's arm. "I know what you're thinkin', kid, and it ain't healthy."

Dion glared at him, trying unsuccessfully to break free of the mercenary's hold. "What do you mean?"

"'One man knows who I am'? or words to that effect? Yeah, Sagan knows, all right, but are you willing to risk your life and mine and Dixter's and the lives of everyone else around here to find out?"

"You're wrong! I wouldn't do anything like that! I'm not stupid. Besides," the boy added coolly, twisting free, "I already know the truth."

"Yeah." Tusk grinned. "XJ told me. I got to hand it to you, kid, you threw a lightning bolt into that computer. XJ hasn't had a shock like that since we got caught in a zapping crossfire on Delta Venus. C'mon." The mercenary heaved a sigh. "Let's get this over with."

Dion allowed himself to be persuaded. He cast a backward glance at the van. He hadn't really been plotting what Tusk suspected him of plotting. In fact, he hadn't consciously thought of it at all until Tusk brought it up.

Consciously thought of it.

The plan must have been in his subconscious, however, because the minute Tusk accused him of trying to communicate with the Warlord, Dion recognized the idea and knew it for his own and knew he had rejected it for all the reasons Tusk had mentioned. Which meant that Tusk knew Dion better than Dion knew himself. The boy found this disconcerting.

The two shoved their way inside GHQ, trying—along with two other pilots—to enter the door as two humans and an alien

were trying to get out. Fighting his way inside, Dion was
smothered by the heat, the noise, and the crush of people. He
didn't like crowds. He felt himself apart, separate, distinct
from other people.

I don't belong, he thought. I'll never belong.

After a considerable wait, during which the young man
became so absorbed listening to the conversations around him
and trying to make sense of the military jargon that he forgot
his uneasiness, Bennett shouted into the packed room. "Tusk!"

More pushing and shoving, and finally the two left the heat
and the noise and entered Dixter's office, which—by comparison—was almost cool and almost quiet. Bennett shut the door.

General Dixter sat behind the desk. Across from him, sitting
in a chair, reading a mag, was a woman. She looked up when
they entered, then turned back to her reading. Obviously, she
wasn't impressed.

"Tusk, come in. Dion. Sit down."

The general nodded in welcome. If he was surprised that
the mercenary had brought the young man with him, he didn't
indicate it by word or gesture. Dixter appeared to have
forgotten there was anything the least strange about Dion—
either that or the load of more urgent matters had shoved it all
to the back of his mind.

"Tusk, this is your TRUC's driver, Nola Rian. Nola, this is
Tusk, your gunner. You two will be our first team."

Truckin', got my chips cashed in . . .
                    The Grateful Dead, "Truckin'"

It wasn't that Tusk had anything against women. Tusk liked
women, liked them very well, in fact. Tusk respected women.
There'd been several excellent female pilots in his flight
school. When a woman was in another spaceplane, flying next
to his, she wasn't a woman anymore. She was a pilot. What
Tusk didn't like was having a woman in the same plane, having
a woman as a partner. That made him nervous. He was always
inclined, when with a woman, to feel protective and fuss over
her. Leap in front of her with his drawn sword—that sort of
thing. And that sort of thing could get you killed.

So now he was not only being forced to ride shotgun on a
TRUC, he was going to have to share his duties with a female.
Not seeing how matters could get much worse unless the
Warlord should suddenly happen to stroll through the door-
way, Tusk gave a sickly grin, extended his hand, and said the
first dumb thing that came to mind.

"You don't look much like a TRUC driver."

Actually Tusk was thinking that this Nola Rian looked more
like a TRUC. She had a short, compact, square-shouldered
body, with the muscular arms required to handle the cumber-
some, unwieldly freight haulers. Nondescript brown hair, cut
short in a no-nonsense fashion for comfort in the heat framed
a pert face freckled by the Vangelian sun. Green eyes, flecked
with brown, glanced at Tuck without interest and she kept her
hand to herself. What he said had been meant as a compliment, but she apparently took it differently.

"You don't look much like a deserter," she replied.

Was that an insult? Tusk couldn't make up his mind. Mulling
it over, he took back his hand before she bit it.

"Sit down, please, and let's get on with this," Dixter ordered. Tusk hunched himself into a chair. Nola moved away from him. Dion remained standing in a corner, unnoticed, he thought, until he happened to catch Dixter's gaze shifting somberly from the papers on the desk to the young man.

I was wrong. I'm on his mind, Dion said to himself. He's thinking about me more than his war. Look directly at me, damn you! Who is it you see? What do you fear?

But by the time the words flicked through Dion's mind and before his eyes could connect with the man's, General Dixter had turned his attention back to his two reluctant recruits.

"Nola Rian is one of the best drivers around, Tusk. She comes highly recommended by the mining authorities. Over four hundred flawless runs. Tusk is one of my best gunners, Rian. He's also one of my most trusted men. You two will make a good team."

Tusk and Nola were eyeing each other with all the friendly intent of two starving mountain lions standing over a fresh kill.

"You *will* make a good team," Dixter repeated, his voice hardening. "This is the first shipment. If anything happens to it, there may not be any more. If you get out safely, it might demonstrate to the government how useless it is to try and stop us. Rian, do you understand?"

"Yes, sir." Nola sat up straighter, squaring her jaw, which—in Tusk's opinion—was the last thing her jaw needed.

"Tusk?"

"Yes, sir. Any idea what they'll send up against us?"

Dixter nodded, slowly. "According to Marek's intelligence reports, the government's typical of most small-planet oligarchies. They've got a wide assortment of fighters, long- and short-range, mostly old needle-noses from the days of the monarchy."

Dixter paused, and Tusk tensed. "Yes, sir. What else?"

"A very modern, very sophisticated torpedo launcher. Brand-new."

Tusk's jaw dropped. "Where'd they get that?"

Dixter scraped a grizzle-bearded cheek with his hand. "I wish I knew." His face was grave. "I wish I knew."

Tusk started to say something, caught Dixter's flickering eyelid, glanced at Nola, and kept quiet.

The door opened. Bennett stuck his head around the corner.

"Begging your pardon, sir, but there's a message from Mr. Marek—"

"Right. Anything else?"

Dixter swept a questioning glance at Tusk and Nola, who both shook their heads. Chairs scraped. Tusk stood back to let Nola pass in front of him.

"See you in the morning," he said in a friendly tone.

"0400." For the first time, she looked at him directly. Her green eyes were very green. "Be on time."

Slinging a handbag over her shoulder, she stalked out the door without a backward glance. Tusk and Dion, following her out of the crowded HQ, saw her set off alone with confident ease across the tarmac. Her walk was straight-backed, with wide strides. She didn't look like the type who was easily stopped by obstacles and obviously enjoyed going through them, rather than around them. She didn't look the type to sit quietly and do exactly what she was told.

"Damn," Tusk growled.

··◁■ ■▷··

0400 hours.

Tusk zipped up his flight jacket, Dion watching with envy.

"I don't suppose—"

"No," Tusk said shortly. "I got enough problems." He grabbed his helmet and began to climb up the ladder leading out of the spaceplane.

"Same arrangements as usual?" XJ called out.

Tusk paused a moment. "No. Put the kid's name in. Okay with you?"

"Sure," the computer said. "*He* doesn't swear! Good flying," XJ added when it was fairly certain Tusk was out of the plane and couldn't hear.

"What did that mean?" Dion asked suspiciously, staring sulkily at the closing hatch.

"What did what mean?" XJ crackled. "And make it short. I'm going to shut down for the rest of the night."

"What arrangements that have to do with me?"

"Oh, that. Disposition of property after death. Tusk's just made you his heir. Not much to inherit. Half-ownership with me in this crate. At least now. Tusk's old man was pretty well fixed and left his mother a bundle. I suppose when she dies Tusk will be pretty well heel—"

Grabbing an old jacket of Tusk's, Dion climbed out of the

plane. He could see, in the harsh white of the nuke lights, the hoverjeep waiting to take Tusk to the TRUC launching site, which was located near the mining operations. Standing around it were General Dixter and three other people Dion didn't recognize.

Swiftly he clambered down the ladder and, keeping to the dark shadows held back by the pools of light, made his way across the tarmac.

"These are your escort pilots, Tusk. Nigol from Anwar 33."

Tusk and the alien, whose thick hide required no protection, touched hand and claw.

"Captain Link Jones."

"Link." Tusk held out his hand. "Where're you from?"

"Less said the better, eh, Tusk?" The handsome pilot grinned and shook hands.

"And Captain Mirna Anrim, Ahna 2335."

A grim-faced woman shook hands with Tusk without comment.

"All flying Scimitars," Dixter continued. "All under your command, Tusk. They'll stay with you until you're within range of the fleet's tanker. Then the fleet's own fighters will have you under cover. If the government forces try something, it won't be under the guns of the Warlord. The TRUC driver has instructions to unload and get back here quickly. Everybody clear?" The pilots nodded. Dixter handed out sealed envelopes. "Inside you'll find the rendezvous point. Don't open these until you're airborne. Any change will be transmitted to you in the code you'll find inside. Anything you want to add, Tusk?"

The mercenary shook his head, and the pilots left for their fighters. Dion moved nearer. Dixter had seen him and hadn't said anything, so the young man assumed it was all right for him to stay.

"Tusk, a word with you."

The general, glancing at Dion, made an oblique motion for the boy to join them and led Tusk away from the jeep so that its driver couldn't overhear their conversation.

They walked over to the security fence surrounding the tarmac. Dixter stepped into a pool of light. He looked tired; his eyes blinked with the burning that comes from lack of sleep.

"Tusk, we picked up a Priority Code One signal from the Warlord's flagship. They've issued a Class A seize and apprehend for you. They have your description, including a vid—

your old military I.D.—*and* your plane's description down to the last carbon streak and rivet."

Tusk's shoulders hunched. "So they *did* make me when we left Syrac."

"It gets worse, I'm afraid. There's a price on your head, my friend. Ten thousand golden eagles."

Tusk, staring at him, gasped.

"Ten thousand! Damn! For that kind of money I'd turn myself in!"

Dixter smiled wearily. Dion glanced at them in confusion, only partially understanding, biting his tongue to keep from interrupting.

"What about the kid?"

"Nothing. You at least achieved that much, Tusk—you and Platus. My guess is that Sagan either doesn't know he's with you or he has no idea what the boy looks like and can't put out a description."

Tusk nodded in gloomy satisfaction.

"You still want me on this job, sir?" he asked calmly. "Or is this my pink slip?"

"No, I need you. You're not flying your plane and there's no reason for you to leave the TRUC. When you arrive at the tanker, let Rian handle the docking and do all the talking. They know her, after all. You stay on board, out of sight of the vid sensors. Keep your helmet on, your mouth shut. They may have—probably do have—voice prints. You should feel flattered. Sagan's spent a lot of time and money on you."

"And what happens when I get back, sir?" Tusk didn't seem to appreciate the compliment. "I can't just sit here, for God's sake!"

"I'll work on that. Leave it to me," Dixter said reassuringly.

"As if you don't have enough to think about, sir," the mercenary said ruefully. He ran his hand through his wiry black hair, tugged at the silver earring.

"Don't worry, Tusk. Concentrate on this job for now." Dixter clapped him on the back—a gesture Dion had come to recognize as one of dismissal. "Good flying. Give Nola Rian my regards."

"Yeah. I mean, yes, sir." Tusk, not appearing happy, turned to find Dion standing in front of him.

The mercenary started and instantly manufactured a smile. He apparently hadn't been aware of Dion's presence and he cast a reproachful glance at Dixter. "You here, kid? You ought to be in bed."

"I just wanted to say"—Dion couldn't untangle the skein of words that twisted in his mind—"good flying," he finished lamely. He held out his hand.

Tusk smiled. Taking the boy's hand, he gripped it firmly, then—consigning Dion to Dixter with a glance—the pilot loped off, climbed into the hoverjeep, and disappeared into the night.

"What does that mean, sir?" Dion asked. "A Class A seize and apprehend?"

Dixter stood unmoving, staring fixedly into the darkness. A flare of blinding light and a fiery, deafening roar as one of the fighters took off prevented the general from answering. He waited until all three planes were airborne, following their progress aloft with his eyes until they were nothing but flaming dots in the heavens before he spoke.

"It's used only for the most dangerous class of criminals—those who are considered a serious threat to the Republic. There were only a few names on that list, and now Tusk's has joined them."

"What names, sir?"

Dixter turned shrewd, narrowed eyes on him. "You know them, Dion. You don't have to ask me. Danha Tusca, Anatole Stavros, Platus Morianna, Maigrey Morianna—"

"Who?" Dion stared at the general. "Who did you say—"

Dixter, obviously sorry to have spoken, didn't reply. Turning to leave, he stepped out of the light and Dion could no longer see his face. "There's only one name you have to worry about, young man, that of Mendaharin Tusca." Dixter's voice came out of the night and was soft and bitter as the darkness. "Because all the others are dead."

Chapter ·–◦⬤◦–· Sixteen

Put the pedal to the metal!
Trucker slang, circa 1970.

"Where've you been?" Nola pounced on him. "We're thirty minutes behind schedule!"

"The general had some last-minute instructions," Tusk replied.

The two stood eyeing each other grimly, then Nola, lips pulled tight, hit a button and the TRUC's heavy door heaved itself shut with a rumble that shook the gigantic vehicle. Tusk, when viewing the thing from the outside, had come to the conclusion that it looked like a squat, rectangular warehouse some joker had decided to levitate.

"Follow me," Nola ordered, leading the way down a metal-lined corridor.

Tusk did so, noting that the puffy flight suit she was wearing did nothing for her figure. He didn't like short women, anyway. He couldn't stand brunettes. Tall willowy blondes—especially blondes who had more sense than to drive TRUCs for a living—were more his style. Gloomily, he stared around him, oppressed by the sense of several hundred tons of metal-encased rock riding on his tail.

The cabin they entered was tiny, meant for brief journeys into space and back. Brusquely, Tusk shoved the woman aside to get a look. Two people would have been a tight fit under normal circumstances, and the huge lascannon mounted in the center further restricted movement. Reaching up a hand to scratch one's head would be a task that called for serious precalculation.

"It's designed for function, not speed," Nola snapped, shoving Tusk aside in turn with a deft hip and shoulder movement that slammed him face-first into a bank of toggle switches.

"Function!" Tusk snorted. "I know that's something *I* always look for when some S.O.B.'s shooting torpedoes at me!"

He regretted his statement as soon as he said it. He couldn't see her face—her back was turned to him—but he heard the woman catch her breath, saw the hand clutching the back of the pilot's seat tremble. With difficulty, Tusk wormed his way around to face her.

"Look, Rian. I—"

"Get your helmet on!" She slid away from him. "We're thirty-five minutes behind schedule."

Wondering how he got himself into this and deciding to blame it all on XJ, Tusk pulled on his helmet, snapped the chin strap with a vicious click. He took a few moments to inspect the lascannon, not because he needed to, but because the delay was obviously irritating Nola Rian. The cannon was a newer model than the ones with which he was familiar, but he noted and highly approved all the changes in design and smiled in grim satisfaction. At least something was going right!

Leaning back in his seat, Tusk watched the woman's hands move skillfully over the instrument panel. He had only the vaguest idea of what she was doing. The TRUCs were anti-grav driven vehicles, and though Tusk knew something about them on principle he had never operated one.

Glancing out the thick steelglass windscreen, he saw the crew scrambling to clear the area as Nola gave a thumb's up to indicate they were ready to go. A rumbling—barely heard through the TRUC's thick metal shields—indicated that the overhead doors to the silo where the monstrous vehicles were housed were slowly sliding open. Nola activated the anti-grav field and slowly and silently the ungainly monster rose up into the air. Absorbed in the remarkable and unexpected beauty of seeing the ground fall slowly away from him, instead of blasting up off it like a bolt of perverse lightning striking out at heaven, Tusk was startled to feel an ice-cold touch on his hand.

Turning, alarmed, expecting a crisis, he discovered Nola reaching out to him, not an easy task considering the lascannon mounted between them. Her eyes, seen through the visor of the helmet, were pretty eyes—sparkling green, wide, with a fringe of brown eyelashes beneath pertly slanting dark brown eyebrows.

"Tusk—" she swallowed, seeming to have difficulty finding

the moisture in her mouth necessary to talk, "I just wanted to say that I'm sorry—about being such a . . . such a bitch—"

"Hey, no. You weren't—"

"I was," she said feelingly. "Last night and this morning both. And you didn't do anything to deserve it— Well, maybe that crack about not looking like a TRUC driver. But I'm sensitive about that. I was fat when I was a kid and they used to call me TRUC. Maybe it's one reason I took up driving them. Now I'm babbling. First a bitch, then a babbler. The truth is, Tusk, I'm scared. So scared it took all my bitchiness this morning to keep me running to the head and throwing up—"

"Rian, hush, take it easy," Tusk said, catching hold of her hand and squeezing it. "Jeez, your fingers are like ice. Hell, you got a right to be scared. I'd be worried about you if you weren't!"

"I've flown through cosmic dust storms and never lost either my nerve or my cargo," Nola continued, gripping Tusk's hand tightly. "These TRUCs could fly through the side of a mountain and come out intact. But cosmic storms don't shoot at you—"

"You're gonna do fine, Rian. And everything's gonna be all right." Tusk hoped the helmet obscured the expression on his face. "They wouldn't dare shoot at us. Think of the repercussions. Reporters crawling all over them."

The green eyes crinkled in the corners. "Uh-huh. There's always the chance that whoever got that fancy new torpedo boat is planning to use it as a prop for filming a war vid. Right?"

Before Tusk, somewhat taken aback by her perspicacity, could think up an answer, the woman had turned her attention to steering or whatever one did to maneuver the vehicle, if one maneuvered it at all.

"And if it isn't a breach of discipline, you could call me Nola."

"N-no. Not a breach, Ria— Nola . . ."

Lord! Now who was babbling? Tusk sought refuge in plugging his helmet into the TRUC's crude, antiquated communications system.

"Twenty-six minutes to rendezvous," Nola reported. "No, the other channel. That one's mine to my ground crew and later to the freighter. This one links us—you and me—that's what we're talking over now. Just leave it alone. This one is yours to the fighters and it's clear. I made sure of that. You've got to flick the switch every time from sending to receiving. I know. It's a damn nuisance but the bastards running the company wouldn't spend the money to upgrade. Marek would have. Whatever we said we needed, he bought. No questions asked. Trusted us to know our end of the business best."

"So now you're up here, risking your life for him."

Tusk experimentally flipped switches, hoping he wouldn't forget in the tenseness of battle and end up talking to himself.

"Not just for him, for all of us workers," Nola corrected. "You picking anything up from your friends yet?"

"No. We won't until we reach the point."

Nola nodded, but didn't answer him. She was conferring with her crew below, and making adjustments to her instruments. It was amazing, Tusk thought, how fast they were actually moving. He could see the curvature of the planet's surface and one of its small moons peeping over the edge.

"Rendezvous . . . now," Nola said, peering out through the windscreen.

And there they were, all three. Tusk breathed a small sigh. One fear down. A couple hundred more to go.

"Hey, Tusk." The voice crackled in his ear.

"Yeah, Link, I'm here," Tusk answered without enthusiasm.

"Oh, Tusk, where are you? The flamin' speed of that thing hasn't caused you to black out, has it?"

"Flip the switch!" shot Nola out of the corner of her mouth, her hand motioning.

Swearing roundly, having forgotten as he'd known he would, Tusk switched from receiving to sending.

"I'm here. Everything okay from our end. What about yours?"

"Picking up company, old buddy. You see 'em?"

"Just on my radar. Yeah, that's what I said—radar. We're talking dark ages. And this damn windshield's so thick I won't be able to see them until they're on my—" He glanced at Nola and stuttered, "uh . . . right in front of me. And I'm not your 'old buddy.' What have we got?"

Looking at the radar screen, he could see four blips, one considerably larger than the rest, and he guessed the answer.

"Visual sighting," Mirna reported. "Three needle-nose fighters. No modifications. One torpedo boat. Whewww!" she whistled in awe. "New model. Got those new hypermissiles."

Nola, who was apparently monitoring Tusk's transmissions as well as her own, glanced at him and raised an eyebrow.

Tusk hesitated, then decided, what the hell. Might as well let her know the worst.

"They move faster than light," Tusk said, staring out the screen, trying to get a fix on his enemies, trying to keep from looking directly at Nola. "You never see what hits you."

Nola's tongue flicked twice over her lips, before she could ask casually, "Where the devil did they get something like that?"

"Beats me. Dixter'd like to know, too, from the looks of it. But don't worry. They're not about to blow their prize up."

"Maybe the Warlord sent it."

"Naw! The Congress wouldn't bother outfitting a small-time government like this one with prototype torpedo boats. Lots cheaper to step in and take over. Look, Nola"—he wanted to pat her hand reassuringly, but the hand was busy—"don't think about the missiles. Let me take care of that boat. You just keep this thing moving, no matter what. From what I've heard, you can do that better than anyone around."

He was rewarded with a smile that rearranged all the freckles on her cheeks and nose and did a little minor rearranging with his heart. Reminding himself sternly that he didn't like short, stockily built brunettes, Tusk turned his attention back to the job at hand. The fighters had taken up their positions—one behind the TRUC and one on either side.

They were well above the planet by now, surrounded by the eternal starry night of space. The torpedo boat hove into view. Spotlights shone on its bristling weapons and illuminated the myriad whirling, flashing, revolving, and oscillating instruments sticking out from it in all directions. It was small, built for the speed and maneuverability that would give it the advantage over a larger opponent. The torpedo boat floated in front of them, well out of range of most weapons the TRUC might be likely to have, but not the lascannon. Good. That was gonna be a nice little surprise.

"Tusk," Nola said, "I've shut off the anti-grav. If I don't fire my rockets soon we'll drift off course."

A streak of flame zipped past them. Nola started; her hands on the instrument shook.

"Warning shot across the bows," Tusk said. "They want our attention."

"They got it!" the woman muttered.

"TRUC 4," an official-sounding voice came over the radio.

"By orders of the—" there was a slight hesitation on the part of the voice, "Mectopian Council, you are under arrest. You and the mercenary pilots with you will surrender yourselves to our jurisdiction. The mercenary pilots will be escorted back to our base. We will see that you reach the Republic freighter safely. If you cooperate, this will be taken into consideration in your sentencing."

"This bastard wants a fight," Tusk commented.

"That's an off-world accent," Nola said in a low voice, "and he mispronounced the name of the government."

Tusk nodded, frowning. "Stall," was all he could think of to say.

"Hello, out there. I'm experiencing instrument malfunction," Nola said into her mike. "Would you repeat your instructions?"

"You heard me, TRUC 4," was the cold response. "You have thirty seconds to surrender or we open fire."

"Two fighters closing on me, Commander," Nigol reported.

"Get into position but remember orders—let them shoot first. Nola, put up the deflector shields everywhere except the front so that I can fire." Tusk rose to his feet and positioned himself behind the lascannon—an extremely tight fit.

"I only *have* front deflector shields!" Nola snapped. "To protect the cab."

"Damn!" Tusk swore. Dixter'd told him that during his briefing on the TRUC. "Keep talking, then. Link, Mirna, you handle the freighters, and throw what you can at that torpedo boat."

"Righto," sang out Link.

"Yes, sir," returned Mirna.

"Are you from the Republic?" Nola was shouting.

A flash of light and bone-jarring jolt was their answer.

"Ordinary missiles." Tusk held onto the grips of the lascannon for support. "Hit us somewhere in front and below. Any damage?"

"No." Nola was white-faced but steady and calm. She even managed a weak grin. "It takes a lot to damage a TRUC."

"Thank you, Creator!" Tusk murmured.

Flares and flashes outside the windscreen indicated the Scimitars were attacking. Tusk crouched behind his gun, lining up the computerized sights that were being fed readings from the radar.

"Hold tight, Nola. Don't pay attention to what I'm doing or

to those birds out there. Do you have to warm up your engines or anything like that to start this tub moving?"

"No. When I fire, we go. Real simple."

The beginnings of a plan were lurking about in Tusk's mind. It was desperate and not to be thought of until things were . . . well, desperate.

Another shot slammed into them, knocking them around a little but no damage. That captain must realize he isn't accomplishing anything except making a nuisance of himself, Tusk thought. Off-world, is he? Probably answering to a couple of government flunkies aboard his ship. He'd do what they said to a point. Then he'd take matters into his own hands—or at least that was how Tusk read that cold, impersonal voice. He could almost hear it saying, "I regret very much the action I was forced to take which led to the total destruction of the TRUC but as you see we were unable to impress upon them our determination not to let rebel-held shipments through—"

"Hey, Tusk," came Link's voice, "get this S.O.B. off my tail, will you, ol' buddy?"

Tusk, shaking his head, opened fire.

Flaming bolts shot from the usually inoffensive TRUC. The needle-nose chasing Link caught one and went spinning out of control. Its partner, realizing suddenly he was facing a lascannon, pulled up so sharply he did a roll over and flew out of range to consider the matter.

Another shot slammed into the TRUC. The captain must not have known about the lascannon. He did now, which was unfortunate but couldn't be helped. Tusk would have liked to have him come in a little closer.

"I'm going in for a hit," Mirna reported.

"I'll cover you." Tusk opened a steady barrage of fire at the torpedo boat. Its deflector shields were up. He was doing little damage but hoped at least to make them keep their heads down, perhaps even score a lucky hit. Did they have to lower their shields to fire the torpedoes? He—

A bright orange flash, and Mirna was gone.

There was nothing left of her Scimitar. It had been vaporized. All over in less than a second. Tusk hadn't seen a thing. He couldn't even tell the part of the ship from which the torpedo had been launched.

"Sweet, holy mother. Did you see that?" Link sounded awed.

"I saw it."

In anger and frustration, Tusk fired another ineffectual burst at the torpedo boat.

"TRUC 4." The captain was back on the air. "You have seen a demonstration of our weapon's superiority over your own. I ask you once again to surrender."

"Do it, Nola," Tusk ordered,.

"What?" She turned to stare at him, her face strained and incredulous. "You can't be serious! I'm not going to!"

"Do it!" Tusk growled. "Link, Nigol? You two clear out. Run like you're scared as hell. You can't do anything against that torpedo boat."

"I wouldn't say that," Link protested.

"I smell one of the famous Tusk scams," Nigol struck in. The alien added something in its own language that Tusk assumed was good luck but which sounded as if someone had dumped a bucket of frogs into a pond.

"Okay, we're outta here." Link was disgruntled. "Make sure you get Nola home on time tonight. We got a date."

The two fighters peeled away, spiraling out of the skies and drawing off three of the needle-noses after them.

"A plan? What plan?" Nola was glaring at him suspiciously.

"A date? With Link?" Tusk glared back at her. "What do you see in that two-timing hotshot?"

The woman's face flushed to the roots of her brown hair. The green eyes flashed. Before she could reply, Tusk added, "I thought I gave you an order, Rian."

"You could at least tell me what's going on!" Another shot thudded into the hull.

"No time," Tusk said, which was a lie. He didn't want her having to think about what she was going to have to do any longer than necessary. "Go ahead. Surrender. Make it sound convincing."

Nola, shooting him a frustrated, helpless glance, spoke into the mike. "This is TRUC 4. Don't fire anymore. I—I surrender."

"Good," Tusk whispered. "Now, more panic. Tell them we've been hit and that I'm dead."

Her anger faded, replaced by astonishment. Completely mystified, Nola spoke into the mike, her eyes on Tusk. "We've been hit. My gunner's dead. I've—I've got his blood all over me!" Her voice rose shrilly. "Don't hurt me, please!"

Tusk held his breath. Everything hung on the torpedo boat captain's next command. The mercenary was counting on the fact that this man was a professional, as tough and experienced as he'd already shown himself.

"TRUC 4, raise your deflector shields."

"Hot damn!" Tusk crowed.

"But that means we can't use the cannon!" Nola hissed.

"Do it!" Tusk commanded tersely.

Returning to his seat, he strapped himself in securely, taking extra precautions. Nola, sighing, yanked on a lever. A scraping and rumbling sound and the deflector shields lurched into place. Tusk was happy to see that they were every bit as old-fashioned and massive as he had hoped. No invisible force fields for the TRUC. Reinforced steel plate that they couldn't even see through, leaving the driver to steer by instrument readings.

Good, Tusk thought. That'll make it easier for her.

"My shields are up," Nola reported unnecessarily, knowing that the torpedo ship could see them.

"I'm going to send an armed party aboard, TRUC 4," returned the captain of the torpedo boat. This guy was taking no chances.

"What's he doing?"

From where he sat, Tusk couldn't see Nola's radar screen, and he fidgeted nervously.

"He's moving toward us, closing fast," Nola reported.

"That's good. Now, Nola," Tusk said, keeping his voice even and calm, "when he gets closer still, right in front of us, I want you to start this baby up."

Nola sucked in her breath, her eyes widening. The freckles on her face were vivid brown against her pale skin.

"But that will mean—"

Tusk nodded. "Ramming them—an old and honored tradition in the history of naval warfare."

"Tusk!" Nola gasped. "It won't work! We'll all end up dead."

"I thought you said this thing could fly through a mountain."

Nola, looking sick, shook her head.

Tusk considered taking over, but he didn't know anything about flying one of these contraptions. Nola's hair clung in loose, damp ringlets to her sweating forehead. Her eyes shimmered with tears that she had too much pride to shed. Her full lips trembled.

Date with Link!

Reaching out, Tusk took hold of the woman's chilled hand. "You can do it, Nola! You have to do it! There's no other way now. You don't want to let Marek down? Or all the rest who're depending on you? Think of them, Nola. Don't think of anyone or anything else. Where's the torpedo ship now?"

Nola looked unwillingly at the screen. "Almost— Going around to the portside."

"He must not have a launch vehicle. That or he wants to lock onto us. When he's in range, head this mother straight at him."

For a tiny moment, Tusk thought she was going to fail him. Then her head lifted, her lips tightened. Nola drew a deep breath, straightened her shoulders, and put her hand on the ignition button. The hand made some minute adjustments to the instruments, changing the direction the rockets would fire to take the TRUC straight into the path of the torpedo boat.

Nola knew her vehicle. She alone could best gauge how near the torpedo boat would have to be so that it wouldn't have time to react and get out of the slow-moving TRUC's path. There was nothing for Tusk to do but sit back, brace himself, and wait.

Those were the worst few moments of his life.

Now that he had convinced the woman to take this drastic action, he was having second thoughts. She was right. It didn't matter that the torpedo boat was about thirty times smaller. It would blow up and take them with it. The TRUC, after all, wasn't indestructible. Even with the deflector shield protecting them, the cab was vulnerable. He was an idiot. A damn fool. He'd let down everyone. Dixter. Marek. The kid. He'd get himself killed and—worse—he'd kill this woman who trusted him, who was depending on him. She'd know, in those last few horrifying moments, that he'd been wrong . . .

Nola's finger jerked spasmodically. A roaring blast from the rear told him the rockets had fired. The TRUC lurched forward.

An indrawn breath, holding it, holding it—

A jarring thud, blinding light, a concussive blast—

··◁■ ■▷··

A constant beeping was making his head hurt.

"Shut up!" Tusk told XJ, flapping about with his hand to give the computer an extra little reminder.

He couldn't find it.

"XJ?" Sitting up, he opened his eyes. "What the—?"

Where was he? Whoever was playing this joke better cut it out. He turned his head to locate the sound of the beeping and end its days forever when he saw a figure slumped over the control panel. Memory returned in an aching torrent.

"Nola!"

Shoving aside the broken lascannon, which had toppled to the deck, Tusk leaned over the woman's comatose body. Gently removing the helmet, he felt her neck and found a pulse—strong and even. Exhaling a deep sigh, he eased her back into the chair. There were no holes in the flight suit, no signs of blood except for a cut on her lip where the mike had driven into her mouth when she fell forward. Like him, she must have been knocked unconscious by the explosion.

Glancing out the windscreen, Tusk saw the wrecked and mangled deflector shield. The screen itself was cracked, but its seal held. Tusk recalled guiltily all his uncharitable thoughts about that thick windscreen.

"Bless you!" He reached out and patted it. He could have kissed it. No, on second thought he'd rather kiss something else.

"Nola." He brushed back the damp brown hair. "Nola!"

Slowly, she opened her eyes, blinked, and looked up at him with a hesitant smile that set freckles dancing over her face.

"Nola Rian," Tusk said, "you're beautiful!"

"Not only that," she said, grinning up at him shakily, "I'm the best goddam TRUC driver you'll ever meet!"

Chapter ❖ Seventeen

When the stars threw down their spears . . .
William Blake, "The Tyger"

Dion hung around outside the communications van, fidgeting, jittery. The hot early morning sun blazed down on the tarmac, evidently warming it up for the truly hot afternoon sun. Sweating, his clothes sticking to his body, the young man crouched in a scrap of shade cast by the GHQ building and waited for word of Tusk. Gadgets and devices on top of the van revolved swiftly or slowly rotated or just pointed straight into the air. Dion watched them until he was half-mesmerized by the movement. Odd, disjointed thoughts flashed in and out of his mind in time with the rotations.

A month ago, I wouldn't have been able to believe I was doing this . . . Tusk left me his spaceplane. If he doesn't come back, I'll . . . He'll come back. I shouldn't be thinking things like that, the bad luck word. At least I didn't say it aloud. Platus would laugh. Our joke, the bad luck word. Dear God! What was it I said that killed him? No, stop it. Don't think about it. . . . I could fly the plane, I know I could. I did for a while that time back when we first came out of the Jump. Tusk said I handled it like a pro, too. Maybe Dixter'd let me fly with the others. I could avenge Tusk . . . That's stupid. Nothing's happened to Tusk, nothing's going to. And they wouldn't be likely to let a kid with no training up there. Shoot yourself in the foot and we're all dead, that's what Tusk would say. I— Someone's coming out. Running. Something's happened. Something's wrong.

Dion was on his feet, following the soldier dashing from the van. The boy slammed into the GHQ office right behind the man, nearly taking the door from its hinges. Bennett's eyebrows jumped up into his hairline with such force it was a wonder they didn't scalp him.

"The general—" the soldier said.

Bennett nodded, motioned to the office, and fixed Dion with a stern gaze. Dixter, hearing the commotion, came out, nearly colliding with the soldier coming in.

"Sir, radar's picked up what looks like a squadron of bombers closing in—"

"Nukes?"

"No, sir. Nothing that sophisticated. Looks like a bunch of the old garbage scow model, sir."

"That figures. They'll dump whatever they've got on us. Well, this means we're getting our hands slapped. I take it the TRUC mission was successful, then?"

"Yes, that was my next report. There was one casualty—"

"Casualty?" Dion stepped forward.

Bennett was packing up the portable computers and obviously preparing for a hasty departure. But he managed to clear his throat and frown at the interruption, pausing in his work as if expecting to be asked to toss the young man out on his ear.

"Captain Myrna—"

Dion heaved a sigh and missed the rest of the report. Dixter issued several orders that made little sense to the boy, who didn't understand what was going on. Bennett was shutting down systems and unplugging plugs and packing things away with an efficiency which indicated this was all routine procedure. The soldier left and Dixter turned to enter his office, then seemed to remember and looked over at Dion with a smile that was kind but preoccupied.

"Tusk's all right. They made it through safely and hooked up with the Warlord's tankers."

At that moment, what sounded like the throaty howl of some wild animal rose in pitch to the wail of the three Furies. The awful sound made the hair stand up on Dion's arms.

"Air raid alert," Dixter said, by way of explanation. The man's eyes, fixed on the boy, narrowed. "What the hell do I do with you? Bennett?"

"Almost finished here, sir. Your office—"

"Yes, yes. I'll take care of it. We've got time. We spotted them early."

"Please, sir, what's happening?" Dion broke in.

The siren's wail was unnerving and yet oddly exhilarating. The ground began to shake and he saw out the window some of the spaceplanes powering up and heading for the takeoff zone.

"Bombing run. A damned nuisance, that's all. We'll have the planes off the ground, but it'll tear hell out of the tarmac. Have to find a new location. Bennett—"

"I have one, sir. Do you want—"

"No, go out there to the van and relay it to commlink." Dixter moved toward his office. "Come with me, boy, while I get ready to roll—"

"Bombs." Tusk's plane. XJ. But all Dion said aloud was, "Bombs."

Dixter entered his office. "You can ride with us. It's a little bumpy—the shocks in this damn thing need overhauling but there never seems to be time. I—"

He glanced around behind him. The kid was gone.

Dixter charged out of his office to find Bennett, returning from relaying the air base's new location to the communication's van, backed up against the doorjamb. From his indignant expression, it seemed the aide had been nearly run down.

"Dion?" the general demanded.

Bennett pointed.

"Damn!" Dixter exploded, realizing where the boy was going and what he was planning to do. He headed for the door only to find his aide standing respectfully but firmly in his path.

"Get out of my way."

"Excuse me, sir, but were you going to attend to the breaking down in your office or shall I? We have less than fifteen minutes, sir."

"That damn kid—"

"Yes, sir. Begging your pardon, sir, but it would be physically impossible, without stimulants, for someone your age to catch up with someone his age. I'll just go take care of your office—"

"You know damn well I can't stand anyone pawing through my papers. Don't look so smug. I'm not going to forget that crack about my age. Where's my driver?"

"Warming up the engines, now, sir."

"Use the cab's link. See if you can establish communication with that spaceplane before the kid tries to take off. If you can raise him, tell him to let the fools pound it into dust. We'll get Tusk a different one. This'll work out better anyhow, the Warlord will lose him."

"Yes, sir." Bennett was out the door.

Dixter entered his office, shut his computer down, and began to pack up everything that wouldn't survive rattling around in a trailer lurching over the desert at high speeds. The roaring of spacecraft blasting off was deafening, even this distance from the launch zone. The ground shook and several maps slid from their places on the walls. Dixter glanced out the window. Through the blowing dust and drifting smoke, he could see what looked like red hair streaming in the wind— flame burning in the desert.

"What the devil's that quote?" Dixter said aloud. "'The Lord went before them by night in a' what—pillar of salt? No. Pillar of five. 'To lead them.' What put that into my mind? Blasted kid's going to get himself killed. Tusk'll never forgive me. I said I'd take care of him. Why didn't I go after him? That's the quote:

"'. . . and by night in a pillar of fire.'"

Dixter finished his work. Straightening, he looked back out the window. The boy was gone.

"And that's why," he said to the patch of vivid burning color he could see in his mind, "I guess, kid, I really don't think you're destined to be pounded to pulp by some third-rate oligarch. I almost wish you were. I think it'd be easier—on all of us."

··◁▸ ▶◦··

Coughing, blinking in the stinging dust raised by the blasting force of the spaceplanes, Dion ran half-blindly through the smoke, searching for someone to give him a lift. He found a hoverjeep filled with pilots in the same predicament as himself. It was already starting to move by the time he reached it. Shouting for them to wait was out—he couldn't hear himself think, let alone talk. He hurled himself forward and landed on the jeep's back end with a thud that knocked the wind out of his body. One of the passengers grabbed hold of him, hanging on to him just as the jeep roared into life and hurtled through the air.

There was nowhere to sit; Dion clung to the flat back of the jeep, the woman'd who'd caught him keeping hold of his arms so that he didn't fly off. The wild ride ended before he quite knew what was happening. The woman let go of him before the jeep stopped. Dion slid off the back, landed face-first in the dust. He was up and running without giving himself time to find out if he was hurt. The siren wailed and sobbed; the sound was in his blood, surging through his body.

He scaled the outer ladder to the spaceplane, fumbled with the hatch, and nearly fell in head over heels when XJ opened it for him. Slithering down the ladder, he bounded through the living quarters, jumped down to the bridge, and threw himself into the pilot's seat.

"Prepare for takeoff," he managed to gasp. Breathing was like a sharp knife being driven into his side.

The lights blinked; life-support made a kind of coughing sound.

"My circuits shorted out," XJ snapped. "I thought you said prepare for takeoff."

"Don't you hear that . . . damn siren!"

"You're hyperventilating. Stick your head in a paper sack and take a deep breath. It's just another scramble. Happens two, three times a day—"

"It isn't . . . either! Bombers—"

"Bombers! Real ones? C'mon, kid. I'll get in my remote. You carry me, that way I can shut down. We'll head for those rocks—"

A round remote unit, bristling with electronic eyes and wiggly little arms that had been perched near the edge of the instrument panel suddenly came to life and landed with a plop in Dion's lap.

"No!" Lifting up the remote, Dion glared into what he assumed was its camera lenses and shook it. "We're going to take off, save Tusk's plane. Either that, or we sit here and get bombed."

Which wasn't a bad idea. Dion grabbed the bottle of jump-juice. Tilting it to his lips, he took a swig and gasped as the foul-tasting stuff burned down his throat. It seemed to help his breathing—once he *could* breathe—and the pain in his side went away.

The remote unit flashed eratically and emitted a series of loud, static-laced sounds that were, however, perfectly understandable. Tusk would have been impressed.

"I'm going to tell him you said that." Dion grinned shakily and took another drink. This stuff wasn't bad, once you got used to it. Tucking the bottle under one arm, he went to work. The remote whirred viciously to itself for another second, then hopped back to its perch. The computer's blank face came back to life, lights flashed on the control panel, and he heard the clanging sound of the hatch sealing shut.

"They're coming in," XJ said. "I've got 'em on my screen."

Dion jammed a helmet on his head, strapped himself in, and tried to remember what to push and what to flick in what order. His hands had quit shaking, but the tips of his fingers had gone numb.

There was a jarring thud and the ground seemed to lift up around them. Dion stared at the instrument readings.

"What did I do? I didn't do anything—"

"It was a bomb, you idiot!" XJ was practically howling. "Ignore it. Just get us the hell outta here! Push that one and there, no, to the left. That one! Damn Mendaharin Tusca to the Correlian gasworks. Noooo! Yes, yes! That's it! And—"

The spaceplane's engines rumbled. Tremendous forces flattened the boy back in his seat. The jump-juice surged up from his stomach and into his mouth and he completely missed his first takeoff because he was leaning over the arm of the chair, heaving up his guts.

···◁■ ■▷···

The bombers saw the spaceplane fly up right in front of them but they let it go past. Once a plane was off the ground, it was beyond their reach. They had their orders and those orders didn't come from the government, as Dixter had assumed.

Up in the heavens, far above the planet's surface, a hunter waited to see what prey his dogs flushed out of the brush.

Chapter ·❦·❦· Eighteen

So pale, so cold, so fair.
"St. James Infirmary Blues"

Maigrey had no idea how much time had passed since she had been taken aboard the *Phoenix*. Prisoners lose a sense of time, even when they are able to experience day and night—one runs into the next and a day is as long as a month, a month as short as a day. Maigrey's days were routinely, interminably, endlessly the same. She was allowed to walk about the ship, but not allowed to speak to anyone, not even the centurions who guarded her.

It is easy to be courageous during brief and terrifying moments of crisis. The body leaps with a surge of adrenaline, the mind dances with brilliance. When the danger is over, you are a hero and can't say how or why. But to face danger day after day; to keep up your courage hour after tedious hour; to sleep with fear and wake up with fear; to live in constant doubt, both of the future and of yourself, drains the body and the soul.

Maigrey obeyed the commandment for silence not out of defiance, as the Warlord supposed, but out of despair. The trumpet sounded the end of each day and began the next and every time Maigrey heard the notes she thought, "To-morrow he will ask me about the boy. Today he will ask me about the boy." But Sagan never did. He didn't speak to her at all, never came near her. But he was aware of her, as she was aware of him. A haunting fear took ghostly form and stalked her.

What does he want from me, if not the boy? she wondered. Could it be I've mistaken him, misjudged him, misread him? Fatal. Fatal.

177

Maigrey attempted to exorcise the ghosts by turning to old friends, long-lost friends—books. She had been without books during the entire time of her exile. Old favorites were rediscovered and enjoyed as much as or more than when she'd read them years ago. How, she wondered, could she have ever deserted Mr. Micawber?

There were new works to be read, although she didn't much care for the modern authors who had surfaced after the second Dark Ages. They seemed to think that if they didn't reduce a reader to a state of hopeless depression they hadn't written a novel. This led her to wonder what the Warlord had been reading. It might give her a clue to his plans. Despair had not reduced her to inaction, and an hour spent at her computer enabled her to access the ship's library file.

She and Sagan did not share a similar taste in novels—he considered them, with few exceptions, frivolous—she was interested to note he had been rereading Plato's *Republic* and Machiavelli's *The Prince*, an odd combination and one she found disquieting. Several recent historical texts and commentaries brought her up to date on the current galactic political situation, plus she found a fascinating technical text written by the Warlord himself describing his development of the long- and short-range Scimitars. When Maigrey had completed that one, she had no doubt that she could fly the planes with ease.

Music was her best source of consolation. She had dreamed music in her exile, waking to find melodies running through her head, trapped in silence. Now she could fill her life with music. Always alone, with her music the prisoner found she could bear loneliness.

What Maigrey could not bear was a reawakened love—a love she thought she had conquered but which she realized had always been and would always be a part of her. Her love of spaceflight.

Spaceflight was a lover whose charm was in his mystery, his excitement, his danger—a lover who cared nothing for the one who loved him. His beauty could pierce the heart, his cold could freeze the blood. He drew you to him, made you his own, then killed without pity, without mercy.

Aboard *Phoenix* was a small lounge located on a deck in a part of the ship set aside for the use of visiting diplomats or planetary governors or members of Congress on some of their "fact-finding" missions. Sagan had little use for diplomats, less use for planetary governors, and no use at all for junketing

Congressmen. This portion of the ship was therefore rarely used, off-limits to all nonauthorized personnel. Maigrey had wandered into it during one of her restless roamings and had discovered that the view from the vast steelglass windows was breathtaking.

Her guards, of course, reported. "My lord, should she be allowed here?"

Sagan, after some thought, gave his permission. Maigrey returned to the lounge often to watch the spectacular panorama of the ships of the fleet traversing space, their tiny, bright, twinkling man-made lights dwarfed and made humble by the black void through which they sailed.

"This fleet could have been yours," Maigrey said to herself—the only person to whom she was allowed to talk. "This galaxy could *be* yours! You have the power, the strength, the will to make it yours!"

The specter appeared before her suddenly and now she could put a name to it.

It was herself. It stretched out its bony hand and in it was a crown.

Maigrey quit going to the diplomat's lounge.

··◁■ ■▷··

"My lord, we are within communication's range of the planet Vangelis."

"We are not close enough that they can detect our presence?"

"No, my lord," Captain Nada replied. "Not with this planet's limited technological capabilities. Vangelis is a "C" rating, my lord." ["A" is the highest—a planet whose people have developed intergalactic travel. Class "B"—interstellar travel, relatively close to home. Class "C"—interplanetary travel within one's own solar system, and so on down to "X," which had been the classification of what was now the penal colony of Oha-Lau.]

"Thank you, Captain Nada. Send for the Lady Maigrey."

"Yes, my lord. And where will the prisoner be brought?"

"Here, Nada. To the bridge."

Captain Nada's lips pursed, the folds of his pudgy cheeks sucked inward. He was displeased. Prisoners, especially royalists, had no business upon the bridge of a Republic warship. Not that Nada believed seriously for one moment that they were in any danger from this middle-aged woman. It was the principle of the thing. The captain had no choice—now—but to carry out his orders. He would, however, put this in his report.

Nada descended from the navigation bridge to communications below. "Have Citizen Morianna brought to the bridge."

The captain refused to refer to her by that abhorrent title of a nobility that was dead and gone. It was bad enough, being forced to "my lord" this and "my lord" that. The words sometimes stuck in his craw. Every time he said them, they left a bad taste in his mouth. A message was handed to him. Reading it, Nada returned to the bridge.

"We just received this communication, my lord. The Scimitar has been sighted."

"Where?"

"Vangelis, my lord. It is with mercenary forces under the command of one"—Nada was forced to refer to some hastily scrawled notes "—John Dixter, a so-called general in the employ of the rebel Marek. As you suggested, my lord, the government ordered bombing runs made on all mercenary spaceplane squadrons currently operating in the area. The Scimitar left the planet's surface and was sighted by an employee of a private concern. We were unable to get the name."

"That's not important." Sagan knew the name—the Adonian, Snaga Ohme. The oligarchs were not the only ones on Vangelis to have received orders from the Warlord. "Was the sighting confirmed?"

"Yes, my lord. A fighter was sent to verify. It did so and tracked the spaceplane back to its new landing site. The fighter maintained its distance, as you commanded, my lord, and did nothing to arouse Tusca's suspicions."

"You hope it did nothing. My commendations, Captain."

Characteristically, Sagan made no mention of the fact that he had been the one to put his dogs on the correct trail. Turning on his heel, he started to walk away.

"But, my lord!" Nada stared after him. "What are your orders?"

"Orders, Captain? You have my orders. My orders stand."

"I was not referring to that, my lord. We are maintaining our current position in deepspace. I was referring to the deserter, Tusca. Shouldn't I send a squad to arrest him, my lord?"

"Have you gone deaf, Captain? *My orders stand.* You will do nothing. And make no mention of this in the hearing of Lady Maigrey."

Nada's cheeks sucked in, puffed out. His brows would have met over his nose in a frown had they not been kept apart by a roll of fat. This smacked of intrigue. Admiral Aks had hinted that this search for a deserter was being performed with the President's knowledge and approval. Nada wondered, however. He knew the Warlord was in communication with someone on the planet. These communications were coded Red, which meant that no one, not even the admiral, could understand them. Was this a proper action for a citizen of the Republic who lived, after all, to serve the people? One of the tenets of the revolution had been "No secrets from the people!"

Believing in this tenet strongly, Captain Nada had made certain secret reports himself to the President. The reports had been well received. It was about time, he thought, that he make another.

··❖· ❖··

The main viewport aboard *Phoenix* was a gigantic porthole, its diameter over one hundred meters in length. Several decks bisected the viewport—the relaxation lounge for the crew looked out of the lower part of the circle, the lounge for officers was on the deck above that, the porthole's top formed an arched window that extended from deck to overhead in the Warlord's chambers. The bridge had the benefit of the view from the viewport's very center.

The traditional "captain's walk" on the bridge was a narrow catwalk built in front of the gigantic porthole so as to obtain full benefit of the magnificent view. The "captain's walk" was suspended above the command center of the ship and it allowed those privileged enough to set foot upon it the privacy sacred to the workings of their mighty brains. At the same time, it enabled them to keep themselves appraised of all the functions of the ship that were being controlled and monitored on the deck below them.

On a flagship, the captain's walk could be somewhat crowded, since both captain and admiral came here to stroll about and enjoy the panorama of suns, double suns, nebulae, distantly seen galaxies, comets, asteroid belts, insignificant planets, moons. On a flagship such as *Phoenix*, with a marshal present in addition to a captain and an admiral, the three might find themselves bumping into each other on the catwalk had not protocol dictated that whenever a marshal was using the walkway, no one else was allowed on it except by invitation.

Pacing the bridge alone, Lord Derek Sagan caught a glimpse of pale hair on the deck below. Pausing in mid-stride, he watched the woman walk toward him, and for the first and only time in his life Sagan regretted his sarcastic speech to the admiral. Seeing Maigrey, he understood why work came to a halt in her presence, why his men could do nothing except stare.

If Corasians, in their horrible trundling mechanical bodies, had boarded his ship, Sagan's men would have responded swiftly and efficiently, reacting as they had been trained. But how were they to react to this? How were they to react to the sight of that pallid face set in rigid calm, the fixed, staring gray eyes? The only life visible in that face was the blood that pulsed in the scar.

Sagan had won. The woman who stood before him was crushed, beaten. But the Warlord felt cheated in his victory. He didn't want a lifeless corpse. A corpse wasn't useful to him, and he needed to make use of this lady. Somehow he had to jolt the body back to life. The guards brought the woman to the foot of the ramp ascending to the catwalk. The Warlord descended to greet her.

Their eyes met—his shadowed behind the helm, hers gray as the sea beneath a winter sky. Two enemy commanders taking up position on opposite ridges, the field of battle spread before them, each trying to spy out any weakness in the other.

Sagan bowed, a courtly gesture. "Lady Maigrey, a rosette nebula is currently visible from the viewport. You shouldn't miss this sight. I would be honored if you would join me." He held out his hand to her.

Both were fully aware of the eyes of the crew watching them; both were reacting to the crowd. This is what they had been born to. The tragedy of their lives had been played out before thousands.

"Thank you, my lord."

Very precisely and coldly, she placed the tips of her fingers on his open palm and walked up the stars beside him, making it quite apparent by her stiff back and high-held chin that she was a prisoner obeying a command. Her cheeks were flushed, there was a spark in the eyes.

The Warlord experienced the elation of Dr. Frankenstein. The corpse was coming to life.

Glancing behind him, Sagan indicated that the lady's guards were to remain below. Together, in silence, he and Maigrey walked up the ramp. The murmured low voices of the men watching was their applause. A sharp, biting rebuke from Captain Nada recalled the crew to its duties, but both lord and lady were aware they held their audience still.

Arriving on the bridge, Maigrey removed her fingers from the Warlord's palm and stood staring silently out the viewport, her hands clasped before her. Sagan crossed his arms behind his back, beneath the folds of his cape, and settled into a relaxed stance. Both gazed out at the nebula with such rapt attention it seemed neither had ever seen one before. Neither was—in reality—seeing this one now.

"It's beautiful, isn't it, my lady?"

"Yes, my lord. I know how highly you value beauty. What do you intend to do—blow it up?"

The upper part of his face was covered by his crested helmet, but Maigrey could see clearly—though she was not looking at him—a faint smile widen the lips that were a dark slash across his face. Like a severed limb sewn back on the body, the mind-link—newly joined—was still raw and bleeding at the edges, sensitive to the touch. Each kept bandages wrapped around the wound, to hide it from the view of the other, but this wasn't completely successful.

Maigrey had been six years old by her planet's reckoning when the two of them had met and their minds had first, by accident, been joined. Sagan had been fifteen. The melding had lasted nearly twenty years before his sword slashed it apart. Now, reestablished again, it was natural that, however well protected, certain thoughts and feelings must seep through.

"No. I think I'll leave the nebula as it is, my lady. It serves a useful navigational function. Because of it, in fact, I can tell you the name of the planet over there." The Warlord pointed to a speck of light, indistinguishable amid a myriad specks of light. "Vangelis."

Maigrey felt the probe of his mind flick into hers, a surgeon's scalpel touching the wound. Involuntarily she flinched. What did he want? What was on that planet? Was it supposed to mean something to her? It didn't, but she wasn't going to let him know that if she could help it.

"How interesting, my lord. Named for the twentieth century composer, I presume?"

Music. She filled her mind with music, one of the techniques their teachers had taught them to use to enable them to retain a sense of their own identities. Sagan could make out nothing in her mind except a cascade of bells and swooping melody. Something by the very Vangelis of whom she'd spoken, no doubt. The Warlord did not recognize it.

"More likely it was named after some whore," Sagan commented. "The planet was established as a mining colony—it's composed almost entirely of uranium."

Maigrey's mind touched his—not a probe but delicate, cool fingers. Sagan allowed her to touch, allowed her to find part of what she sought—the boy. Maigrey snatched her mind back. The Warlord saw, by the sudden livid appearance of the scar against her skin, that she had cut herself.

"If you will excuse me, my lord, I am extremely tired. I wish to return to my quarters."

Maigrey turned to leave. Sagan, politely, gave her his hand.

"I was hoping you would be my guest for dinner this evening, my lady," he said as they walked slowly to the ramp.

Maigrey, keeping her eyes anywhere but on his face, saw the sinew, muscle, and bone of his arm clearly delineated beneath the tanned skin crisscrossed by the battle scars. Some she remembered, others were new.

"Thank you, my lord. I prefer to dine by myself."

"I have no doubt," he said in a low, wry tone for her hearing alone. "Betrayal leaves a bad taste in the mouth."

"I'm surprised you noticed, my lord. I should think *you* would've become accustomed to it, by now."

In silence, they walked together down the ramp—the lord brilliant in shining gold and flaming red, the lady pale as the moon beside him. The centurions snapped to attention; the eyes of every man in the crew that were not absolutely required to be somewhere else were on them.

"I have been remiss in my duties as host," Lord Sagan said loudly, for the benefit of the audience, when they arrived on the deck. "My officers have been eagerly awaiting the opportunity of dining with you, Lady Maigrey. This night seems a fitting occasion."

"What is the occasion, my lord?"

"One which you will have cause to celebrate, I trust, my lady."

The Warlord handed the woman over to the custody of her guards. "Dinner this evening is formal, my lady." He glanced somewhat scathingly at the nylon, zippered men's gym suit she was wearing. "I have arranged for suitable attire. You will find it when you return to your quarters. We dine at 2200. I will send my orderly for you. My lady." He bowed.

Gravely, she returned the courtesy. "My lord."

For an instant the eyes met, the mental blades touched, but it was in salute, not contest. Not yet. The combatants parted, the Warlord ascending back up the ramp, the lady leaving under guard for her quarters.

"Pass the word for Admiral Aks," Sagan commanded.

The message was sent, and the admiral appeared. Aks and his lord walked together the length of the catwalk. Nada, out of earshot on the deck below, would have given his pension to know what was being discussed up above him.

"The Scimitar's been sighted."

"Yes, I am aware of that, my lord. Captain Nada wanted to send a patrol to arrest Tusca."

"Nada's a bungler. He wouldn't get within ten miles of the mercenaries. They're undoubtedly monitoring our transmissions. By the time we arrived, they'd have ducked down some other hole. We'd lose them again and maybe not find them so easily."

The admiral glanced around to make certain they could not be overheard.

"What of the boy, my lord?"

Sagan paused in his pacing; his gaze went to the bright speck in the blackness that was Vangelis. "I see him, Aks. Not clearly, he's a shadow on my mind, but I see him. And she sees him, too."

"Doesn't that make it conclusive, then, my lord? Only those of the Blood Royal could touch each other—"

"I don't know! That's the hell of it! My desire, her fear. Maybe those are the shadows we're seeing. I can't put a face to him, Aks, and I don't believe she can either."

"Then how are we to resolve this dilemma, my lord? We can't go in and seize him because we have no idea what he looks like, who it is we're supposed to seize! Not to mention"— Aks's voice sunk even lower—"Snaga Ohme."

"The damn fool," Sagan was bitter, "reacted with typical Adonian paranoia. Someone's bound to wonder where the devil those stone-age oligarchs came up with a prototype torpedo boat." The Warlord stared out the viewport at the glittering nebula. "Do you remember what I said to you the other day, Admiral, in regard to God?"

"I beg your pardon, my lord?" Aks had not been prepared for this sudden leap from the mundane to the metaphysical.

"'The Lord works in mysterious ways, his wonders to conceal.' The Creator is working, Aks. He is bringing all together—my greatest desire, my most dangerous enemy, and my gravest threat."

"Your greatest desire is, I presume, the boy." Aks, seeing his lordship was in good spirits, decided he would be safe to indulge in a bit of sarcasm. "I suppose God's going to drop him into your hand, my lord?"

The Warlord glanced at the admiral from out of the corner of his shadowed eyes. "Precisely."

Chapter ·──◆◆◆──· Nineteen

Footfalls echo in the memory
Down the passage which we did not take
Towards the door we never opened
Into the rose-garden. My words echo
Thus, in your mind.

T. S. Eliot, "Four Quartets"

Returning to her quarters, Maigrey slammed shut the door and stood leaning against it. She had to sort out her thoughts and she was reluctant to disturb them by even the simple act of walking across the small area of floor space and sitting down in the one chair provided for the "guest's" comfort.

Outside, she heard the boots of the centurions take up their accustomed places on either side of her door. On the bed Maigrey saw what she assumed to be the "attire" Sagan had mentioned. It was wrapped in white linen, like a shroud. Maigrey was reluctant, suddenly, to touch it.

This is nonsense! Since when are you afraid of a dress?

But she didn't lift the white linen covering to see what was beneath. She did move away from the door. Walking over to her nightstand, Maigrey pulled up the chair, sat down before the mirror, and told herself she was going to fix her hair.

"The boy," she said quietly. "That was the thought in Sagan's mind, the thought he wanted me to find. The boy is there, on that planet. He can see him just as I can, a shadow on the mind. Why is he letting me know? Why is he telling me? Surely he must know I'll do everything I can to keep the boy safe."

Maigrey's hand touched the scar, the fingers following its line from her cheekbone to her lip. From the pain she felt, she would not have been surprised to see that touch draw blood. She could have masked the scar—plastiskin could make a

187

human of one hundred appear no older (at least on the surface) than one of twenty. But Maigrey knew that nothing would cover it, nothing would blot it out. Were she to put a metal helmet over her head, the scar would burn through.

Picking up the brush, she began to smooth the tangles from her long, pale hair. "And what is safe? For the boy to live his life in ignorance? To never know who and what he is? Is that what you truly want for him? But if you really believed this, why did you hide away the child? He was to be our hope. 'Sick of ourselves, we have dreamed a king.'

"But not like this. Not Sagan taking him to that man who calls himself President." Maigrey's hand jerked. The brush turned, the bristles missed on a hard downward stroke, and she let it fall. "Of course! Sagan doesn't intend to take the boy to Robes! He's going to keep him, use the boy himself!"

Her gaze went to the white linen shroud.

Kicking the brush aside, Maigrey rose to her feet and walked slowly over to the bed. She knew, yet she was afraid to know. She reached down, grabbed a handful of the linen, and tried to tear it off. The shroud was tightly wrapped around whatever it covered and she was forced to fumble at knots. Maigrey could feel the gown beneath the covering. Its weight was heavy; made of thick fabric. The knowledge increased her certainty and she tore at the knots that refused to give way to her trembling hands. Finally they came undone, and hesitantly, afraid to breathe, she lifted one corner and peered beneath it.

Maigrey closed her eyes. She sank to the floor, suffocating, the pain in her chest constricting her breathing. Let me die, Creator! she pleaded silently. Let me die as I should have died then!

Her hand remained on the bed. Beneath its fingers she felt fabric so soft and smooth it was almost warm to the touch. Blue. Indigo blue velvet. A ceremonial gown, worn on state occasions. Worn by the Guardians on state occasions. State occasions such as a dinner given in their honor by King Starfire. A dinner in the palace. A dinner in the palace on the night of the revolution. Indigo blue velvet, matted black with blood.

Her hand clutched the velvet, crumpling it between her fingers. She saw them entering, moving with quiet, ordered assurance to their places at the long tables set out in the palace ballroom. Each man, each woman dressed alike in robes of shimmering indigo blue. On each breast glittered the star-jewel; the Guardians wore no other adornment, no jewel ever mined was of greater value. Stavros walked in front of her, Platus behind her. They moved to their table, the king's table, for tonight they—the Golden Squadron—were being specially honored. But Sagan wasn't there. He hadn't entered with them. He was late. Stavros made a joke; he was always making jokes. Maigrey couldn't remember it. It hadn't been funny. Nothing was funny. The room was too crowded, the voices rose in a mindless hubbub and gave her a throbbing headache. She wanted them to be quiet. Couldn't they tell? Some dreadful calamity hung over them. Why couldn't they understand? She would tell them! Warn them. Before she could do so, Sagan entered. All the Guardians were seated except him and he was there, standing in the doorway. He, alone, was not clad in indigo blue. He was wearing battle armor. . . .

Darkness.

And then the hospital and pain and bandages and fear. And the worst pain, the most terrible pain was discovering that she was still alive.

Dr. Giesk and his infernal machine with its wires and bits of adhesive plastic could have inflicted no more exquisite torture on this victim than did the Warlord, using nothing but a few yards of blue cloth. And even Sagan might have been amazed at his success. He knew the pain he must inflict by summoning memory. He couldn't know how much greater the torment of *not* remembering!

I won't wear it, was Maigrey's first coherent thought. I won't go to his dinner. I won't leave this room. I am a prisoner and I will *be* a prisoner! I won't set foot out. I'll hide—

Pulling herself to her feet, barely able to stand, Maigrey backed away from the bed. She was forced to open her eyes and all it seemed they could see was indigo blue. Before she fell, she caught herself on the back of the chair and, leaning against it for support, stood staring at the robes.

And then Maigrey sensed Sagan's mind. He had hit her, drawn blood. Weakened, she had lowered her guard. Would she fall down now and die?

She sank into the chair and moved her hand to pick up her comb. Her fingers brushed against the rosewood box that stood in an honored place on her vanity. The wood was smooth and warm, warmer and smoother than the fabric of what had come to be known as the robes of death. Her hand closed over the box.

Memory's sword is a two-edged blade.

··◁▷··

The formal dining rooms on *Phoenix* were located in the portion of the ship devoted to the rare and occasional visitor. The Warlord cared nothing for what he considered worthless civilities, but he did demand that his officers dine with him once every ship's month. The room's furniture was severe—all steel and chrome and glass with sleek lines and sheered-off angles. It was designed to be uncomfortable; visitors were not encouraged to linger. There were no decorations or adornments. You were never allowed to forget this was a ship of war. Each piece of furniture could be dismantled almost instantly, to be stowed away when the ship was cleared for action. Huge steelglass viewports provided ever-changing vistas of black space that were breathtaking but somehow seemed to emphasize the chill atmosphere of the room.

The dining table, made of steel, bore an unfortunate resemblance to a table in an operating room. Covered with a white cloth, as it was this evening, it did, however, manage to look quite elegant. The plates were of pewter and marked with the emblem of the phoenix rising from the flames. The heavy crystal goblets bore the same emblem embossed in gold.

The room's lighting was indirect. Spotlights were hidden in recesses in the overhead. Beaming downward in a straight, direct line, they had the effect of illuminating only small areas of the room at any one time, leaving the rest in dimly lit shadow. So cunningly placed were these lights that when the guests were seated at the table, the Warlord's face was left in almost complete darkness while the faces of those dining with him were harshly exposed.

This trick lighting often served Sagan well. It was at such times as these when the guard is lowered, good wine and good food loosen the tongue. A journey down what appears to be a well-worn conversational path often leads the unsuspecting victim right off the edge of a cliff. A covert glance, a guilty blush, a cheek gone pale in anger or fear—all are visible to the eyes watching from the shadows. It was no wonder his officers came to dread these evenings. Even Nada, who considered himself ten times more cunning than his lord, never attended without a supply of small white pills prescribed by Dr. Giesk for internal disorders.

This evening, the gentlemen had gathered by the time Maigrey arrived. Admiral Aks and Captain Nada were in attendance, as well as the captain in charge of the centurions and several wretched lieutenants, sweating in their tight-collared dress uniforms and wishing heartily that they were somewhere else. Derek Sagan was clad in the Roman costume he admired, this particular breastplate and armor having been copied from those said to have been worn by Julius Caesar. The Warlord's gold-trimmed red cape swept the deck. At his side, he wore the bloodsword.

Nada's eyes flickered when he saw the sword. A remnant of the old royalist days, its use was outlawed by the Republic. To even own one was to court charges of treason. Sagan not only retained the sword that was his by right of birth but he flaunted it openly. Nada made a mental note for his secret report. Derek Sagan, watching the captain's swift change of expression, made a mental note of Nada.

An orderly entered the room. All eyes turned toward him as he announced the honored guest waiting in the antechamber to make a formal entrance.

"Citizen Morianna," the orderly said, standing stiff and rigid, his back to the door.

The expectant silence was broken by a few coughs and clearings of throats. This and a swift exchange of glances between the men informed the orderly that no one had appeared to lay claim to that name.

The orderly maintained his stance but darted a look behind him. He saw the woman standing calmly outside the door, gazing around her with interest, obviously waiting to hear her name announced. Perhaps his voice hadn't carried.

Swallowing, endeavoring to moisten his dry throat, the orderly tried again.

"Citizen Morianna."

The officers stirred uncomfortably. Derek Sagan put his hand to his twitching lips. Walking over, he leaned down and spoke a word into the orderly's ear, then returned to his place in the shadows.

Flustered, the orderly said in low tones, "Lady Maigrey Morianna."

Maigrey stepped forward into the room, into the light.

It was well that Sagan had retreated to the shadows, for not even his iron will could control the tremor that sent tiny cracks through his stone facade. It was not the sight of the indigo blue robes of ceremony which Maigrey wore; he had already steeled himself to that and had taken a vicarious pleasure in knowing the anguish the sight of those robes must have cost her. It was all part of his design, his intent to weaken her and wear her down. He had been rather hoping she might refuse to wear them, perhaps refuse to come to him at all.

Maigrey wore the blue robes—he had forgotten how well that color suited her. But her return attack had not only parried his blow, but it managed to slide beneath his blade, touch his soul, and draw blood. Sparkling on her breast was the Star of the Guardian.

An eight-pointed star, carved of the precious gem known as adamant, the jewel's value was calculated in terms of planets. Indeed, the wealth of entire solar systems might not purchase it. Not only was adamant extremely rare, but it had, by royal decree, been used only in the making of these jewels—the Stars of the Guardians. In addition, the gems had supposedly been granted mystical properties by the High Priests of those days, priests who had long since been put to death by orders of the President.

No force in the galaxy existed that could harm a starjewel; the gemstone would submit to being carved only after it had been blessed by the priests. A starjewel possessed its own inherent light that was quenched only upon the death of the wearer. The starjewel was either buried or cremated with the body of the Guardian who possessed it. There was a curse on any who robbed the dead of the jewel—as many looters had discovered to their intense horror following the carnage in the palace the night of the revolution. Yet such is the perverse nature of humanity that the demand for these rare jewels was high, the supply practically nonexistent, their value enhanced by the knowledge that the illicit possession of one was—according to the law of the Republic—a capital offense.

Two were known to Derek Sagan to exist. One was locked away in a vault whose access code were words he had spoken long ago and had long ago told himself to forget. He was staring at the other.

Sagan knew Maigrey had brought it with her. He had recognized the rosewood box when she showed it to him on Oha-Lau and he had given her permission to bring it on board. He could have done nothing else. The jewel did not permit itself to be lost or left behind. It would have found its way back to her. Sagan had not suspected, however, that the lady would have the audacity to wear it.

So strict was the law on the wearing of the starjewels that Derek Sagan had not only the legal right but the obligation to terminate the life of the woman where she stood. Maigrey knew it. She was not only courting death, she was flirting with it shamelessly. Death was the one way she could defeat him.

From the rigid, lockjawed expressions on the faces of his officers, Sagan knew they expected him to carry out the sentence on the spot. If he didn't, they would say nothing, of course, but they would be amazed, they would start to wonder, their faith in him would be shaken. Nada was watching him closely. Aks, who knew that the lady's value was in her life, not her execution, was casting his lord swift, worried glances.

Sagan stepped forward, his left hand resting on the hilt of the bloodsword. The officers fell back before him, some of the lieutenants so hurriedly that they tripped over their own feet. At the sound of his footsteps, Maigrey turned to face him.

Her eyes were gray as a storm-darkened sea and sparkled more brilliantly than the jewel. Her lips parted in a smile. The scar on her cheek was a livid streak against her flushed skin. Sagan was forced to admit to himself pleasure in confronting, for the first time in many years, a foe he deemed worthy of him.

"Lady Maigrey," he said, emerging from the shadows. "The wearing of that jewel is against the law of the Republic, punishable by death."

"I am well aware of that, my lord. All of the crimes of which I have been accused and which amount to nothing more nor less than remaining faithful to a vow I took to serve my king are now punishable by death. Many crimes, yet I can die only once."

"'It is not death, but dying, which is terrible,' according to the poet."

"The Guardians met death with courage. I won't disgrace their memories. It is for them that I wear the Star this night, my lord."

Sagan fell back to bind up his wounds. Due to the circumstances, his opponent was incapable of following up her advantage and he was able to return and strike back.

"Yes, my lady. The Guardians died bravely . . . most of them."

He had not meant to score a direct hit, and even now he wondered what it was that so affected her. Maigrey's eyes dilated; her face paled so that the scar nearly vanished. For a moment Sagan thought she was going to retreat, which wouldn't have suited his purposes at all. Fortunately the Warlord could always count on Captain Nada to stumble out onto the field of combat and commit verbal mayhem.

"My lord, it is my duty as a citizen of the Republic to point out that this citizen is wearing a piece of royalist trumpery expressly forbidden by law. It is an offense against us all that she be allowed to wear it and I insist that it be removed and confiscated."

"Thank you, Captain Nada, for bringing this infraction to my attention." Lord Sagan stepped back, away from Maigrey. "You, Captain, may remove the 'trumpery.'"

Captain Nada took a step forward and raised his hand. Maigrey, facing him, neither moved nor spoke. The starjewel lying on her breast burned with a brilliant, white-blue glow that grew brighter as it captured and held the attention and imagination of all in the room.

Captain Nada hesitated, his hand in mid-air.

"What's the matter, Captain?" the Warlord inquired. "Surely you don't believe those nonsensical stories about the curse? Or about the Blood Royal—that they had powers far above those of ordinary men? We are equal, aren't we, Captain? All citizens of the Republic."

Captain Nada stretched out his hand, the fingers trembling. The Star's light was blinding. It might have been pure flame he was about to grasp. Sweat beaded on his upper lip and glistened on his face. Suddenly, he snatched his hand back. Nada's skin flushed a deep, ugly red. He flashed his Warlord a look of hatred and enmity. Turning on his heel, the captain stalked off to the opposite end of the room.

A collective sigh breathed among those assembled. An alert steward hastened in with glasses of champagne. The Warlord abstained, as was his custom. Maigrey took a glass. She decided she deserved it. The officers, by silent accord, moved away from their Warlord and the woman, leaving them standing together near the door.

That man hates you, Sagan. There was no need for the two

of them to speak. Their thoughts—those that they wanted to share—came to each other clearly.

As much as he hates me, he fears me more, my lady.

And, as Machiavelli says, "It is much safer to be feared than loved." Is that what you believe, my lord?

I have always found it to be so. Haven't you, my lady?

The blade of his thoughts whistled past her too closely. Maigrey was forced to fall back and give herself a moment to catch her breath before she essayed her next attempt. No one approached them; the other officers mingled among themselves. She and Sagan were alone together. All their lives, it seemed, they had been alone together. She felt a sense of shared intimacy with the Warlord, much as they had known before, only now it bothered her, it was different because beneath it was hatred. Why? Why was he doing this? Sipping her champagne, she spoke aloud to make it seem that they were guests thrown together at a dull party. Nothing more.

"The remarks you made to Captain Nada, my lord, come rather strangely from one who was willing to sacrifice everything, even his own honor, for the sake of the revolution."

"The subject of honor will never be discussed between us, my lady. As for Nada, I merely pointed out to him the fallacy of his beliefs."

"Beliefs that were once yours, my lord. Or should I say, citizen?"

"You agreed with me, Lady Maigrey, that Starfire was an inept ruler and that we could expect little better from his younger brother. Come, it's no use turning away. You can avert your face but not your thoughts. I know the truth."

"He was your king. If you didn't like the man, then you should at least have believed in what he stood for and honored that."

"What? Divine right? That he was intended by the Creator to rule? I have more respect for our God than that."

"So much respect, my lord, that you murdered his priests!"

"That was not my doing."

The room had been filled with quiet talk and muted laughter, but the tone of the Warlord's last words cast a pall of silence over the assembly. Deftly Maigrey slid the verbal blade from his flesh, wiped off the blood, and sipped her champagne. The Warlord stood silently, his face once more hidden in the shadows. Maigrey could feel the tense rigidity in the body so near hers. He had not once looked directly at her during their conversation. Perhaps the Star's light hurt his eyes.

Moving slightly nearer the Warlord, Maigrey smiled like a good hostess at the officers to encourage a return to gaiety. Her conversation with Sagan continued, but silently.

If what you say is true and you don't believe the Starfires were given a mandate from heaven, then why do you want the boy?

I should think the answer to that would be obvious, my lady. He will be the marionette at the end of my strings. If he is as spineless as the rest of his family, he will need my help simply to stand up straight.

So you intend to use him to put yourself in control, Maigrey replied. *Then why bother to search for the true heir? Why not just snatch up some kid off the streets?*

Only the true heir will start the stampede that will soon sweep away this mockery of a government. The genetic tests, all must be in order. There must be no doubt in anyone's mind that this young man is a Starfire.

And that's where I come in, my lord?

That's where you come in, my lady. Your cue. Enter, stage left—the only one who can recognize and verify for me that this boy is truly the king.

After so many years? I only saw him when he was a baby—newborn, at that.

Maigrey set the glass down on a chrome table behind her. She was trying to behave calmly, but her shaking hand betrayed her. She tipped the glass, dropped it. The goblet bounced on the thick-carpeted deck and bounded away under a table, from where it was retrieved by a watchful steward.

That's true, my lady, but you would have given him something to know him by, years later. And even your brother would not have been so foolish as to have done away with it. The boy doesn't know who he is. Therefore I assume he knows nothing of his gifts of the Blood Royal.

"The curse," Maigrey murmured aloud.

The steward announced dinner. The Warlord extended his arm with courtesy. Maigrey accepted it with dignity, and they walked together to the head of the table, past the officers who were faceless nonentities.

And what of me? she asked him silently.

Can't you guess that, as well?

I think perhaps I can, my lord. I am a danger to you.

A very great danger. You see, my lady, I pay you the compliment of not underestimating you.

And so once I have served my purpose—

Once I am prepared to move—

—you will rid yourself of me.

Sagan led her to the head of the table. The other officers took their places as they were assigned, all remaining standing in respectful attention. The Warlord himself drew out her chair.

I had a dream, Maigrey. You know that my dreams are portents.

Yes, she knew. She remembered.

In this dream, I see your death . . . at my hands, my lady.

Maigrey sank into the chair. Sagan paused a moment to see that she was settled comfortably, then took his own seat at her right hand. The others sat down and the stewards instantly came around with water and wine.

The dream came in answer to a prayer, he continued silently. She could see of him only his hand that reached out from the shadows in which he surrounded himself and lifted the glass of water. *I asked the Creator to give into my hands those who betrayed me. One by one, they have all fallen to me. You are the last.*

Why didn't you kill me that night? Maigrey asked in the privacy of her own thoughts. The scar on her face ached and throbbed. She covered it with her hand, feeling that it must be pulsing burning red. Only your sword could have done this. Only your hand could have struck me down. Yet why didn't you end it? Why let me live? Dear Creator, if only I could remember! Then, startled, she wondered if that was truly what she wanted. One had to be careful when asking of the God. What was that prayer accounted to Socrates? "Avert evil from me, though it be the thing I prayed for; and give me the good which from ignorance I do not ask."

It was a comforting thought and reminded her that although Sagan was a priest, he did not know the mind of God. Somehow, she supposed, this tragedy must make sense. She wondered if it did to him.

The Warlord's thoughts had, fortunately, turned away from her, and conscious of eyes upon her, Maigrey made some attempt to eat and drink. Ship's food is ship's food the galaxy over. It tasted the same to her now as it had twenty years previous, which meant that she could not lose herself in gastronomical delight. At least the wine was good. She had only to remember not to drink too much or she would receive a rebuke from her commander. And then, sipping at the warming liquid, Maigrey reminded herself that Sagan was her commander no longer. She could do what she damn well liked.

Just what she'd mostly done anyway.

Maigrey finished the draught and, with a smile, indicated to the steward to refill her glass. The steward did so with alacrity. Lifting the goblet to her lips, Maigrey was conscious of Sagan's stern, reproving glance, though she couldn't see it. Some things, she supposed, never changed. She was actually beginning to enjoy herself. Though wounded a few times in their last encounter, she'd managed to penetrate her opponent's guard and knew she'd drawn blood. It was exhilarating to be back in action.

The Warlord leaned forward, looked across her to Admiral Aks, who was seated on her left.

"Any word on that Scimitar, Admiral?"

"Scimitar, my lord?" Aks, having imbibed two glasses of wine, almost missed his cue. "Oh, the one belonging to the deserter, Tusca. Yes, my lord. We have located its position on Vangelis and are currently monitoring it."

"Circumspectly, I trust."

"Yes, my lord, of course. As you commanded."

"And where did it finally set down?"

"In a small valley in the midst of a large mountain range. An excellent site, well fortified."

"John Dixter is a good general. Marek chose wisely when he selected him to lead this little insurrection." All Maigrey could see of the Warlord were his hands. They held a knife and were cutting into a piece of meat with deft, swift slicing strokes. "John Dixter. I believe you knew a John Dixter at one time, didn't you, my lady?"

The food was ash in Maigrey's mouth, the wine vinegar. She put the table napkin to her lips, fearful that she would choke. Plutarch relates that Portia, the wife of the traitor Brutus, killed herself by snatching burning charcoals out of the fire and putting them into her mouth. Maigrey knew then in what agony the woman had died. She tasted fire. She felt stifled, her throat burned. Tears stung her eyes.

Sagan's thought touched her. *They know I was your commander, lady. Don't disgrace me by crying!*

Anger gripped Maigrey with a cool, steadying hand. Sagan

had taught her the techniques of withstanding torture and torment, even as cruel as this. Disgrace *him?* She wouldn't disgrace herself.

"I once knew a John Dixter, my lord. But it is a common name in the galaxy."

Beneath the table where he couldn't see, Maigrey's hand clenched, her nails digging into her flesh. The steward would later find traces of blood upon the linen napkin.

"It would be a remarkable coincidence if the son of Danha Tusca were to be found with another John Dixter, a John Dixter who was *not* a friend of the members of the famed Golden Squadron. It is a common name, but this time, my lady, I am convinced that it belongs to a most uncommon man."

"If it *is* the same John Dixter, my lord, then he was a loyal commander, both to his king and to those whose honor he held in his care—those whom he commanded. I agree with you. He is an uncommon man. Certainly I know *no other* like him."

Very deliberately, the Warlord laid down both fork and knife, forming a cross upon his plate, a tradition among priests.

"Admiral Aks, you will send a squadron of marines to the planet's surface and arrest, in my name, the deserter known as Tusk and the royalist John Dixter. I want Tusca for questioning, but Dixter is expendable. If he resists, terminate him."

"Yes, my lord." The admiral made as if to rise from his seat. A lieutenant of the marines, who was also a guest, looked somewhat startled, but started to do the same.

"Leave Dixter out this, Sagan!" Maigrey said softly. "He had nothing to do with us!"

"I warned you long ago, lady, what your friendship might cost that man. You have only yourself to blame."

Maigrey stood up, hoping, as she did so, that she would find the strength to stay on her feet. The linen napkin slid from her lap and fell unheeded to the floor. "If you will excuse me, my lord, gentlemen."

There was much fumbling, clattering of tableware and scraping of feet, and a few coughs; the woman had caught most of the men in mid-mouthful. Admiral Aks held her chair. The other officers did her the honor of standing. Last of all, the Warlord rose slowly.

Maigrey could not see his face, but she could see the light of the starjewel, reflected coldly in his shadowed eyes. Catching hold of the gem, she wrapped her hand around it tightly, quenching the blue-white glow, and left the room without a word.

"Will she do it, my lord?" Aks inquired in a low voice.

"Yes. She must, she has no choice. I have made it a matter of honor."

Honor? Aks had seen the woman's face when John Dixter was mentioned. In the admiral's opinion, honor had very little to do with the matter. But, whatever the reason, the Warlord appeared to have won this contest. Aks glanced at Sagan to see if he could detect an expression of satisfaction on the stern face.

If there was, the shadows hid it extremely well.

Chapter ⋯✦◗◒◗✦⋯ Twenty

Can this be death? there's bloom upon her cheek . . .
                    George Gordon, Lord Byron, "Manfred"

"The kid handled the plane like a pro, sir. Oh, sure, he did some minor damage on landing, but that's to be expected with a first-timer, though to hear XJ carry on, you'd think the kid'd run the plane into the ground and brought it out again on the other side of the planet."

Dixter smiled. The general would have liked to point out to Tusk how paternal the mercenary was sounding, but, looking at the eight-pointed star glittering in the man's ear, Dixter kept quiet. That might be striking a little too close to the heart. Better to forget the past; maybe it'd go away.

"I've had him up a few times since in that reconditioned Scimitar you found for us, sir. It's about to melt XJ's microchips. I caught him trying to break into the other plane's computer files to see what was going on."

"How's the boy doing?"

Tusk pulled thoughtfully and absentmindedly at the earring. "It's just plain weird, sir. Now, I've never trained pilots or anything, but I remember my own trainer flights and this kid is uncanny. There's a helluva lot of things to do when you're flying. Things not to do, too. Just figuring out how to add what the computer's telling you with what your instruments are telling you and what your eyes are telling you—when most of the time the three don't agree—takes a military year. You get to do it by instinct, but that doesn't come except with experience."

The two were standing in one of the modular hangars that had just been constructed on their airfield. An alien had its RV in for work and at that moment a generator roared into operation, followed by the sound of furious banging and hammering. Shaking his head, coughing in the fumes, Dixter led the way outside.

"The kid already has the instinct," Tusk shouted over the noise. "It's like he had it before he ever set foot in the plane. No, maybe that's not right. It's more like he absorbs everything all at once and processes it and, bam! It's all right there for him. He knows exactly what to do and how to react. I've never seen anything like it, sir."

I have, John Dixter said to himself. It's bright and beautiful, Tusk, and the flames will reduce you to ashes. It's what happens when we dare to love a god.

"I gave him an old Scimitar pin of mine. The boys and I made it a regular ceremony, sort of like they do in the Air Corps. You'd've thought I crowned him king—"

Dixter raised an eyebrow.

"Sorry, sir," Tusk grunted. "Bad metaphor, Uh, say, General. The real reason I came. Where has . . . uh . . . Nola—that is, Ms. Rian—been keeping herself these last few days? We were going to get together to discuss some . . . uh . . . technical modifications on the TRUC before we take out the next shipment."

"Technical modifications." Dixter kept a straight face. "I see. Well, Tusk, I don't think we have to worry about flying shotgun on any more of the shipments. Not since you made scrap metal of that torpedo boat. We'll keep sending escorts, but I doubt they'll run into any trouble. And speaking of the torpedo boat, that's where Nola is. Marek and I got to wondering about that fancy device and I sent Rian to do a little investigating. Nothing dangerous, Tusk, so don't get your shorts in a knot. She'll poke around a few files, eat at a few TRUCer diners, ask a few questions. She knows just about everybody in the industry. This is strictly between us, all right?"

"Yes, sir." Tusk appeared somewhat shamefaced. "Thank you, sir. That's all I wanted to know."

The alien had ceased his work for the moment to search for a tool. The noise temporarily subsided.

"While I've got you, here's the new flight schedule." Dixter removed a computer printout from an antiquated file folder he was holding and handed it to the pilot. "See that everyone gets a copy. I'm glad to hear Dion is keeping occupied— Well, well. Speak of the devil."

"Tusk! I've looked all over for you! Say, can Link and I— Oh, sorry, General Dixter. I didn't see you!" Dion came dashing around the corner of the hangar building and pulled up short at the sight of the general.

"That's all right. We've finished. See you at the briefing tonight, Tusk."

"Yes, sir. What is it, kid?"

Dixter, walking away, heard Dion say something about provisions and Link giving him a ride into town. Heading back to his headquarters, the general's mind ran over everything Tusk had told him about Dion. Dixter understood and was wishing he didn't when he heard a wild yell behind him.

Turning, he saw Tusk waving his arms and shouting. Dion lay sprawled on the tarmac on his feet.

"What happened?" Dixter ran up.

"My God! I don't know, sir. One minute he was standing there talking and the next he pitched down on the ground. Look at him, sir!" Tusk clutched Dixter's arm. "D'you ever see anything like that?"

No, Dixter hadn't. And he'd seen just about every kind of casualty that could happen to a living being. The boy lay on his back, looking straight up intently at something no one else could see, seemingly listening to something no one else could hear. And he was answering. Or thought he was. His lips moved.

A chill went through Dixter, starting in his gut and spreading through his body. He glanced around. They were attracting a crowd, of course. Any distraction was welcome to break the monotony of war, which had been likened to drinking jump-juice and water—one shot of gut-wrenching excitement mixed with a glassful of boredom.

"The kid's having some sort of fit. Get a blanket, you men. Don't just stand there gawking. Make a litter and we'll carry him to my office. I suppose the rest of you haven't anything better to do than stand here?"

"Look, sir. He's trying to say—"

"Shut up, Tusk!" Dixter commanded in a low voice, bending over the boy, seemingly to help him but in reality to shield him from curious eyes.

The men dashed up with the blanket and gently transferred Dion from the concrete to the makeshift stretcher. The general covered him well, to keep him warm, and managed at the same time to slip the blanket up over his mouth. A startled Bennett ushered the men into Dixter's inner office, shoving maps and files off an old battered couch that occasionally doubled as a bed. Laying the boy down on the couch, they made him comfortable, and Bennett cleared the office of those who would have been more than happy to hang around and wait for the kid to either come to or kick off. Dixter sent Bennett on a search for a medic and locked both the door to the outer office and that to the inner when his aide had left.

"He's coming to himself, sir," Tusk reported.

Dixter returned in time to see Dion shove aside Tusk's restraining arms and try to sit up. The red-golden hair burned like flame. The boy's eyes were a startling blue against his pale face. Looking up at Dixter, he reached out clutching hands.

"Leave! We've got to leave! Sagan knows!"

"What the hell—" Tusk stared at him.

"Hush." Dixter gently pried loose the fingers that seemed to be trying to rip his shirtsleeve from his arm and sat down beside the boy. "Steady, son. You're not making sense. Tell us what happened."

"There isn't time!" Dion glanced around fearfully. Sweat trickled down the boy's face. "We've got to leave! Sagan's coming. Didn't you hear her, sir?"

"The kid's been in the jump-juice again," Tusk muttered.

"Shh. Calm down, Dion. Everything's under control. The Warlord isn't coming yet and we'll be ready for him when he does."

"Where is she?" the boy demanded. "Did you send her away? I was going to ask her—" he paused, frowning, "ask her something. I can't remember. Get her back! Get her back here!"

"Sufferin' Crea—"

"Tusk, keep quiet and get him some water."

Dion glared at the general angrily. Dixter was firm, his face grim. "Here, Dion, drink this." He held out the water and the boy finally did as he was told and seemed calmer when he'd drunk it down.

"Now listen to me, son. Look around you. Don't you remember what happened? You were standing outside the hangar. You asked Tusk about going into town with Link—"

Dion's eyes widened; he stared around confusedly. "Yes, that's right. How'd I get— What—"

"You passed out. The boys carried you in here. But you didn't faint, did you? You weren't really unconscious."

"No." Dion felt limp and drained. He lay back on the couch, his head propped up on a roll of maps. "Then you didn't see her? She wasn't here?"

"Who, son?"

"The woman! I was talking to Tusk and . . . then . . . she was standing right in front of me! She was . . . so real! She was as close to me as you are now, sir. She said, 'Sagan knows where you are! He's coming after you. If you need help, you can trust John Dixter. God be with you.'" Dion frowned. "But then you couldn't have seen her, or she would have told you yourself instead— Sir, are you all right?"

Dixter sat back on his heels. The general's face muscles were rigid, his skin was gray, the eyes staring at Dion were like the eyes of a corpse—wide open but unseeing. Tusk jumped up.

"Sir, are you all right?"

Dixter ignored him. Tusk, glancing from the general to the kid, muttered, "I think we could all use a drink," and headed for the bottom drawer of the general's battered desk.

"What did she look like?" Dixter's question was almost unintelligible. His mouth barely moved. Dion answered it only because he heard it more with his heart than his head.

"She was dressed in a blue gown—a blue that kind of shimmered when she moved. She wore a beautiful jewel, shaped like a star. Her hair was long and straight and fell from a part in the center of her head down either side of her face."

"What color was her hair?"

"Damn! Where's the bourbon?" Tusk was banging drawers. "Brandy. That'll do. Here, sir!" He sloshed a thick viscous green liquid in a glass and handed it to the general. "Drink it, sir. You don't look good."

Dixter didn't touch the glass, didn't even look at Tusk.

"Her hair's hard to describe, sir. It wasn't golden, it was lighter than that. But it wasn't pure white. It was—"

"Sea foam," Dixter said so softly that the boy leaned forward to hear. "The color of sea foam against blue water."

"I don't know, sir," Dion murmured, beginning to shiver. "I've never seen the sea."

"Go on."

"There . . . was a scar on her face—"

"General, sir! Where the hell's Bennett!" Tusk leapt for the door.

"No!" Gritting his teeth, Dixter stood up and made his way over to his chair. He lowered himself into it and closed his eyes. "I'm fine. Don't call anyone, Tusk. Don't let anyone in." He motioned for the brandy. "I'll take that now."

Tusk, looking dubious and half-determined to disobey, shoved the tumbler across the table.

Lifting the glass to his lips, the general managed a twisted smile. "The pain's an old one." He swallowed the fiery green liquid, gulped, and drew a deep breath. "The scar. Did it run . . . like this?" Slowly, as if he were inflicting the wound on himself, Dixter drew his hand along the right side of his face from the cheekbone to the corner of the lips.

"Yes!" Dion threw off the blanket and sat up. "Who is she? Do you know her? I have the feeling I should. There was something familiar about her, but—"

Tusk motioned him to be quiet.

Dixter was staring at the glass in his hand. For a moment, he rolled the glass around between his fingers, watching the green brandy coat the sides, then he tossed the rest of the liquor down the back of his throat.

"I know her. Or rather, I knew her. She's dead. She's been dead these seventeen years."

Rising from behind his desk, Dixter walked over to stare out the window of his mobile headquarters. It was cooler, down in the flat bottom of the mountain bowl that he'd selected as their new site of operations. The fans no longer kept the maps rustling. But the maps seemed to stir anyway, as if whispering to themselves.

"Shit," Tusk said and reached for the brandy bottle. "Begging your pardon, sir."

Dixter drew a handkerchief from his back pocket and wiped chill sweat from his face. Turning, he sat back down at his desk. Tusk passed the bottle. The general studied it, as if wondering if it was real or a figment of his imagination. He looked at Dion.

"And you recognized her. You thought she looked familiar."

"She reminded me of someone—"

"I'm not surprised. Platus. Your mentor. I never thought they looked that much alike. But other people did. She was his sister."

"Maigrey Morianna!" Tusk coughed and blinked back tears. The green brandy of Laskar was potent stuff. It made jump-juice taste like lite beer. "My father talked about her some.

Uh, I hate like hell to ask this, sir, but just how sure are you that she's dead?"

"I didn't see the body, if that's what you mean," Dixter answered with a wry smile. "But I was sure, all the same." The eyes, from their web of wrinkles, looked at the wall and saw right through it, clear back through space and time. "She was scared, and I'd never seen her scared of anything. She disappeared in the night. She gave me the slip, stole a plane, and tried to get off-planet. The press reported that she'd been shot down over Minas Tares." Dixter poured and drank brandy. "I never heard from her again. Yes, I believed she was dead. Why not? Everybody else was."

"Then, sir, do you think there's a chance that she's alive? Maybe what the kid saw wasn't a ghost. Maybe she was using that telepathic projection stuff that the Blood Royal used to use on each other. And if that's true"—Tusk peered nervously out the window—"then shouldn't we be doing something? Like leaving?"

"Where would you go?" Dixter's words were glazed with liquor. "If Sagan knows where we are, you can bet that he's waiting somewhere up there for you, probably just out of range. That bombing run. I wondered about that. Why bother? Unless you want the quail to leave the thicket."

Tusk got to his feet, heading—somewhat unsteadily—for the door. "That reconditioned Scimitar. I'm taking it. C'mon, kid. We can make Mannheim XI by 0600—"

"Not you, Tusk. Sagan's made you. Link. Send the boy with—".

"Link! That ego-inflated blob of hair gel? He's not a Guard—" Tusk stopped, his tongue asking his brain if he really wanted to continue. "Thanks for the suggestion, sir, but Link didn't make the promise to the kid's dead friend. I did. It's my responsibility."

"Not anymore. She made it mine. Send the boy with Link, and that's an order—"

"It doesn't matter, either of you," Dion interrupted coolly. "I'm not going anywhere. Not till I get some answers."

"Kid—"

"I mean it, Tusk. Don't argue with me. You don't understand."

"Goddam right I don't! Dead ladies talking to you. Sagan coming to haul us off and shove us in the disrupter and you and the general sittin' here on your—"

"That'll do, Tusk," Dixter interrupted. "The boy's right. We're all in this too deep to wade out now."

"I just hope like hell the water doesn't close over our heads in the meantime," Tusk muttered. He stood near the door to the office, irresolute and unhappy.

The boy's intensely blue eyes were wide and clear and glittered with an unholy radiance. The red-golden hair, swept back from the forehead, was like a cascade of flame in the cold sunshine that filtered through the trailer window. He sat forward, staring at Dixter, his lips slightly parted as if to take a deep, long, and satisfying drink.

"This proves it, doesn't it, sir? It proves who I am! Beyond all doubt."

"It doesn't prove anything, son, except that you're of the Blood Royal." The general poured himself another brandy.

Dion looked downcast, but gamely tried again. "That promise you talked about making—to 'someone very dear. Someone who was dying.' That was to her, wasn't it? To Lady Maigrey? Now don't you see, sir? She's absolved you of that! She isn't dead. I know she isn't. Please tell me what you know, sir!"

"I'll tell you," Dixter said, staring into the glass. "But I warn you. It isn't much."

The general was quiet. There was no sound except the whispering of the maps. Tusk, still standing near the door, shifted from one foot to the other, gazed longingly outside, and finally threw himself back into his chair. "Link!" He said in disgust and reached for the brandy bottle.

"What do you know about comets?" John Dixter asked.

Chapter ·–◦○◦–· Twenty-one

Go and catch a falling star . . .

John Donne, "Song"

"Comets? Sir, you were talking about . . ." Dion paused.

Dixter hadn't heard, hadn't even looked up. Rolling the brandy on his tongue, he swallowed. "They're made of ice, you know. Flaming ice, they streak across the sky, touch you with fire, and then disappear. You ever been to Laskar, Tusk?"

"Where they make this stuff?" Tusk upended the bottle. "Yeah, sir, I've been there."

Dixter, reaching into a drawer, pulled out another bottle, uncapped it, and poured himself a generous glass.

"A hell-hole, Laskar. A planet where any sin known to human and alien is for sale at any price. I haven't been there in years, but I don't suppose it's changed."

"Worse, sir," Tusk said. "The cities are wide open. No law. But the casino owners and such pay their taxes, if you know what I mean."

"I heard as much. Well, in the old days we used to try to keep the place in order—taxes or not. We had a base near the capital—"

"It's still there, sir. That's where they collect the taxes." Tusk swigged brandy.

"The king's army used to assist the locals if things got out of hand, which things did on a pretty regular basis. It was a great place for R and R, one of the hot spots in the galaxy."

"Off-limits now, General. Has been ever since pirates hijacked that naval destroyer, murdered the crew, took off with the ship, and started attacking the commercial fleets. There was a big public outcry. People wanted the President to shut Laskar down or maybe just drop a couple of nukes on it but all that happened was to declare the planet an official, no man's

209

land. 'Citizens, go there at your risk. The government will not be responsible.' Like I said, Laskar pays its taxes."

"Somebody's paying, that's for sure. It'd be interesting to know who and for what. Still, that's neither here nor there. Another drink, Tusk? Sure you won't have one, Dion?

"Well, where was I? Laskar. Yeah. I was on Laskar. Stationed there, when I was a colonel. Thirty-two years old, by my planet's calculations. I was due for reassignment and it couldn't come fast enough. Some men liked that tour. I knew guys who volunteered for it. I hated Laskar. It's got a green sun. Something about the atmosphere. Turns everything you look at green. You learn to sleep days. First because you can't take the sight of everything bathed in a sickly gangrenous glow. Second because you're up all night anyway. Life on Laskar begins at dusk. Life ends at night, generally alone, in an alley.

"Lovely place, Laskar. You never went to the grocery store without one hand on your lasgun and a friend walking behind to make sure you weren't stabbed in the back in the frozen food aisle."

Dixter watched the brandy swirl in the glass.

"My orders for transfer came through, finally. I was scheduled to ship out on a battle cruiser orbiting on routine patrol. Some buddies and I went to celebrate in a bar we'd found that was relatively civilized—for Laskar. We were standing around the bar when some of the Royal Air Corps pilots from this cruiser swaggered in. We knew there'd be trouble. A lot of the base soldiers were in that bar, and ground troops've got no use for hotshot fly-boys. My friends left. They were officers and had their stripes to think about. But I was getting off that stinking planet and I just plain didn't give a damn. Besides, the owner was a good guy. I'd done him a few favors and I knew where the back door was and the combination to the lock that opened it. I decided to stick around and see the fun.

"Sure enough, the pilots had a few and then started in on 'land-bound lubbers.' The soldiers told the fly-boys where they could fly their planes and it wasn't deepspace. I don't know who threw the first punch. It didn't matter, 'cause within seconds it was every man for himself. I stood at the end of a bar, drinking brandy. This brandy." Dixter held the glass to the light. "Occasionally I'd duck a bottle or convince some private that he didn't really want to hit a colonel and shove him back into the fracas. The pilots were getting the worst of it.

There wasn't a stick of furniture left intact unless you count my barstool. The owner was on the phone, screaming for the cops. It would be just a matter of time before the M.P.'s arrived to bring down the curtain. I was thinking about heading for the door in back when one of the Air Corps officers walked through the door in front."

Dixter took a mouthful of liquor down the wrong way, coughed, and covered his mouth with his handkerchief. Tusk started to reach out unsteadily to pound the general on the back, thought better of it, and latched onto the bottle instead. Dion sat on the edge of his chair, his hands clasped tightly in his lap, his penetrating gaze fixed on Dixter.

"The officer was a female. I'd known women officers before and I could take them or leave them. Some were good. Some were bad. Just like men. Just like aliens. But this one—" Dixter drew in a soft breath, "she was young. Too young. And fragile. Hair the color of sea foam. Eyes that changed color like the sea, too. Sometimes they'd be green, sometimes sparkling blue, sometimes dark and gray. Not that I noticed the color of her eyes then. I just remember thinking that it must have been that hair and those eyes that got her those major's bars she was sporting and she'd probably take one look and beat it. Hell, there were fists punching, feet kicking, fingers gouging. There wasn't room for the bodies on the floor; they were starting to stack up in the corners.

"But she didn't leave. I saw her lips tighten and suddenly, from the expression on her face, I knew how she'd won those bars. She waded into the melee, grabbed hold of the first pilot that came flying her direction, and smacked him hard to bring him to his senses.

"'Get out, Fisher,' she ordered. 'The M.P.'s are coming.'

"The fly-boy was thinking about arguing until he saw who had him.

"'Yes, sir, Major,' he mumbled and staggered toward the door.

"She was back in the midst of the fight, as cool as you please. Someone—like me, I thought—should get her out of here before she gets hurt. But I just sat there. Somehow I knew, by the look of her, that she wouldn't thank me for coming to her rescue. Besides, she didn't need rescuing. One guy took a swing at her. In less time than it takes to tell, he was on the floor wondering what had run him over. But she wasn't there to fight. She was there to get her men out before they landed in the lockup and she did. When they saw her, they forgot about their brawl.

"'Out!' was all she said, and they slunk out, those who could walk carrying those who couldn't.

"She turned back, going through the debris, lifting up the overturned tables to make sure no one got left behind. Satisfied that she had all her boys, she headed for the door.

"I'm not a praying man. But I said a prayer then—the kind a kid prays. You know, 'Grant me this, God, and I'll do anything you want in return.' And my prayer was answered. Sirens and whistles. The M.P.s were right outside. That broke up the fight in a hurry. Guys began leaping through the windows. Too late, of course. They were being nabbed on the sidewalk. She was trapped. If she walked out, she'd walk right into their arms and, what with the blood spattered on her and her hair down in her face and her uniform torn, it wasn't likely she could pass herself off as an innocent bystander. The room spun around me and it wasn't the brandy. Somehow, I managed to cross the floor and I caught hold of her hand.

"'This way,' I said.

"She never hesitated. We were out the back door just as the M.P.'s came in the front.

"'Quick!' she said. 'They'll be back here, too.'

"We ran down the alley, knocking over boxes, scattering stray cats and bottles and bums. When we reached the street, we let the crowd on the sidewalk catch us up and take us with them. Behind us, I could hear more sirens. We ducked into the shadows of a doorway. I was still holding her hand.

"'Thank you, Colonel.' She caught her breath. Her eyes were brighter than the street lamps. 'I would've been in real trouble if my commander'd had to come get me out of jail.' She laughed, though, when she said it. I wondered why, at the time. 'I owe you one, Colonel—'

"'Dixter. John Dixter.'

"'Where's home base?'

"'Here, but I'm shipping out tomorrow. Reassignment.'

"'Good. You'll be traveling with us.' She slipped her hand out of mine. 'Thank you again, Colonel Dixter. I won't forget.'

"She was gone. Vanished into the crowd.

"I didn't even know her name."

Dixter's glass was empty. He didn't refill it. Tusk lolled in his chair, his face lit by a warm glow. Dion never moved, never took his eyes from the general's face. Outside he heard

Bennett pounding on the locked door to the trailer, but the sound wasn't real, not nearly as real as a decadent city beneath a green sun.

"I hate spaceflight," Dixter growled suddenly. He glanced at Tusk, who blinked and made some attempt to sit up straight. "You wouldn't understand. No pilot ever does. I guess that's the real reason I stayed in that bar to watch the fly-boys get the flak knocked out of 'em. Oh, I know all about the beauty, the mystery, the romance of space. To me, it's just a cold and lonely place to die. Where's the romance in sudden decompression—your brains gushing out of your nose? Or in being blown to pulp or drifting endlessly, marooned, to die of the cold or starvation or by your own crazed mind?

"Plus I always get space sick. The first three days out for me are hell and I'd been dreading the flight to my new assignment. But not now. When it came time to board, I was the first one in the shuttle. Of course, I was still sick as a dog. For three days I couldn't move off the bed, except to crawl to the head. Finally, when I decided I might live after all and I could keep water down, at least, I made my way out into the ship and began to search for her.

"I found out where the pilots bunked, where their officers' quarters were. I hung around, hoping to see her. I came to know every major by sight, but I never found the one I was looking for. Maybe she hadn't meant this ship, but there weren't any others. Besides, I saw a couple of her boys, their faces cut and swollen from the beating they'd taken. A week went by and then one day a pilot I'd met—I got to know a lot of them, as you can imagine—and I were walking down a corridor to the rec room . . ."

Dixter filled his glass, but he didn't drink it. He rubbed his eyes and ran his hand through his graying hair.

"I saw her and knew in that moment the answer to everything: why she wasn't quartered with the other pilots, why those boys of hers turned white at the sight of her, why she had those major's bars and she couldn't have been more than twenty, why nothing would ever be the same for me again.

"She was coming down a corridor, walking toward me, and she was dressed in the shining silvery armor of the Guardians. Around her shoulders was the blue cloak with the silver edging that marked her rank, around her neck was the starjewel, at her waist was the bloodsword. At her side walked a man—tall and strong and proud. He was dressed in silver armor and wore the blue cape, only his was edged in gold.

"'Derek Sagan,' said my friend, seeing me staring and thinking I was looking at him.

"When he said the name, I did look. 'Sagan?' Even on Laskar, we'd heard of him. 'What's he doing on board a cruiser?' It was the first time I'd ever heard of the Guardians being directly involved in combat.

"'He's been given command of a special squadron—an idea he proposed. It's made up entirely of members of the Blood Royal, because of those touted mystical powers of theirs. I'm thankful I'm not part of it. He's a brilliant commander but a real bastard to serve under. A perfectionist. Can't tolerate mistakes. They say he's as hard on himself as anyone else, but that doesn't make it any easier to be around him.'

"'Who's the woman?' I asked. All I could see were her dark eyes and that glittering jewel.

"'The Lady Maigrey Morianna.'

"This guy I was with had spent some time at court, I found out. His father was a minor potentate of some sort and he considered himself an expert on the Royal Family.

"'Major Morianna, I should say,' my friend said. 'She's a pilot, too. My guess is she'll be in the new squadron. A member of the Blood Royal, of course. The king's a first cousin on her father's side, I believe, and Sagan's a cousin once removed or something like that—despite the fact that he's a bastard. I mean a real one.'

"He spoke in a whisper. I didn't blame him. Looking at Sagan's face, I wouldn't have said those words aloud within a light-year of him.

"'What about her?' I asked casually, trying to be cool.

"I guess I failed, 'cause he grinned at me and shook his head.

"'Forget it, friend. You might just as well have fallen in love with a comet. Fire on the outside and cold in the center. She's a warrior from a family of warriors. On her planet her people ride horses and fight with arrows and spears. She was thrown out of the Royal Academy for Women when she was six for nearly knifing one of the Sisters. King ordered her sent to the men's academy with her brother. That's where she met Sagan.' He leaned closer to me, lowering his voice even further. 'They're mind-linked.'

"'What the hell's that?'

"I was only half-listening. Her hair was so soft and fine it floated when she walked. It was long, almost to her waist. She must have had it braided under her cap the day I saw her.

"'Watch the two of them,' my friend said. 'It's really uncanny. They can share thoughts. Their eyes meet and you can almost see the energy flash between them.' He rambled on, but I wasn't listening.

"Fall in love with a comet. That was true. I saw it now. She'd flash through my life and leave only an aching blackness when she was gone. I saw it all as she walked down the passage, coming toward me. I had been going to say something to her, but I put that thought out of my mind, just as I put her out of my life at that moment.

"They strolled through the ship as if they owned it. Hell, maybe they did, for all I knew. People made way for them without even thinking about it. I flattened myself back up against the bulkheads, hoping to fade into the ductwork. Sagan was saying something to her. Her eyes brushed over me without a glimmer of recognition and then she was past me. That was that, I supposed. I was almost relieved when Sagan stopped, his attention drawn to someone else. Maigrey turned her head. She looked at me—directly at me—through that mist of hair and she grinned. It wasn't a smile. It was a grin—one conspirator to another. She raised one finger in a warning kind of gesture. Like this—'keep quiet.' I remembered what she'd said about her 'commanding officer.' Then she turned and walked away.

"And that was that." Dixter toyed with the half-empty glass. "We became good friends on that trip. We were friends for years. Her friendship wasn't what I wanted, of course, but I took that over losing her. She was Blood Royal, after all. Her ambition burned in her. It had been born in her, she'd been raised for it. Politics bored her, she didn't want that. She wanted to fly. She and Sagan and the others in the squadron were the first members of the Blood Royal the king allowed to become pilots. Usually, you know, they were married off to others in the royalty to keep the bloodline pure. But this was when things were starting to fall apart for the monarchy. I guess the king figured he needed all the help he could get.

"And the help turned around and stabbed him in the back."

Dixter fell silent. The banging and yelling had increased in volume and ferocity. He glanced vaguely in the direction of the outer door.

"Confound it, Tusk, make 'em stop that racket!"

Rising to his feet, Tusk lurched forward, fumbled with the lock, flung open the door, and staggered into the outer office. Dion heard the mercenary conferring with Bennett. Whatever he said obviously didn't have much effect, for Bennett himself appeared in the doorway.

"General Dixter, sir—"

"It's all right," Dixter said. "Just"—he waved his hand—"leave us alone."

"Yes, sir," Bennett said. "Would you like some coffee, sir?"

"No, Bennett. I'd like to stay drunk."

"Yes, sir. Very good, sir."

"Find Captain Link and tell him to report to HQ on the double. And send Tusk back in."

"That will be difficult, I'm afraid, sir. He's passed out."

"Good. That'll make it easier. Take him back to his plane. And tell XJ that Tusk's grounded until further notice."

"Yes, sir."

Dion started to stand up, but Dixter waved him down. "Bennett'll take care of Tusk. You stay here. You should . . . know the rest. While I'm still sober enough to tell it."

"Yes, sir." Dion subsided back onto the couch.

They heard a sound as if someone had thrown a glass of water into someone else's face. A groan and then a scuffling sound and a crash, swearing. The door slammed and everything but the rustling maps were quiet. Even Dixter's voice, when he spoke, seemed to Dion not so much to disturb the silence but to flow into it and become a part of it.

"I've never told anyone about that night at the palace. And it's not me talking now. It's the booze. I lied when I said I wasn't there the night of the revolution. The night that came to be called 'die Freiheit.' Freedom! Hah! I was there." Dixter lifted the brandy bottle with a shaking hand and poured. Most of the liquor made it into the glass.

"God help me! I was there."

Chapter ··❦··❦·· Twenty-Two

Where sceptered Angels held their residence
And sat as Princes . . .

John Milton, *Paradise Lost*

"Minas Tares—the royal city. God, it was beautiful. Maybe it was everything else they say now—decadent and extravagant. People living in unimaginable wealth while millions went hungry. All I know is that for me it was the center of everything that was wonderful and lovely. Music, art, literature, architecture—the best came to Minas Tares. It was all destroyed in the name of 'democracy.'

"We knew what was coming, I think. The king knew, certainly. But he either didn't want to believe it or he couldn't decide what to do. Starfire was a good man, but he was weak. His ministers weren't much better. As Yeats says, 'The best lack all conviction, while the worst are full of passionate intensity.'" Dixter stared at the brandy, then drained the glass all in one gulp. He closed his eyes, drew a breath, and expelled it in a sigh. "Anyway . . . I was there that night for two reasons. One, I'd just been made a general. Me and about five hundred other human and alien commanders from all over the galaxy. It was quite a ceremony. 'For meritorious valor.' The king himself pinned the stars on my collar.

"So I was on Minas Tares for that, and I was there because she was there. It was the night the Golden Squadron was being honored by their peers—the Guardians—for their battle against the Corasians on some planet, somewhere. Maigrey was attending, but her most important reason for being there was to be with her best friend, Semele Starfire, wife of the crown prince, who was due to have her baby anytime."

Dixter didn't look at Dion when he spoke. The boy flinched

but kept quiet. It seemed to him that the general had forgotten he was there, had forgotten their danger. Dion remembered but he didn't want to remind the general, fearful of breaking the spell. Besides, to Dion, it wasn't danger, it was deliverance.

"I guess you've heard all about the traitors within the Royal Army who detected the rebel fleet entering orbit around the planet and didn't report it. The base fell. There wasn't even a fight; most of the soldiers joined the rebels. When Robes's army held control of the city, he ordered them to march on the palace.

"I was in the palace . . . or rather on the grounds. The palace was a city in itself. Beautiful buildings, tree-lined boulevards, galleries, shops, restaurants. Thousands of people lived and worked there. It was filled with light and music, day and night. I was there by invitation—it was the only way you could get in. Maigrey's invitation, of course. She wanted to congratulate me. We were going to celebrate."

Dixter reached for the bottle, but it was empty. He gripped it, hard, and stared into the past.

"The rebels hit the palace with everything they had. I'd just come through the first series of gates when the first wave struck. I knew in an instant what it was—there'd been rumors and civil unrest for months. Some of the king's own personal troops switched over to the rebel side. Most of them stayed loyal, though. It was chaos. No one knew whose side anybody was on. People shot each other down like dogs in the name of freedom.

"We were outnumbered a thousand to one. They came out of the skies, poured like rats up through the sewers. What fighting there was wasn't resistance so much as plain frustrated anger. I was unarmed but I grabbed a lasgun from a corpse and fought until what I figured would be my end. A mortar round saved my life. The explosion blew me into a ditch. It was nighttime. In the confusion, no one noticed me, or if they did they must have thought I was dead. When I came to, it was all over.

"I could see flames on the horizon and I knew it was the palace. My one thought was Maigrey. I took the uniform off the body of a rebel solider, a sergeant, and put it on, grabbed his blaster, and headed for the palace.

"The night's like a horrible dream to me. I'd been hurt in the explosion, but the pain didn't seem to register. It just made things unreal. Still, I don't think that even death will blot out my memory of what I saw that night. Robes's troops were out of control—drunk on liquor and blood. Rape, torture, burning, looting—I saw it all and yet I didn't see it. I made myself *not* see it because I knew if I looked I'd open fire and keep on blasting until they cut me down. I had one idea in my mind—Maigrey.

"After a while, I welcomed the confusion, because it let me go where I pleased. I kept heading straight for the palace. I could see it now—its steelglass spires glistening in the flames. Whenever I came up on someone who seemed halfway sober, I asked what had happened there. I heard all sorts of gruesome rumors—the king was dead, murdered. Everyone in the palace was dead, the Guardians slaughtered. One soldier came past, wearing one of those blue robes. It was torn and black with blood. I don't know how I stayed on my feet. The unreality, I suppose. Part of me still couldn't believe it was happening.

"When I reached the palace, I got a shock. Here, everything was under control. The troops were cold sober, disciplined—an army, not a mob—and they were standing guard against their own. I found out later who their leader was. I might have expected. Derek Sagan. They all wore that new crest of his—the phoenix rising from flames.

"I picked out a side entrance and waited for my chance to get inside. Fortunately, a brawl among the rebel troops drew the guards away from their posts. The soldiers'd heard rumors of loot inside the palace and were trying to break in. The guards beat them back with the butt ends of their guns or stunned them. During the confusion, I slipped through the door.

"I'd been in the palace before—Maigrey'd taken me around. But I damn near didn't recognize the place. Some of it had burned; Sagan's troops were busy putting out the fires. There'd been explosions, holes blown in the walls, floors knocked down, staircases hanging out in the middle of nowhere. I was standing there, staring, trying to orient myself, when one of the soldiers came up to me.

"'What's your business here, Sergeant?'

"'Dispatches.' I spoke automatically. I don't even remember thinking about it. I put my hand over my breast pocket. 'For the commander.'

I didn't care anymore. I knew, now, she was dead. I *prayed* she was dead, after what I'd seen. I was dead myself, inside, and I just plain didn't care. The soldier looked at me and must have decided that since I was sober I was telling the truth. He motioned me on.

"'Commander Sagan's in the computer center. Up those stairs and turn to your right.'

"Sagan! My mind reeled. Derek Sagan. A traitor. Of course, by now he knew me. Maigrey'd introduced us. I wondered if she'd known he was going to betray his king. If so, that alone must have killed her.

"You can be sure that, once the soldier was out of sight, I *didn't* go in Sagan's direction. I made my way to the hall where she'd told me they held the royal banquets. The chamber was enormous. It took up almost half one whole floor. And it was filled with bodies. The Guardians hadn't been armed, you see. That was part of the plot.

"I searched among the dead for what seemed like hours. I saw the body of the king, lying in his throne. Robes put it out that Starfire had died of a heart attack, but that wasn't true. I saw the hole—burned through the crown, burned through his skull. But I didn't find Maigrey. I couldn't find any of the Golden Squadron, and I began to hope. I went out into the corridors again, searching—for what I'm not sure. There was even this crazed idea in my head to go find Sagan and ask him.

"It was quiet in the palace; the silence seemed eerie after the noise outside. There was almost no one around—a few soldiers moving about on business, a few standing guard, but most of them were outside. There were no medics, tending to the wounded. There were no wounded. Only corpses. Whenever someone passed me I looked purposeful. I walked quickly, like I knew where I was going. Amazing, what that'll do for you.

"Not really thinking much about it, I made my way to the king's private living rooms. Of course, I'd never been up there. I couldn't have entered now except his own personal guards were dead. I'm not sure why I came. It seemed to me later that I was stumbling around in a fog of pain and despair, but I guess I must have had some kind of rational thought process. I think it was in my mind that if Maigrey could have escaped she would have gone looking for her friend, Semele. And that would have brought Maigrey here. And it was here I found her."

Dixter's voice was thick, but his words were clear, obviously coming from somewhere deep inside him that the liquor couldn't touch.

"She was lying across a doorway, the bloodsword in her hand, as if she'd been holding that door against attack. Her hair covered her face and it was matted with blood. I sank down onto the floor beside her. There was no strength left, nothing left in me. I knew she was dead and I was thankful she'd died quickly. I lifted her hand and put it to my lips and the flesh was warm. That jolted me. I found a pulse. She *wasn't* dead!"

Dixter looked at Dion, bringing the boy back into focus. "She wasn't dead. Do you understand? None of the other wounded had been allowed to survive. Everyone had been ruthlessly slaughtered. But not her. Of all the things I saw that night, that seemed to me to be the strangest. Her enemy had struck her down and then left her. But I couldn't take time to think about it.

"The wound on her face was terrible, I could tell that much, though I didn't dare examine it. Her blood-soaked hair had stuck to it, formed a kind of bandage over it. Carefully I stripped off her blue robes—that would have marked her for death for certain—and I dressed her in the clothes of a murdered nurse, whose body I'd seen lying in the hallway. I carried her out of the palace.

"Once back in the confusion outside, I was in more danger than when I'd been in the palace. But when anyone stopped me, I leered and joked about my 'prize' and said I was just looking for a quiet place where I could have some fun. No one tried to take her from me. I think they thought she was dead and I was some sort of crazed pervert.

"A terrible storm was raging. Rain fell in torrents; the lightning was brighter and more deadly than the artillery. God must be really pissed, I thought. But I guess He wasn't mad at me, because I carried her safely through the turmoil to the hospital in the city.

"It was hell in there. You can imagine. The rebels had taken it over. They were permitting their own people and civilians be treated, but I saw them kill a wounded royal officer, who was brought in on a stretcher. Fortunately, my stolen uniform gained me safe passage.

"When the doctor examined Maigrey, he saw the starjewel hanging around her neck. There was a nurse and another young doctor with him. They all saw it and they all looked at each other. I held my breath. The doctor glanced around, saw the rebel soldiers standing right outside the door of the emergency room.

"'This woman's dead,' the doctor said. 'I need this space for the living. Get the body out of here.'

"I was on my feet. The doctor, walking past me, jabbed me hard, in the ribs. 'Shut up and wait for me in there!' he hissed, nodding at the visitor's room. The nurse drew a sheet up over Maigrey's body, covering her face, and she and the young doctor wheeled her out right past the rebels.

"Dazed, I went into the waiting room. Somebody cleaned and dressed my wounds. That was the first I think I knew I'd been hit. I sat there in a stupor for hours. Finally, the doctor came to find me. He led me to a ward filled with wounded. Maigrey was there, her face bandaged. The nurse I'd seen with her handed me a medicine bottle. Inside, swathed in cotton, was the starjewel. I heard later they'd operated on Maigrey in the morgue.

"When she came out of the sedation, she looked around and seemed just as amazed as I'd been to discover she was alive. She asked me where I'd found her, what had happened. I told her I'd found her lying in a doorway, alone.

"'There was no one else?' she persisted. 'Not Platus? Not Stavros or Danha. Not . . .' she hesitated before she spoke, 'not a baby?'

"When I told her no, she seemed relieved and lay back. 'Forget I asked you that,' she said, gripping my hand tightly. 'Promise me, John.' I promised.

"She didn't say anything else to me after that. She just lay there, holding on to my hand, staring into nothing. A few days later, when she was stronger, I asked her what had happened in the palace that night. The doctor had told me she might feel better if she talked it out. But she only shook her head.

"'I don't remember, John. I've tried, but I don't remember anything except— I don't remember anything.'

"The next day, when I came to visit, she was gone. She'd fled in the night. Then came the news report that Maigrey Morianna, former Guardian and enemy of the people, had been attempting to escape in a stolen spaceplane. She'd been shot down over Minas Tares.

"I managed to make my way off-planet and I started life over, though lots of times I wondered why I bothered. But years pass, wounds heal. The pain subsides and you find out you can laugh again. But it's never quite the same. Never quite the same."

Dixter passed his hand over his face. He looked aged, haggard. Dion hardly recognized him.

"So it could have been her I saw, couldn't it, sir?"

"Yes."

"And it makes sense, now. The baby she talked about was the son of the crown prince who was born that night."

"Possibly." Dixter was noncommittal.

"Lady Maigrey rescues the baby and gives it to the person she trusts—her brother Platus. He takes the baby off-world, to the most isolated planet he can find, and we live like criminals, hiding away until Stavros, who knows where we're hiding, is forced to tell. When you saw me for the first time, sir, you looked at me as if you knew me. Who do I look like? Who do I remind you of?"

Dion stared dreamily at the boy. "All the Starfires had those intense blue eyes of yours, eyes that seem to be able to see through walls. And you have your father's red hair and something of your mother's look. She was a renowned beauty, Princess Semele. You could be her son."

"Heir to a throne that no longer exists."

"Except in the minds and hearts of many."

"Was that why they did it, sir—saved the baby? To bring back the king?"

"If that's even *what* they did. I don't know, Dion. I've told you all I can."

"I saw her. I saw her as plainly as I see you now, sir. How?"

"The Blood Royal had the gift of telepathic communication, but it could only be with those they knew or with someone who had an object that had once belonged to the one communicating."

Dion's hand reached up to touch the ring he wore around his neck. That made it conclusive. But whose ring was it? Why did he have it? And why, if he was who he thought he might be, had Platus never told him? Indeed, Platus had made his lineage sound like something to be ashamed of! And here was this lady, Platus's sister, warning him away.

Dion felt anger stirring within him. Platus had concealed the truth from him. This woman was trying to do the same thing. There was only one person he was beginning to feel he could trust, one person who could understand.

"Where the devil's Link?" Dixter glanced impatiently out the window.

"I think I'll go back to the plane, get my things together so that Link and I can leave right away," Dion said, standing. He felt little remorse about lying. They'd lied to him for seventeen years, but he discovered it wasn't quite that easy. Tusk would wake up, realize he was gone. "If you'd tell Tusk, sir, that I thank him and I wish— I wish . . ."

Dixter made a deprecating gesture. "He'll understand."

No he won't. None of you will. But is that my fault? Dion swallowed, trying to force the pain down his throat. He thought there must be something he could say, something that could make it all right.

He looked at the general's haggard face, the man's gaze that was unfocused but not quite enough. The general was all too sober.

"Good-bye, sir."

"Be careful what you wish for, Dion." Dixter glanced up at him, then drained the last of the brandy. "You may get it."

La cadence est moins lente, et la chute plus sûre.
Gabriele Fauré, "Pavan"

Maigrey sat curled up in the only chair in her small quarters, her head leaning against the side, her scarred cheek resting on her hand. Melancholy music accompanied her thoughts—the sad, familiar melody causing her to remember a time when she had not paid much attention to the words because she had not understood them. She wished she had listened more closely, heard what the voices were telling her.

"The cadence is less slow, and the fall more certain."

The dance was nearing its end, the pace increasing, growing frantic. . . .

The door to her room slid open silently and Sagan entered, just as silently. The music swelled, the voices were sad, but the regret was mingled with a joy that there had been so much.

The door slid shut. Sagan stood near her, loomed above her. She did not move or look up at him, but only listened. What if youth had never been?

"I know I'm your prisoner, my lord, but you could at least have knocked."

"I heard the music. I didn't want to disturb you."

The Warlord walked over to the computer screen that printed out the title of the piece the person had selected from the ship's music library, but just as he bent down to look, the name flashed out. "What was it?"

"Fauré's 'Pavan'—a 'grave and stately dance.'"

The Warlord moved to stand behind her and placed a hand upon her shoulder. She flinched at his touch, though it was gentle and matched his voice. "If so, my lady, then you must take your final turn upon the floor. For you, the dance is coming to an end."

Maigrey was not surprised, nor was she frightened. She was very tired and only wanted to rest. His hand was warm, a contrast to her chill skin.

"The boy is on his way," Sagan added.

"You've lost him, then, my lord."

Maigrey was surprised he wasn't angrier, but then he'd always been expert at controlling his emotions. She didn't bother to search his mind or she might have been prepared for his next statement.

"No, my lady, though you did your best to warn him. He's on his way to me."

Maigrey raised her head, stared at him. Her movement caused her pale hair to brush across the back of his fingers and he withdrew his hand away from the touch.

"I don't believe you."

"Yes, you do, my lady. We can keep our thoughts hidden from each other, but we can't lie. This shouldn't come as a shock, Maigrey." Sagan rubbed one hand over the other, as if the flesh had been burned. "You should have anticipated it. I did. He is, after all, of the Blood Royal."

Slowly, not taking her eyes from him, Maigrey rose out of her chair and stood, facing him. "A trap! It was all a trap."

"Traps are clumsy. I prefer to think of it as a finesse that, if it succeeds, gives me an extra trick."

"And if it had failed?"

"I still make my bid. You see, Maigrey, if the boy had taken your warning and fled, I had decided that I did not want him anyway."

"The taint in our blood. That's what's in him!" Maigrey began to shiver. Clasping her arms, she huddled within herself, turning away from him. "You've won, seemingly, my lord. If he's who you think he is. Why don't you leave? There's no need to torment me further, I suppose."

Sagan came near her. She could feel the warmth of his body, the heat of his mind. His hand touched her, his thoughts enveloped her, both drew her near.

"Perhaps the dance doesn't need to end. We could be partners again, like we used to be." His breath stirred against her hair; his hands closed, painfully tight, over her flesh. The name of the music she heard in his voice was power, its melody was ambition, its theme—conquest. And the hell of it was that she was enjoying it.

"I am going to the assembly hall to meet him. In one hour,

I shall send for you." Sagan's grip tightened imperceptibly. Maigrey couldn't breathe. He might have had his hands around her throat instead of on her arms. "You will make the identification."

No need to tell him she couldn't. He knew better.

Maigrey hung her head and did not answer. The hands left and took their warmth with them. She thought she heard Sagan over near the computer but she couldn't imagine why. Then the door opened and shut and he was gone. After a moment, music began to play again, something *he'd* programmed. She recognized it—the opening of the second act of Puccini's *Tosca*. Baron Scarpia's voice, rich, smooth, pleased with himself and the world.

"Tosca è un buon falco. Certo a quest'ora i miei segugi le due prede azzannano!"[1]

··◁■ ■▷··

The assembly hall was the largest chamber on *Phoenix*. Located in the very center of the ship, it was used only when the President arrived to address his troops. At other times, it was sealed off. The corridors leading to it were silent and empty. Maigrey's footsteps and those of her guards echoed through it with a hollow sound.

Lighting had been switched to the lowest level possible to conserve energy. Nuke lamps positioned in the ceiling at intervals of about ten meters illuminated circles of about three meters. The remainder of the corridor was in semidarkness, the lights' reflections shining in the metallic walls like small suns.

Maigrey wasn't surprised to see this portion of the ship deserted. Sagan had never been one for public exhortations to the troops to give their all for the fatherland. Under the Warlord's command, a soldier didn't fight and die for some faceless politician and dust-covered rhetoric. A soldier fought and died for his own honor and that of his commander's.

"As he was valiant, I honor him . . ." the quote from Shapespeare's *Julius Caesar* began in her thoughts.

Courage was something you couldn't give a man in a speech but only by example. Sagan was their example. Once, he'd been hers.

---

[1] Tosca is a good guide to our victims. Surely by now my bloodhounds have seized their double prey.

". . . but as he was ambitious, I slew him."

Maigrey hadn't meant to finish the quotation and wished she'd never thought of it. She forced her mind to walk the dark and shadowy corridors of the ship, not those of memory. This meeting would be accompanied by enough ghosts without her bringing along extras.

The guards came to a halt in front of what appeared to be a blank wall. One pressed his palm against a security device and a huge steel panel rumbled open. The gap it created would have admitted an army. Maigrey felt small and abashed walking through it alone and smaller still when she set foot in the vast, windowless, circular chamber.

Hundreds of tiny spotlights positioned high, high above her in the ceiling imitated stars, were reflected off metal walls that had been covered with a dull gold alloy. The domed ceiling was ribbed with bands that rose up from the floor to meet at a circle in the center. The huge room reminded Maigrey of nothing so much as an overturned battle helmet.

At the circle's very top, illuminated by a single bright spotlight, was the seal of the Republic. Directly beneath the seal, on the floor below, stood a dais, and on that dais was a throne, fashioned with the arms and crests of the President. Moving nearer, studying it curiously, Maigrey saw that the dais was operated by hydraulic lifts and could be raised above the heads of the crowd. She guessed that it could also be slowly rotated, so that the President could be seen by all. Maigrey understood more fully than ever why this place was never used. The wonder of it was why Sagan hadn't been able to foresee, years ago, that the revolution would come to nothing but this—empty hallways filled with echoes, a politician's gimmick.

The doors boomed shut and Maigrey, starting nervously, turned to see that she was alone. The centurions had not followed her inside. Sagan, although he had said he would meet her here, was not in the hall, or at least not visible. She felt his presence, but then she always felt his presence now. He could be across the galaxy and she would still feel his presence.

Heat had not been wasted on this vast room. Maigrey shivered in the cold, and to keep her blood stirring and her thoughts from wandering off down forbidden paths, she walked across the floor toward the throne. The walk was a long one; the room's size was immense. She could imagine the boy making this same walk, under the scrutiny of herself and

Derek Sagan. She pitied the young man, but it was a pity that was cool and dispassionate. He had chosen his own end.

Maigrey climbed the dais and, turning, looked out upon the empty chamber. She was forced to admit to herself that she admired the boy. Like Sagan had said, if he'd run, she would have understood, but she would have had no use for him. The taint in the blood. It burned like a fever—in some, not in all. Platus had never been afflicted. He'd tried to purge the boy of it, seemingly. Slowly, hardly realizing what she was doing, her mind on the young man whom she'd seen only briefly and indistinctly through a ring of flame, Maigrey sat down upon the throne.

"Power becomes you, my lady. But, then, it always did."

The voice came from without and from within and drove the hall's chill deep into her bones. Sagan emerged from the shadows of the room's far distant perimeter. He was clad in burnished golden armor; the golden helmet hid his face except for the mouth. A red feathered crest burst like flame from the top of the helmet, his red cape edged in gold and decorated with the phoenix swept the floor behind him. Around his waist, he wore the bloodsword.

Maigrey was clad in the indigo blue robes of the Guardians. The light of the starjewel gleamed like a pale moon on her breast. Around her waist, she wore the bloodsword.

Sagan stood at the foot of the dais, looking up at her. Through the slits in the helm, she could see the starjewel's light glitter in the eyes as if on a blade of steel.

"This was the reason why I let you live that night, Maigrey. Killing you would have been like cutting off my sword arm. I once cursed the mind-link that bound me to you, but I was young then. I didn't understand. We were a power, lady, a force that nothing could stop. Don't you remember, Maigrey? When we were together, we were invincible. The Creator intended it to be so. As proof, He has brought us together again. Will you continue to thwart His will?"

Slowly the life drained from her body. Maigrey couldn't move, couldn't take her eyes from him. His words conjured up the past, brought back hopes and dreams, brought back exultation and victory and pride. Once again it could be like that. She could have it all and more. Join together—Warlord, Warlady. Overthrow this mockery of a government and rule as they'd been born to rule. It would be easy. Nothing had ever defeated them.

Nothing, except themselves.

A small side door, invisible in the metal wall panels, slid open. One of the Honor Guard appeared and saluted, closed fist over his heart.

"The boy is here, my lord."

"At my signal, send him in alone. You and the others take up your posts outside. No one is to disturb us for any reason."

"Yes, my lord."

The centurion disappeared, the panel slid silently shut. Sagan climbed the steps of the dais. Maigrey would have risen to her feet, but she was afraid that if she did so, she would crumble in a heap at the foot of the throne. It took all her courage, all her resolve just to keep sitting there. The Warlord took his place beside her, standing at her right hand.

"My lady?" he questioned silently.

"My lord," she replied without a voice.

Sagan touched a tiny control on his wrist.

The huge doors slowly rumbled open.

Chapter ❖ Twenty-Four

By his shining and his power she knew
him . . .

Mary Renault, *Fire from Heaven*

Stealing the old reconditioned Scimitar and flying it out of the mercenary base was an easy task. No one tried to stop Dion, or even seemed to notice his leaving, for that matter. Fighters were coming and going at all hours of the day and night, running escort for the TRUCs and whatever other functions the war on Vangelis called on them to perform.

Dion ordered the plane's computer to secure him clearance so that his voice wouldn't give him away in case there was anyone in the tower who knew him. The computer did as he commanded. An updated edition of the XJ model, it was extremely polite and subservient and performed its job without comment. The boy thought it boring.

Once outside of the planet's gravitational pull, Dion searched space for the Warlord's ship and couldn't find it. So all the young man's lies and plans had come to this—nothing. He felt a baffling, frustrated disappointment and was just trying to make up his mind to go back to base, tail between his legs, when he caught sight of an officially marked, short-range Scimitar streaking across the starlit darkness. He followed it, hoping it would lead him back to its base.

It did.

Be careful what you wish for.

Dion laughed. What did that old man know? At the age of seventeen, having just discovered he was heir to a galactic empire, the boy felt equal to anything. He was young; he was immortal.

The awesome sight of the Warlord's fleet was the first pin to prick ego's bright bubble.

Dion had never imagined anything so magnificent, so beautiful, so deadly—the gigantic *Phoenix*, its white surface gleaming brightly as a sun. Its escort ships surrounded it, planets basking in the reflected radiance. Heading toward this wondrous sun, flying his reconditioned, shabby Scimitar, Dion wasn't a planet, much less a sun. He was an insignificant dot, a speck of dust.

"I don't belong here. What a fool I am," he murmured to himself, but he didn't turn back. A tractor beam latched onto his ship and pulled him ignominiously toward a destroyer circling the outer perimeter. The tractor beam wasn't necessary. Another force—a force much more powerful than any created by man—was pulling Dion inexorably closer. He hoped, very much, that it was destiny.

Four soldiers were waiting for him when he emerged from his Scimitar. He recognized them by their Roman panoply and red-crested helms—the Warlord's centurions, the ones who had surrounded his house on the night Platus had died. They didn't say a word to him; it seemed—from the stern, impassive look of them—that they didn't intend to waste their breath. On orders from their captain, they formed ranks around Dion and marched him off.

Impressed by them, irritated at himself for being impressed and even a little frightened, the young man lagged behind once to see what would happen. An iron hand clamped painfully over the flesh of his upper arm and a rough but efficient shove kept him moving. Something in the captain's eyes, flicking his direction, told Dion that the man's orders were to get the boy there—in what condition was left entirely up to the captain's discretion. After that, Dion kept in step.

They marched him on board a shuttlecraft that carried them from the destroyer across a vast expanse of space to *Phoenix*. He had a long time to look at the warship. Viewed up close, it was unbelievable—the most colossal object the boy had ever seen.

The shuttle waited in line to dock behind several others which apparently had more important business. What was he, after all, but heir to the galactic throne—a throne that didn't exist? Slumping into a chair, Dion felt his confidence ooze out of him. Guilty thoughts of his gentle, beloved mentor came to him.

Platus knew. He tried to save me from this. He gave his life to keep me away from Derek Sagan. And here I am, running to the very man who murdered him.

Surely Platus would have understood! Surely he must know how important this is to me! No, what am I thinking? Everything he taught me, everything he wanted for me was just to be a simple, good, ordinary man—like himself.

Dion tried once again to summon up his anger over being cheated out of what was rightfully his. But—looking around him at the visible, outward signs of incredible, ruthless power—he was beginning to realize that his anger was the frustrated anger of a little child whose father refuses to allow him to thrust his hand into the fire.

The shuttle docked on *Phoenix* at last. The guards escorted Dion out and marched him into and out of elevators and through a seemingly endless maze of corridors. Not one of the men moving purposefully about glanced at him or paid the slightest bit of attention to him. So much for the king of the galaxy. Dion stumbled and nearly fell. The iron hand propelled him onward. It wasn't defiance now; it was his heart, down around his shoes, tripping him.

The guards led him into a part of the ship that was empty of people. The corridors were cold and lifeless, their silence oppressive. Here, at the end of a passageway, he was met by four more of the Roman-clad centurions. One, whose feathered crest was black in comparison to the others' white crests, gestured to Dion to step forward. The young man did so, his own guards falling behind and to either side. The black-crested guard gripped him by the arm, led him in front of a blank wall, and stood silently, waiting. The guard didn't speak. Dion wasn't even certain the man was breathing.

Beneath his feet, the young man could feel the slight vibrating thrum of the ship's engines. He thought, almost, that if he listened closely enough he might hear them. But that was wishful thinking. The silence dinned and echoed around him. When a small beep went off on the black-crested guard's wrist, Dion nearly climbed up the sheer-sided walls.

The guard placed his hand, palm down, over a security panel. A massive door rumbled aside, revealing a vast, domed, circular chamber. A rush of cold, purified air blew past Dion, ruffling the flaming red-golden hair and drying the chill sweat on his body.

Looking within the hall, he saw—far away—a dais, and on it

what seemed to his dazed and blurred vision to be the embodiments of the moon and the sun.

He looked at the guard.

"In there," the man said—the first words anyone had spoken to Dion in hours.

The young man stepped inside, hoping his legs wouldn't collapse beneath him. The door slid shut behind him. He was alone, except for the two people on the dais, and they only made him feel more alone than he'd ever felt before in his life.

"Come forward," the man said.

Not "Come forward, Your Majesty." Not "Come forward, Your Highness." Just "Come forward."

Dion wondered if he could. He recognized the man: the one who had driven the shining sword through Platus's body. He recognized the woman: the one who had warned him away.

The sun and the moon. He was in the presence of both and he felt their pull on him, felt his blood surge like the tide, his body move in response. It would be very easy, he realized, to take his place in orbit around these two. And he realized in the same instant: But I want them to orbit me.

He walked across the metal floor, his thick boots making an unholy noise that jarred every nerve in his body. There was no help for it but to grit his teeth and end it quickly. When he came to stand before them, in front of the dais, the echoes of his footfalls seemed to linger on long after he'd stopped walking.

Dion looked into the eyes of the woman because he could see her eyes. They drew him and held him. Too late, he discovered that they were peeling him, laying back his flesh in layers, cutting open bone to see the heart and brain beneath. She tore out every secret and held them up to the light of the glittering jewel she wore and examined each carefully. She tucked them back within him and sewed up the gashes, but Dion knew he would always carry the scars, the marks of her probing—like the scar on her face.

He sensed approval and pity, expressed in a small, whispering sigh. The woman did not take her eyes from him, but their scalpel cutting ceased. She passed the knife to the man.

"What is your name?"

"Dion, sir."

The Warlord stepped from the back of the throne where he'd been standing. He made a polite, if chill, gesture toward the woman. "I would introduce Lady Maigrey Morianna. But then, I understand that you two have already met."

Dion flushed. He didn't know what to say. His tongue went stiff. Maigrey smiled at him, her eyes grew warm, and he relaxed cautiously. Apparently he wasn't supposed to say anything.

"I am Lord Derek Sagan. We have *not* met."

Oh, yes, we have, Dion said, but only to himself. Lady Maigrey seemed to understand him, however. He saw one of her eyebrows lift; the smile was sad and shared sympathy. He remembered, then, that Platus had been her brother.

"Who gave you your name?"

It was a startling question. Dion was momentarily confused. "The man who raised me, l-lord." The title came clumsily. He felt reluctant to talk about Platus to his murderer.

"His name?" Sagan's voice was cold and sharp, doing more damage than the woman's gaze, for the man was leaving wounds he obviously didn't intend to close.

Dion swallowed, his throat burned, his tongue was thick and didn't fit inside his mouth. "Platus, my lord. Platus Morianna."

"And what is the derivation of your name?"

Dion blinked at the man, staring stupidly.

"Who were you named for?" Sagan said with a touch of impatience. "Why this particular name?"

"I was named for Dion, ruler of Syracuse in Earth's fourth century B.C., my lord."

"A ruler who was betrayed and assassinated by those who claimed to be his friends. Truly a worthy namesake."

"That wasn't the reason, my lord!" Dion cried, stung to courage. "I was named for him because Dion was the student of Plato and was considered by the philosopher and those of the Academy to be the embodiment of what they considered ideal in a king—"

Dion's voice died. Why had this never occurred to him? This name Platus had given him was a clue to his destiny. He'd never seen it before now. He'd always been too absorbed in his anger over the question of a last name to understand that the first was his answer. Platus hadn't despaired of him or his heritage. The name Platus had given him was his blessing— and his warning.

Memories—the two of them sitting together, reading together, his master's gentle voice expounding, explaining. Tears burned Dion's eyes and he was frightened of them, for he knew Sagan would have no patience with them. He thought of running, flinging himself out from under the cruel knife of the man's gaze. But he knew if he ran away that would be the end. He would always be running, not from the Warlord, for he would no longer care, but from himself.

A bright, cold light—half-seen through a shimmer of tears—caught his gaze. Lady Maigrey had lifted the starjewel in her hand and held it so that it would capture his attention. Its cool, pure radiance eased Dion's grief and pain. His tears could not shame him; if anything, they shamed the man who had caused them.

The drops itched as they dried on his cheeks, but he didn't wipe away the traces.

"Very good," Lord Sagan said in a voice so soft that Dion wondered if he'd heard the words or imagined them. "Lady Maigrey"—the helmed face turned toward the woman—"the night the king died, you and the Guardians stole a baby from the palace at Minas Tares. Whose child was it that you took?"

The starjewel's light was no longer clear and beaming but was suddenly splintered and jagged, refracted. Dion saw the woman's hand tremble and she clasped her fingers around the jewel tightly. The light almost completely disappeared and the hall seemed dark and barren without it.

"The baby was born to Semele, wife of the Crown Prince. The child was a boy." The lady's voice, heard for the first time, was dark and barren as the hall.

"The child, for some reason I will never fathom," Sagan continued, "was given into the care of your brother, Platus Morianna. I presume, my lady, that there was some token you sent with the child so that, in the eventuality that something unforeseen occurred, the Guardians would know the child, the heir to the throne, at a later date?"

Maigrey's answer was inaudible. Dion understood it only by the movement of her lips. "Yes, my lord."

"What was that token, my lady?"

The hand holding the jewel tightened visibly, the knuckles white. Dion, thinking of the sharp points of the star, knew they must be driving into the woman's flesh. He felt them pierce his own flesh as well. Her words, these next few seconds, must irrevocably decide his fate.

Be careful what you wish for.

"A ring of . . . his mother's. There was no other like it,

because I'd had it made especially for her . . . on her wedding."

The Warlord stepped down from the dais and approached the young man. Dion gritted his teeth and concentrated every nerve in his being to hold himself perfectly still. He had forgotten how tall the man was, how massive the body. The golden armor radiated heat and it was truly as if the sun had left the sky. Dion was scorched and dazed and almost sick.

"Do you own a ring that might be this token?"

The baritone voice boomed next to him, coming from the chest, resonating through the golden armor. Dion glanced up once at the face but couldn't keep his gaze on the gleaming helmet and immediately lowered his watering eyes. His hand fumbled inside the collar of his shirt; he scratched himself on the little Scimitar pin that Tusk had given him a lifetime ago. Dion hadn't remembered that he was still wearing it.

The boy drew out the ring, hanging from its silver chain.

Sagan's hand took it and he held it in his palm. Dion flinched away from his touch and involuntarily drew back as much as possible, with the result that he nearly strangled himself.

"Describe the ring, my lady."

"You know what it looks like, Sagan." Maigrey's voice had changed; it was grinding.

"Describe it." His ground against hers. Rock against stone.

"A circlet of flames, done in fire opals and rubies, banded with gold."

Sagan's hand let the ring drop. It struck Dion's chest with a thud and the boy drew a deep and shuddering breath.

The Warlord walked back to the dais, his eyes fixed on the lady. It seemed Dion was forgotten.

Sweat poured off the boy, rolling down his face, obliterating the traces of his tears. His legs were weak and there was a twisting in his bowels. The room tilted, sending him sliding across the floor.

"Sagan!"

The man turned with incredible swiftness and agility. A strong hand gripped Dion by the back of the neck and shoved his head down.

"Take a deep breath. No, keep your head lowered."

Those were the only words Dion heard clearly, but he thought there was something added about "typical" and "fine choice for a king."

Then soft, cool hands were holding him and comforting him.

"He's had a shock. My God, Sagan, how would you have reacted? He's only seventeen."

"When I was seventeen I was commanding a flight squadron. When you were seventeen you fought in the bloody Battle of Shiloh's Sun. *This* one nearly faints in my presence. Your brother has raised us a poet for a king!"

Dion raised his head, he could breathe again. The star's light shone clean and bright in his vision.

A pale and slender hand reached up to touch the ring he wore around his neck. He saw, on the palm, five tiny spots of blood. Maigrey was tall; her gaze was level with his.

"Are you feeling better, Dion?"

"Yes," he managed. "Thank you, my lady."

They stood together in silence, each glancing at the other, and Dion was suddenly aware of a shared consciousness among the three of them, of an unspoken question: *What do we do now?*

Suddenly, Sagan stirred. "I asked you to make a decision, Lady Maigrey, before the young man entered. Do you have an answer for me?"

Her hand lingered on the ring. The opals flashed their blue-orange fire, the rubies their blood-red flame. It was reflected in her eyes—the fire of the ring and the cold light of the starjewel. Maigrey looked into Dion—far, far into him—and once again he felt her approbation and her pity . . . yearning, heart-rending pity.

"Yes, my lord. I have made my decision."

Maigrey let go of the ring gently. She took a step back from the young man, facing him. Her hand went to the scabbard of the bloodsword she wore at her side. With an easy, graceful motion she drew the scabbard from around her waist and, holding it out hilt first toward Dion, she sank to her knees on the metal deck at his feet.

"You are my liege lord. From this day forward, I live only to serve you and those you take under your protection. Accept my sword, that it may defend the innocent in time of war. Accept my sword, that it may stand as a symbol of your strength in time of peace. Accept my sword, my king, and with it accept my honor and my life."

Dion stared, dazed and uncomprehending. He hadn't expected to become a sun quite so soon.

"What do I do?" he whispered.

"Take the damn sword." Sagan was angry, bitterly, lethally angry. Not at Dion, but at the woman who knelt at Dion's feet. "She's a Guardian, after all."

Maigrey kept her eyes on Dion. Her face was solemn and ethereal; the pale hair flowed over her shoulders like the sea he had never seen, it stirred about her in the whispering air. And she knelt before him, at his feet, pledging her protection, her love, her loyalty. Slowly, with a trembling hand, Dion reached to grasp the strange-looking weapon.

"It will not harm you," Lady Maigrey said, thinking, perhaps, that was why he hesitated. "Not while it is sheathed. Be careful, and do not remove the hilt from its scabbard. Do not touch the needles."

Dion didn't understand, but he couldn't ask questions. This wasn't the time to reveal ignorance. He wasn't afraid of the sword. He was reluctant to take it because doing so meant taking the responsibility.

But wasn't that why he'd come?

Dion's fingers closed gingerly around the hilt, carefully avoiding the five razor-sharp needles protruding from it. He nearly dropped the blade. Not from pain. He'd expected it to be heavier and was surprised at its light weight.

Neither of the two watching him said a word, though he saw Maigrey cringe, just slightly, and make a swift movement with her hand that she checked, holding herself back, letting him learn.

Dion fumbled with the weapon and finally managed to get a firm grip with his sweating hands. He remembered hearing stories from Platus about kings of ancient days who knighted subjects by tapping them on each shoulder with the sword's blade. The young man wondered if this ceremony was still appropriate, but he didn't know what else to do and he had to do something. Was it right shoulder first or left, and did it matter? What was he supposed to say? Something resounding and memorable; but all he could think of, as he clumsily and fearfully brought the blade down upon the blue indigo velvet, was, "Thank you, my lady."

Maigrey rose to her feet and took her weapon back, somewhat hurriedly, Dion noticed. She was probably afraid he'd cut off his hand.

"Kings are made, not born," Derek Sagan said. "You will note, young man, that my sword stays at my side."

Dion was stunned, fearful. "Then you don't believe I'm . . . I'm the heir?"

"I believe you're the son of the crown prince, let's put it that way. The lady and I, by the way, are both your cousins—though just what the relationship is I can't begin to explain to you. Had those I trusted long ago not betrayed me, I might have raised you, young man, and then you would truly have been prince of a galaxy. But now—" Sagan shrugged and turned on his heel to leave.

"What are you going to do to me?" Dion knew he sounded like a frightened child, but he couldn't help himself.

Sagan paused and glanced back over his shoulder. "I'm not going to do anything *to* you. I might do something *with* you or *for* you. I haven't decided yet."

He continued walking, his cape billowing out behind him, his anger whipping like a storm wind around him.

Dion felt Maigrey, standing near him, breathe a small sigh.

Sagan halted. Golden flame and red fire, he faced her.

"Enjoy the final set, my lady. For you, the dance is drawing to an end."

He bowed and turned. By some unseen, unspoken command, the doors rumbled open and the Warlord walked through them. The doors did not, however, close after him. They saw him say a word to the guards and gesture toward them with a gloved hand. Then he was gone. The guards took up positions outside the door.

Dion shivered and glanced around, feeling helpless and disheartened. This hadn't turned out as he'd planned. What had he expected? Anything from immediate arrest and execution, he supposed, to sudden adulation and success. What he had was nothing. He hadn't expected nothing.

Oh, sure, now Dion knew who he was, but then he'd known that for a long time, anyway. His one small bit of comfort was Platus's message to him from the grave. But even that was bittersweet. Hope. Hope for what? Hope for a wise, compassionate ruler? Hope for a king who ruled by justice tempered by mercy? Hope for the millions being kicked in the faces by heavy boots? Hope for those ground beneath the wheel of corruption? Yeah, hope—brought to you by a seventeen-year-old orphan who couldn't hold a sword without dropping it.

"What a fool I was to come here! I should have done what

Platus wanted, what he gave his life for. I should have lived my life an ordinary person. That's all I am or ever will be."

Dion spoke bitterly. It was only when the lady answered him that he realized he'd spoken aloud.

"No life is ordinary. Each, no matter how small or insignificant, is a tiny spark of divinity."

Maigrey drew nearer to him. He saw himself suddenly as protected and protector all in one, and felt warmer, better.

"If it is any comfort to you, Dion," she continued, looking at him with grave intensity, "you were drawn here, not by him or by me, but by what you are."

"You mean fate? A Higher Being? Destiny?" Dion shook his head. "I don't believe in that. Platus taught that man is his own destiny, he is free to choose his own path in life."

"My brother was an idealist. We can never have complete freedom to choose what we are or become. We aren't born into a void. We are born to parents in a city in a world on a planet and each of those are links in a chain dragging us through life."

"But the chain can be broken."

"By some, perhaps, but not by us. Not by those known as the Blood Royal. How do you think you came to be, Dion? Did your parents meet and fall in love? No, their DNA met. It was a match discovered beneath a microscope. The matchmaker was a computer. It's how all of us were 'produced.' *Almost* all," Maigrey amended, glancing toward the door. Though Sagan had left them, his presence lingered around them still.

Dion's head throbbed and he put his hands to his aching temples. "Why the hell didn't they just build androids? It would have saved them all a lot of trouble!"

"The spark of divinity, Dion. The spark that can burst into the flame of greatness . . . or a devouring fire. But I shouldn't keep you talking. You're tired and it's cold in here. I'll call the guards, they'll escort you to your quarters."

"Wait! What if I don't want to stay on this ship, my lady? What if I want to go back?"

She looked at him and he saw again the cool pity in her eyes. "It's too late for that now, Dion. Don't blame yourself. I think it was too late from the moment you were born."

"I'm a prisoner, you mean." But if she was right, who was his jailer?

"For a time. You're not what Lord Sagan expected, Dion. I can tell you that much. The reason I know is that he and I . . . our minds are linked. It's difficult to explain—"

Dion nodded. "I know, my lady. The general told me about you, about both of you. General Dixter. John Dixter."

The young man watched the woman out of the corner of his eye, hoping for a reaction, although he had decided that the rumpled, brandy-soaked old man wasn't worthy of her.

No blush crimsoned the lady's pale cheek, no smile touched her lips. She gave no indication that the name held any meaning for her at all. Ice. Flaming ice. Dixter had been right. The warmth Dion'd first felt around her began to seep away.

Maigrey turned from him and gestured. The centurions had left their posts and were marching into the chamber toward them.

"You're his prisoner, too," Dion said, edging near her. "What he said about the dance—that means he's going to execute you, doesn't it, my lady?"

"He can try," Maigrey answered, her gaze on the guards.

Dion was somewhat nonplussed at her coolness, but he forged ahead, lowering his voice. "We could escape . . ."

Maigrey turned, looked at him, the gray eyes smooth and placid and fathoms deep. "We could, Dion. Would you come?"

He started to answer "Yes, of course," but she'd seen inside him, seen his secrets. She held them up before him, one by one, illuminating them in the harsh, brilliant light of the starjewel.

The "yes" wouldn't be spoken; he was ashamed to say the "no" aloud. And so he averted his face from the gray-eyed gaze and said nothing.

"God be with you, Dion."

Coolly bowing her head, Lady Maigrey left him. Her guards fell into step behind her and with her dignity, her regal posture, and the respect the men accorded her, she gave the impression that she was their commander, not their prisoner.

Alone with his own guards—and that was tantamount to being alone, for they didn't even look at him, much less attempt any form of conversation—Dion stood in the huge, round, empty hall.

"At least now I have a name."

Chapter ·◄◊►· Twenty-Five

Even in heaven they don't sing all the time.
Lawrence Ferlinghetti, from *Pictures of the Gone World*

A million dark suns revolved erratically around in Tusk's brain. Suddenly and without warning, they all exploded into fiery life.

"*Good* morning!" sang out XJ. "Rise and shine!"

"Sufferin' Satan! Damn and blast you to hell and back again!" Tusk clutched his head, squinched his eyes shut.

"No swearing!"

The computer turned the lights up to full power and opened the viewport. A flood of blazing sunlight drowned Tusk. Groaning, he staggered to his feet and vanished precipitously into the head.

XJ hummed to itself and lay in wait.

"Where's the kid?" the computer demanded when Tusk reappeared. "You didn't lose him in some game of seventy-eight, did you?"

Tusk fell face-first onto his hammock and lay there wondering if his head was going to remained attached to his neck or just float off into the sky like a balloon. He found himself devoutly hoping it would leave before it exploded.

"I asked you a question!" XJ snapped.

"I'll answer it as soon as I shave the fur off my tongue," Tusk mumbled into the pillow. "Whadaya mean, where's the kid? He went into town with Link."

That didn't sound right, Tusk thought. I should tie a string on my head. Tie the other end around my wrist . . .

"That was yesterday afternoon, you rummy! The kid didn't come home all night. I've been worried sick! You're no help. You stroll in after a hard day at the gaming table boozed to the—"

"Didn't come home?" Tusk sat up, holding onto his head with his hand. Someone was trying to stick a pin into his balloon. "I didn't play cards. I was with Dixter." The explosion sent shattering pain through his throbbing temples. "Dixter! The kid! Sagan!" The mercenary staggered to his feet and headed for the hatch.

"You can't go see the general looking like that!" the computer cried, scandalized. "Put on a shirt! And a pair of— He's gone." XJ sounded disbelieving. "Everybody'll blame *me*, I suppose! Well, it's not my fault he goes around looking like a refugee!"

··◁▭ ▭▷··

"That's as far as I could get, General," Nola Rian said. "The door was sealed shut, from the inside. No one in that factory knows a damn thing except that they went to work one day and there was nothing there. No furniture, no computers, no files—nothing except the electric outlets. You understand, sir, that the people I talked to were the ones who wouldn't be likely to know much about the business—maintainence, groundskeepers. The people who did, the people who knew things— Well, they're gone."

"Gone?"

"Just . . . gone." Nola spread her hands, encompassing empty air. "The business was obviously a front for something else, something really big. I came up with a name. It may or may not mean anything. One of the secretaries had to bring coffee to a meeting of the general managers one day and he heard the name 'Snaga Ohme—'"

"Ohme!" Dixter stared, his heavy eyebrows meeting in a frown.

"Yes, sir. The secretary remembered it because he'd been reading a mag about a party this Ohme fellow had thrown on Laskar. Apparently he's one of the rich and the beautiful."

"One of the rich and the deadly. He's—"

A buzz made Nola start. Dixter depressed a button.

"Tusk's here, sir."

"Thank you, Bennett. Send him in."

The last was unnecessary. Tusk flung open the door. "The kid's gone! He didn't come home—"

"Come in, Tusk, please, and shut the door." Dixter was calm, unperturbed. "You remember Driver Rian?"

"Nola!"

Looking at her, Tusk saw her looking at him and he realized he was standing in General Dixter's office in nothing but a pair of filthy, stinking blue jeans and rope sandals. His hair was uncombed, unwashed, his body was unwashed and half-undressed. His eyes must look like Tison's twin red suns, and Tison's desert sands were in his mouth.

"I'm sorry, sir, I—"

"Sit down, Tusk. Rian, would you please wait in the outer office? This won't take long."

"Yes, sir." Nola rose to her feet. She cast a worried, concerned glance at the mercenary, who was too upset and preoccupied to return it. The door closed behind her.

Tusk slumped into a chair. He couldn't believe Dixter. The general was cleanshaven, uniform clean and no more rumpled than usual. His eyes were clear. His shoulders were hunched, but that seemed to be from a heavy burden he was carrying rather than the effects of yesterday's brandy. The painful throbbing in Tusk's head moved to his heart.

"Sir, I think we should send out patrols—"

Dixter interrupted, raising a hand. "That won't be necessary, Tusk. I know where the boy's gone."

Tusk knew, too, then. He stared at the general in bitter silence. Suddenly, he jumped to his feet and started to leave.

"You couldn't have stopped him."

Tusk whirled around. "I sure as hell could have tried! Sir!" He grabbed for the doorknob, missed, and nearly fell over backward.

Dixter sighed. "Tusk, sit down and listen to me. That's an order."

Tusk didn't know whether to obey or throw the chair through the door. Discipline and his better sense won out. He relapsed into a seat, his face angry and brooding. He kept his eyes on the floor.

"You know how it is, Tusk, to be one of the Blood Royal."

"I'm only half," Tusk muttered, not looking up. "My mother wasn't. My old man never did anything right."

"But you know—"

The mercenary stirred uncomfortably. His head hurt, bad. "Yeah, I had delusions of grandeur. Once. That's why I joined the Air Corps. Got beat out of me real quick."

"Your father tried to stop you from joining, didn't he?"

"That was a helluva lot different, sir!" Tusk lifted his head, glared at the general. "I was going to flight school, not throwing myself into a terminator!"

"You knew your own name, Tusk. You know who you were, who your father was. And, yes, you were going to flight school. You weren't going out to find a throne."

"The only throne that kid's gonna sit on is the kind you flush. Why did you let him go, sir? The woman—Lady Maigrey, if that's who she was—gave him into your trust!" *I* gave him into your trust, Tusk added, but had sense enough not to say aloud.

"No, Maigrey said that if Dion needed help, he could trust me. The boy did. I answered his questions. I told him all I could. But I can't live his life, Tusk, and neither can you. If it's any comfort, I don't believe Sagan will execute the boy. There's something about Dion. He's got 'destiny' stamped in large letters across his forehead."

"But you let him go, sir!"

"Who would you have sent with him? You? Me? Sagan would have terminated both of us, without a moment's thought. You're a deserter for God's sake, Tusk! I'm traitor. Not to mention the fact that Sagan's carrying a grudge against you for swiping the kid out from under his nose in the first place. I think that was another reason the boy went—to protect us. Besides, Dion's not alone. Lady Maigrey's with him."

"Good!" Tusk grunted. "Great! A ghost."

He was still mad, but he didn't feel like he was going to throw things anymore. What Dixter said made sense—or at least Tusk figured it would when the balloons quit bursting in his head. He wasn't mad at the general. He was mad at himself. And at Dion, he thought. Damn fool kid. I let him down. But why'd he have to make me care, anyway?

Dixter's lips parted in a wry smile. "I don't think she's a ghost, Tusk. I think she's with Sagan, probably a prisoner, too."

He *hopes* she's a prisoner, Tusk realized fuzzily. God, that man's hurting. Love. You'd think, after all these centuries, they could have found a cure. He rose unsteadily to his feet.

"I'm sorry, sir, for the way I acted."

"Apology accepted. I understand. I felt like hitting someone myself when I woke up this morning."

Tusk paused, hand on the doorknob that he managed to find this time. "Sir, do you think I can fly my plane now? The

Warlord's got what he was after, and anyway I really don't give a damn. If he wants me, he can come and get me."

"Sure, Tusk, go ahead. This war isn't going to last that much longer. The government's about ready to negotiate. Marek estimates they're losing twenty million on the uranium shipments daily."

"And when it's finished?"

"I've already had offers from three other systems. I'll take the one that's farthest away. There's nothing here for either of us anymore, Tusk."

Reaching up to his left earlobe, Tusk jerked out the earring that was in the shape of an eight-pointed star. He stared at it, fingering it, then stuffed it into the pocket of his blue jeans.

"Yeah," he agreed. "Not a thing!"

Chapter ·──◦◍◎◍◦──· Twenty-Six

> Necessity and chance
> Approach me not, and what I will is fate.
>
> John Milton, *Paradise Lost*

It was ship's night of the day following the day of the meeting with Dion. Maigrey hadn't seen Sagan, she hadn't seen the boy. She'd kept herself apart from both. Going to the library on board *Phoenix*, she returned to her quarters with a book. She had just started to read it—she'd finished about sixty pages—when she came to this passage:

> "'In our course through life we shall meet the people who are coming to meet *us*, from many strange places and by many strange roads . . . and what it is set to us to do to them, and what it is set to them to do to us, will all be done.'"

The words struck Maigrey and chilled her, and she looked back to reread the paragraph with more careful attention.

My lady.

Sagan's thoughts suddenly entered her mind, startling her as much as if he had suddenly entered the room.

My lord. Maigrey closed the book, keeping her fingers between the pages to mark her place, and waited in trepidation. Sagan had spent the night in prayer; she'd sensed his thoughts. She'd spent the night awake, staring into the shadows.

I intend to initiate Dion.

You can't be serious!

I am, and you will assist me, my lady. You should be pleased. It will lengthen the days of your dance.

248

The boy isn't prepared! It takes years of study, training. The thought came to her reluctant and unbidden. *What if he fails?*

I have no choice. The President and the Congress know that he is in my possession.

Captain Nada, she guessed.

Yes. He has just wit enough to serve my purpose. He feeds Robes's paranoia, and a fearful man is a clumsy man. I am close, very close to gaining what I've always sought. I must know completely the will of the Creator in this, my lady, before I make my final move against the leaders of the great and glorious Republic.

The sneer was almost audible.

If you have so little respect for Robes and his principles, why did you join the rebellion? I know you considered our king weak and unfit to rule. I know you believed he had lost his mandate from heaven. But was it—she hesitated. *Did you truly believe the worlds would be better off under a democracy?*

They could hardly have been worse, or so I thought at the time, Sagan replied. *It seems I recall having this conversation before, my lady. Don't you remember?*

No, she didn't remember. They must have talked that night . . . before the killing started. He must have given her some hint, some indication of what he intended to do. He couldn't have concealed his purposes from her. Which meant she must have known, must have condoned and gone along. . . .

Their silences merged and she sensed him thoughtful; sensed, too, the disillusionment that had corroded the once strong, true steel of his ideals.

Yes, my lady, I believed in Peter Robes. You didn't know him then. You considered him beneath you—

That's not true. I didn't like him. I didn't trust him.

It is true. You could never forgive him for being one of us and yet for renouncing us. I believed in his goals, his principles—or what he wanted us to think were his goals and principles. I believed in the people. Pah! Do you know, lady, that in the last election only twenty percent of the citizenry bothered to vote? And those who did elected the candidate who spent the most money to woo them. Never mind that Robes is proven corrupt. Never mind that the once great empire is crumbling into pieces.

Edmund Burke, Sagan continued, *is said to have predicted that the French revolution would lead to a military dictatorship . . . and there was Napoleon, reaching into the ashes to fan destiny's dying spark. I am reaching, my lady, and it is almost within my grasp.*

Maigrey carefully shut the book and lay it down upon her reading table.

And why the boy, my lord? Why this obsession with him?

Isn't it obvious, my lady? To keep sentimental fools like you from raising up another Starfire—another weak king who couldn't decide if he should part his hair in front or behind.

You'll dazzle Dion with power. He'll come to love and respect and honor you; and then you'll betray him just like you betrayed—

Maigrey checked her heedless, headlong rush down a path she'd never meant to take. She drew a quivering breath, wiped a stray tear from her face, and searched for a handkerchief. She never had one; it was some sort of law with her. Finding none, she wedged herself into the tiny bathroom, grabbed a face cloth and doused it in cold water.

You speak easily of betrayal, my lady. It seems to be the one unresolved question between us. Who betrayed whom?

Did I betray you, my lord? Or did I betray my king? Did I know what you planned and keep silent until it was too late? Maigrey sighed and pressed the face cloth to her eyes.

I refuse to help you, Sagan.

I will need three days to prepare myself. You may have that time to prepare the boy for the ceremony. If you've forgotten it—

"Not likely," she said aloud.

—you'll find it on the computer, in my private files. I'll give you access.

I won't—

You will, my lady. Because you're wondering, too.

He was gone.

Maigrey returned to her chair, picked up the book, and opened it. The computer on her desk beeped to life with a message, and she glanced over at it.

"File: Rite. Type CODE and ENTER."

Resolutely, Maigrey ignored it and returned to her book.

". . . 'you may be sure that there are men and women already on their road, who have their business to do with you, and who will do it. Of a certainty they will do it. . . .'"

Yes, they would. Maigrey couldn't stop that. And the boy had better be prepared, he had better know what he could do. *If* he could do it. Besides, she *was* wondering, she had to admit it. Sagan knew her, knew her very well.

Maigrey started to dog-ear the page, thought of the grim and sour-faced ship's librarian who would glare at her, and dog-eared it anyway. Very few people ever checked out the ancient English language texts. She and Sagan were probably the only ones, and then he wasn't very likely to read *Little Dorrit*. It was a long book.

I wonder if I'll live to finish it.

Three days. The words came from her subconscious as if in answer to her question. Why? Why that time? Maigrey paused, considering. Three days. Sagan didn't need three days to prepare himself! Certain ceremonies required a priest to spend hours in fasting and in prayer—especially if one was going from warrior to cleric—but not this one. He was waiting for something, something that would happen in three days. And he was keeping it hidden from her in the very darkest part of his mind.

Going to the computer, Maigrey stared at the screen and then, sighing, reached out and experimentally hit a key and then ENTER. Nothing happened. A true code was required, and it was like Sagan not to tell her what the code was. Of course, it would be something she knew, something only the two of them knew, for it was forbidden that anyone outside the Blood Royal should have knowledge of the mysteries.

It needed little prompting for her to remember the words, but a great measure of strength to type them, to give them life. She could have said them aloud. That, however, would have been to give them a soul. Her fingers were stiff and fumbled at the keys.

"Two togeher must walk the paths of darkness before they reach the light."

She hit ENTER hurriedly, wanting to see them vanish. Nothing happened.

Maigrey bit her lip and forced herself to reread them carefully. This *had* to be the code he would select.

There it was, a stupid mistake.

She added the *t* in *together*. Hit ENTER.

The screen blanked out and then filled with words. She assumed they were words. All she could see, for long moments, was a shining blur.

··◆■ ■▶··

"An initiation rite, my lady?" Dion appeared dubious. "Isn't that sort of . . . silly?"

Maigrey shook her head. "Lord Sagan isn't talking about a frat party. This is serious. Deadly serious."

Dion looked alarmed at her tone, but Maigrey did nothing to soften it. She wanted him to be scared. Scared as hell.

The two were together in the empty diplomat lounge. Maigrey had gone back to watching the ever-shifting, ever-same magnificence of the universe and she had brought Dion with her. The lounge was cold and almost devoid of furniture—just a few chairs that looked as if they'd been cut out of a circle, then the halves turned upside down and stacked on top of each other. Sitting in one of these, her arms resting on the high sides, Maigrey stared at the stars glittering in the deep blackness and pondered her words.

Dion, sitting in a chair across from her, found his gaze drawn irresistibly to the scar on her face. It seemed to him that when the flesh had knit to close the wound, it had caught up the soul and bound it in as well. The face might try to hide her thoughts, her emotions, but they were clearly visible in the scar. He could see her blood rise and fall in it, see the pulse of her heartbeat. He knew he shouldn't be staring. It was impolite. But he couldn't help it. When she turned her eyes upon him, suddenly, he flushed and made believe he had been looking with intense interest at one of the centurions, standing in the doorway.

Maigrey's hand moved unconsciously to touch the scar that sometimes ached with an unbearable pain.

"The initiation rites began years ago as a test—"

"A test?" Dion bounded to his feet. "Lord Sagan doesn't believe me, does he, my lady? He doesn't believe who I am—"

"Sit down, Dion. And allow me to finish."

Flushing more hotly, shamed by the cool rebuke in her tone, the young man subsided, sitting back in his chair.

"During the second Dark Ages that occurred in the early twenty-first century, the intelligentsia saw only two beacons of light in the future of mankind—space travel, whereby they could escape the repressive governments, and genetic tampering, whereby they could create their own superhuman leaders to come back and take control. Over future generations, they proved successful in achieving both goals.

"But when the process of genetic improvements began, the repressors tried to imitate it, tried to create their own superhumans for their own purposes. The scientists had foreseen this and reacted to keep the process under control. They developed tests that enabled them to determine who was one of the Blood Royal and who was, so to speak, a cheap imitation."

Dion stirred restlessly, scowling, and Maigrey paused a moment to study him. She knew well enough what he was thinking and he would have his answer. He had to learn to be patient. But it wasn't that which drew her notice. It was the cobalt blue eyes, the flaming red-golden hair that tumbled about the face like a lion's mane, the crease between the feathery reddish brown brows, the high forehead and cheekbones, the sensually curving lips. Looking into his face was to look into the face of another, the face of her one, dear, true friend. Maigrey seemed to see that face against a backdrop of flame and horror. . . .

Swiftly, she looked away.

"As time went by, and the process of genetic altering evolved, the Blood Royal began to control itself. They wanted to keep their line pure. Marriages were arranged only after the most rigorous computer searches. A man who was weak in certain areas sought a woman who made up for them. Occasionally, of course, this didn't work. The divine spark, as I said.

"By this time, the test had become a part of the culture of the Blood Royal, getting mixed up along the way with rites of passage and bar mitzvahs and eventually, in some parts of the galaxy, the test lost all of its original intent. About this time, the Order of Adamant began its rise to power.

"The Blood Royal were designed to be rulers, but no one foresaw that they would become rulers of the soul as well as the body. Charismatic, strong, and powerful, the priests and priestesses of the Order of Adamant spread the worship of the Creator throughout the galaxy.

"They brought continuity and conformity into the lives of people of varying cultures, particularly into the lives of the Blood Royal, who were often called upon to leave one world and marry into another that was vastly different. Religion was often the only thing the wedded couple had in common.

"The old test became one of the first rituals to be taken over by the Order. They standardized it and added their own touches, so that, in the time of your uncle, the king"—Maigrey added that little touch to calm the boy and subtly remind him again of the serious nature of what she was saying—"the test had become a true rite of passage, a solemn ceremony that was often attended by prophecies and . . . and such like."

Maigrey coughed and cleared her throat. One of the guards, with quiet efficiency, brought her a glass of water.

"Thank you," she said, smiling at the guard.

The centurion, from his expression, took that smile as a gift. Dion knew how he felt. Cold and proud and strong, the woman seemed at the same time vulnerable and fragile. The boy longed with every fiber of his being to comfort her sorrow, protect her from danger. Yet the idea of putting his arm around her, of touching her seemed appalling, irreverent. He would have as soon embraced a . . . comet. The young man was consumed more by the impulse to offer his body to her as a living shield, to throw himself between her and whatever threatened her. Dion saw on the face of the centurion that same desire. And Maigrey had probably never spoken five words altogether to the man.

Before Dion knew quite what he was doing, he was out of his chair and down on his knees beside her.

"My lady, you're so unhappy! Let me— Tell me what I can do—"

Maigrey smiled at him. Then her lips tightened, the scar flamed red. Reaching out, she took hold of his jaw in her hand and gripped it tightly. Her nails cut his flesh. She turned his face to hers.

"Look within yourself, Dion! What you are experiencing is the power of the Blood Royal. Someday, the way you feel about me is the way other people will feel about you."

She shoved him backward, away from her, and curled up in her chair, brooding.

Catching his balance, Dion rubbed his stinging skin and stared at her. He was half-angry. He'd been brutally rebuffed, his pride had been hurt. He wasn't certain he understood her words. Maigrey didn't glance at him, but sat wrapped in a shroud of dark and bitter silence. Slowly, Dion rose to his feet and made his way back to his chair. He sat down and, drawing back his hand from his chin, saw blood on his fingers.

"So," Maigrey said abruptly, "that is why Sagan wants you to undergo the rite."

"What's it like? What happens?"

"I can't tell you. It's a secret, sacred to God. A curse is said to fall on those who reveal it." Noticing his exasperated frown, Maigrey added, "I can tell you this much: Often the Creator will speak to the priest or give some sign of His will and intent for the life that comes before Him. This is what Sagan's hoping for, I believe."

"The Creator's will," Dion muttered, wiping the blood on his pant leg, hoping she didn't notice. "I can't believe in some myth." He kept his face averted from her, rubbing his hand back and forth along his jaw where he could feel the scraping stubble of a beard whose golden color rendered it invisible to all eyes but his. "What about me? What about what I want? My own will? You and Sagan seem to think I haven't got one."

"You have a will of your own, Dion. But that doesn't negate the fact that there is another Will, a Higher Power which says 'You can be more than you are. I know, for I made you.' Often the two struggle together—every child rebels against his parent and the struggle is good, for it's only in questioning and pushing and testing our own limits that we come to know ourselves, that we become strong. And we can fight against it all we want, but there comes a time when man must bow his head and say to God, 'Not my will, but thine, be done.'"

"So how do you know which is which?"

"I think, eventually, we come to know." Maigrey sighed and looked far away, into another part of the ship, into another heart. "It is for those who know and who continue the fight that the struggle becomes bitter.

"We like to see ourselves as suns," she added, speaking almost to herself. "We want to be worshiped as life-givers, feared as destroyers. But though each sun possesses an immense, fiery radiance, its light eventually fades over distance and time, and all of the stars together are powerless to illuminate the vast and empty darkness."

Nevertheless, whispered like an echo in Dion's ears, *not my will, but thine, be done.*

Chapter ·◆◦◯◦◆· Twenty-Seven

Lachende Löwen müssen kommen.
Friedrich Nietzsche, *Die Bergrüssung*

As Maigrey had told Dion, the struggle between knowing the will of God and submitting to the will of God was a bitter one. Sagan had followed his Lord's commands because they coincided with his own desires. Now, he was beginning to see that there might be a clash of wills. The Warlord claimed to want to know the mind of God. In reality, he feared he knew and sought to change it.

When Derek Sagan had completed his mental conversation with the lady, he summoned the captain of his personal guard.

"When I shut this door"—the Warlord indicated the outer door that led to his chambers—"no one is to pass. No one. For any reason."

"Very good, my lord."

"Any messages, no matter how urgent, are to be delivered to you. You will deliver them to me when I ask for them."

"Yes, my lord." The centurion saluted, fist over his heart.

Sagan caused the door to slide closed and sealed it from the inside. He shut his computer down, switched off all communications and signaling devices. He took off his armor, packed the bloodsword away.

There was, in the Warlord's quarters, a secret chamber that, if Captain Nada had known of its existence, would have gained him enormous credit with President Robes and ended the career and undoubtedly the life of Warlord Derek Sagan. It was a small, private chapel, and no one, not even Admiral Aks, was aware of its existence. Those who had supervised its construction believed they were building a vault to hold the wealth of solar systems. So it did, but it was a wealth that had

256

been collected over the centuries and had nothing to do with gold.

His body stripped naked, Sagan entered the chamber through a door that was activated by a security device which functioned similarly to the bloodsword. When the palm was placed on five needles protruding from the pad, a virus identical to the one in the sword was injected into the bloodstream. It flowed harmlessly through Sagan's body. Had it entered any other body—Captain Nada's body, for example—the captain would have been writhing on the deck in extreme agony.

Entering the vault, Sagan caused the door to shut and seal behind him. Certain it was secure, he approached an altar made of a block of obsidian that had been left rough on the sides and was ground smooth to a polished finish on top. It was pitch dark inside the vault; no artificial light was permitted to shine on the sacrosanct. Sagan needed no light to see what was before him. A small dish holding rare and costly perfumed oil, a silver chalice decorated with eight-pointed stars, and a silver dagger whose hilt was an eight-pointed star were arranged on top of the altar. Folded neatly beneath it were robes made of the finest black velvet—a priest-father's only legacy to his bastard son.

Standing before the altar, Sagan raised his hands and invoked God. He dressed himself in the robes, kissing the cloth reverently before he put them on as he had been taught. Kneeling upon a black silken cushion fringed with gold, the emblem of the phoenix embroidered on it in threads of gold and crimson, he struck a match and lit the oil. A blue and yellow flame illuminated the dark chapel, filling the air with the heady fragrance of incense.

Sagan stared into the flame long moments, composing his mind. Then he shoved back the sleeve of his left arm, revealing the muscular, sinew-lined wrist and forearm. The smooth skin, always hidden by gauntlets, was marked with numerous ugly scars, all of the same peculiar nature. Long ago, these scars had been the marks of the priests and priestesses of the Order of Adamant. Now they were marks of death, for that order was outlawed and anyone found with these telltale scars was swiftly and summarily executed.

Sliding his fingers through the openings left between the points of the star that was its hilt, Sagan grasped the dagger with his right hand and, with a swift, deft motion, slashed open the flesh of his left arm. Blood flowed, pumped from the heart. The Warlord held his arm over the chalice. The flame's unwavering light glistened off the pulsating liquid dripping into the cup. When the chalice was full, Derek placed his wounded arm in the fire and whispered a prayer, his lips pressed tightly together to keep from crying out with the pain. The fire seared the flesh, sealing the cut; the bleeding ceased.

Light-headed from blood loss and the agony of the burn, Derek leaned his elbows on the altar for support, lifted his head, and commenced his argument with God.

··◄■ ■►··

Dion was confined to his quarters, not by any orders of the Warlord's, but on Maigrey's recommendation that he take this time to meditate and think and try to resolve the turmoil in his soul. The young man lay on his bed and stared up at the underside of the metal deck above his head.

He wished he had his syntharp, but it was aboard Tusk's spaceplane. The young man'd had no choice but to leave it behind. Dion tried to listen to the ship's music, but it was Platus's music he heard, and that made him feel angry and then guilty because he felt angry. He finally shut it off and listened to the silence that wasn't silence in the gigantic battle cruiser but a composite of sounds blended together into white noise which was, he discovered, oddly soothing.

Lying on the bed, Dion wrestled with questions: Who am I? Why am I here? Where am I going? Does Someone know for certain or I am drifting in chaos?

"Mankind has pondered these questions for centuries. I'm supposed to answer them in three days?" Dion asked a light fixture.

The light fixture provided only its own brand of illumination, nothing beyond. Lady Maigrey had been no help either.

"You have to find the answer yourself, Dion. I can't tell you what to believe."

"Platus told me what *not* to believe," the boy countered.

"Did he? Or did he ask you to study, to question, to seek the truth? Instead of seeking it, perhaps you decided that it didn't exist."

Dion recalled the hours he and Platus had spent reading the Koran, the Bible, the writings of Buddha. And then there'd been Thomas Aquinas, Jean-Paul Sartre, Descartes, Schopenhauer, Nietzsche. Yes, he realized, they'd been searching for truth—the teacher as much as the pupil.

Alone in the humming silence, Dion thought he was beginning at last to come to know Platus and, as he did so, his anger started to die. The Guardian had done what he'd thought was right. After all the horror he'd seen, after the tragedy he'd faced, could Platus be blamed for losing his faith? Dion wondered if now, after death, Platus had discovered that for which he was searching.

··◁■ ■▷··

The days passed. Sagan struggled with God, Dion searched for God. Maigrey pointedly ignored Him. He'd brought her here for no purpose other than to torment her. He was allowing the kind and innocent people of Oha-Lau to suffer beneath the lash. He'd dropped the boy right into the palm of Sagan's hand.

She possessed all the touted mystical powers of the Blood Royal—the mental gifts that made locked doors a mockery, guards laughable. She could walk out that door—hell, she could walk *through* that door—this instant and no one except Derek Sagan could stop her. And he was, she knew, completely preoccupied, locked in battle with a redoubtable foe—her foe. The Foe that had given her the means to escape a prison of steel and then chained her to the walls with a silken thread. She could batter down the steel doors, she could flee *Phoenix*, flee this solar system, flee the galaxy, but the thread would be impossible to break. It was wound around her soul.

Maigrey continued reading *Little Dorrit*.

··◁■ ■▷··

For others do I wait . . . for higher ones, stronger ones: . . . laughing lions must come!

The words were disjointed, no longer made sense. Laughing lions. Dion flung Nietzsche across the room. He'd had enough. He showered and dressed himself in an Air Corps pilot's uniform Sagan had sent to him to replace his faded blue jeans. The young man dragged a comb through the tangled mane of flaming red-golden hair; having no patience with the snarls, he yanked them out, though it brought tears to his eyes. He smoothed minute wrinkles from the high-collared, black, red-trimmed uniform. Its impeccable tailoring accentuated his height and his lithe, muscular form. Dion studied himself in the mirror and decided that, when all was said and done, he looked like a king. Going to the door, he slammed his hand hard on the control. The panel slid open and he sprang out swiftly, hoping to startle the guards who were standing at relaxed attention on either side.

Beyond a flicker of the eyelid and the glance of the eyeball his direction, neither man moved a muscle. Dion wondered what *would* make them respond. The detonation of a nuclear warhead right in front of them, he decided, or the sudden appearance of the Warlord.

"I suppose," the young man said, shaking back the flame-red hair out of his face, "that there is some sort of recreation lounge on board?"

"Several," the guard answered. He did not, Dion noticed, say "my lord" or "sir" or even "young sir." The young man might have put such a lack of respect down to the fact that he was a prisoner, except that Lady Maigrey was always "my lady," spoken with almost the same inflection of near reverence that the men accorded to Lord Sagan.

Dion chafed against his youth and inexperience, but Platus's teaching had taught him enough to realize that such respect must be earned and could not be dictated. Swallowing his resentment, he clarified. "A bar?"

The guard raised an eyebrow and glanced at his fellow. Dion felt a moment's elation. At last he'd gained a response—even if it was only surprise.

"I want to go there," he said before the surprise wore off. "I believe Lord Sagan gave orders that I am to have complete freedom of the ship, provided, of course, that you accompany me."

One of the guards spoke into a commlink. The answer came back almost instantly. "Lord Sagan has left orders not to be disturbed."

"Come on," Dion urged. "What can it hurt? It's not like I want to visit some classified or restricted area. I'm seventeen. I've been to bars before."

Well, he'd been to *one* bar. Link had taken him (making him swear never to tell Tusk). The place was noisy and smoky, dark, confusing, and exciting—all of which sounded quite soothing to Dion now.

"The Warlord did say the kid could go where he chose."

"I can't see any harm in it. You stay with him. I'll go file our daily."

"Okay, kid. This way." The centurion indicated that Dion was to turn to his left, and the two proceeded down the corridor.

"What's your name?" Dion asked the guard.

The centurion appeared reluctant to answer.

"You can at least tell me your name. It gets . . . lonely . . . sometimes." Dion hadn't meant to admit to that, felt his cheeks burn.

"Marcus. My name is Marcus."

Pleased that he'd made a dent in the armor, Dion glanced around at the man. "That name's Roman, isn't it?"

"All of those chosen to be centurions have names of Roman origin. Lord Sagan awards them to us when we are accepted into the Honor Guard."

"I notice you're wearing a Scimitar pin. Were you a pilot?"

"I still am." Marcus appeared amazed that Dion could ask such an inane question. "All Lord Sagan's personal guard are seasoned pilots. The best in the fleet." He spoke with the quiet, unconscious pride of men who know they don't have to boast about their achievements.

Dion began to realize that these men performed menial tasks—such as escorting a prisoner to a bar—without complaint because they knew that at a moment's notice they might be called to escort their commander to glorious victory.

The full implication of what Sagan had accomplished struck Dion with such force he nearly stumbled over his feet. The Warlord had provided himself with his own personal army—an army that was intensely loyal to him and him alone. The hell with the President. Damn the Congress. To the devil with the Republic. These men were Sagan's, body and soul.

"In here." The centurion touched the young man's arm. Dion had been walking along in a dazed fog.

Numerous recreation lounges on board the *Phoenix* helped combat the long hours of boredom when off-duty—the quiet hours that were more deadly to a soldier's morale than the most terrifying bombardment. Gaming lounges, vid lounges, and gymnasiums with swimming pools provided recreation for the body and the senses. The library and classrooms—where qualified professors taught everything from alien thought and philosophy to military history to playing the synthesizer to transferring the magnificent panoramas of space to canvas using paint and brush—provided recreation for the mind.

All these were popular—mainly because they were places where a man didn't *have* to be. In addition, there were the bars. Ever since the days of Admiral Nelson, the "rum ration" had been considered essential to the morale of the naval fleet. These days rum had been replaced by hundreds of other far more exotic concoctions. A computer kept track of what each man drank and how much. Any hint of alcohol addiction and the crew member found himself under the none too gentle care of Dr. Giesk.

Dion entered the bar, pausing a moment to allow his eyes to adjust to the dim lighting after the glare of the corridor. All noises of the ship were suddenly left behind, replaced by soft, nerve-soothing music.

The bar was comfortable, inviting, designed for talking and relaxing. Stuffed couches arranged in semicircles undulated in mauve waves throughout the room. Indistinct and shadowy forms talked quietly, erupted into sudden laughter. Glasses clinked on the tables, cool air fragrant with artificial smells of anything but the antiseptic smell of the working part of the ship wafted from unseen vents. Dion stood in the doorway, looking around and feeling suddenly homesick for Tusk and Link and his other friends. He was unaware that he was beginning to attract attention until the talking and the laughter and the glass clinking ceased.

The bar suddenly grew quiet, except for the soft whoosh of air, and everyone in the place stared at him.

Dion had been the subject of rumor for a week: the search for him, his eventual surrender, his dramatic meeting with the Warlord and the Lady Maigrey. The young man should have felt intimidated by the staring eyes—the eyes that met his, then slid away to look knowingly into other eyes, the eyes that were skeptical or curious or laughing. The young man should have felt shy, awkward, embarrassed, perhaps even angry. Dion didn't feel any of this. A tingling sensation spread from his fingertips through his arms, pulsed from his heart to the rest of his body. He could scarcely breathe for the excitement.

Dion didn't need to drink liquor. He was tasting a stronger, more addicting wine—power. He breathed it in and sucked it up. He stood there a long time, saying nothing, meeting the eyes, drawing them to him, feeding off them. It was exhilarating, like the first time he flew the Scimitar.

The spark of divinity—flame or devouring fire.

Without saying a word, Dion turned and left the bar. Marcus glanced at the bartender and shrugged.

"Kids!"

··◁═ ═▷··

The ship's bells chimed the watches and three days came to an end at last.

Derek Sagan emerged from the chapel. He'd spent the entire time in the tiny altar room. Nothing but water had passed his lips, and that sparingly. He'd slept on the bare, chill metal of the deck. He was gaunt and grim and looked as if he'd fought all the legions of heaven.

He bathed and broke his fast. Putting on his armor and a pair of gauntlets—hiding the old scars and the new—he concealed his ravaged face behind the cold metal of his helmet and unsealed the door.

"Send for your captain," he ordered the man standing guard-duty outside.

The captain entered, fist over his heart.

"*Ave atque vale,*[1] my lord."

"And to you, Captain." Sagan returned the salute. "You bring a message."

"I do, my lord." The captain paused. He did not understand what he was saying—it was in an archaic language. He had committed it to memory phonetically and he needed to be certain in his mind he had it absolutely correct.

"'The blood-dimmed tide is loosed.'"

Actually it came across more as "ze blud-dmmmmd tid iz luuzed" but Sagan understood the garbled words of the line from Yeats's poem *The Second Coming*. He knew who had sent it; he knew what it meant.

"Satisfactory, Captain. When it is 2300 hours, bring Lady Maigrey and the boy, Dion, to my chambers. Request Admiral Aks to report to me now."

"Yes, my lord."

The captain left upon his assignment. Derek Sagan poured himself a glass of water and raised it in salute to the door of the chapel.

"I am well on my way to victory. Any further argument?"

[1]"Hail and be well." Ancient Roman salute.

·◁ ▷·

Alone in her room, Maigrey finished *Little Dorrit*:

They went quietly down into the roaring streets,
inseparable and blessed; and as they passed along in
sunshine and shade, the noisy and the eager, and the
arrogant and the froward and the vain, fretted and chafed,
and made their usual uproar.

Chapter ◄◗◍◗► Twenty-Eight

> In vain man's expectations;
> God brings the unthought to be,
> As here we see.
>
> Euripedes, *The Bacchae*

Maigrey's guards escorted her to the double doors decorated with the phoenix rising from the flames that guarded the chambers of the Warlord. The centurion standing outside the doors spoke a few words into a commlink set into the wall, and Maigrey heard the harsh answer, "Let her enter."

The guard started to push open the door, but Maigrey halted him. "Wait," she murmured. She smoothed the folds of indigo blue velvet, adjusted the cowl over her hair. The centurion would think, no doubt, that she was preparing herself to be ushered into the presence of the lord. Maigrey wasn't; she was stalling. She didn't want to enter his room, his private chambers, his sanctum. It would be *him*. All *him*, all memories, and she didn't think she could bear it.

But what am I going to do? she thought. Stand here in the corridor, looking like an idiot? If I don't walk in there, he's beaten me. How do I expect to defeat him, destroy him if I can't summon the courage to walk into his bedroom?

Lifting her chin, disguising her fear beneath an imperious air, she stepped toward the door, and the guard—caught by surprise at her sudden movement—hastened to open it for her.

I would know this room anywhere, Maigrey reflected. If I were set down upon a strange world and entered these chambers, I would know them for his.

There were the same familiar objects, objects she had forgotten, yet if they'd been missing she would have noted their absence. The collection of Roman artifacts—armor,

265

swords and daggers, shields. An ancient helmet, a broken sandal worn by some long-dead plebeian, a statue of Apollo Loxias, the god of the longsight. There were no new additions to his collection, which Maigrey found odd and foreboding. He paid homage to his past, but was not bringing it into his present . . . or his future.

The furnishings were more numerous and more luxurious than he'd been able to afford when she'd known him. But they were in the same style, arranged in the same way with taste and simplicity. Had Maigrey been blind, she could have walked around this room without hesitation. She knew where everything was; everything was in its place. She could have sat down in a chair and wept.

Instead, she clasped her ice-cold hands together and took a step forward. A robed figure emerged from behind a plain black screen.

"You kept . . . that?" Maigrey stared.

Sagan was dressed in black robes, his father's robes. His head was bare; the cowl rested on his shoulders. He wore his long black hair loose; it fell in heavy, gray-streaked waves to his shoulders, curling slightly at the ends. He looked older, more haggard without the strong shielding of the armor. Maigrey glanced at the dark, cold eyes, then looked involuntarily at his wrist, knowing what she would see and seeing it, she swiftly averted her gaze. The sight of the new scar unnerved her. He was still practicing his faith. Somehow, she had presumed that following the revolution, he would have renounced it, as he had renounced everything else he had once believed in. The past, apparently, *was* intruding upon the future.

"Come this way, my lady."

With an abrupt, commanding gesture, Sagan beckoned her around behind the screen.

Drawing a deep breath, Maigrey followed him. The screen hid from view a large open area. This part of the chamber had been cleared of all furniture except a long metal table covered with a black cloth marked at each corner by a silver eight-pointed star. Another black cloth shrouded several objects in the table's center. Tall, thick, beeswax candles stood in silver candle holders at either end. Lifting the black cloth, Sagan allowed Maigrey to see the objects beneath it.

"Is it all correct, my lady? Is it as you remember?"

Yes, it is as I remember. Their own investiture came back to her clearly. The two of them, because of the mind-link, had gone through the ordeal together. The voice of the priest, Sagan's father, had reverberated around her, around the room. It had been the first time he'd spoken since he took the vow of silence—an act of penitence for his great sin. It was to be the last time anyone would ever hear him speak:

Two together must walk the paths of darkness before they reach the light.

Maigrey pressed her hand over her mouth. She couldn't read Sagan's thoughts; they were heavily shielded, and she hoped he couldn't read hers. Not that it mattered; he could undoubtedly see the pain on her face.

"My lady?"

His impatient voice came from a great distance, through a thick and blinding mist.

"Yes, it's all correct."

She tried to say the words but the mist was too thick, robbing her of breath, of strength, of sanity. It was billowing, blinding, suffocating, and she was sinking beneath it when she felt him near her, felt his hand upon her arm, steadying her.

His voice was in her ear, his breath warm and moist on her skin. "When this rite is ended, so is your usefulness to me. You will not know when, for I will not give you opportunity to thwart me, but sometime soon, rest assured, my lady, I will come for you."

Maigrey tensed; anger and excitement and the need to keep her plans hidden from him burned away the mists. She wasn't succeeding well. He gazed at her, amused.

"You're going to fight me, aren't you, my lady?"

"You'd be disappointed in me if I didn't, wouldn't you, my lord?"

Calm and composed again, she glided away from his touch and saw a smile flicker across the thin, stern lips.

You challenged me deliberately! She marveled. Neither spoke, except in their minds. *To give me back my courage! Yet you could kill me now, without a moment's hesitation. You hate me that much. Or is it me? No, not me but what I remind you of, what I am to you. Your past, our past. And more than that—the future. A future that was bright and glorious and full of promise. Now it's bitter and dark and stained with blood. By erasing me, you erase all that and, with the boy, you once again have youth and hope.*

You were always a romantic, my lady. You should have listened to the prophecy. There was nothing in our future except darkness, betrayal, death. By ridding myself of you, Maigrey, I rid myself of the one person who possesses the power and the understanding necessary to stop me. It is that simple.

That simple? Then why the doubt, why the confusion? I see your mind, my lord, and your purpose is not clear. Something clouds it, casts a shadow over it—

Sagan turned from her abruptly. The chain of thought severed, leaving behind a bleak emptiness. Maigrey remembered the sensation. It had always occurred when they broke the close mental contact between them. Even if they had been miles and miles apart, they both felt as if a chill wind were roaring through the hollow tunnel of their minds. Each was forced to concentrate a moment, force each one's own soul to move back in to fill the void.

This had not happened to them since the mind-link had been reforged. It only indicated how strong the link had grown—despite themselves.

"My lady?" He wondered if she was ready.

"My lord." As ready as she'd ever be.

··◅ ▻··

The clock's digital readout lacked a few minutes of 2300. Dion sat nervously in a chair, staring at the computer chess game he'd started days ago and never gone beyond three moves. When the knock came at his door—the knock he'd been expecting ever since he'd received Sagan's message— Dion didn't move but stared at the screen, brow furrowed in concentration as if he had nothing on his mind except his gambit.

The knock was not repeated. The hatch slid open; Sagan's centurions had no intention of bringing their charge late.

"It's time."

The centurion who spoke was Marcus. Dion would have greeted him by name, but the soldier's face was stern, forbidding any attempt at familiarity.

His mouth dry, his hands wet, the young man rose to his feet, nearly overturning the chair in his nervousness. It had been a foolish thing to do, he realized—sitting there for over two hours speculating, guessing, imagining, trying to recall if Platus had ever dropped one tiny hint about this ritual. Now

I'm stretched taut as a string on Platus's old harp. If someone touches me the wrong way, I'll snap.

Marcus eyed him with cool curiosity. Dion did not know, but the centurions had themselves been speculating what the Warlord wanted with the young man at this hour of the night. Everyone on board ship knew who Dion was, by now. They knew he was the heir to a throne stained in blood. They knew he was wanted by the President and Congress. They knew—or thought they did—that he might very well face execution unless he renounced his birthright. Perhaps Lord Sagan was going to discuss that issue with the boy right now. A "discussion" with the Warlord was rarely pleasant—he could make a man renounce the fact that he was a man at all. It was even money among the crew that—when they saw this young man again—Dion would be lucky to remember his name, much less the fact that he was king.

The ride up the Warlord's private elevator was accomplished in silence broken only by the soft hissing of life-support and the almost inaudible whoosh of the hydraulics. The centurions escorted Dion to the golden double doors decorated with a blazing phoenix and turned, silently, to leave him.

"But—what?" Dion felt helpless, paralyzed. He could barely force words from his parched throat.

"You are to enter alone," Marcus said, from the shadows. "Go ahead. The door will open. You are expected."

Dion heard the words as ominous, whether the man intended them to be or not. He hesitated and the thought came into his mind that he could turn and run and no one would stop him. And he realized, at the same moment, that this was Part I of the test. Raising a shaking hand, he pushed on the door and it slid silently open.

Dion stepped forward and was almost immediately blind, swallowed up by darkness. The door shut behind him. He held still, afraid to move until he could see, not wanting to impair his dignity by bumping into something. Listening, he heard a soft sigh and the rustle of smooth cloth and he knew Maigrey was here. She did not wear the starjewel. Perhaps its light was considered intrusive.

Within the thick blackness, a darker, heavier shape moved—the Warlord. "Stretch out your hand."

Dion did so, hesitantly.

"You feel the cloth at your fingertips?"

Groping, Dion found it—some sort of coarsely woven fabric.

"Strip off your clothes, drape that over your body."

Flushing in embarrassment, despite the darkness, Dion did as he was commanded, struggling with folds of the fabric, trying to figure out how it was worn. At last he found an opening he figured was for his head. He slipped it on and the crude robe fell over his shoulders and touched the floor. It left his arms bare and he shivered in the room's icy chill. The fabric was like rope. It itched and, when he moved, scratched irritably against his skin.

A strange scent made Dion's nose tickle. Incense. He was afraid for one panicked moment that he might sneeze. Rubbing his nose with his hand, he prevented it.

A candle flared. Above it, Dion saw Sagan's face clearly for the first time. Queasy fear gripped the young man's bowels. The metal mask of the helmet had been cold and impersonal and unfeeling, but that was natural. He had assumed that the face beneath it was warm and alive.

He had assumed wrong.

Holding the candle in one hand, the Warlord lifted the cowl and covered his head. His face vanished beneath the fabric that seemed made of woven night.

Dion started to speak, to stammer out some sort of greeting, but Maigrey, moving into the candlelight so that she might be seen, made a slight negating gesture with her hand and shook her head.

"Do not speak, Dion." Her voice was soft and low. The pale hair, lying on her shoulders, was white and cold as moonlight. "Your thoughts turn inward"—her hands moved to her heart—"and outward." Her hands extended to the open air. "You look within, to yourself. Without, to the Creator."

Fear wrung Dion. His flesh was soggy pulp, his blood water. He was shivering with terror; he was desperately, horribly afraid. Think of himself? The Creator? The young man could visualize only fearful pain and death and oblivion.

"Come this way," Sagan ordered, gesturing.

Dion willed himself to obey but his feet wouldn't move. He ducked his head, covered his lips with his hand, and prayed to a God he had never believed in that he wouldn't spew out the bile filling his mouth.

He was dimly aware of Maigrey whispering, "What have you told him would happen? He looks as if he's going to his death!"

And he had to suffer the Warlord's stern, frowning displeasure. "Nothing. I've told him nothing."

Then Maigrey was beside Dion, her hands on his arms. Her touch was cool and soothing.

"Dion, it's a religious rite, a ceremony, nothing more."

"No!" He gasped the word, almost choking, staring wildly at the black screen behind which lurked some unknown horror. "I'm going to die!" When he spoke the fear aloud, he was filled with a sudden peace and the shivering stopped, the sickness eased. Dion gently put aside the woman's hands.

"I'm going to die," he repeated and looked into her eyes to see reflected there a ghastly, livid face—his own.

Imbued with a terrible calm, almost light-headed, Dion moved without hesitation to the screen and, at Sagan's gesture, stepped around it and saw before him the table covered with the black cloth.

Maigrey cast a swift, questioning, fearful glance at the Warlord, but if he answered her, it was an answer given in silence, for he did not meet her eyes. She stood a moment, irresolute, staring intently at Dion, trying, it seemed, to penetrate to his soul. The young man gave back nothing; he had nothing to give. The Warlord placed his candle in one of the silver candle holders and, moving to the opposite end of the table, lit the other. Now he looked at Maigrey, and the look was one of irritation.

Sighing, she lifted the hood of her gown and covered her fair hair. Her face was hidden in shadow and Dion knew, suddenly, that he was alone.

"Stand in the center of the circle," Lord Sagan said, indicating a white line on the floor. "Step over—not on—the edge."

The circle was made of some sort of powdery, crystalline substance. Dion did as he was told, lifting his feet gingerly, one after the other, careful not to break the line.

Sagan took his place behind the table, behind the objects that were concealed beneath black cloth. Maigrey drew near him, standing at the Warlord's left.

Clasping her hands before her, Maigrey bowed her head. Sagan raised his, lifting his eyes and arms to the heavens. Neither gave any indication to Dion of what he was supposed to do, but he knew that it didn't matter. Nothing mattered, for soon he was going to die. Calm, uncaring, empty of thought and feeling, he stood alone in the center of the circle of salt and waited.

"Creator, one comes before you who is on the verge of

manhood and who seeks to understand the mystery of his life."

Maigrey tried to concentrate, tried to keep her thoughts on the words of Sagan's prayer; she couldn't help but dart swift, furtive glances at Dion. What had come over the boy? She might have suspected the Warlord of deliberately terrorizing him, except she sensed Sagan was equally perplexed by this strange behavior. Maigrey wondered, somewhat guiltily, if she could have been responsible. She had meant for Dion to take this seriously, but surely recommending that he read Nietzsche could not account for a reaction like this!

Dion's face glimmered white; his eyes were wide and stared ahead at the candle flame. His hands clenched tightly, gripping his courage. His breathing was quick and shallow. The red-golden mane of hair clung damply to his forehead and neck. Sweat trickled down his temple. He looked like a man going to his own execution.

". . . we of the Blood Royal have been granted talents beyond those of other men. In return for your blessings, Creator, you have given us additional responsibility. You have given us responsibility for the lives of other men. . . ."

And you, Sagan, abrogated that responsibility, Maigrey silently added. You threw it away. You're mouthing the ritual. In your heart, you don't truly believe the words you speak. God exists for you and you alone, exists for the sole purpose of putting the universe within your grasp.

". . . use our mental and physical prowess to protect and defend—"

"And to conquer." Maigrey didn't realize, until she felt the sudden stiffening of the man's body beside her, that she had accidentally spoken her thoughts aloud.

"Use it to create—"

"To destroy!"

Sagan paused, drew a deep breath, then said in a voice that was low and shook with the effort of his self-control, "My lady, you blaspheme!"

"I blaspheme!" Maigrey forgot where she was, forgot her purpose, forgot everything but where she had first heard those words he spoke. "You're the one who's making this ceremony a mockery!"

"Stop it!" Dion's eyes went from one to the other of them, from Maigrey to Sagan, his gaze wild and staring. His face was covered with a sheen of perspiration; the words burst from him in agony. "Stop it!" His hand closed spasmodically over his chest, as if he were trying to hold himself together, trying to keep from being torn apart.

Maigrey pressed her shaking hands to her temples to calm the blood throbbing in her veins. What had come over her? What had made her say such things? Her fury subsided quickly, leaving her weak and shivering with cold and a numbing awe.

"This is all wrong, Sagan! We should stop—"

His hand closed over hers, nearly crushing the bones.

"We've gone too far. The Creator is with us. Can't you feel His presence?"

Yes, God was with them. He was in the darkness and the light, within them and without. He was too far, too near. Maigrey's chill fingers clasped tightly around Sagan's. For a moment he held on to her, she held on to him, neither knowing what they did, both knowing that they needed to cling to something real and solid.

Before them stood the boy, alone, waiting.

Waiting to die.

Sagan let go of her hand. He stepped back, behind her. This she must do on her own.

God. God is with us. His will be done.

Calm. Calmly, Maigrey, she told herself. The boy is watching. He'll need your strength, your support. It won't help if you crumble to the floor and curl up in a ball and wail like a terrified child. You can do that on the inside.

Maigrey lifted the black cloth. Beneath it were four objects—a silver pitcher filled with water, a silver dish filled with oil, a silver globe, and a silver wand.

Facing Dion, Maigrey forced the boy to fix his wild-eyed gaze on her, using the strength of her will to keep it there.

Waves, waves washing upon the shore. Eternal, unending, one after the other. Receding, gathering, surging forward, receding. The sand, smoothed by the water's endless caress, is cool beneath your body. The water over your skin is warm.

Dion's locked jaws relaxed; his limbs ceased to tremble. He brushed the red-golden hair back from his forehead and watched her expectantly, anxiously.

Maigrey drew a breath, let it out, and was about to begin when she realized the words had gone clean out of her head. She stammered. Sagan moved up, standing right behind her, their bodies almost—but not quite—touching, and Maigrey remembered.

"In the time of the Ascendancy of Man, on a distant planet chosen by the Creator as one to cradle life, it was written that four elements bound the universe together. These were called"—she spoke in the ancient tongue "—earth, air, fire, and water.

"From the dawn of time, man sought ways and means to control these elements. He discovered he could control them physically, by inventing devices that would serve him, devices to rule the elements. Centuries later, man discovered that, if he were made strong enough, he could rule the elements with his mind and his soul.

"This night, Dion Starfire, you come to us to be initiated into the mystery. You seek control of that which is beyond the control of most. If the Creator deems you worthy, you will be granted that control. That is what we are here tonight to learn. Pray to the Creator, Dion," Maigrey added softly. That wasn't part of the ritual, but she felt a desperate need to communicate to the boy the presence of God. "Pray to Him for guidance."

Dion continued to stare at her. What was transpiring in his heart and in his soul was known to two alone—himself and God.

"We bring to you now the four elements. Concentrate on each, come to understand and realize that you are one with each. Only through understanding can you gain ascendancy."

Reaching out her hand, Maigrey picked up the silver wand and held it above the table, level with her own heart.

"Air. The breath of life. The wind of destruction."

She moved the wand in a slow circle and the air around them began to stir and whisper. The wind she summoned grew stronger, swirled around them, rustling her robes, setting the candle flames flickering. The breeze lifted Dion's red-golden hair and stirred it with gentle hands. The wind began to die down. The first part of the rite was nearing its end. Maigrey, relieved, was about to return the wand to its place on the table when she saw that Dion was suffocating.

The boy, clutching his throat, was gasping for air and not finding any. There was terror in the eyes that were bulging from his head. His lips were turning blue, his chest jerked, the muscles fighting frantically to sustain life. Dion staggered, reaching out a hand to her for help.

Maigrey started to move around the table, started to go to him, but she felt firm hands grip her shoulders. A voice breathed into her ear, "Wait!"

The boy dropped to his knees. Crouched on the floor, he sucked in a breath. Panting, he gasped in another and another. Sitting back on his heels, closing his eyes, he threw back his head and just breathed.

"Derek, what—"

"I don't know, lady." Sagan's hands, tense and rigid, gripped her shoulders. "I don't know. Keep on. We must keep on."

Then let go of me, she knew she should say, but she didn't, she didn't want him to let go. Once again, lost in darkness, they were each other's strength.

Dion rose unsteadily to his feet and came back to stand in front of the table. There were dark smudges beneath his eyes; his skin was so pale the blue and purple lines of the veins stood out clearly. It took Maigrey several tries—looking into that frightened face—to speak the next words.

"Earth." She cleared her throat. Sagan stood close behind her, their bodies warm together, pressed near each other for comfort. "Matter. You can control matter."

Maigrey lifted the smooth silver globe from the table. Tossing it lightly up into the air, she exerted her will upon it. The globe hung suspended, inches above her hands. Its appearance began to change. Razor sharp metal spikes, several centimeters long, emerged from the sides until the ball was studded with them.

Withdrawing her hands from beneath the globe, Maigrey commanded, "Place your hands beneath it."

Dion, after a moment's hesitation, stretched out his hands. The globe started to fall and, by frightened instinct more than conscious thought, he controlled it, caused it to remain suspended in the air.

Dion gasped in elation, his eyes—glistening with triumph—went to Maigrey. His lips parted.

She shook her head slightly, warning him not to speak.

"You can control matter with your mind, but there are forces in this universe over which you will have no control. Then you will be required to withstand pain—mental and physical. Such a force you will face now. The globe will drop. I cannot stop it. Neither can you. Will you have the courage to catch it?"

This was the most difficult part of the rite. Maigrey could remember quite clearly staring up at those flesh-rending spikes, her imagination portraying with vivid clarity what would happen if those spikes tore through her palms. It took every measure of courage she possessed to stand and let that

globe drop and not snatch away her hands at the last instant.
And, even then, she admitted to herself later, if it hadn't been
for Sagan standing there, prepared to catch the ball without
hesitation, she would have failed. The thought that she might
fail where he would succeed had goaded her beyond what she
had known to be her limits.

Illusion, Dion. She attempted to give the boy a telepathic
message. *It's all illusion. The spikes aren't really there. They're
illusions—*

Only they weren't.

The globe fell; the knife-sharp spikes made an eerie whis-
tling sound in the air and a dull, soggy, plopping sound as they
drove through flesh and muscle, tendon and bone. Blood
spurted. Dion screamed. His hands were impaled on the silver
globe.

"My God!"

Maigrey could only stare. Sagan flung his arm around her,
holding her tightly, keeping her from going to the boy. His
precaution was needless; she couldn't move.

The spikes suddenly withdrew; the globe rolled from the
boy's torn hands, fell to the floor, and bounded into the
darkness.

Dion raised his head and looked at Maigrey. Slowly, he held
out his hands. Blood oozed from the palms, severed fingers
dangled by strips of skin. He had ceased to scream, he was in
shock.

Sagan withdrew his arm, shoved her forward.

"Continue!" His voice was harsh and unrecognizable.

"I can't, Derek! I don't know what's happening!"

"Continue, lady! Or the boy *will* die!"

"Water."

Maigrey wondered if she had strength to lift the pitcher and
was not surprised when she very nearly dropped it. *The boy
will die.* The words she spoke next came from a place inside
her that was acting completely on its own, of its own volition.
She no longer had any conscious idea what she was saying.
"Water—from which comes life."

Upending the pitcher, Maigrey poured the water on Dion's
injured hands. The cool liquid flowed over the palms, bringing
relief to the pain, seemingly, for he closed his eyes, tears
sprang from beneath the lids. The water mingled with the
blood, washing it away.

"Fire. Sustainer. Destroyer." The oil lamp burst into bright
flame.

Maigrey lifted the oil lamp, uncertain what to do, for in this part of the ritual the initiate passed his or her hand through the top of the fire. Sagan reached out, snatched the lamp from her grasp. Grabbing hold of the boy's hands, he thrust them into the flames.

Maigrey caught hold of the Warlord's arm, trying to stop him, but he flung her aside and poured the burning oil directly onto the flesh.

The smell was nauseating. Dion never made a sound, but stared with a calm, terrible fascination at the flame covering his hands. The fire blazed, finally died. When it was out, the flesh of his hands was left whole, untouched, unblemished, healed.

Dion looked up at them, at each of them, smiled brilliantly, radiantly, and dropped, lifeless, to the floor.

"Is he—" Maigrey couldn't find breath enough to speak the word.

Sagan walked around the table. Standing over the boy, he stared at him a moment, then leaned down and put a hand on Dion's neck.

"No. He's fainted." The Warlord straightened. "He'll be all right . . . in time."

Maigrey walked slowly around the table. The cloth was wet with water. The pitcher lay where she'd dropped it when Sagan knocked her aside. The silver globe had disappeared; she doubted they'd ever find it. The One who had made use of it was gone and had probably taken His tools with him. If there was blood on the cloth, she couldn't see it, couldn't distinguish it in the darkness from the oil and the water.

This wasn't what the script called for. This hadn't been the way the scene was supposed to be shot. No one had requested these special effects. What did it mean? Pain, suffering. Yes, that was to be expected of those who lived to serve, that was the rite's lesson. But initiates were given the power to compensate, to turn the pain into illusion, to prove that the mind could overcome outside forces. Dion was given the power, but apparently he wouldn't be allowed to use it, just as he had not been allowed to use it during the rite. Or, if he did use it, it would be turned against him. He would be expected to sacrifice . . . everything? For nothing in return?

Sagan's thoughts were turmoil, darkness, confusion. He was staring into the stars, into the night, into nothing. Maigrey looked at the young man lying at her feet.

"What was that ritual, my lord? The rite for a king?"

Sagan stirred, returning from whatever dark realm he'd been traveling. "A king? Yes."

His lips tightened. The struggle was bitter indeed.

"And more. A savior."

Chapter ·◆つ◎◯◆· Twenty-nine

I am born.
Charles Dickens, *David Copperfield*

The guards knew that today she would die. Maigrey saw the knowledge, saw respect mingled with sorrow, in their eyes when they met her that morning for her customary walk. There was no shame, no guilt, however. They were devoutly loyal; they believed implicitly in their lord. They would die themselves if he ordered it. They would see her put to death with equal equanimity.

"Please take me to the sick bay," she requested.

"Yes, my lady," the centurion answered, and she heard a softness in his voice. Yes, they knew. It was to be today.

Dion was still unconscious. Dr. Giesk, flitting around her like a bat, assured her that the boy would sleep for days. Good. Whatever happened, however this encounter ended, it would be hard on Dion. Maigrey had seen, last night, the darkness and the light enter his soul. All his life, the two would fight within him, each striving for dominance, each bringing its own strengths, its own weaknesses. He would never be free of the conflict. Never, from this moment, be truly happy.

Leaning over the bed, Maigrey brushed back the red-golden hair from the white forehead. A sudden, vivid, flashing memory came to her. Semele, lying in my arms, dark hair tousled. Her face is deathly white, streaked with tears and blood. So much blood, and the flames are getting nearer. . . .

Maigrey's soul shrank back, appalled. The memory sank and she did not try to dredge it back up.

The young man stirred and cried out in his sleep. Maigrey clasped his hand and held it fast. Her touch seemed to bring him ease, and he sighed and slept. Leaning down, she kissed him on the cheek.

279

Rising suddenly, briskly, she turned and saw one of the centurions blinking his eyes with unusual rapidity. Maigrey carefully kept from observing him and laid the book she had brought with her down upon the bedstand.

"Please see that the boy is given this," she said to Dr. Giesk.

The doctor's eyes were fixed not on her but on the scar on her face. When Giesk realized she had spoken to him, he started and gave her a deprecating, guilty smile.

"Oh, yes, my lady. Certainly."

Firmly resisting the impulse to grab the man's necktie and knot it around his scrawny neck, Maigrey brushed past him. She saw his glance go from her to a set of double swinging doors at the far end of the sick bay. Maigrey knew what was behind those doors—a shining steel table standing on a tile floor with a drain beneath it; instruments to cut and remove and slice; shining steel basins. This night, her body might be lying there. This man, gloating over his prize. . . .

"Come away from here, my lady."

One of the centurions had hold of her arm and was guiding her firmly away from the autopsy room, out of Giesk's odious presence.

"The stench in here is enough to make anyone feel giddy," added the centurion.

Well, well, Maigrey thought, gratefully accepting the man's assistance, perhaps they wouldn't watch her die with equanimity after all.

·━◆ ◆━·

"How are you feeling, young man?"

The pinched, weasel-like face of Dr. Giesk loomed over the boy. A scrap of necktie escaped from beneath the doctor's white coat and flopped onto the blanket. Giesk rescued the tie, tucked it neatly back, and continued to peer into the boy's face. Dion blinked, involuntarily moving away.

"I'm fine."

Dion tried to push himself up to a sitting position in the bed, only to discover wires attached to his wrists, leading to a winking, blinking machine that stood nearby. The young man glanced around, saw sterile beds standing in orderly, well-dressed rows, their blankets folded and tucked to exact specifications, their crisp, smooth, white sheets overlapping by just the proper width, no more and no less. Even with a patient between them, the sheets did not relax. Dion had to squirm to ease himself out from beneath his sheet's rigid grasp. He was, he realized, in a sick bay.

"What happened to me?"

"You suffered a shock to your nervous system. A thing not uncommon for those who are guests of the Warlord." Giesk giggled and peered intently at the readings on his machine.

Dion remembered. Fearfully, he lifted his hands and stared at them, turning them over and over. There was not a mark on them. But the pain had been real, the tearing flesh, shattered bones, severed tendons. And then the horrible moment when he saw his flesh withering and burning in the fire. The memory of the horror overwhelmed him and he began to shake. Cold sweat covered his forehead.

"Mmmmm," Giesk murmured, frowning. "I think you had better keep to your bed today. I'll give you a sedative."

"No, wait!" Dion reached out a hand to grasp the doctor's lab coat. "Who brought me here? Did they say anything?"

"The Warlord brought you himself," Dr. Giesk said, giving Dion a shrewd, penetrating look. "Carried you in his arms and you're no lightweight. He's kept his strength up remarkably for a man of his age. Comes from exercise and the proper diet. I limit his intake of red meat, you know. And he has never in his entire life touched a drop of alcohol. The priests don't, or perhaps I should say *didn't* . . . but we're among friends."

One half of the doctor's face suddenly performed the most grotesque contortions. Dion was considerably alarmed until he realized Giesk was winking at him.

Shivering, the boy pulled the blanket up around him. Every object in the room was either metallic or white; the place even smelled cold. "But didn't he say anything? What about Lady Maigrey? Was she with him? Didn't *she* say anything?"

"Lady Maigrey? Now, there's a fascinating woman. Have you noticed that scar on her face?" Giesk perched his thin behind on the edge of the bed. "Remarkable. Quite remarkable. She came to see you shortly after the Warlord brought you in for treatment. The lady didn't say anything, but she left that for you." Giesk pointed at a book lying on the bedstand.

Dion snaked an arm out from under his blanket and grabbed it. Lying propped up on his elbow, moving awkwardly so as to keep from tangling himself in the wires, he opened the cover.

"There's some writing on the inside and a few lines marked. I couldn't read the inscription. It's in one of those old languages." Giesk turned and motioned to a medicbot that was filing charts. "QUAC, over here, please."

Casting the doctor an angry glance, which went right past Giesk, Dion carefully brushed the cover of the leatherbound book to rid it of the man's touch. The medicbot trundled across the floor. Giesk punched several buttons on its chest. A mechanized arm moved over a tray, selected an item, and stuck what looked to be a wet dot on Dion's arm. The young man, absorbed in studying the book, paid little attention to it.

The book was *David Copperfield*. Hurriedly he flipped the pages to find Maigrey's inscription, for he guessed it must be some sort of message. He hoped it would let him know how he'd fared with the test. He wondered uneasily if he'd disgraced himself by passing out. He couldn't imagine Sagan flopping down on the floor like a dead fish.

Dead . . . The memory of his ordeal became suddenly cloudy and hazy, not nearly as frightening. Dion felt his muscles relax and he stopped shivering.

Preface. Introduction. A long introduction, written by some scholar. Table of Contents. Chapter One. "I Am Born." And there, lines marked. First lines. Dion read them carefully.

> Whether I shall turn out to be the hero of my own life, or whether that station will be held by anybody else, these pages must show.

Written in feminine handwriting on the margin were the words, "My love and prayers are with you always. *Dominus tecum*, Dion Starfire." It was signed with Maigrey's name.

Dr. Giesk, still sitting on the edge of the bed, was rattling on.

"That scar of hers. I think it was made by the blade of a bloodsword. Whoever handled it was extremely skilled or she was extremely lucky, since a blow like that should have split open her head. I haven't had a chance to examine the scar closely—not yet, anyway."

Dion puzzled over the inscription. It seemed as if she were saying good-bye. He rubbed his eyes; he was drowsy. He couldn't think. Giesk rambled on. There were, at present, no other patients in the ward, so the boy was in for the full brunt of the doctor's bedside manner.

"They'll bring the body to me afterward, however. I've specifically requested it. I'll be able to study it quite closely, see just how they managed to close the wound so that the skin grew back so smoothly. I think it was probably glued—"

"Body?" Dion raised his head. It took an effort. Someone seemed to have filled his skull with rock. "What do you mean—body?"

"She's to be executed today," Dr. Giesk said. "There's nothing you can do to stop it, young man, so you might as well lie back down and let the drug take effect. When you wake up, it will be long over."

"Wake up . . ." The rocks were tumbling around and around, crashing into each other. "That . . . wasn't . . . sedative." Dion fumbled his way out of the sheet, ripping off the wires attached to his hands. Slowly, he swung his legs over the side of the bed. The rocks left his head, tumbled down his body, and landed in his feet.

Dr. Giesk made no move to stop him, but sat watching, the cold eyes observing the boy with detached, clinical curiosity. "That's a very powerful sleeping drug. You won't make it to the door."

Matter. You can control matter. I kept the silver globe in the air. I willed it to stay in the air and it did—until . . . until . . .

Dion gritted his teeth.

"I'll make it!"

Why was the floor floating ten meters beneath the bed? He'd have to jump for it. The floor leapt up to meet him and he landed heavily on his hands and knees. Standing, reeling against the side of the bed, Dion took a step and realized he was naked.

"Can't be a hero . . . naked. Can't go . . . t'rescue . . . 'thout clothes. All . . . laugh. Sagan'd . . . laugh."

Peering around, Dion discovered his jeans, neatly folded, on a shelf beneath the bedstand. He made a grab for them, but they drifted away from him. He tried again and this time snagged them. But, holding them up, he was confused by the sight of two legs. He had no idea how to put them on.

Seeing a patient needing aid and receiving no orders to the contrary, the medicbot set down its tray of medicines and went to assist. Dion allowed it to dress him like a child. Dr. Giesk watched all this with intense interest, never moving to stop him. Once his jeans were on, Dion lurched toward a door leaning at an odd angle at the end of a long metal and white tunnel.

"Follow him, QUAC," Giesk ordered the medicbot. "Don't interfere with him. What a marvelous research opportunity! I want to see where he goes, what he does. Switch on your camera and your remote scanner. Keep a record of brain activity. Monitor his heart rate and, when he collapses, extract a blood sample."

The medicbot whirred off in pursuit of its patient.

Giesk stood staring after the two of them, his hands fiddling with his necktie. "I wouldn't have believed it. I wonder how far he'll get? I almost think I'll go along . . . No." He smacked himself on the hand. "Naughty, naughty. You have work to do. Must prepare for the autopsy. It isn't every day you get a chance to observe a dead Blood Royal. And I'll be able to review the medicbot's vid tapes of the young man. That kid! Doped to the gills and still functioning. Remarkable! Absolutely remarkable."

·◄■ ■►·

Maigrey sat in the empty lounge on the deserted level of the ship, watching the stars glittering in the darkness of the universe's cold and endless night. Her guards had retreated back near the door, standing well away from her, unobtrusive, respectful of her desire to be alone.

She wasn't alone long. Her back to the door, she heard behind her the muffled footsteps of several men, the soft tread of one pair of booted feet walking across the carpet. She knew that tread; it matched the beating of her heart. Maigrey didn't move, didn't turn her head. Calm and relaxed, she waited, never taking her eyes from the stars.

Heavy hands rested on her shoulders with unwonted gentleness.

"It is time, my lady."

Sagan's fingers brushed softly through the pale hair. Maigrey closed her eyes, her courage almost failing her. Why keep on fighting? Wouldn't it be easier, better, just to let it end?

Yes, and he would despise her forever.

The Warlord backed up a pace. Maigrey rose to her feet, turned, and stood facing him. She wore the indigo blue gown; the starjewel gleamed with its own light, brighter and warmer than any of its namesakes. At her side, the bloodsword.

"And how am I to die, my lord?"

"The beam. It's swift, painless. I owe you that much, at

least." He frowned slightly as he said this, then shook his head, to rid himself of a disturbing thought.

Maigrey wondered very much what that disturbing thought had been, but she couldn't see his mind.

The beam. Laser through the forehead. There were worse ways to die. She knew; she'd seen most of them.

Maigrey nodded gravely. "And what is the crime of which I'm accused?"

"If I read the list, my lady, we'd be here for a light-year," Sagan evinced some impatience. "But, since you insist, the crime for which you must pay with your life is the crime of treason against the state."

"I have not committed treason, my lord. My king lives and I am loyal to him. It is you, my lord, and your state who have committed treason."

Sagan's eyes narrowed. "If you're trying to stall—"

"It's my right to know with what I'm charged, my lord."

The Warlord's lips compressed; his jaw muscles tightened. "Very well, Lady Maigrey. You are charged with breaking your oath of allegiance to a superior officer. You are charged with refusing to obey his commands. You are charged with betraying those who trusted in you."

For an instant, it seemed the laser beam had struck her. Maigrey's face went livid, her eyes rigid and staring. Her breath stopped. It took her a moment to find the breath to speak, but when she did, her words were clear and strong.

"According to the law of your state, I have the right to be tried and convicted by a jury of my peers."

"You have been tried by your peers, my lady," Derek Sagan said. "I am your peer—the only one left alive."

"Then, my lord, you can have no objection to a trial by combat."

The Warlord's well-disciplined, well-trained guards stirred, turned their heads, and exchanged glances.

Sagan heard them, if he could not see them. His lip twitched slightly. He leaned close to her and whispered, "I am pleased to see that time cannot stale, nor custom wither your infinite variety, lady. I wondered what you had in mind. I compliment you."

Maigrey lowered her eyes. "Thank you, my lord."

Sagan said aloud, "I have judged you, my lady. I have found you guilty. I have sentenced you to death, and I will carry out that sentence."

"I dispute that, my lord. And it is my right, being of the Blood Royal, to take my case to the Supreme Judge, the Highest Judge, the Judge who will someday judge us all. I challenge you, my accuser, to prove your charge against me on the field of honor. Through my valor and my skill at arms, I will prove my innocence. God alone will be my judge."

The men behind them had fallen silent, too silent. Every man was waiting, each seemingly holding his breath, to hear his lord's answer.

"You can't turn me down, Sagan," Maigrey said to him softly. "They would always wonder if you were afraid to face me—the first crack in the solid shield of their loyalty. And you're going to need that loyalty when you commit your own brand of treason."

"Reconsider, Maigrey. You can't win. Even if you do manage to slay me, my men will kill you where you stand."

"One thing at a time. That is what you always taught me, wasn't it, Commander?" Maigrey looked into his eyes, saw reflected there the blue-white light of the starjewel.

Sagan's thin lips twisted in a bitter smile. "You have been very clever. I hope you won't live to regret your cleverness." Reaching out his hand, he touched the scar on her face, running his fingers down the smooth skin. "This time, I will not be merciful. My lady." He bowed, turned on his heel, and left her.

"My lord." Maigrey pressed her hand against her cheek. The skin, where he touched it, burned.

Chapter ❖❖❖❖ Thirty

Die now!
Ancient Greek response to good fortune

Dion wondered fearfully if the ship was under attack. The deck canted away beneath his feet, the corridors slanted at impossible angles, making it difficult to walk them. He was continually dashing himself against the bulkheads, hurtling into blast doors. But if the ship was being fired on, no one seemed the least bit concerned. Everyone continued going about his business. Those who noticed Dion at all regarded him with either amusement or disgust.

"Please . . ." Dion lurched toward the two officers. "Lady Maigrey, tell me—"

But the men continued past him, regarding him with disgust.

"Drunk! The Warlord won't tolerate that!" one said to the other.

Dion leaned against a wall to recover his balance and try to rediscover the floor. He could hear the medicbot whirring along behind him, its metal fingers clinking together, plucking at him if he allowed it to come too near. Whenever he stopped, it sidled close to him. He could see himself—a grotesque, curved, and convex reflection—in its round, lifeless lenses. Pushing away from the wall, filled with a vague terror, he stumbled on.

"Dion!"

The voice was familiar.

The boy stopped in his headlong rush to nowhere and turned—too quickly. His body couldn't maintain its balance and he fell. The medicbot's motors whined in triumph, and Dion tried to scramble up and get away. He managed to make it to his knees.

"Dion, what's wrong? Look, it's me, Marcus."

Strong arms had hold of him. Strong hands supported him. Peering into the man's face, Dion knew him . . . one of his guards.

"He drank his lunch," someone else said. "That's what's wrong with him."

"No!" Dion protested, choking on his swollen tongue. "It's a . . . drug!" He waved his hand at the medicbot, hovering over him with a syringe in one metal claw, a ball of wet cotton in another, and a glass vial in a third.

"Giesk?" Marcus asked, eyeing the medicbot with a grim and unfriendly expression.

"Can't fall . . . asleep!" Dion clutched at the man. "Maigrey . . . execute. Must . . . stop."

"So that's it," Marcus muttered. "Get away!" he ordered the medicbot. "Back off, you metallic ghoul!"

The medicbot slid backward, clicked to a stop, and remained standing, staring at them through its myriad lenses.

Marcus said to his companion, "Help me get the kid back to my quarters. Then you—" he added something in low tones that were lost on Dion, who was beginning to feel himself spiraling down into a deep pit.

He started awake, grasping frantically at the edges of consciousness, trying to pull himself back.

"I can walk," he mumbled, shoving the men's hands away from him.

Marcus helped him to stand and guided him, offering a steadying hand when the boy's knees began to sink beneath him. The centurions' quarters weren't far away; Marcus and his friend had just left them when they ran into Dion. The two guided the boy inside, the other guard left on his errand, and Marcus shut the door in the medicbot's blinking face.

Dion gazed longingly at the neatly made bed and planted his back firmly against a wall. "Lady Maigrey . . . is she . . . dead?"

"No," Marcus said.

Dion closed his eyes, almost sobbing in relief.

"Not yet," the guard added in a low tone. He stood in the center of the small room in which there was a bed, a computer, a desk, a locker, and a chair. "What did Giesk give you? Do you know?"

Dion shook his head muzzily. "Sleeping . . . something."

The wall was starting to tilt over backward, taking him with it. Marcus put out his hand, caught hold of him.

"You better sit down before you fall. You might hurt yourself."

"Can't. Must . . . rescue . . . lady."

"There's nothing you can do, Dion. She's chosen trial by combat. Against Lord Sagan."

Dion's eyes flared open. He stared at Marcus—who was beginning to separate and become three people. "I don't . . . understand."

"You won't understand much of anything under that drug. I—"

"Take me . . . to her!"

Marcus shook his head. "I've broken the rules, bringing you here. By rights I should have marched you right back to sick bay."

"Then I'll go . . . myself—"

Dion stared at the door and willed his body to walk over to it. It was going to be tough going, because someone had cut off his feet. At least he assumed that was what had happened, since he couldn't feel them anymore. The door slid open—

Shining gold and fiery red filled his vision.

"My lord! Please! You can't—"

Dion lurched forward, clasped hold of metal, cold and unyielding. Flames burst in his skull and he began a sickening, slithering fall . . .

The Warlord caught the boy in his arms.

"You can put him on the bed, my lord," Marcus offered.

"What's the matter with him? Did he say?"

"Yes, my lord. Apparently Dr. Giesk gave him some sort of sleeping drug. One of the doctor's medicbots was following the young man."

Sagan gazed at the boy in frowning thoughtfulness, then snapped into the commlink, "Giesk!"

"My lord."

"I'm with Dion. Did you—"

"You're with him, my lord? Excellent. I have a complaint to register against your guards, my lord. They interfered with one of my—"

"Giesk, shut up."

"Yes, my lord."

"Did you give the boy the drug?"

"Yes, my lord. As you ordered."

"Then what the hell is he doing up walking around?"

"Remarkable, isn't it, my lord? His system is fighting it and was almost actually winning! So to speak, my lord. In medical terms, I'd say it was his chromosomes—"

"Damn his chromosomes! What's the prognosis?"

"I couldn't say, my lord." Giesk sounded hurt. "If my medicbot had been allowed to take a blood sample—"

"Make a guess."

"Well, my lord, I would guess that his system has successfully acted to dilute the drug. Just as your system would, my lord, were I to give it to you."

"Thank you, Doctor, but I'm not the one under sedation. I asked you—"

"Yes, my lord. What's the young man's condition now?"

"He's sleeping."

"That probably won't last long. I can't give him any more of the drug without risking serious harm. He'll wake up suffering the galaxy's worst hangover, but beyond that, my lord, he'll be all right."

The Warlord stared down at the boy in grim silence. Marcus had retreated to a far corner, the centurion letting it be known that he was here if needed and was not if he wasn't.

"I tried to spare you this, Dion. But—so be it. You might as well see that the shining toy you want so much has a dark and lethal heart. Giesk!"

"What were you saying, my lord? There's nothing wrong with his heart—"

"Don't be any more of a fool than you can help, Giesk. Can you give the boy something that will bring him around now?"

"Yes, my lord. A pep shot. He won't feel very good—"

"Where he's going, he won't feel good no matter what kind of shot you give him. You have your orders."

"Yes, my lord. I'll send the medicbot—"

The Warlord broke the connection. Rising to his feet, he looked around the small room.

"Centurion."

"My lord."

"When the boy regains consciousness, bring him to the arena. But see to it that he doesn't interfere."

"Yes, my lord."

Sagan started to leave. The door slid aside, the medicbot hovered just beyond. Pausing, the Warlord turned around and fixed his shadowed gaze upon the soldier.

"Your name is Marcus, isn't it, centurion?"

"Yes, my lord."

There were one hundred men in the Honor Guard. Sagan knew every one of them by name.

"Tell me, Marcus. Why didn't you take the boy back to sick bay? Or just allow the medicbot to do its duty?"

Marcus hesitated, swallowing, passing his tongue over dry lips. This could earn him a reprimand—if he was lucky. Punishment, if he wasn't. It might get him thrown out of the Guard, dishonorably discharged from the service. Men had killed themselves rather than face that fate.

It was always best, with the Warlord, to tell the truth. He knew when a man was lying. He could, it was said, see inside the brain.

"My lord, the young man asked about the Lady Maigrey. He could have let the drug put him to sleep, but he didn't. He was fighting against it to come to her aid. Such courage shouldn't be thwarted."

Marcus had no idea if what he'd said made any impression. Sagan did not immediately respond. He might not have been paying attention. He was looking at Dion, lying on the bed, the flame-red hair tousled on the pillow.

"Centurion," the Warlord said suddenly, "if I fall this day, the Lady Maigrey will be in considerable danger. Would you be prepared to defend her—against your own comrades?"

Marcus, completely confounded by the question, stared at the Warlord, uncertain how to answer. "My lord—"

"The truth, centurion."

"Yes, my lord. I would defend her with my life."

What Marcus had said amounted to treason. Sagan could very well put him to death for such a statement. But the Warlord had commanded his soldier speak the truth, and though Sagan was known to be unmerciful, he was not known to be unjust.

The Warlord glanced outside the door. The medicbot hummed in its impatience to carry out its instructions.

"Very good, centurion. If I fall, see to it that Lady Maigrey and the boy are taken to a place of safety."

Marcus couldn't speak. His face must have registered his astonishment, however, for the Warlord, glancing at him, smiled wryly. "Don't worry, centurion. That's one command I don't expect you to have to carry out. However, it's well to be prepared." He reached out his hand; the tips of his fingers touched the red-golden hair.

"Yes, my lord." Marcus saluted, fist over heart.

The Warlord nodded, returned the salute, and stalked out. His red cape, billowing behind him, nearly engulfed the medicbot coming in. It whirred irritably and began puttering around the boy, drawing blood samples and surreptitiously carrying out numerous other tests for the benefit of Dr. Giesk. Finally it planted a small wet dot on the boy's arm and, clicking and clanking, whirred itself out of the room.

Marcus sighing, wiped his hand across his sweat-beaded upper lip, and sank down into a chair.

··◁■ ■▷··

"Admiral Aks requests permission to see you, my lord."

"Let him enter."

Aks strode through the golden double doors. Seeing the Warlord clad in a tight-fitting body suit that he used only for physical exercise, the admiral stopped dead in the entry hall.

"So this ridiculous rumor I've heard is true, my lord?"

"Not knowing to which ridiculous rumor you are referring, Aks, I couldn't say."

The body suit slid over the Warlord's smooth muscles, emphasizing his strong build and girth. He flexed his arms, to make certain the suit allowed suitable freedom of movement. Satisfied, he tied back his long, gray-streaked black hair with a leather cord.

"You've actually agreed to fight the Lady Maigrey in a duel! My lord, I must protest. This is preposterous." Aks was red in the face with the exertion of his emotions. "You're far too valuable to the Republic to risk yourself in this manner."

Sagan flicked him a glance.

"Hardly an argument conducive to forcing me to change my mind, Admiral. You know better than anyone aboard this ship that I am *not* valuable to the Republic. I am, in fact, a distinct menace to the Republic."

"Damn it, Derek, you know what I mean!" Aks rarely resorted to swearing and never in front of his liege lord. He had never called Sagan by his given name. "You're our hope. You can squash this imbecilic democracy and put power back into the hands of those who deserve to hold it. You've made your plans. You've spent years on them! Now, when all is nearly ready—"

"—I remove the last obstacle, Aks."

"But at such a risk to yourself, my lord!"

"Thank you, Admiral, for your vote of confidence. Are you suggesting the lady might defeat me?"

Aks paused, nonplussed, but his fear overrode his usual strong sense of self-preservation. Or perhaps it was his sense of self-preservation that goaded him on. The admiral was well aware of Captain Nada's spying. Aks knew that he himself had figured largely in Nada's reports of Sagan's treasonous actions. At the moment, the admiral stood safely behind his Warlord. He didn't like to think what would happen to him if that secure bulwark was removed.

"My lord, of the two of you, she *was* the better swordsman."

Sagan looked at himself in the mirror. The muscles of the arms and legs were well rounded, smooth. There was not a stronger man on the ship, not a man—even among the young ones—who could keep up with him in running, swimming. There was not a wrestler who could bring him to a fall, not a fencer who could come within his guard. Yet every day it took a little more effort to keep up his pace. Every race he ran, the Warlord wondered if this would be the one in which he would slip, falter. He put his hand on his abdominal muscles, felt them not rock hard, as in his youth, but softer, beginning to sag.

Lifting his right hand, he stared at five white marks in the palm. In his mind he could hear the chanting of an unseen crowd. "Die now!" they cried. "Die now." The shouts of the ancient Greeks to one who had achieved some great triumph in his life. "Die now, while you are happy, for nothing in your life can be better than this moment." Or, in other words, Go out in glory, it's all downhill from here. Angrily, Sagan shook his head, physically shaking off the thoughts. What a fool's notion. He hadn't yet reached the pinnacle of his success. "The blood-dimmed tide is loosed." He had it in his power, now, to conquer the galaxy.

The Warlord's open palm clenched slowly to a fist.

"I've waited seventeen years for this moment, Aks. Don't tell me it isn't worth it! She's the last. The last who turned on me. My victory over her is assured. God has given her into my hands. I've foreseen it."

The Warlord turned abruptly and, lifting a pair of fencing

gloves, pulled them on. The Admiral, though daunted by Sagan's anger, was frightened enough to blunder ahead.

"My lord," he said, lowering his voice, though he knew they couldn't possibly be overheard, "there are ways. . . . No one could ever say you had anything to do with it. One of the men, gone crazy. A fanatic, killing her to protect you. You could be furious, outraged—"

"—and live with myself the rest of my life?"

Sagan's anger had cooled. He appeared amused and he laid a hand on the admiral's shoulder.

"The men would always wonder, Aks. I'd see the shadow of doubt in the eyes that now regard me with fear and respect. No, it's fitting, after all, that we meet this way, as we met that last night. I wonder, Aks, if I didn't know what she was planning. I think I must have. It came as no surprise to me, when she issued the challenge. I knew, when she said the words, that this was our destiny. I saw again the vision of her death in my mind when she spoke. And yet—yet—"

"My lord?"

Sagan lifted the bloodsword, held it in his hand, staring at it. "Something isn't right, Aks. You know that when I have these glimpses into the future, they are clear and accurate to the last detail. And, in that vision, she is wearing armor—silver armor. An exact copy of mine." The Warlord cast a glance at his gold armor, carefully arranged by his orderly on its stand near his bed.

The admiral failed to see what silver armor had to do with anything. He had never really given credence to his lord's visions, considering them dreams and nothing more. Aks spread his hands deprecatingly.

"Women's fashions change with such rapidity, my lord—"

"Aks, you're a dolt."

I may be a dolt, my lord, but I'm not the one risking my life for some worn-out notion of honor. Aks did not say this aloud. He didn't say anything, and the Warlord didn't notice his silence.

"Such armor as that doesn't exist, Admiral. It couldn't possibly exist, unless I had it made for her. And, in my hand, I'm holding a dagger—a silver dagger of ancient make and design—"

The chiming of the ship's bells interrupted him. Sagan straightened, glanced around. "Leave me, Aks."

"You're determined to go through with this, my lord?"

The dark line of the Warlord's lips expanded slightly. "Don't worry, Aks. If I fall, you can always claim that you were going along with me simply to gather evidence to use at my trial for treason. Instead of hanging around, annoying me, you might want to spend this time erasing any incriminating computer files."

"You have completely misunderstood my intentions, my lord. I can assure you of my undying loyalty. I wish you success, my lord."

Hurt and indignant, Aks turned on his heels and marched stiffly out of Sagan's chambers. But, once he was alone in the Warlord's private elevator, the admiral happened to remember the existence of certain files on the Adonian, Snaga Ohme. Aks was loyal, but there was no sense in carrying it to extremes. Emerging from the elevator into the corridor, the admiral hurried posthaste to his own quarters.

Derek Sagan removed the hilt of his sword from its protective platinum and palladium scabbard, which also served as an energy recharger for the weapon. The Warlord checked the sword out of habit, though he knew that it was up to full power. He hadn't used it since the night he'd slain Platus Morianna. Balancing the sword in his hand, making a few passes to limber his arm, he halted and stared at it.

Silver dagger. Of ancient make and design. *Not* a bloodsword.

Sagan fitted the hilt back onto its scabbard, unbuckled the scabbard from around his waist, and carefully laid the sword upon his bed. One did not come armed into the presence of God.

Entering the chapel, the Warlord looked down upon the black cloth, the objects resting there: the chalice, the lamp, the dagger.

Yes, that was it. That was the dagger. A ceremonial blade, blessed by the Priests of Adamant, intended for use in the worship of the Creator, never meant to take life.

Cursed, he thought. I would be cursed, my soul damned for eternity to use it for such a purpose.

Sagan touched the dagger, traced the pattern of the eight-pointed star with his finger. He wondered that he hadn't recognized it when he first had the vision, but it had been unclear then. He had dreamed it many times since, and each time it became clearer in his mind, each time he saw more details.

What is God trying to say to me? What is God doing to me, anyway? To tell me this boy—this heir of the Starfires—is a savior! Sagan lifted the dagger, held it in his hand.

A savior!

With a bitter curse, the Warlord hurled the dagger back onto the altar. He heard a ringing clatter and something metal fall onto the deck, but he didn't look around. Walking out the door, he sealed it behind him and, grabbing the bloodsword from his bed, he summoned his guard and left for the arena.

In his mind, he could hear the voices, "Die now!"

··◄■ ■►··

"How do you feel?"

"Like warships are blasting off in my head and using my mouth for a landing pad." Dion groaned, sat up, and clutched his throbbing temples.

"Can you walk?"

Dion opened his eyes. The light was like spears flying into his brain, but the walls at least were where they should be and seemed likely to stay there. The overhead was up and the deck was down. When he stood, Marcus was at his side, to keep him from falling.

"Yeah, I can walk." Dion remembered, and looked around fearfully. "Where's the Warlord?"

"Relax. He's not hiding in my footlocker. He was here and ordered Giesk to give you a shot. That's what brought you around." Marcus grew more serious. "I'm to take you to the arena."

Dion shivered. The small room was cold and he had nothing covering his chest and arms. He was barefoot, too, standing on the cold metal deck.

"The arena. That's where . . . this fight . . ."

"Yes." Marcus rummaged in his locker. "Here, put these on. Your feet are some bigger than mine, but I wear these in the gym and they're stretched out. I've got a shirt, too."

"Thanks." Dion struggled into the shoes and pulled the shirt gingerly over his aching head. He saw Marcus putting on his armor. "Aren't you coming with me? Are you on duty?"

"Yes. You *are* my duty. And I'm coming. Everyone on the ship who isn't manning some critical station—or dead—will be there. And I bet even the dead are lined up to watch this contest."

Dion's face grew dark and shadowed. He turned away and

would have shrugged off Marcus's comforting hand, but the man gripped the boy's shoulder tightly. "Dion, there's an old soldier's saying. 'We live for the day, and we die for it.' They're both soldiers." Marcus put on his helmet, buckled it beneath his chin. "We should be going. It's nearly time."

The two left the centurion's quarters and walked into the corridors, joining a flow of men that were all moving the same direction.

"See," said Dion, waving his hand. "Everyone hurrying to view the show! It's like the gladiators, only worse, because we're supposed to have another three thousand years of civilization behind us."

"It was the lady's decision. It was her choice, as it must be, according to the law."

"What?"

Dion stopped in the corridor, and was immediately in imminent danger of being run down. Men cursed him and shoved him out of their way. Marcus, grabbing hold of the sleeve of the boy's shirt, pulled him to one side, out of traffic.

"I don't believe it!" Dion retorted.

"Would you have her die like a sheep led to the slaughter? That would have been the easy way for her, Dion, and you can bet that she knows it. This gives her the chance to fight for her life, but if she fails—" Marcus shook his head.

"Fails? She can't win!" Dion cried. "If she—"

"Lower your voice."

"If she wins, if she kills . . ." Dion paused, unwilling to say the bad luck words, and then wondered why the thought of Sagan's death was difficult for him to accept. He made himself continue, speaking coldly. "If she kills the Warlord, then you centurions will kill her. Won't you?"

Marcus did not answer aloud, but he turned his face toward the boy. The eyes were barely visible beneath the shadow of the helm, the face was stern and expressionless. But Dion understood. The man's silence said more than words.

My God! She knew this; she's been planning this all along. Dion felt her nails, digging into his flesh. *What you are experiencing is the power of the Blood Royal.* What a dumb, stupid . . . kid . . . I've been.

The two continued on, walking in silence for several paces. Then Dion asked in a subdued tone, "You said her right by *law.* What law are you talking about?"

"It's sort of the final appeal. You see, on board a ship like this, with thousands of men living side by side, justice has to be swift and thorough. A man is tried by his superior officers, who determine his sentence. But sometimes, when a crime is committed, it's one man's word against another's. When this happens, the Warlord deemed that the accused has the right to trial by combat. God is considered to be the final judge, for it's known that He wouldn't allow an innocent man to pay for a crime he didn't commit."

But that's a superstition that dates back to the Dark Ages! Dion started to say. The centurions—like their commander—were pious men. The boy wanted Marcus's respect, so he swallowed his blasphemous words. "It just doesn't seem fair," he said instead. "Lord Sagan's a strong and powerful man and Lady Maigrey's . . . well . . . a woman."

"Strength doesn't count. Agility, stamina are what's important. The bloodsword makes all else equal."

They were halted by a gigantic crowd swarming into the arena. Dion stopped, dismayed. Marcus grabbed hold of the boy and bullied his way forward.

"My lord's command, let us pass!" he called, and men, turning, seeing the bright helmet and flashing armor of the Honor Guard, hastily did what they could to make room.

The arena was a large, circular, domed hall with tiers of seats extending around a huge playing field. In the starship, participation in organized sports was not only encouraged, it was mandatory. Not only did sports provide an outlet for pent-up energies, they kept minds quick and alert and the body in shape. And, when not needed for some game, the officers used the arena to keep the troops drilled, for practice formations, and to rehearse the military band. Some type of activity was going on in the arena almost any time of day. But there had never been, in the memory of anyone on board *Phoenix*, a crowd gathered in the arena equal to the size of this one. No one had ever personally dared challenge the Warlord.

As Marcus said, even the dead must have come to watch.

Chapter —— Thirty-one

O, that a man might know
The end of this day's business ere it come!
But it sufficeth that the day will end,
And then the end is known.

William Shakespeare, *Julius Caesar*

Maigrey stood by herself at the far end of the arena. Opposite her, about ten meters distant, was the Warlord. A circle had been drawn with chalk in the artificial dirt between them. Maigrey was dressed in a body suit similar to the one the Warlord was wearing, except that hers was silver and his was gold. Sagan was noted to scrutinize this costume of hers, but at length shook his head slightly. Those standing near the Warlord saw his face was shadowed, sterner and grimmer than usual.

The Lady Maigrey was very pale, but composed and calm.

Marcus shoved and pushed his way through the crowd, dragging Dion after him. Most of the men, when they saw the boy and recognized him, did what they could to make way for him. The arena was packed. It was standing room only. Dion hadn't imagined there were this many men on board *Phoenix*, and he wondered who was left to run the ship. The noise level, at least, was tolerable. Voices tended to be hushed in the presence of the Warlord; there was no cheering or yelling but awed, almost reverent silence among those gathered to see their lord's moment of triumph . . . or his crushing defeat.

By the time Dion and Marcus had reached the front of the crowd, the young man had surged ahead of the centurion. Dion burst through the open doors and was out onto the floor of the arena before Marcus could catch up with him.

"Let me go!" Dion attempted to shake off the man's hand.

The pep shot seemed to give him unusual strength, but it was, he discovered, an illusionary feeling. Marcus had a grip like iron. "I'm going to stop this!"

"How?" the centurion asked in a low, cool voice.

Frustrated, Dion paused to consider. Or try to consider. His head throbbed, the crowd confused him; the arena was hot and the air stale. He was dimly aware of hundreds of pairs of eyes fixed upon him, expecting, perhaps, some entertainment before the main event. This attention didn't fill him with the same sense of elation he'd experienced in the bar. He felt like a fool and knew, from the expression on Marcus's face, that he looked the part.

"I don't know," he said, sick and miserable. He could see Sagan and Maigrey standing not five meters from him. Both must have noticed him, but if they did, neither gave any sign. They seemed completely oblivious to everything going on around them. The Warlord placed the hilt of his sword carefully in his gloved hand. Dion remembered, vividly, Sagan performing the same action in Platus's small house. The boy saw the blade blaze to life, and the blood flow down bright armor. . . .

Marcus was leading him to a bench that stood on the edge of the field.

"At least let me talk to them," Dion mumbled, sinking down, his shoulders slumped, head in his hands.

"Neither would thank you for breaking their concentration. Using the bloodsword takes tremendous mental control." Marcus, standing beside him, suddenly smote Dion on the shoulder. "Brace up, boy. Do you have less courage than your lord and your lady, who are fighting for their lives?"

The word "boy" stung Dion's pride; the blow stung his skin. Sullenly, he sat up straight and shook the red-golden hair out of his face. Marcus stood at attention beside him—hands clasped behind his back, his feet planted firmly apart, his head facing forward. When he spoke, it was out of the corner of his mouth and in a voice so low, Dion had to strain to hear him.

"If your lady wins, she will need your help. You are of the Blood Royal, aren't you?"

"Yes." Slowly Dion rose to his feet, to stand next to Marcus.

"You can use the sword, then." The centurion flicked him a glance from the corner of his eye, half-shielded by his helm. "But you had better be certain you have a king's blood flowing in your veins. To handle the bloodsword otherwise is death."

"I'm certain," Dion said, but not without a flutter in the pit of his stomach. Of course he was. He was the son of the crown prince. Reaching up, he clasped hold of the ring he wore around his neck. "I'm certain," he repeated more firmly.

"Good. Then, if my lord falls, you must be prepared to take his sword. I will be with you, but I can't use the blade."

Dion tensed, trying desperately to will himself to feel better, to banish the ache in his head. "You'd do that, you'd help her? Us? Why?" There was a tinge of suspicion in the boy's voice.

"Because it is my lord's command," Marcus said simply.

Dion forced down a rush of sickness and dizziness. He was sweating, but his body was shaking with chills. "I don't . . . know anything about . . . those swords," he said through lips so stiff he could barely talk. "Could I even use one?"

The arena blurred in his vision. He blinked his eyes, focusing on the weapon in the hands of the Warlord. The two combatants were walking forward to take up their places directly opposite each other within the center of the chalked circle.

"She's so pale," Dion murmured. "There's something wrong. Look—"

Maigrey started to step into the circle, but she halted and put her hand to her forehead, swaying slightly on her feet. A low murmur passed through the crowd. Dion took a step forward. Marcus's hand reached out and gripped him so tightly Dion could hear the bones in his wrist crunch.

"No one is allowed to assist a combatant. If she falls, she falls."

Dion bit his lip with the pain.

A breathless moment passed, then Maigrey looked around, confused, as if wondering where she was. She shook her head, almost angrily, and with firm step, her slender shoulders squared in resolve, she entered the ring. Sagan entered it at the same time. The two walked forward to meet each other.

"By the law, they must remain in the ring and fight in the ring," Marcus said, relaxing his grip on the boy's wrist. "They are allowed to step outside to rest, and when one does, the other is not allowed to pursue him. But only two rest periods are permitted. Then it is a fight to the finish."

Maigrey and Sagan came to stand face to face. The combatants were required to salute each other before they took up their battle stances. Dion, standing near, every nerve and fiber of his being attuned to each of them, heard their softly spoken words.

"The last of the Oath-breakers. After seventeen years, Maigrey, I take my revenge."

"It isn't vengeance, Sagan." Dion saw Maigrey's lips part in a smile whose sorrow pierced his heart. "Let us admit the reason we are truly here. Life is too painful for each of us to tolerate, if both of us still live."

The Warlord stared at her intently for a long moment, and Dion wondered what was passing between them silently. Sagan bowed, with true respect.

"My lady."

Maigrey bowed in turn.

"My lord."

The arena seemed to Dion to echo with those words. There was a hushed silence, coughs were stifled, no one spoke or even appeared to breathe. The two combatants, stepping back about five paces, took their places and fell into the battle stance.

"They should at least wear some sort of armor," Dion said, in an agony of apprehension.

Marcus cautioned him to speak softer. Dion saw Maigrey glance his way, saw her frown slightly, and, fearful of breaking her concentration further, he gulped and kept quiet. Marcus leaned near him.

"It wouldn't do any good," the centurion whispered. "There is no protection from the bloodsword. It can slice through solid, zero-gravity forged steel as neatly as it will slice through the flesh of your arm. Those who use it rely on swiftness and agility and their own mental power to protect them."

"Tell me how it works." Dion moved closer, their shoulders touching. He never took his eyes from the two in the center of the ring.

Maigrey and Sagan circled each other, trying to draw the other into making the first move. The sword blades glowed an almost blinding blue color, then suddenly Maigrey made a feinting strike inward and in the precise instant the Warlord's blade appeared to disappear. She fell back from the attack. Sagan's blade reappeared and struck out and Maigrey's weapon blinked out of sight.

"What's going on?" Dion stared in confusion. "Why does the blade vanish?"

"It doesn't. Not really. That's the weapon's defense shield. It will protect against the enemy's blow, but to use the shield requires almost double the energy needed to use the blade. They're playing a mental game with each other, trying to drain each other's strength."

"I don't understand."

"You had better, for you may be called on to use it."

The two were circling, feinting attacks now and then. The swords blazed blue, then disappeared and then were blue, switching from offense to defense with the swiftness of a thought.

"Have you ever seen one of the swords?"

"Yes." Dion did not tell Marcus where or under what circumstances. He saw it clearly, though, in Platus's hand.

"You've seen that there are five prongs on the hilt. When the user grasps the hilt, these prongs penetrate the flesh and inject a virus into the bloodstream. In a person with the correct blood type and DNA structure, this virus opens channels that parallel the normal nerve channels and eventually reach the brain. Micromachines are injected, making connections with the lymphatic systems to draw energy from the body's cells to power the weapon. The energy used comes from ATP, adenosine triphosphate. The sword has its own energy source, but once that is depleted, it begins to draw on the only other source available—your body."

"What happens if you don't have the correct blood type and you pick up the sword?"

Sagan made a sudden lunge at Maigrey, who didn't meet him with a block as expected, but who swiftly and agilely dodged, whirled, and sent her blade slicing through the air with a vicious downward stroke that would have cut the man in two had he not guessed her attack and reacted in time, falling back away from her. The two paused a moment, eyeing each other, then resumed their places in the center of the circle.

Dion resumed breathing.

"The virus injected into a body that doesn't have the proper bloodline turns into a particularly nasty form of cancer," Marcus said quietly. "It mutates rapidly. There is no cure. Death, if you're lucky, comes in about three days. At least there's one thing you won't have to worry about. If my lord falls, no one will be eager to take possession of his bloodsword. You'll have it all to yourself."

Death, if you're lucky, in three days. The inside of the palm of Dion's right hand itched unpleasantly. He rubbed the skin. "But Sagan's wearing gloves. How could—"

"Doesn't matter. The prongs will penetrate the heaviest gauntlet. And the hilt is weighted in such a way that, in order to use it, you must hold it so that the prongs dig into the flesh. Oh, good exchange. Well done!"

The crowd was losing its awe, getting into the spirit of the battle. A rapid series of attacks made the air hum with the blade's energy. The afterimage of the blue light burning the retina of the eye made it seem as if the two were surrounded in red streaks and it was difficult, for an instant, to see what had happened.

Both emerged unscathed, though each was sweating profusely and their breath was visibly coming quicker and shorter. They took up their positions again when Maigrey suddenly made the same gesture that had drawn Dion's concern earlier. She put her hand to her temple, blinking her eyes. She had just presence of mind left to stumble out of the circle. Sagan, standing in the center, his sword arm relaxed, watched her closely, warily, apparently suspecting some trick.

But Dion, who could see Sagan's face clearly, saw a tiny frown appear between the thick black brows. The man was puzzled, obviously wondering what was going on.

"That will cost her," Marcus said in grim tones. "She should have taken the rest later in the battle when she'll need it more."

"There's something wrong with her! That's obvious. Why don't they stop?"

"There's no way they can. The only way to stop now is for one to yield to the other, and that would mean not only death but dishonor."

"What honor is there in this? Fighting someone who's sick?"

"The lady doesn't appear sick to me. She fought with too much energy. There, she's going back. I don't know what the matter is, but she better control it."

The fight seemed, to Dion, to drag on for hours. The tension was unbearable. It was, as Marcus said, a battle of wits as much as of physical prowess. Eyes were focused on each other, the brain endeavoring to penetrate the mental shield while the body tried to penetrate the physical. Each was growing visibly tired, each making tiny mistakes, saving themselves only by sheer bursts of energy, skill, and intuition. Blood oozed from wounds each had taken.

And then Sagan slipped, the aching muscle of his legs giving out. Maigrey was on him in an instant and only the fact that he was standing next to the circle and could throw himself out saved him.

Picking himself up from the dirt, he jumped back into the circle, and those who knew him knew that he was furious. Unlike other men, the Warlord's rage did not kindle a fire, but rather seemed to quench one. He was cold and remote and intent on ending this contest that had, in his estimation, gone on far too long. His attack was vicious. He hammered at Maigrey's sword again and again until it seemed impossible that his arms would possess the strength to keep inflicting such blows . . . or hers to absorb them.

Maigrey was forced to keep her shield switched on continually and her strength was waning fast. But she defended herself bravely. The shouting in the arena was deafening and seemed not to be for either one in particular but in homage to the valor of both and the eager, brutal expectation that is humanity's worst failing—the thirst for blood.

Dion strained forward, his heart thudding in his chest, his throat burning. Marcus, mindful of his duty in the midst of the excitement, had hold of him, or else the young man would have hurled himself into that circle of death. The noise reverberated off the walls, sending the blood pounding in his head until he feared something inside him must burst from the pressure.

And then suddenly Maigrey collapsed. She sank to her knees in the dirt of the arena, her head bowed, her shoulders slumped, the sword gone lifeless in her hand.

"Get out!" shouted many, on their feet, urging her to seek the sanctuary outside the edge of the circle.

Lord Sagan paused, flaming sword in hand, waiting to see if she would make the attempt to save her own life. But Maigrey didn't move. She had fallen in the classic pose of one who faces execution, and the Warlord, taking this for her surrender, raised the blade above her head.

The crowd roared. Some shouted for Sagan to finish it. Others shouted for the lady to find her courage.

A scream of rage welled up inside Dion. He leapt forward, only to feel Marcus's arm around his neck, throttling him. The young man fought viciously, hopelessly, and Marcus was forced to nearly choke the breath from Dion before he could calm him down.

"Look, boy! Look!" Marcus's hissing voice finally penetrated.

"She's in a trance!" Dion whispered.

Maigrey seemingly had no idea where she was or that her own death was standing over her. She was staring at something no one else could see, a look of tense concentration on her face. The Warlord hesitated to strike; it would be like killing her in her sleep. Still thinking it might be a trick, he kicked the sword from her hand out of her reach. Maigrey didn't move, didn't appear to notice her weapon was gone. The expression on her face had changed to one of horror. Whatever visions she was seeing must be terrible.

The shouting in the arena had changed to a murmur, puzzled and ominous.

Hurling his own sword into the dirt, Sagan knelt beside the woman, and taking hold of her by the shoulders, he shook her. Maigrey's head snapped back, her hair straggled over her face. Her eyes were gray; the scar was a leaden streak across her skin. Her lips parted to gasp for breath. She didn't speak. Blinking, she focused on Sagan and a shudder went through her body. Reaching out her hands, she caught hold of him, clutching at him as she were drowning.

The Warlord's black hair had come undone and fell about his sweat-streaked face. He held her, supported her.

"What is it, Maigrey? What do you see? Share it with me!"

Looking up into his eyes, her expression ghastly, Maigrey placed both hands on either side of the Warlord's face.

The murmur of the crowd became a muttering, an exchanging of glances, grim and fearful. The arena seemed to grow darker. A shadow was spreading, emanating from the two unmoving figures in the center of the arena, like a perverse sun that brings night, not day.

Dion freed himself from the centurion and started across the arena. Marcus, uncertain what was happening or how it affected his orders, allowed the boy to go and followed him. His lord did not look like himself.

"My lord!"

Captain Nada had entered the arena. Making his way through the dirt toward the two combatants covered with grime and sweat and their own blood. A disdainful expression on his face, Nada paused inside the ring to flick a bit of soil from the pants leg of his uniform. Like the fool who comes on before the last scene in a tragedy, he gave the audience a chance to relieve their pent-up feelings. Nervous, stomach-clenching laughter burst from the watching men. The captain's face flushed purplish red. He glared around at the men in silent rage, but it was obvious he blamed this insult on the Warlord. He gave the man and woman kneeling in the circle a look of complete and utter disgust.

"My lord, we have received a message from outpost B545 on Shelton's Planet I. They are under attack. Enemy unknown. Battleship *Diana* is on patrol in that vicinity. I have ordered *Jupiter* to reinforce—"

"Call it back." Lord Sagan's voice cracked harshly, from exhaustion and strain. He freed himself from Maigrey's grasp and rose wearily to his feet. Glancing around, he caught sight of Marcus's bright armor. "Centurion, take the lady to sick bay—"

That threat was enough to rouse Maigrey from her trance. "No," she murmured, holding out a warding hand, waving Marcus away. "I'm fine. I'm all right. Just . . . let me rest a moment."

The Warlord was strolling rapidly out of the arena. The men were breathlessly silent, straining to hear.

Nada, obviously incensed, followed. "My lord, I protest—"

"I said order *Jupiter* back, Nada. Their mission is pointless."

"I hardly call going to the aid of an outpost under attack pointless, my lord. We have received no further reports from Shelton but—"

Sagan spun on his heel. Captain Nada, nearly tripping on the Warlord's feet, was forced to backpedal swiftly to avoid a collision.

"Nor will you, Captain. Ever. The outpost no longer exists. I've seen it. It has been wiped out—to the man."

"What—"

"Corasians, Nada. They've entered the galaxy." Sagan, turning again, continued walking. His centurions were hurrying to him, eager to be of use, and he was issuing orders as he walked. "Put the fleet on alert and get hold of the President. I'll use the emergency channel. Where's Aks? Send for the admiral and tell him to meet me in the war room. Alert the outposts on Shelton's Planets II and III, but don't be surprised if they don't respond."

Maigrey, forgotten, brushed the pale hair out of her face. Her eyes were on the Warlord. She looked drained. Dion, kneeling beside her, heard her sigh. She closed her eyes, overcome with a weariness that was not of the body but of the spirit.

"And so we go on." He heard her murmur.

Book II

Where All Life Dies

. . . while I abroad
Through all the coasts of dark destruction seek
Deliverance for us all . . .
                    John Milton, *Paradise Lost*

Chapter ·❖◦○◦❖· *One*

I wish to have no connection with any Ship that does not sail fast, for I intend to go in harm's way. . . .

John Paul Jones

Derek Sagan stood in the war room aboard *Phoenix*. On the vidscreen before him, President Robes sat at the oval table. He was alone. Robes was attired in a white, cable-knit, V-necked sweater, striped at the neck, and with cuffs of bright lines of red and blue. The white set off his tan, which in turn set off the touches of gray at the temples; the entire effect looked extremely good in the newsvids. He had apparently been taking some sort of gentle exercise which Sagan's urgent message had interrupted.

The President leaned forward, nudging to one side a silver water pitcher that sat on the table before him in order to get a better view of the vidscreen. The Warlord, glancing at this water pitcher, saw the image of another person reflected in it, someone who was keeping out of range of the camera, someone standing directly across the room from the President. Robes did not look in this person's direction, but clasped his hands before him—a gesture which meant he was giving you his full and complete attention. His face was expressive of grave concern.

Derek Sagan swiftly depressed a series of buttons on the control panel before him. Robes's face disappeared, replaced by the silver water pitcher that was, with every shot, growing larger on the screen.

"You have, of course, verified this news of an attack, Citizen General?"

"Yes, Mr. President."

The silver water pitcher was revealing a curved and distorted magenta blob. Sagan ordered it brought closer. Magenta. The Warlord's blood congealed in his veins.

"This is an outrage," the President was saying. "I'll take it to the Congress, of course. I'll call an emergency session. I've no doubt that we will declare war on the Corasians."

"Yes, Mr. President."

The person reflected in the water pitcher could be seen clearly. Sagan hadn't been wrong. Magenta robes, edged in black, the zigzag of black lightning—dark lightning—running down the front. It *was* him! Mentally, the Warlord staggered.

He was reported dead! What's he doing here? Of course! Robes. He has Robes! Perhaps he's had him under his control from the very beginning. It would explain much.

"Citizen General Sagan? Have we lost communication?"

"Excuse me, Mr. President." Sagan wrenched his mind back to his duty. The silver water pitcher dwindled in size and on the screen, once again, was Peter Robes. "I was . . . receiving further news on the enemy."

"I understand your interest, Citizen General. But perhaps you could favor me with your full attention?"

"Yes, Mr. President." Sagan ground the words with his teeth.

"It is likely, if the Corasians follow their usual plan of action, that they will use Shelton's Planets I, II, and III as bases and strike out at the rest of the galaxy from there. Wouldn't you agree, Citizen General?"

Sagan agreed.

"Then," the President continued, "we are fortunate that the enemy has picked a relatively worthless and out-of-the-way system—"

"There are seven million people on Shelton's planets, Mr. President."

Robes's face crumbled instantly from grave concern to gentle grief. "You misunderstood me, Citizen General. Of course, I didn't mean worthless in terms of human life. That is a terrible tragedy, certainly, but . . . let's be brutally realistic."

Yes, since the press isn't around, Sagan thought.

"Seven million people is a mere drop in the ocean of the life of the galaxy. And, in terms of resources, Shelton's planets are, I believe, devoted mainly to scientific research. There are vast numbers of scientists in this galaxy.

"I intend—once Congress has declared war, of course—to command the generals of the other sectors to pull back and guard the dense population centers of our galaxy. I want you, Citizen General Sagan, to stop the Corasians from penetrating further into the galaxy."

"Yes, Mr. President. I will need reinforcements—"

"Impossible, I'm afraid, Derek." Robes leaned forward, his face revealing complete and absolute confidence in his commander. "Let's drop the formalities. We're old friends, after all. The inner circle of the defense will need all the galaxy's current resources in case—and I don't mean this to be negative thinking, I'm only being realistic—in case you fail to stop the enemy."

"I would say, Mr. President, that fighting the Corasians with the force I have means failure is a foregone conclusion."

The President's face exhibited gentle sorrow, extreme disappointment. "I'm sorry to hear that, Derek. You are my ablest commander. I expected better of you." Robes's eyes flicked, almost involuntarily, to the unseen person standing across the room from him. Their gaze returned to the Warlord immediately. Sagan might not have caught the glance if he hadn't been watching for it. "You have your orders, Citizen General Sagan."

"I have my orders. Yes, Mr. President."

"Our best wishes and those of the galaxy are with you."

Are they indeed, Mr. President? Sagan silently commented.

The screen went blank. The Warlord stood staring at it in profound silence for a long, long time.

··◁ ▷··

In the forgotten lounge on the diplomatic deck, Maigrey and Dion were alone. There were no guards in attendance—an oblique compliment to the lady, and one which she found depressing. The threat to her galaxy was holding her prisoner now more surely than Sagan ever could. She sat limp and lifeless in a chair, staring, unseeing, out at the stars. Her head rested wearily on her hand. Dion watched her with grave concern. She had drunk nothing, eaten nothing in the several hours that had passed since the duel. She had not spoken at all.

An orderly entered the room, padding softly, not breaking the heavy silence. He bore a tray and set it down on a table at Maigrey's side. On the tray was a porcelain teapot of fanciful design—the spout was the head of a dragon, the pot was its body, and the handle was the dragon's tail. The pot rested on four small clawed feet. Steam curled from the dragon's parted mouth. Two cups, shaped like dragon eggs, without handles, stood near the pot, along with a bowl of fruit and a plate of plain, unsalted crackers.

"From his lordship," the orderly said and left.

Dion, leaning over, sniffed at the tea. It had a faintly tarry aroma and his nose wrinkled. He glanced up at Maigrey, who was looking at the pot with a wan smile.

"You don't think he's trying to poison us?" The young man was half-serious, wholly in earnest.

Maigray's smile widened slightly. "No, Dion, it's supposed to smell like that. It's called lapsong souchong." She traced her finger over the dragon's head. "Even the teapot looks familiar. But it couldn't be the same one. It couldn't." Sighing, she closed her eyes.

Dion carefully and awkwardly lifted the teapot. "Here, let me pour you a cup. You should drink something."

"Why? To keep up my strength? To keep on living?"

Her bitterness and anger startled the young man. He tried to set the teapot back down gently, but it struck against one of the cups and made a frightful clatter. Maigrey opened her eyes, saw his face, and sighed.

"I'm sorry, Dion. It's just—" She paused, thinking, then said softly, "Once, I knew a man, a renowned poet, who fell down an elevator shaft. He was rescued and they brought him up alive, but the doctors diagnosed some sort of internal injury to the brain and said he only had a few months to live. The man bid his friends and family good-bye, completed the book of poetry he was writing, and then prepared himself to die. But he didn't. He kept on living. Five years later he was still alive. It was his biggest disappointment."

Dion said nothing. The story appalled him, though he didn't understand its point. He picked up a cracker, broke it in two, started to eat it, then tossed it back down onto the plate.

"Lady Maigrey," he said abruptly. "What did the test tell you about me? Did God . . . er . . . speak?"

What a superstitious fool he sounded! Might as well ask a Ouija board.

"He spoke, but not quite what we expected to hear." Maigrey lifted the teapot with a sudden, brisk gesture. "Will you try this? It doesn't taste as odd as it smells and it's good for queasy stomachs. How are you feeling?"

"The drugs seem to be wearing off. I was feeling hungry, in fact, until the food came in. Now, I'm not certain." Dion looked at the hot brown liquid in the dragon's egg cup. "If you don't mind, my lady, I think I'll go see if I can find some water."

So that's all she plans to tell me, Dion thought. Bah! God talking! What kind of fool do they think I am? What's God supposed to say—that I'm going to be a great king because I passed out on Sagan's floor? Probably all the Warlord meant to do was torture me and see how I reacted! Well, if you ask me, I think I came through it pretty fine. Now if I could just figure out how I managed to make that silver ball float in the air. . . .

When he returned, he found Maigrey standing by the viewport, staring thoughtfully into a distant part of the galaxy.

"I saw the Corasians before the fight began, you know." Maigrey didn't turn, didn't look around at him. "Black shapes, blotting out the stars. I'd seen them in my mind before, but it was years ago, and I couldn't remember what they were, I couldn't concentrate. I didn't dare concentrate on them."

"But—you *saw* them!"

"Our altered blood structure does quirky things, sometimes, things scientists can't explain. I can see images in my mind of events happening somewhere far distant. Sometimes I can control it and see what I want; sometimes the visions come to me unbidden, as this one did today. It was how Sagan hoped to be able to use me to find you. But, as it turned out, that wasn't necessary."

Dion stirred uncomfortably, angrily, feeling that he'd been accused of some misdeed. Shaking the red-golden mane of hair out of his face, he shoved his hands in the pockets of his jeans and stared moodily out at the stars.

"What about sharing this vision with Sagan? That hand-on-the-face business." Dion hadn't meant to sound jealous and only realized he'd done so when he saw her glance at him, amused.

"Because we're mind-linked, he and I can share the visions, but only if we are physically touching." Maigrey lifted her palm. By the dim light of the lounge and the lambent light of the stars, he could see the five small white marks that were now slightly red and swollen from contact with the blood-sword. "It happened only after we'd been given our swords. I think it probably has something to do with the virus. Two people of the Blood Royal who aren't mind-linked can experience a certain amount of mental telepathy when they are using the swords. This can be good or bad, depending."

"Depending on what? It seems good to me."

Maigrey looked at him fully, intently. "On the minds using the swords. The stronger, you see, has the ability to control the weaker."

He hated it when she looked inside him like that. Dion flushed and rubbed the palm of his right hand. Ever since he'd seen the bloodswords, he'd felt those five marks on his skin. Clearing his throat, he turned away from the window, wandered over to the table, and absentmindedly devoured all of the crackers. He heard a sound, a faint jingle of armor, and was almost relieved to see Lord Sagan standing in the door.

Maigrey turned back to staring out the steelglass.

Sagan glanced at the young man. "How are you feeling, Dion?"

"Fine, my lord." The young man spoke coldly. He was furious at Sagan and his anger vied with his intense admiration. The conflicting emotions were confusing and painful and he didn't know how to handle them. Standing straight and stiff, he clasped his hands behind his back.

The Warlord's face was drawn and tired-looking; there was a gray tinge to the skin. The lines around the mouth and nose and on the brow were deeper, darker.

"Fine or not, I want you to report to sick bay."

"Why?" Dion's anger flared. Sagan was obviously trying to get rid of him. "I feel fine. I—"

"I said, you are to report to sick bay. There are some tests Giesk wants to run. Guards." Sagan made a peremptory gesture. "If he won't go, take him."

Dion glanced at the Lady Maigrey, but she was no help. She stood with her back to him, looking out at the stars. The young man swallowed the hot words that came flooding to his mouth and, after a moment's bitter struggle, did as he was commanded. Stiff-necked, red-faced, he stalked out of the room.

The Warlord indicated with a gesture that the guards were to follow.

"My lord," said one of the centurions, "should we send for replacements?"

Sagan shook his head.

The guard saluted and left. Maigrey could hear their booted

feet ringing on the steel deck, then the sound faded and she and the Warlord were alone.

"You were hard on the boy, my lord."

Sagan came to stand beside her. "He better get used to it. Things are only going to get worse."

"So it's as bad as that?"

"Don't you know? I haven't kept my thoughts hidden from you. I've been too damn busy."

"I didn't want to see them." Maigrey's voice was soft. Her hands were clasped before her. Tensely, unconsciously, she twisted her fingers.

"The Corasians are attacking in force. We had a treaty with them. Don't blame me, lady. I had nothing to do with it. It was Robes's first act as President, guaranteed to win him popularity. For the past fifteen years, our spies—mine and those of the other Warlords—have reported to him that the Corasians were not holding to the terms of the treaty, that they were building up their forces. Robes always refused to comment directly, but his mouthpieces in Congress accused us of war-mongering, of using the Corasians as an excuse to keep our fleets and armies strong."

"This attack surprised you, then?"

"To be honest, yes. I had expected them to strike, but not this soon. According to my last report before I lost contact with my agent, the Corasians couldn't possibly have been ready to make a full-scale assault. But I think," Sagan added, his voice dry, "I was the *only* one surprised."

Maigrey turned, stared at him incredulously.

"You think Robes knew?"

"I'm convinced of it."

"And he let hundreds of thousands of people on those planets die? I can't believe that, even of him!"

The Warlord shrugged off the question. "What are thousands to him when he has trillions of votes in the inner circle of the galaxy? Shelton's planets were inconsequential—mostly inhabited by soldiers and scientists, their families, a few scientific stations, and the usual population centers that grow up around military bases."

Pausing, Sagan leaned near, lowered his voice. "You must understand, lady, that my agent in the Corasian galaxy was good. Very good. He'd been there for years—a slave in one of their chemical factories, that was his cover. They'd never come near discovering him. Then he disappeared. In his last report he indicated that there was someone on to him."

"Robes's agents?"

"*Someone's* agents. And not, I think, the Corasians."

Turning, the Warlord left the viewscreen and went over to seat himself wearily in a chair. Suppressing a groan, he rubbed a knotted muscle in his thigh.

Maigrey turned away. She found she couldn't look at him—weary and beaten—without feeling a wrenching pain in her heart. Plus she sensed him afraid, and his fear unnerved her. But what was he afraid of? Certainly not the Corasians, not impending battle, however uneven the odds. It was something else, something buried that had just been recently brought to the surface—like an exhumed corpse.

"The tea's cold, I'm afraid, my lord." She spoke just to fill the silence. "You never liked the lapsong much, anyway. I could send for oolong—"

"No, it doesn't matter. Come sit with me, lady, like the old days. We have much to discuss. Pour me a cup of this stuff. I won't taste it anyway."

Dying would have been so much easier.

Maigrey turned from the window and walked over to the table. Pouring the tea, she handed the cup to him and he gulped it down thirstily. Silently, she poured him another. He drank half of this cup, then sat, holding it in his hand, staring at it. The delicate porcelain looked fragile as an eggshell in his large hands.

"Robes has ordered me to make a stand. To stop the Corasians here and now. No reinforcements."

Maigrey seated herself in the chair opposite that of the Warlord. "And he kills two birds with one stone."

"Not precisely. Let's say that he allows the birds to kill each other."

"He knows you're plotting against him?"

"Yes, he knows!" Sagan beat a clenched fist softly against the arm of the chair, emphasizing his words. "Damn the man! He's clever, Maigrey. I keep forgetting how clever! And there's another more clever—" he broke off abruptly.

Maigrey wondered what he had been going to say, but she kept clear of his mind. The last thing she wanted right now was to get too close to him.

"The President orders us to stand and fight the initial assault out here, where there are few populated systems—a command that will be applauded by the Congress and the press."

"And the other marshals?"

"He's pulling them in to form a second line of defense around the major populated zones."

"We're on our own."

Sagan's mouth twisted. "We?"

Maigrey flushed and looked down at her hands.

"Yes," the Warlord added quietly, "we're on our own."

"But the enemy could penetrate anywhere! A thousand different places!" Maigrey gestured to the stars. "How can he be certain—" But she knew the answer, the moment she asked the question.

"They'll come straight for us, lady. I would bet all my fortune on the fact that somehow, undoubtedly through a leak in security, the enemy knows our exact coordinates, knows all our moves. That's why they've attacked before they were ready. They didn't need to be ready. Undoubtedly they've promised Robes they'll turn and run after they've destroyed us. If he believes that, he's a bigger fool than I thought. You know, of course, what the enemy's really after?"

"*Phoenix.*" Maigrey's hands curled over the arms of the chair. Her eyes glanced around the ship.

"And the rest of the ships. The reports we've received from the survivors fleeing Shelton's system tell us that the Corasians are following their same pattern—rounding up the people, using them either for food or slave labor, destroying everything else except the machines. It's our technology they want. They'll come straight for us, all right. We have the unique distinction of being both bait and trap."

"You know their numbers?"

"I can estimate them, from the early reports."

"Can the fleet survive?"

"The computers say no, not with our current strength. But we can do a significant amount of damage before we die. By God, I'll blow up this ship myself before I turn it over to them!"

"You've never been one to give a damn about orders, Sagan. You could retreat, fall back."

"I'd be branded a coward—disgraced forever. Not but what I might do it; I can handle the newsmedia, and Robes knows it. But you see, my lady, there's a possibility I can win this.

And, if I do, I'll be the galaxy's hero. Nothing will be too good for me."

"Not even the galaxy itself." Rising to her feet abruptly, Maigrey left the Warlord, returned to staring out the window. Her back was to him, her arms crossed across her chest. "It's quite a risk Robes is taking."

"He's a gambler; he knows the odds and they're in his favor."

"What about the local systems? Won't they send help?"

"They'll be too concerned for their own safety. We're keeping this quiet, but the news will break soon and then we'll be deluged with pleas for *us* to rush to *their* aid."

Maigrey stood at the window, her hands rubbing up and down her arms. Sagan, suddenly realizing what she was thinking, rose to his feet.

"You're wrong, Maigrey. Dixter and his people won't join me."

"Would it help if they did?"

"Yes, of course. Any addition to our manpower would help."

"His people are good, from what I've heard."

"They're good. I trained most of them myself. Three-fourths are deserters from my air corps!"

Maigrey smiled slightly at the bitter edge in his voice. "John Dixter will come."

"He might if *you* asked him, is that what you mean, Maigrey?"

"No." She shook her head, the pale hair falling around her face, hiding it from view. "Dion."

Sagan was caught off guard. He hadn't seen that one coming. Moving close behind her, he rested his hands on her shoulders. "Nice try, my lady, but it won't work. Even if Dion did go, he would come back to me. What do you call it? The taint in our blood? Ambition, the lust for power burns in that boy. And I have what he wants."

Maigrey held herself rigid beneath his touch. Hours ago, they had been intent on killing each other. Still alive. Her biggest disappointment. Setting her jaw, she turned, breaking his grip, and faced him stolidly.

"And what will you do with him now? What will you do with a boy our God has told us is His chosen. A boy destined, perhaps, to be both king and savior of his people?"

Sagan clasped his arms behind his back, beneath his cloak. "A foolish question, my lady. You know that—like Lucifer—I would far rather reign in hell, than serve in heaven."

"You dare to defy God?"

"Let us say, my lady, that I am working to persuade Him to change His mind."

"I'll stop you in this, Sagan!" Maigrey advanced a step. "I fought you for Dion once, long ago. I'll fight for him again."

"Be warned, my lady, I can rid myself of you right this moment—"

"No, you can't. That's an empty threat, my lord. You could have killed me this afternoon, but you didn't. You hesitated, held back. I see into your mind clearly now. You're torn two ways. God has granted you a glimpse into the future and you've forseen my death at your hands. But not now. Not yet. Something wasn't right today, was it? Something I wore, something I said— Killing me today *would* have defied God, and you don't dare do it! He has brought us together for a purpose, perhaps to fight together against this new peril."

She took a step nearer; they were practically touching.

"Our motives will be different, my lord. You think of your own glory, your lust for power. I'm thinking of the people, the millions who will die. Like it or not, we're shackled to each other. There's no way to break the chain. We've tried it, and it didn't work. The only way it seems we'll ever escape this hellish prison is to help each other climb the walls! I'll help you, Sagan, but only if you keep your chains from entangling Dion. If you don't, I'll drag you down myself!"

"And you'd drag the boy down with us. It's too late, Maigrey. Dion's bound, body and soul. He was from the day he was born." Sagan backed away from her. Reaching into the bowl of fruit, he selected an apple, and held it up to the light. "I accept your premise, lady. But I question your motives. I don't believe they are as pure as you pretend. Since we're peering into others' minds, I see you, standing behind Dion's throne . . . *very close* behind his throne." He tossed the apple into the air. "I think I'll take this to the boy. He's probably hungry."

"Yes," Maigrey said, biting the word. "He probably is."

The Warlord turned to go, paused, looked back. "But I like your idea about Dixter. I'll consider it. Thank you, my lady."

He turned, and was gone.

Still alive. Maigrey sighed. Still alive.

Chapter ·◄>○○◄>· Two

'Great are thy virtues, doubtless, best of fruits.'
John Milton, *Paradise Lost*

A sudden buzzing roused Sagan from the deep meditative state he used in times of emergency, preferring it to that of sleep. He came out of his meditation mentally alert, physically ready for any type of action. No action was called for at the moment, however, except to respond to a flashing red light on his personal computer.

A message, coded for him, beamed directly to him.

He gave the voice response and the message flashed on the screen. His security was absolutely unbreakable, his computer being programmed to seek out, identify, and attack any other system trying to surmount his innumerable defenses. But Sagan had taken the additional precaution of carrying on his clandestine dealings in twentieth century English—a wordy, clumsy, and confusing language now almost totally, but not completely, forgotten.

"Gad, Sagan, what a beastly language. I quite abhor it. Can you imagine the barbaric types who used it? I assure you, I get quite nauseated just thinking about them. In response to your question, my agent reports that after my removal from Vangelis, a young human female was discovered snooping around my offices. She is one Nola Rian and she is a—if you will believe it—TRUC driver. Isn't that too ridiculous? Further investigation has linked her to a human male, one John Dixter, commander of the mercenary forces. There is, of course, always the possibility that I could have been the teeniest bit careless and let something slip but, gad, Sagan, I'm a genius. What do you expect? Is this a problem, dear boy? If so, I assure you, it can be rectified."

322

"It's a problem but not for me. For you, Snaga Ohme." The
screen had gone dark. The Warlord was talking to the night. "I
will do the rectifying. You will pay the price."

Returning to his bed, Sagan stretched himself out, crossed
his hands over his chest, interlacing the fingers, and drew a
deep breath. Releasing it, he murmured, "Yes, lady, your
suggestion is an excellent one. John Dixter's assistance in our
cause will be invaluable. Truly invaluable."

--◁■ ■▷--

"Dion, a moment's word with you."

"Certainly, my lord. Please come in."

The boy's voice was cold and stilted; he was nurturing his
anger. The Warlord, seeming not to notice, stepped inside the
young man's living quarters. Sagan was clad in his gold
ceremonial armor, the golden helm with the red-feathered
crest on his head, his red cape, trimmed in gold, fluttering
behind. He was holding something in his hand, keeping it
concealed beneath his cloak.

The Honor Guards took up their stance, the door sealed
shut, and the two were alone. Dion rose to his feet, and
remained standing, rigid, defensive.

Sagan, glancing around, saw that the young man had been
reading a book—*David Copperfield*. The Warlord's lips tightened, but he said nothing. Now was not the time.

"There's to be a meeting of the fleet's officers, 1800 hours. I
want you to attend."

Disarmed, Dion's mouth sagged. He blinked and brought
his gaze to bear on the Warlord. "Me?"

"As the Lady Maigrey and I were discussing last evening,
this current crisis engulfs us all. There is, in fact, an important
mission I'm going to be asking you to undertake. And since
from now on, wherever we walk, we walk with danger, I
thought you should have this."

The Warlord threw aside his cloak, revealing the object he
had hidden—a bloodsword.

Dion gasped, then drew a shivering breath. His hands
itched to touch it, but part of him wanted to put those same
hands firmly behind his back and have nothing to do with it.

Before he could make any sort of intelligent response, the
Warlord had come forward and—with all the deference of a
squire to his knight—buckled the sword in its scabbard around
the young man's slender waist.

"When wearing this sword, you should at least dress like royalty." The Warlord glanced scathingly at Dion's blue jeans. "You can change to your uniform later. Now, if you like, I have an hour to spare. We could go to the gymnasium and I could begin to instruct you in the sword's use."

"If you want, my lord."

The young man's response was hesitant. His gaze was fixed on the sword, fear and desire vying within him.

"There *is* some risk involved. Do you understand?"

"About the—the virus?" *Dead in three days, if you're lucky.* Dion replied in a steady voice, "Yes, my lord. I understand."

"You don't have to do this, if you don't want to. You don't have to take the risk. Even though your parentage seems certain and you were given the rite of initiation, there remains, still, this final test." Sagan did not mention that he'd had Dr. Giesk run a blood sample. The boy was in no danger, none at all. His blood was pure. Or it was "tainted," depending on how one looked at it. This moment—though the boy would never realize it—was the true test.

"I know about the risk, my lord. I want to take it."

"Good." Lord Sagan's cool smile was hidden by the shadows of the helm. "I thought you would."

··◆▮ ▮◆··

Maigrey sat in the bar, watching the light reflect off the bottles. She was glad they'd kept the bottles. There were more modern, convenient means of dispensing liquor available. Hell, almost any two-byte computer could mix an old-fashioned. But there was something about the bottles and about the bartender mixing his magic from the bottles that was comforting to her. Rather, Maigrey supposed, like the wizard from ages past, working in his laboratory, mixing the weird and the wonderful to weave his spells.

"Another?" the bartender asked, whisking away the soggy cocktail napkin, his hand hovering over the glass.

"Yes. But don't take that yet. One more swallow."

Maigrey drank it, returned the glass to the bar. The empty disappeared, a full one took its place. Magic. She stirred the ice cubes around and around, admiring the various colors of the liquors in the bottles—amber, bright green, gold, clear; the different shapes of the bottles . . .

Out of the corner of her eye, she saw flaming red-golden hair, the face white in the indistinct bluish, purplish lighting of the bar. She saw what he wore around his waist. He walked with self-conscious pride, somewhat awkwardly, his hand holding the scabbard as he moved through the lounge in an effort to keep it from banging into tables. Maigrey stared back into her glass and continued stirring the ice around and around.

"I've been looking all over for you, Lady Maigrey." The boy's voice was accusing.

"I knew where I was."

The young man was silent a moment, probably trying to figure out what she meant, most certainly trying to decide how to respond. "Lord Sagan's guards told me you were here."

"See? *We* knew where I was, then."

From his expression, Dion didn't see, not in the least. Maigrey smiled faintly. There was another pause, the young man waiting for her to say something.

"What are you drinking?" he asked finally, when she didn't.

"Vodka martini. Very dry. On the rocks. With olives. You've got to mention the olives specifically. If you don't, they stick a piece of lemon in it."

"Lord Sagan doesn't drink." Accusation had become reproof. The boy was sanctimonious as only youth can be when descrying the faults of their elders.

"I know. I do it for both of us." Maigrey swallowed vodka. Holding the glass in her hand, she shook it gently, to hear the ice cubes clink against the sides. "Where'd you get the bloodsword?"

"Lord Sagan gave it to me." Dion flushed with pride. His right hand touched the hilt, somewhat gingerly.

Maigrey glanced at it, looked back into her drink. "It's Platus's, you know. I wish I could say he'd have wanted you to have it."

She heard the swift intake of breath. When she lifted her eyes and looked at the boy, she saw that he had gone white to the lips. Dion stared at her, his brilliant blue eyes, surrounded by white rims, glistening with the shock.

"I'm sorry," Maigrey said, shrugging. Fishing the olive from her glass, she ate it, then carefully placed the toothpick on the bar in front of her. "I thought you knew."

"Damn it! How could I know? I never saw it, except for that . . . that night!" Dion's hands fumbled with the buckle of the sword belt. His fingers were numb and shaking and he couldn't unfasten it. Maigrey's fingers closed over his, suddenly, and he shivered at the chill touch.

"Don't take it off. I'm sorry, truly sorry." She looked at him earnestly. "It's right you should have it, right you should know how to use it. Only, remember what I said about the mind control. Be careful." Keeping hold of his right hand, she turned it palm up. Five puncture marks marred the skin. Swelling, they were beginning to turn an angry, fiery red. "He's using you, you know, Dion. He'll use you to gain what he wants, then he'll throw you away like so much rubbish."

Dion snatched his hand away from her grasp. The boy's voice was hard and brittle. "It's a game two can play at, my lady. Or maybe three."

He glowered at her from beneath lowered brows. She'd hurt him, hurt him badly, and he had to strike back.

"Your arm ache?" Maigrey asked.

"No."

"It'll feel numb for several days, but the sensation won't be permanent. Next time you use the sword, it'll be easier."

"I know that. Lord Sagan told me."

"Ah, yes." Maigrey took a drink and swallowed. "'Satan was Christ's elder brother.'"

"What?" Dion only half heard her.

"'Satan was Christ's elder brother.' Robertson P. Davies. *Fifth Business*. Twentieth century author."

The young man didn't understand. "How many of those have you had?"

"'How many of those have you had, my lady?'" Maigrey corrected reprovingly, lifting her chin, fixing him with an imperious gaze.

Her eyes were clear, Dion saw, and focused, though shadowed with indescribable sadness. The young man had the grace to be ashamed. "I'm sorry," he mumbled, ducking his head and flexing his hand. It hurt abominably. "My lady."

"It seems all we're doing is apologizing to each other. Forget what I said, Dion. I'm tired. I couldn't sleep. I keep seeing . . . them. The Corasians. And I don't know if I'm seeing them from the past or if I'm seeing them from now. Either way, it's awful." She shivered and shoved her empty glass forward. "How many toothpicks do I have in front of me?"

"Four, my lady."

"Then I've drunk four drinks, unless the toothpicks're breeding. Do you know, in thousands of years of progress, we've never been able to improve on the toothpick? I suppose when man was slogging his way through the swamps, beating his dinner over the head with clubs, he picked up a stick and poked what was left out of his teeth. And here we are today, traveling beyond the speed of light, proving Einstein wrong, and scattering toothpicks throughout the universe. A marvelous creation, man."

Dion glanced around the bar, hunched closer to her. "Lady Maigrey," he said in low tones, "can I ask you a question about that initiation?"

"Shhhh," she warned, and he leaned nearer.

"During the rite, I kept that . . . ball . . . in the air. I willed it with my mind to stay floating above my hands."

"Yes?" she said, arranging the toothpicks in a square on the bar.

"I've been trying it, in my room. I can't even keep a paper cup up in the air!"

Maigrey folded in one side of the square. "You did what you did out of desperation, duress, adrenaline. It takes years of study and training to learn to break the laws."

"Break the law? But I don't want—"

"Physical laws. The laws of the universe."

"Can you do it? Break the laws?" he asked in almost a whisper.

Maigrey smiled, rearranged the toothpicks into an M.

"What could you do, if you wanted, my lady?"

"What could I do?" Her voice, her smile, were soft. "I could split the bulkheads open. I could short out all the electrical systems. I could make each man in this bar rise up and slay himself."

Dion stared at her, skeptical, dubious. "If you could do all that, you could have escaped, any time you wanted!"

"Yes, I suppose I could have," Maigrey said, reversing the toothpicks, forming a W.

"Then why—" he paused, licking his lips. "Me, isn't it?"

Maigrey nodded, reached for her glass, and took a drink. "Yes, you, Dion Starfire. I am a Guardian, after all."

"You want something, kid?" The bartender came over.

"What? Oh, no, thank you." Dion waited until the man left. "This power—can you teach me to use it?"

"No."

"No?" Dion was disappointed, angry. "Then Lord Sagan will."

"I don't think so. You see, that was the message of the rite, Dion. One of the messages, at any rate. You have the power, but you are destined never to be able to make use of it."

"Why? How do you know?"

The gray eyes fixed on him, their gaze cool, dispassionate. "Because it turned on you. Because it damn near killed you!"

"But that's not right, not fair! It's a . . . waste!"

Maigrey's gaze went back to the glass in her hands. "Yes, a waste. All such a waste." Rousing herself, she sighed and said, "It's almost time for the meeting." She slid off the barstool.

"Wait a moment." Dion, rising, blocked her way. "If you have these wonderful powers, why don't you use them? Like"—he gestured angrily, frustrated—"to pick up that glass or open doors—"

"We can't live without order in our lives. One group of the Blood Royal tried it. They became outlaws, running—not from the laws of man—but from the laws of the universe. They plunged into chaos and never managed to find their way out."

"Who were they?"

"They called themselves the Order of Dark Lightning, a mockery of the priests' Order of Adamant. They were 'mind-seizers.' Their order was destroyed during the revolution. I suppose you could say, after all, some good came out of evil." Maigrey waved to the bartender, who bowed in return. "Thanks, Merlin."

"Is that his name?" Dion turned to stare.

"God, I hope not."

She walked out of the bar. Dion was amazed to see every man rise to his feet as she passed. He imagined her standing in the midst of them, her long, pale hair flowing over her shoulders, her arms raised to the heavens, commanding, "Die. Die for me. Die for me now!"

Dion saw the expressions on the faces of the men, heard the murmured words of respect and admiration that fell at her feet like rose petals, and he began to believe in her. His belief shook him to the core of his being.

··◆ ➡··

"You've fought the Corasians before, haven't you?" Dion said, hastening after the woman, who was traversing the corridors at an incredible rate of speed. Men cleared her path, but they didn't clear Dion's, and he was continually caroming off people and muttering apologies.

"Yes," Maigrey answered, glancing over her right shoulder. Not finding him there, she looked over her left, saw him attempting to dodge a servicebot, and slowed her pace to allow him to catch up. "The Corasians used to raid the galaxy on a regular basis, hitting the planets on the outer fringes, mostly. They're desperate for new technology. They're an intelligent species, but they haven't a creative bone in their bodies. In fact, they haven't any bones in their bodies."

Maigrey stopped and peered around the maze of corridors. "Where's the conference room?"

"This way." Dion steered her down a passageway to their left. "What are they, then?"

"Creator only knows. To me, they look like something a volcano spit up. Some sort of intelligent form of energy, kind of like a flaming amoeba. That sounds like a drink, doesn't it? A flaming amoeba. We made the Corasians what they are today, you know."

"We did? How? We take this elevator to level nine."

"My, those doors shut fast, don't they? What level's the flight deck on?"

"Level sixteen. Why?"

"No particular reason. Just handy to know these things. Where was I? Oh, yes. Bringing the Corasians into the twenty-second century. It happened around the middle of the twenty-first, when hyperdrive had been perfected and humans were happily zipping all over the universe, spreading toothpicks. A bunch of priests— That sounds funny, doesn't it? A bunch of priests. Perhaps it should be a flock.

"Anyway, these priests were sent off to bring not only toothpicks but the Word of God to the poor benighted souls in the galaxy next door who'd never heard it. Discovering intelligent minds on the planet of Corasia, the priests promptly landed and realized almost at once that they had made one of history's all-time great mistakes. Sort of like the enterprising life insurance salesman who sold policies to the men of the Seventh Cavalry right before the Battle of Little Big Horn.

"The Corasians were delighted to see the priests. So delighted that they refused to let them go."

The elevator came to a halt. The doors opened.

"The Corasians kept the priests prisoner until the day they died and, from what we have gathered, the good fathers must have prayed daily for death. You see, at that time, the

Corasians were just molten blobs, roaming around their planet, sucking up the energy they needed to live. They'd just about depleted the sources. The priests were—no pun intended—a godsend."

"This is the level," Dion said. Maigrey hadn't moved. He looked at his watch. "We should hurry, my lady."

"Yes, I guess we should." She walked out of the elevator, took a wrong turn. Dion drew her back. "The first thing the Corasians did was to take over the priests' robots. The Corasians discovered that they could fit their bodies inside these machines and use them for the hands and arms that they lacked. Their own energy powered the bots, they supplied the intelligence. Once they'd done this, they had the ability to take apart the robots, figure out how they were built, and start building their own.

"By 'interrogating' the priests, the Corasians learned about our galaxy and the marvels of technology we'd created that were just sitting around, waiting to be picked up. Using the priests' taped voices, the Corasians sent out distress signals and trapped ships that came to their rescue. Once they had these ships, they were able to scavenge more equipment, build more robots. Eventually they sailed forth and attacked other ships, which led them to the human and alien colonies that were springing up on the fringes of their own galaxy.

"The Corasians used the humans they captured as slaves, forced them to build more machines, and within a century had become a completely mechanized populace spread out over hundreds of planets in their galaxy."

"This is the conference room," Dion said in a low voice. "Through those doors."

"The doors that are closed and guarded." Maigrey crossed her arms, and leaned back against a bulkhead. "I guess we're early. I'm always early. It's a compulsion. Just as bad as people who're always late."

"We're not the only ones," Dion muttered, returning the stares of the other early arrivals—ship's officers, gazing curiously and with interest at the woman and the young man— the subject of the fascinating rumors currently circulating throughout the fleet. Dion moved nearer Maigrey, who was regarding them all with amusement, as if enjoying a private joke.

"The Golden Squadron was being honored for heroism

against the Corasians the night of the revolution, wasn't it, my lady? At least that's what Tusk said. I'm sorry. Maybe I shouldn't have brought that up."

Maigrey had gone exceedingly pale. The indigo blue dress she wore emphasized the pallor. The elation of the alcohol was fading, giving way to depression and the beginnings of a bad headache.

Seeing the young man's chagrined expression, Maigrey flushed self-consciously. "There you go, apologizing again."

More officers appeared, milling about in the corridor, talking in low voices. They were waiting for the Warlord, who hadn't yet arrived. And though everyone stared at Dion and Maigrey and it was obvious they were the subject of much of the whispered discussion, no one spoke to them.

"I don't mind talking about it," she said. "It'll tell you something about the enemy. The renowned Gold Squadron, famous in story and song, had been sent on—of all things—a recruiting mission. Sagan was furious. He considered himself above all that nonsense. But the king had commanded us to go and we couldn't disobey. . . ."

Her voice trailed off; she was silent, looking back. The voices faded around her, the walls of the ship dissolved. Once again, she was standing on that beautiful planet with its trees and birds and gently rolling sea, the white sand beaches, the water that glittered with phosphorus in the long, warm, soft nights. What was the planet's name? She couldn't recall. And there'd been a time when she'd thought she'd never forget.

And then had come the shadows.

"I saw the enemy, in my mind, much like yesterday. Only I didn't know what they were. We'd fought them before, but I'd never seen them in my visions. I was nervous and upset, which was odd, because all the others—even Sagan—had begun to relax and enjoy . . ."

Her eyes closed. She shook her head. "But never mind that. I knew something dreadful was going to happen, some sort of terrible calamity was sweeping down on this planet. Sagan, through the mind-link, came to share my fear. We went to the authorities, tried to convince them to take precautions, to mobilize their defenses. By then I knew what the enemy was, I could see the Corasians clearly. But this planet was a happy place, a sunny place. And what were we but a bunch of royal brats—too smart for our own good?

"We returned to our base. Sagan had decided, orders or no orders, we were getting the hell out of there. But it was too late. The Corasians came out of hyperspace and hit the planet before it knew what was happening.

"It was a pilot's worst nightmare—being caught on the ground during an assault. The Corasians don't use destructive nuclear weapons. God forbid that they should hurt the machines or ruin a perfectly good food source. They drop chemical bombs; that paralyze all living organisms. Then they move in and take over. Some of the people—the strong ones—are restored, used as slaves. Others—the old, the weak, the children—well, they're marched, like cattle, into the slaughterhouses. And for the same purpose."

"My God!" Sweat beaded Dion's upper lip. The lines around his mouth were tinged green.

"The Corasian fleet was sighted and the planetary government had just time enough to send everyone into terror-stricken panic. The first battle we fought wasn't against the enemy. We fought our own kind. They wanted our planes. They wanted to escape. It was awful. I remember Danha Tusca, weeping, as he shot them down. Sagan saved our lives that day . . ."

"Maigrey," Dion said softly.

But she didn't see him or hear him. She didn't see or hear the Warlord come up and stand right in front of her. She was blind to the present. Her eyes saw only the past.

"He was calm, frighteningly calm. He said we couldn't survive an encounter with an invading fleet; he ordered us to delay our takeoff until most of the Corasians had landed and were occupied in conquering the planet. Our helmets protected us from the paralyzing gas.

"Sagan's plan worked. When we finally lifted off, the main body of the enemy fleet had been dispersed and was scattered all over the solar system. We fought our way out easily, flew to the nearest battlecruiser in the vicinity and alerted the king. The Royal Army attacked and eventually drove the enemy from the planet.

"Sagan saved our lives," Maigrey repeated. "His will held us together when we were falling apart. He was our commander and we revered and respected him. We would have followed him anywhere."

She became aware of her audience, of the man standing before her, clad in golden armor, golden helmet hiding the face in shadows. Her voice faltered when she realized what she'd been saying and who'd been listening.

"We revered and respected him," she repeated steadily, "and we would have followed him anywhere—except down, into dishonor, disgrace. Into hell."

Chapter ··❈◯❈·· Three

The lion is alone, and so am I.
George Gordon, Lord Byron, "Manfred"

The conference chamber aboard *Phoenix* was a large, oval room whose walls were decorated with a gigantic composite photograph of the galaxy taken from the side and focused inward. One gigantic arm of the galaxy's spiral began at approximately the place the Warlord was standing. The myriad stars swept around the room, bunching up and becoming thicker and thicker above the door at the room's far end, which was directly opposite Lord Sagan. On the opposite side of the door, the stars flattened out and the other spiral arm extended around the room, vanishing into darkness, both arms nearly meeting right above the Warlord's head. It looked to Maigrey as if the stars were engulfing them and she began to feel slightly claustrophobic. Not to mention a throbbing headache.

"And that, gentlemen, is the updated report on the enemy's strength. They are formidable, to say the least."

To say the least. The officers were avoiding meeting each other's eyes. Those who couldn't hide their appalled expressions stared down at their hands. The rest kept carefully impassive gazes fixed on their Warlord.

"I have been in contact with the President. He has ordered us, essentially, to stand in harm's way. If we cannot stop the enemy, we are to inflict severe damage, force them to halt their advance."

"My lord." A young officer, the youngest present, raised his hand.

"Williams."

"Begging your pardon, my lord, but why doesn't the Republic support us? They could have fifty cruisers here within a ship's week."

An intelligent young man. Maigrey noted Sagan reward him with an approving glance. Of course, the Warlord couldn't tell him the truth, tell this young man that he and his compatriots were being sacrificed to their liege lord's dangerous ambition.

"Such a move would leave the densely populated systems at the galaxy's heart virtually unprotected. A second line of defense is being thrown up here"—the Warlord moved along the wall, to stand near one panel at the center of the galactic map—"and here." There was some muttering and low exchanges of conversation. The Warlord allowed this to continue for only a certain length of time, then his deep baritone overrode them. "We have our orders, gentlemen. There is no use whining about them."

The officers appeared chagrined, some—among them young Williams—flushed angrily. "My lord—" he began in protest.

"I have not yet finished, Captain. There is, of course, another alternative to the two I have mentioned. We damage the enemy, we stop the enemy, or we destroy the enemy utterly. I have decided on the latter. In other words, gentlemen, I intend to win."

Three rousing cheers, Maigrey thought, leaning her aching head on her hands. She could feel the wave of enthusiasm break over her, sweeping them all along with their Warlord to, what? Inevitable destruction. We would have followed him anywhere. . . .

"Are you feeling quite well, my lady?"

The Warlord, walking back to his place at the head of the table, paused behind her chair. He was furious with her, but whether over what she'd said or the fact that she'd been drinking was beyond her current mental capacity to figure out.

"Yes, thank you, my lord. A slight headache. It will pass." Maigrey didn't bother to look up at him.

The Warlord continued past her, pausing a moment to answer a question put to him by Admiral Aks. What in God's name had caused her to bring up that ancient history anyhow? It was that cursed wizard's potion. She'd asked for one to make her forget the past, not present it to her in living color.

". . . our strategy will be to wait. We'll take up stations outside the Vangelis solar system, to protect our supply sources, particularly the uranium. We have some time in which to prepare ourselves. The Corasians, following their customary procedure, are establishing bases in Shelton's system. They'll need to obtain fuel and to repair whatever equipment was damaged in their attack on Shelton."

The faces of the officers were grim. Many of them had fought the Corasians and knew what they did to a conquered planet. One of them—Williams again—raised his hand.

"My lord, why don't we attack them now, on Shelton's planets, before they recoup their strength?"

Sagan's lips were a straight dark line beneath his helmet. "I don't like the thought of what's happening to the people on Shelton's planets any more than you do, Captain Williams. But to rush heedlessly to their rescue would serve no one. We will let the Corasians stretch *their* supply lines. We will let them come to us and we will spend our time preparing to meet them."

There was a struggle in young Williams's face. He wanted desperately to argue. Perhaps he knew someone on Shelton's planets. Or maybe he was just a young warrior who longed for the glory of the charge, who lacked the patience to crouch down in the foxhole and wait. Dion, next to Maigrey, stirred restlessly. He must agree with the captain, Maigrey realized. Why is it always the young, who have the most to lose, who want to rush headlong to death?

Because they are immortal, Maigrey answered silently. Once, I was immortal. . . .

Williams managed to control himself and the meeting continued.

"I will not hide from you gentlemen the fact that we are in desperate need of manpower. The local systems can be of no help to us. They have put their own military on alert and will be providing for the defense of their own planets. The Lady Maigrey has offered a suggestion which I have considered and have decided to act upon. You know, of course, about the conflict being carried on between one Marek and the government of Vangelis. Marek called in mercenaries to assist him. Lady Maigrey proposes that we ask these mercenaries— particularly those who are fighter pilots—to join us."

"My lord, I must protest!" Captain Nada, of course. "Even if this scum could be scraped up out of the gutter and molded into some sort of viable fighting force, it would be impossible to trust them!"

"What do you mean, scum?" Dion was on his feet, his chair crashing to the floor behind him.

"That will do, Dion." Sagan's tone was stern.

"Viable fighting force?" The young man was in a rage, past hearing. "They can outfight you, you fat—"

"Dion, sit down."

The Warlord did not raise his voice. It penetrated the young man's fury, however—that and Maigrey's cool fingers touching his forearm. Swallowing his wrath, Dion picked up his chair and sullenly returned to his seat.

"Perhaps with any other troop of mercenaries, I would agree with you, Captain Nada. But these are led by a man known to myself, to Lady Maigrey, and, I believe, to Admiral Aks."

The admiral nodded.

"His name is John Dixter. He held the rank of general in the old Royal Army. I have served with Dixter. He is a capable commander, a good judge of men. I can assure you that his people will be disciplined, skilled, and—if Dixter gives me his word—I believe they can be trusted."

Maigrey stared at Sagan. What a commendation! It was no more than John deserved, but still— The knowledge made her uneasy. Any man Sagan rated that highly would be a man he would consider dangerous. She probed his thoughts but discovered them roped off, barricaded. She sensed duplicity; this wasn't the innocent overture for an alliance of desperation that it appeared. But, if not, then what? Surely, even Sagan, when driven into a corner and fighting for his life, would not expend his energy in taking potshots at an apparition from his past? Maigrey, frustrated, was suddenly sorry she had ever made the suggestion. She had the distinct impression that, somehow, she had played right into Sagan's hands.

"As you say, my lord, I know John Dixter," Admiral Aks was adding. "I know him from the old days. I agree with you, my lord, that he is a good officer and that he can be trusted. However, I do not think he will join us. His hatred and defiance of the Republic is well known. It is not a question of us trusting him, but of him trusting us." Aks made his speech smoothly; he'd been well coached.

"That is true, Admiral, and therefore I propose that we send this young man, Dion Starfire, to act as intermediary. The young man, as you have witnessed from his impassioned, if ill-timed and ill-mannered defense, is acquainted with John Dixter and those in his command. He will inform the mercenaries of our mutual danger and offer them our proposal of a temporary alliance."

Dion's mouth fell open. He stared at Maigrey, then at Sagan. Maigrey was no help. She would have liked to tell the young man to refuse, but she had no grounds to do so, nothing but a vague feeling of disquiet. And we need the pilots! she reminded herself. We need their planes. Maybe I'm just being paranoid.

"Of course," the Warlord was continuing, "Starfire is a civilian. I cannot order him to undertake this mission, but I would take it as a great personal favor if he would."

The Warlord smiled, the dark line of the lips lengthening.

By thy cold breast and serpent smile . . . Maigrey shivered.

Flushed with pride, stammering with confusion, aware of the cool, measured observations of the officers, Dion rose awkwardly to his feet, his chair scraping the deck.

"My lord. I— It would be my honor. What about sending Lady Maigrey with me? I really don't know General"—Captain Nada snorted at the use of this title and the Warlord cast him a swift, frowning glance—"Dixter all that well, but he and the Lady Maigrey were friends—"

"An excellent suggestion," Sagan answered gravely, "but I find her ladyship's presence on this ship necessary. She has fought the Corasians before. I value her advice. She will remain here—safely, I assure you."

Dion opened his mouth to argue, felt Maigrey's hand on his, and said instead, "Very well, my lord."

"You will leave at once, when this meeting is ended. There is no time to be lost. Gentlemen, I have told you everything I can. If you have questions, ask them now. All ships are to be rigged for silent running until the battle begins. No ship-to-shore transmissions are to be either sent or received. Communication between ourselves will be handled by courier. The enemy can see us, there's no need to let him hear us, as well. Oh, and by the way, Captain Nada, I'm afraid this means President Robes will have to miss his daily reports. He'll be annoyed, but then, this is war and we must all make our little sacrifices."

By thy unfathom'd gulfs of guile . . . The lines of Byron's poem, *Manfred*, came to her.

The officers looked at each other, puzzled, not knowing what this meant. Nada knew. The captain's eyes bulged with outrage; his choleric face was purple. He sputtered, attempted to stare down the Warlord, to bluster his way out. But as far as Nada was concerned, Sagan had sealed off all the exits. The eyes, shadowed by the helm, ran their steel gaze right through the wretched man. Nada slumped back in his chair. The purple faded from his face, leaving it the color of the underbelly of a dead fish.

The silence became acutely uncomfortable. Admiral Aks, acting on a subtle cue, responded with a question. Sagan replied and the conversation lapsed into clarification and discussion of strategy and tactics. Dion, leaning forward in his chair, listened with eager, intense excitement. Maigrey settled back and let her head hurt. Only when the talk switched to spaceplanes, and in particular the Scimitar, did she pay close attention. And then she had to be careful not to allow Sagan to notice.

By that most seeming virtuous eye . . .

The meeting ended. Chairs scraped, the officers were on their feet, some hoping to talk further to the Warlord, others speaking into their commlinks, commanding their shuttles to be readied. Captain Nada, without a word to anyone, slunk out of the room. No one made any attempt to speak to him. It was obvious to all of them that he was out of favor with the Warlord. From now on, Nada was nothing.

Maigrey stood up. The Warlord cast her a glance, commanding her to stay. She would have liked to remind him that she, too, was a civilian, and therefore not subject to his command, but she supposed that wasn't really true. She couldn't remember a time when her life had been at peace. She'd seen her first battle when she was five years old, perched on the back of her father's horse. She was and always had been a warrior.

Maigrey started to sit down, saw Dr. Giesk edging his way through the crowd toward her, and hastily moved to join Dion, who was standing near the Warlord. Giesk was, fortunately, captured by a captain who wanted to discuss a pain he'd been suffering in his left side.

With practiced ease, Sagan spoke with those who had legitimate questions and politely dismissed those who merely wanted to insinuate themselves into his notice. Maigrey lost track of the conversation. How did the rest of the *Manfred* poem go?

By thy shut soul's hypocrisy . . .

Admiral Aks, remembering his duties, recalled the more persistent questioners to theirs and personally escorted them from the conference room. When the three were alone, the Warlord turned to Dion.

"Your Scimitar is being readied. Can you leave within the hour?"

"I can leave now, this moment, my lord!"

Dion flamed with eagerness, excitement. His eyes were on the Warlord. Maigrey recognized the look of admiration in them; she'd seen it reflected often in her own.

> By the perfection of thine art
> Which pass'd for human thine own heart . . .

Sagan glanced at Maigrey. It was nothing more than a glance, he said nothing, not even in his thoughts. But she knew it for what it was—his trumpet call of victory.

What was he plotting? Dear God, what was he up to?

"I have had placed in your spaceplane a complete report on the situation. I've provided John Dixter with full information on the status of my fleet, on my strength, numbers, everything. That should convince him, if nothing else will, that I am to be trusted.

"A meeting between Dixter and myself can be held on the planet's surface. Neither he nor any of his people need come on board the ship. Should he be willing to discuss my proposal, I am certain that the Lady Maigrey would be pleased to take part in the final negotiations."

Sagan looked at her for her approbation. What could she say? "Yes, of course, my lord."

> By thy delight in others' pain . . .

"Do you have any message for me to take General Dixter, my lady?" Dion turned; his blue eyes were intense, enflamed.

"Perhaps Lady Maigrey would prefer to give you her message in private," Sagan suggested. His eyes burned with a darker fire.

> And by thy brotherhood of Cain . . .

"That will not be necessary, my lord. Dion, ask John—General Dixter—if he recalls the human impersonator on Laskar."

Dion looked disappointed. At his age, he'd been expecting Elizabeth Barrett Browning. This message would tell John what he needed to know. As for the other, it was too late for that. It always had been.

Maigrey was suddenly extremely tired. "If you no longer need me, my lord—"

"No, my lady. Thank you. Come, Dion. I'll walk you to your ship. I've had a few modifications installed—"

> *I call upon thee! and compel*
> *Thyself to be thy proper Hell!*

Perhaps, after all, she'd go back to the bar.

Chapter ❈❖❖❈ Four

Here comes the prince.
William Shakespeare, *King Henry IV*, Part II,
Act V, Scene 2

Bwaamp! Bwaamp! Bwaamp!

The blaring siren blasted Tusk out of his hammock. Enemy alert! He dropped the mag he'd been reading, stumbled forward, and fell over an empty bottle, stubbing his toe. Swearing, he hopped across the deck. The plunge from his quarters on the upper deck to the cockpit on the lower was a harrowing experience, but he made it almost safely. His body acted while his mind attempted to fight its way up from the fogs of jump-juice and he was seated in his chair in the cockpit, flipping switches and muttering commands, before it occurred to him that something wasn't quite right.

For a base that was under enemy attack, the night was remarkably peaceful and quiet.

"Hey! What the hell's going on?" Bwaamp! Bwaamp! Bwaamp! "And shut that damn thing off!"

The siren faded away with a deathlike rattle in its throat. There was something wrong with it. Tusk had always meant to fix it, but had just never gotten around to it. He didn't really use it all that much, anyway. It was his own private invention, to get him going in case of an emergency.

"Goddam it," Tusk swore, peering outside the viewport and seeing the other spaceplanes in the encampment sitting dark and silent, their pilots undoubtedly peacefully relaxing. "There had better be ten thousand enemy fighters bearing down on us right now, XJ, or so help me I'll drop a bomb on you myself!"

"There's no attack," the computer stated.

"No attack! Then what was this? Just a little test for my nervous system?" Struggling to his feet, Tusk shook his fist at the blinking-eyed, monkey-faced computer. "I'll tell you how my nervous system is! It's shot to hell! My pulse rate's one-ninety! I think I'm having a goddam heart attack!" The mercenary staggered across the deck and over to the ladder. "I'm going back to bed."

"Dixter wants you," XJ said.

"It can wait till morning."

"This *is* morning. 0200 hours. And it can't wait. The kid's back."

Tusk had his foot on the first rung of the ladder. The metal was cold on his bare flesh. He paused, and in the silence he could hear his heart thumping in his chest.

"The kid?" He looked over at XJ. "Dion?"

"What is this, a nursery? How many kids you think we got stashed around here? Yeah, of course, Dion. He—"

But Tusk didn't listen, didn't hear. Scrambling up the ladder, he hit the deck running, dragged on a pair of jeans, stuck his feet into his sandals, hauled a disreputable shirt over his head, plunged his head and face into a sink full of cold water, and was up the ladder and out the hatch before XJ could complete his harangue.

The computer, left behind, comforted itself by replaying a vid tape it had just made of Tusk leaping out of his hammock when the siren went off.

⋯⋯⋯

Tusk saw lights in the general's trailer and quickened his pace. He knocked on the door, barely waiting for a reply before he flung it open. A bleary-eyed Bennett was brewing coffee.

"The general sent for me?"

"In there." Bennett nodded. "The general will be here in a moment." The aide cast a stern and disdainful glance at Tusk's outfit. "*He* is dressing."

Even at two in the morning, Bennett managed to look as if he could go on parade in the next twenty seconds. His uniform was crisp, shoes polished, hair combed. Tusk did note, however, that the aide had missed buttoning a button, third from the top, on his shirt. Bennett wasn't infallible. There was, after all, justice in the universe. Tusk shoved open the door to the general's office.

"Kid!" he cried, bounding into the room and preparing to fling his arms around the boy.

Only it wasn't a boy who stood facing him. Tusk stopped, staring, confused and uncertain. He would have as soon flung his arms around an open flame.

Dion came forward, an eager light in his blue eyes, to shake the mercenary's hand. "Tusk! How are you? How's XJ?"

"Fine," Tusk mumbled.

He eyed the young man—the black and red-trimmed uniform, the sword on his hip. The wild flame-gold mane of hair had been neatly trimmed and slicked down.

Tusk pulled up a chair. Dion resumed his seat. On his lap he held a slim metal case—the type used for carrying important documents. Tusk recognized the symbol that stood in raised relief on the outside of the case—a phoenix, rising from flames. The mercenary crossed one leg over the other, uncrossed it, scratched his head, and wished Dixter would get here.

"You seen the general, k— Dion?" he asked, after a moment.

"No. I just landed a few minutes ago." The young man looked apologetic, glancing at Tusk's disheveled appearance. The smell of jump-juice was strong in the air. "Did I take you from a party? I hadn't expected it to be the middle of the night. It was only the middle of the afternoon when I left the ship."

"Ship's time." Tusk was feeling increasingly uncomfortable. "I wonder if that coffee's ready yet." He stood up and started for the door, only to fall back as it opened and General Dixter stepped through.

Tusk saluted, hand to his forehead. Dion saluted, too, fist over his heart. Dixter looked at the young man, noticing everything Tusk had noticed. He smiled slightly, his eyes remaining grave.

"I'm not a Warlord yet, Dion," he said.

The young man looked startled, then, realizing what he'd done, he hastily relaxed his salute and held out his right hand. "I'm sorry, sir. I guess I got into the habit."

General Dixter took the young man's hand, but he did not shake it. Instead, he turned it palm up, to the light. The skin was marred by five red swollen marks.

"At ease, Tusk. Sit down."

Feeling bleak and empty, as if he'd found something

precious he'd lost only to discover it had never been his, Tusk subsided into a chair and sat, fidgeting.

Dion radiated a self-conscious self-importance that was both attractive and repellent. It seemed to the mercenary as if the kid had raised his shields, was protecting himself from attack.

Dixter took his seat behind his desk. The night air was crisp and chill. Bennett, entering the room, brought cups of coffee; the steam rose from them in spirals. Before he left, the aide switched on a small space heater.

Dixter, sipping his coffee, looked intently at Dion and said nothing.

The young man suddenly appeared embarrassed, uncertain where to begin.

"So, uh, kid, how'd you escape?" Tusk asked.

"I didn't," Dion said. "The Warlord sent me."

Dixter held very still, then slowly set the coffee cup down on the desk.

"Tusk, you know what to do."

"Yes, sir." The mercenary was rising to his feet. "I'll alert—"

"No, wait! Please!" Dion reached out his hand, grabbed hold of Tusk's arm. "Listen, it isn't like that! I haven't betrayed you! I wouldn't. Lady Maigrey wouldn't, either." He held up the metal case. "Please, look at what's in here. Then you'll understand."

"Lady Maigrey?" Dixter's expression didn't change, but the lines on his face seemed to stand out more noticeably. "What about Lady Maigrey?" He didn't look at the case the boy held out to him.

"I've seen her, sir. I've been with her. You're right, sir. Everything you said about her. A comet. Flaming ice. Only she's so sad. So unhappy. I wish—" Dion stopped, drew a deep breath, and kept silent.

Dixter stared, unseeing, at the steam rising in a long, thin, unbroken line from the coffee. "She's alive."

"Yes, sir. It was her idea that I come to you, her suggestion. Please, sir, read what I've brought."

Dixter took the proffered case, laid it down on the table. Dion leaned over and punched in a combination on the locking device. There was a click, a whir, and the case's lid opened. Inside were a few sheets of paper, bearing the official letter-head of the Republic, and a computer disk. Lifting the papers, the general began to read.

Tusk, watching the man's face, saw the flesh around the lines sag and grow haggard, the skin go pale beneath its weathered tan. Eaten alive by curiosity, barely able to contain his impulse to snatch up the papers, Tusk tried to contain himself by swallowing a large gulp of coffee. He'd forgotten it was hot and yelped in pain, the steaming liquid burning his throat, tongue, and the roof of his mouth. The mercenary hastily covered his mouth, but the general never looked up.

Dixter's coffee gradually grew cool. He didn't notice, didn't touch it. He read the papers carefully—there were only three; Sagan was always concise—and then replaced them carefully in the case.

"So that's what's been going on." The general picked up the disk, but made no move to insert it into his computer. He tapped the disk against the top of his desk.

"Please, sir, *what's* been going on?" Tusk pleaded.

"Two days ago, we intercepted a series of distress signals being sent from a remote system on the fringes to any warships in the vicinity. They were in code; we couldn't make out what was being said or where it came from. And then they ceased. Shortly after that, there was a flurry of transmissions from the *Phoenix* back to headquarters. Again in code, but one of our operators, who used to serve aboard the battleship *Diana,* said she thought *Phoenix* was in direct contact with the President himself."

"Yes, sir," Dion said. "As you see in the report, it's all there. What the President said—"

"What's all there? Sir, for God's sake—"

"The Corasians, Tusk," Dixter answered. "They've invaded the galaxy. They've attacked and taken Shelton's system. Sagan believes that they're preparing for an all-out assault on the galaxy. He thinks they'll strike this direction next. The War-lord has been ordered by President Robes to make a stand and, if unable to stop the enemy here, then he is to do as much damage to them as possible."

"Holy shit," Tusk said reverently and with awe.

"Lord Sagan"—the general's voice was expressionless, impassive—"has asked for our help."

Tusk scowled. Reaching for his coffee, his hand jerked and he spilled it over his legs. "Hah! That explains it, then. It's a trap, sir."

"No, it isn't!" Dion protested earnestly. "Lady Maigrey *saw* them in a vision! Lord Sagan could have killed her, but he didn't because of the invasion! You have to believe me, sir!"

"I believe you, son. I heard the distress calls myself."

Dixter lapsed into silence. He kept tapping the disk on the table. It was the only sound in the night. Snick, tap, snick. Tusk, gritting his teeth, thought he might crawl out of his skin if that noise didn't stop.

Dixter rose slowly to his feet. The space heater was pumping out hot air and it was growing uncomfortably warm in the small office. Without thinking of what he was doing, the general switched on a fan, and stood staring out the window, into the night.

Dion prodded. "Lord Sagan wants to meet with you, sir, to discuss the alliance. It has to be soon. We have a little time, he thinks, but not much. All the details, statistics, everything he knows about the enemy force is on that disk. The meeting can take place on this planet, anywhere you choose. Lady Maigrey will be there."

"She will?" Dixter turned his head around, looked at the young man over his shoulder. The fan whirred softly.

Tusk was on his feet. Going over to stand near the general, he spoke in a low undertone. "Sir, he's wearing one of those damn swords. You saw the marks in his hand. I know something about them; my father had one. It can do weird things to your brain—"

Dion stood up. His face was pale, resolute. "General Dixter, sir, I want to tell you something. You and Tusk, both."

The men turned to face him, Dixter's expression thoughtful, Tusk scowling and unhappy.

"I know who I am, sir. I have a last name. It's Starfire."

Dixter nodded. Tusk coughed and started to make some remark, but the general halted him with a slight gesture.

"That means that I'm king. The people in this galaxy are my people, my responsibility, given to me by God. I can't, I won't allow them to be hurt without doing everything I possibly can to protect them!"

King! Of what? That square foot of floor space you're standing on, maybe! Grow up! Get real! Tusk wanted to laugh out loud, laugh long and bitterly, and put an end to this. But the laughter never made it past his gut. He saw the young man's face, saw the intensity in the bright blue eyes, heard the earnest, serious tone in the hopelessly young voice. Tusk felt the flame, felt the fire.

"I don't believe this!" The mercenary plopped down in

Dixter's chair and glared at everyone in range. "I don't believe any of this!" But he did, and that was the problem.

The general laid a hand on Tusk's shoulder, its firm grip comforting. Dixter's words, however, were to Dion.

"There's one thing I don't understand, Your—" the general paused; he'd almost said *Your Majesty* and meant it— "er . . . young man. How can Lord Sagan be so certain the Corasians are going to strike out in this direction?" He waved a hand at the stars. "There's a million other possible routes—"

"I think Lord Sagan had better explain that to you himself, sir." Dion flushed. "I sat in on the discussion, but I really don't understand. Will you, at least, agree to a meeting, sir?"

Dixter said nothing. The fan whirred. The heater pumped out hot air. The general absentmindedly opened a window. Cold wind flowed into the room.

Turning, Dixter gave Dion a sudden, sharp, quizzical look. "Lady Maigrey must have sent me a message. What did she say?"

Dion licked his lips. "It's kind of strange, sir. Not, perhaps, what you might suppose—"

"Dion, her message."

"Sir, she said"—the young man shrugged—"to remember the human impersonator on Laskar."

The general switched off the fan. Tusk, sitting at the desk in his shirtsleeves, had goose bumps on his black skin.

"I'll agree to the meeting."

Dion looked startled, then relieved, then elated. "You will, sir? Where? When?"

"Tomorrow. 1200 hours." Dixter walked over to a map, studied it, and put his finger on a spot. "Here. Take down the coordinates." He read off longitude and latitude.

Dion repeated them excitedly. "I have them. I won't forget. I'll go back now and tell him . . . and Lady Maigrey. Goodbye, sir. And thank you! Thank you!" He shook Dixter's hand heartily. "Tusk? You'll be there tomorrow, won't you?"

The mercenary didn't look up. "Yeah, tomorrow."

Dion gazed at him worriedly, a frown creasing his forehead. He started to reach out, to touch him, but Dixter shook his head. "He'll be all right, son. Just give him time. You better go. The Warlord will be waiting for you."

"Yes, sir. You're right. I'll go. Thank you again, sir."

Dion, with a last glance behind him at Tusk, saluted—

correctly, this time—and left the office. "Good-bye, Bennett. It was good to see you again."

They heard Bennett's cool, correct reply, the door opening and closing. The aide peered in.

"Do you need anything, sir?"

"Enter this into the computer, Bennett," Dixter said, handing him the disk. "No hurry. Let me know when I can call it up. And arrange for a meeting of all pilots at 0600."

"Yes, sir." Bennett glanced at Tusk, slumped over the desk. The aide raised his eyebrows questioningly. Dixter shook his head, and Bennett, taking the disk, left.

Outside, through the open window, came the sounds of a spaceplane preparing for takeoff.

Tusk looked up. "What the devil does a human impersonator have to do with this?"

"Interesting." Dixter mused. "An interesting message. I wonder . . ."

"Sir?"

"The human impersonator of Laskar was an alien with an obsession about being human. It hated us and at the same time longed to be one of us. This obsession degenerated into madness. The alien had the ability to shift its form. It would become human in appearance and entice humans—men and women both—into having sex with it. In the middle of the act, the alien would change back to its original body. It was so loathsome and hideous that its victims would sometimes kill themselves rather than have to live with the knowledge that they'd been making love to a grotesque and horrible monster."

Tusk shook his head, too muddled to try to understand, wondering obliquely what this said about the general's sexual habits.

"Kind of a strange message, isn't it, sir?" Tusk spoke guardedly. Glancing around, he hoped to catch sight of the brandy bottle. "From a woman you haven't seen in years?"

The general smiled. "No, not really. She's just letting me know who I'm climbing into bed with."

Tusk gave up the search. Suddenly, he understood.

"Sir," he said in a low voice, "we could always snatch the kid away from him—"

Leaning on the windowsill, Dixter stared out into the night, at Dion's spaceplane, soaring into the darkness in a shower of flame.

"Keep away from him, Tusk. Keep back . . . or you'll get burned."

"Begging your pardon, sir, but it's already hotter'n hell."

The general grinned. Turning from the window, he fumbled in a pocket, pulled out a key, and tossed it to the mercenary. "Third drawer on your left. We'll drink a toast." He waited until Tusk pulled out the bottle, wiped out two glasses with the tail of his shirt, and poured. Dixter raised his glass. "I give you His Majesty. God save the king."

Tusk scowled. "That's not funny, sir."

"I didn't mean it to be."

Tusk held the glass in his hand, stared into it, then suddenly slammed it down on the desk. Brandy slopped over the rim, flooding a map. "Excuse me, sir. I got a lot to do."

He flung open the door and stormed out, nearly knocking down Bennett, whose eyebrows shot up to the crown of his bald head.

"Sir," the aide said, "I've input that file you wanted. You'll find it under 'Sagan.'"

"Thank you, Bennett. That will be all."

"Yes, sir."

The aide left, gently closing the door. Dixter lifted his glass to the heavens and silently drained it.

Chapter ·❊·◦◯◦·❊· Five

> Love bade me welcome, but my soul drew
> back . . .
>
> George Herbert, "Love"

For the meeting between the mercenaries and the Warlord, Dixter had chosen the site of an old deserted fortress built into the top of a cliff on a part of Vangelis considered desolate even for that barren planet.

"It's a remnant of early stellar exploration," commented Lord Sagan, emerging from the shuttlecraft and staring up at it through the swirling dust. "The fortress is somewhat of a mystery to archaeologists. The planet was lifeless when humans first discovered it. Why, then, did those early explorers feel the desperate need to build this gigantic fortress? Who did they think they were protecting themselves against?" He gestured. From horizon to horizon, the land was empty. "There was nothing out there to attack them."

"Why did they, then?" Maigrey asked, accepting his arm to aid her steps over the rough and uneven terrain.

"The only explanation the scientists can come up with is that the explorers were seized by a collective madness—a group paranoia. This theory has received support from rather sinister evidence. It appears that—locked inside their safe fortress—the explorers proceeded to slaughter each other."

"I can understand why," Maigrey murmured, pausing to look around.

The wind howled and shrieked and tore at the hood covering her head. Dust devils raced each other across a barren rock floor, orange clouds scudded across a cobalt blue sky. No wonder those early explorers, coming from years of living in a sterile, controlled, and protected environment, had imagined demon hordes massing to attack them and, after years in this forbidding and wind-blasted place, had found the demons in their own minds.

Sagan cleared his throat. Touched neither by beauty nor awed by desolation, he was impatient to get on with business. Checking a sigh, Maigrey clutched the hood of her cloak, cursed the long velvet skirts that were tangling her feet, and struggled forward against the wind.

Steep and narrow stairs, cut into the side of the fortress's rock wall, led up into the fortress proper. At the top of the stairs, Dion stood, waiting to meet them. He must be tired, Maigrey thought. He had returned to the ship after his meeting with Dixter, made arrangements with the Warlord, and then flown back to finalize the details with the mercenaries. It was unlikely he'd had a chance to sleep in the span of a ship's day and night. But if he were fatigued, she could see no outward sign beyond a slight translucence of the marble complexion that made the blue veins beneath his eyes stand out more clearly. The wind tossed his red-golden hair, a bright flare of color against the gray stone walls. It seemed as if a flaming torch lit their way.

"My lady. My lord. Captain Williams. General Dixter and his party are waiting your arrival, my lord. If you will follow me. My lady?"

Dion held out his arm. Maigrey accepted it, and he led the way into a colonnade whose stone columns cut the wind and provided shade from the hot sun while still allowing the paranoid observer the opportunity of keeping watch on the barren land around him. Sagan's party traversed this porch for a lengthy distance, Dion and Maigrey leading, Lord Sagan and Captain Williams following behind, and the eternal Guard of Honor rhythmically marching in the rear.

"Where's Captain Nada?" Dion whispered out of the side of his mouth.

"He was taken ill last night," Maigrey answered, her face hidden by the folds of her brown cloak. "A very sudden illness, but one that was not, I believe, totally unexpected."

Dion stared at her, shocked, then cast an oblique glance back at the Warlord. "You mean—"

"'You bets yer money and you takes yer chance.' Nada backed the wrong horse."

"What?"

"Nothing, Dion. Never mind."

The colonnade led them through a series of arched doorways that took them deeper into the fortress. It was cool, out of the sun, and quiet, away from the incessantly shrieking wind. Dion brought them to a doorway larger than the rest and halted.

"If you will wait here, my lord," he said, "I will announce you."

Sagan waved his hand; he was involved in a conversation with Captain Williams. Maigrey, left alone, removed the hood from her head and shook out her hair, wishing she'd thought to bring a mirror and a hairbrush. Such things never occurred to her until it was too late. She was anxiously doing her best to smooth down her pale, fine hair and shake the dust from her cloak when she caught Sagan's eye. A crimson flush mantled her face. She was primping like a girl before her first date.

Her hand went to the scar on her cheek, and she was disappointed in herself to discover her heartbeat increasing; the fingers against her skin were chill, her face burning.

John's an old friend. Just an old friend. It's been seventeen years, after all. I've changed. Her hand touched the scar. He's changed, too. Probably married, with ten kids. . . .

Dion returned. He had hold of her arm and was leading her somewhere. Maigrey had an indistinct impression of a large room and movement: numerous people—humans and aliens—rising to their feet from around an oblong wooden table. But it was all a blur because he was standing in front of her and his eyes were on her and he *had* changed, but then again, he hadn't. He took her hand in his and bowed low and she must remember who and where she was and so she could only squeeze his fingers tightly and say with her eyes what she wanted very much to say aloud.

Sagan and the general were being introduced as strangers; easier far than sorting out the tangled relationships of years past, trying to explain them to most of those present. Any constraint and coolness present between them could be put down to a very natural distrust and antipathy between those who represented—ostensibly—law and order and those who represented defiance. All very ironic, considering Sagan's ambitious designs.

One person managed to distract Maigrey's thoughts from John Dixter, and that was a young man introduced to her as Tusk. He came into focus sharply. He was not much like his father in his build—Danha Tusca had been a heavy-set, broad-shouldered man. Maigrey remembered meeting Danha's wife, once, long ago, and saw that the young man took after her—slim, fine-boned, well-developed muscles filling out a compact frame. Tusca lacked his father's resolute and solid presence, too. There was trouble in the young man and, noting the eight-pointed star he wore displayed prominently in his left earlobe and the concerned and frowning glances he darted at Dion, Maigrey guessed she knew some of what was gnawing at him.

Introductions performed—everyone cooly polite if not exactly cordial—those present took places around the table by order of rank. The Honor Guard posted themselves at the door. Maigrey found herself seated at the bottom of the table, far from the general, which was probably just as well for the presence of mind of both of them.

The meeting opened with the Warlord going over the situation, describing the Corasian attack on Shelton's system, emphasizing—Maigrey noted—the horrors inflicted on an innocent populace. He told the mercenaries precisely what he knew of the enemy's plans, and informed the general of the President's order that the Warlord put himself and his men "in harm's way."

Sagan's manner was condescending, contemptuous; he might have been here to clap them all in irons, rather than asking for their help to save his life. Maigrey saw the mercenaries' reactions—lips tighten, brows darken, alien tentacles coil in anger. But John Dixter was relaxed, listening attentively, his face softening into a wry smile. She breathed easier. He knew Sagan; he understood what this was costing the man.

There was some angry muttering when the Warlord concluded, but none of the mercenaries spoke, all waiting for their commander to reply. Dixter sat silently, contemplatively for several moments, his eyes fixed on Sagan. The Warlord's gaze was on the general, each attempting to see how far he could penetrate into the other's skull.

"Your report was most thorough and concise, Lord Sagan," Dixter said suddenly, never taking his eyes from the Warlord. "I have only one question. How is it that you are so certain the Corasians will attack at this point in the galaxy?"

"You know the Corasian lust for modern technology, 'General' Dixter." Sagan managed to surround the man's rank with audible quotation marks, causing Tusk—at one point—to clench his fist and stir in his chair. Dixter laid a hand remonstratingly on the arm of his friend. "We are the largest fleet— Let me amend that. We are now the *only* fleet in this quadrant. I am basing my calculations on the enemy's past actions, of course, but I have received no information about the Corasians which leads me to believe that they have changed in seventeen years. If anything, their need for modern advancements, for parts to repair their aging ships, is undoubtedly more acute."

Dixter nodded his head slowly. He tapped a pen gently on the table. The Warlord's argument was sound, logical, and Maigrey knew John didn't believe it for an instant. She sensed that Sagan understood this, as well.

Tap, tap, tap. The general's pen made the only sound in the room.

"Sir?" It was one of the aliens, speaking through a translator.

"Colonel Glicka," Dixter replied, still not taking his eyes off the Warlord, but ceasing to tap the pen.

"I don't trust him. I say we let him fight it out on his own." This was how the statement came across. Maigrey, who understood the language, heard it in much more colorful and graphic terms. Dion understood it, too, apparently, for he flushed up to his eyes and glanced nervously at Sagan.

The Warlord's cold contempt didn't thaw, wasn't warmed even by anger. "I don't trust you either," he responded, in the alien's own language. "And you can do what you damn well please. I don't need you. We'll fight, with or without you. But remember this. If we're defeated, then so are you—without even firing a single shot. If we fall, they'll come for this planet, they'll come for you. And you'll face them alone. Translate that for me, Starfire, so that everyone understands."

Dion, caught by surprise, did as he was told, somewhat haltingly, stumbling over the words. The mercenaries glowered in anger, the aliens' tentacles twitched, but nobody said anything. Whatever emotions John Dixter was feeling, he wasn't showing, except to glance—once—down the table at Lady Maigrey. He raised an eyebrow; she could only answer with a small shrug. Both were marveling at Sagan. The Warlord was doing the mercenaries the favor of allowing them to die for his cause.

"And what is the arrangement you propose?" Dixter asked.

"You, 'General,' your staff, your pilots, and their space-planes will be taken aboard *Defiant*, commanded by Captain Williams. This is presuming, of course, that you would prefer to fight as a unit, rather than having your men dispersed among my squadrons?"

"Of course. And who is to be in command?"

"You, 'General,' will be under my command. Your men, however, will look to you for their orders. Current squadron leaders among your pilots will maintain their own authority."

Dixter frowned. The pen resumed its tapping.

"You're not a pilot, General Dixter," the Warlord said in cool tones. "You're a ground soldier. You have only limited knowledge of space warfare, of its tactics and strategy. I include you because I am well aware that your people would not consider any other arrangement. But I must insist that you place yourself completely under *my* command."

Again the Warlord's reasoning was logical, made perfect sense. Maigrey, feeling a pain in her hands, looked down and saw she was tensely, nervously, and unconsciously twisting her fingers.

General Dixter tapped the pen, marking his words. "I would agree to those terms only if those of my people who have broken any of the Republic's so-called laws are given unconditional pardons."

"Very well," Sagan said. "I agree."

That was too quick, too easy. The general laid down the pen, sat a moment in silence, then slowly rose to his feet.

"Thank you, Lord Sagan. My officers and I will confer—"

"Over what? I've made my terms, 'General.' Take them or leave them. Time moves and so does the enemy."

"I understand. This won't take long. I've arranged for luncheon to be served in the next room—"

"Thank you, 'General,' but I follow strict dietary rules. I never eat food that has been prepared by strangers. I will return to my shuttlecraft to await your decision."

There was a scraping of chairs and everyone rose to their feet or whatever appendages were used for standing. Dixter made a deprecating gesture. "Your absence will be regretted, of course, Lord Sagan." The general's gaze shifted to the end of the table. "Perhaps her ladyship would honor us with her presence?"

"It is I who would be honored, General Dixter," Maigrey said, coming forward, walking around the Warlord.

"An excellent idea, 'General.' Lady Maigrey can answer any additional questions that might occur to you. I trust it will be satisfactory to you if she relays your decision to me? I see no need for us to meet again."

"Most satisfactory," John Dixter said. Reaching out, he took Maigrey's hand in his and drew it through his arm, unobtrusively pressing it close.

"I remind you again of the shortness of time, 'General.'"

"You will have my answer within two hours."

"'General.'" The Warlord inclined his head.

"Lord Sagan." Dixter answered, not bowing. "Dion, I hope you will stay with us?"

"Yeah, kid, I haven't had a chance to talk with you," Tusk said, the first words he'd spoken.

"Starfire, there are matters I would like to discuss, if you are free," Sagan said.

Dion's blue eyes went from one to another. Slowly he began to rub the palm of his right hand. "Some other time, I guess, Tusk. Excuse me, General."

"Certainly, son," Dixter said, his voice and his expression grave.

The Warlord turned on his heel. Dion walked out with him, Captain Williams accompanying them. The Honor Guard snapped to attention, fists over their hearts, as the three passed. When the three had left the room, the guard followed. Their booted footsteps could be heard echoing along the colonnade.

"This way, my lady," Dixter said formally, leading Maigrey down a hallway that branched off the colonnade. The other mercenaries seemed slow in following. Casting a glance over her shoulder, Maigrey saw Tusk impeding their path, putting himself in dire danger of being trampled by a large and obviously hungry alien.

"Strict dietary rules?" Dixter muttered to her as they walked slowly along.

"He prefers not to be poisoned," Maigrey said, smiling.

Dixter smiled in turn, and Maigrey saw that though the smile smoothed some of the lines in the rugged face she knew so well, it didn't erase them all. Some were too deep. The two walked on in silence.

"Where's the dining room?" she thought to ask, after a moment.

"Back there," he said. "Are you hungry?"

"No. Not at all."

"Neither am I."

An archway at the end of the hall led them into what had apparently been a pitiful attempt at a garden, built out on the top of the cliff. High stone walls protected it from the savage winds. Sunlight poured down from the sky, but the life-giving fire had obviously been too concentrated, too bright. The soil was baked nearly as hard as the rock walls. The blazing sun must have withered anything those early settlers had tried to grow.

But now it was late afternoon, nearly twilight, and the garden was cool, the shadow of the walls stealing softly across the barren soil.

Dixter drew Maigrey into a far corner. Keeping hold of her hand, he turned to face her. "He didn't leave a guard on you."

Maigrey lowered her head; her hair fell forward. But John Dixter was accustomed to this trick of hers. Reaching out, he caught hold of the pale hair and drew it back from her face, causing her to look up at him.

"He knows I won't leave. He knows I can't."

"Dion?"

"Yes," she answered, and wished with all her heart that her answer was the truth.

Then she saw that it didn't matter. It had never mattered. John knew, he understood, better than she did. He clasped his arms around her and held her close. Maigrey laid her head on his breast and felt, for the first time in her years of exile, that she had come home.

Chapter ·✦◗○◖✦· Six

Parting is all we know of heaven,
And all we need of hell.
Emily Dickinson, "My life closed twice before its close"

"All these years, Maigrey, I thought you were dead!"

"I'm sorry, so sorry for the grief I caused! But I had to disappear, vanish completely. You were my closest friend, John. Sagan was bound to watch you!"

Dixter moved his hands to her forearms, gently smoothing the blue velvet fabric. "I remember this gown . . . or one like it. Torn, blackened, stained with fire and with blood." Pausing, he drew a deep, shivering breath. "You might have trusted me, Maigrey."

"Trust you!" Reaching up her hand to his face, Maigrey slowly traced the lines upon the weathered skin. "Don't you know yet, my dear friend, the person I was trying to escape? The person I trusted least? The person who, to this day, I dare not trust?" Her hand moved from John's face to her own, her fingers tracing the scar upon her cheek. "I took that person and I buried her in a place where I thought no one would ever find her again!"

"Maigrey, don't!"

"But it didn't work, you see! I cried out to him and he found me because I wanted to be found. I betrayed everything Stavros and Tusca and Platus died to keep from betraying. I brought him the boy and here I am, still with him, still dancing up and down the hall, hand in hand, in time to some infernal music!"

"Hush, my dearest, hush! We won't talk about it anymore. For seventeen years, Maigrey, there hasn't been a day gone by that I didn't love you."

She blinked her eyes, sniffed, and glanced around as if she

thought someone might have left a box of tissues in the garden. John fumbled in his pocket, brought out a handkerchief, and handed it to her.

"Here, I brought an extra."

Maigrey smiled, wiped her eyes, and, glancing up at him through lowered lashes, said teasingly, though her voice was muffled and half-choked, "So there isn't a wife and ten children somewhere?"

"A wife? What kind of life is this"—Dixter waved his hand back toward the fortress—"for a woman?"

"For a woman who loved you? Come now, John. Like Mrs. Bagnet, she would have put on her gray cloak and shouldered her umbrella and followed you across the sundering seas. I wish you would have married." Maigrey stepped back, moved away from him. "You make me feel guilty. I've left your life like this garden—barren, empty. I never meant to do that—"

Dixter, following her, caught her and drew her near. "I knew what I was doing. I wasn't some kid, having my heart stolen. I was a man and I gave my love to you freely and willingly. I knew precisely what I would get back in return. You were always honest with me, and your friendship was enough, Maigrey. More than enough. I knew my rivals, you see—"

"Rivals? Plural? There were never that many!"

"There were two. Him and one other."

Maigrey, leaning against him, rested her head on his cheek. She followed his gaze; both looked down upon the Warlord's shuttlecraft, sleek and glistening in the fiery sunlight.

"Who was the other?" she asked softly.

"The one I feared most. The one I could never hope to displace."

Maigrey glanced up at him, puzzled.

"Out there." Dixter looked up, straight up, into the heavens.

The day was waning, the sky was still light, but a nearby planet sparkled in the distance.

"I'll prove to you how well I know you, Lady Maigrey. You're not here with me now. You're up there, trying to figure out how you're going to get hold of a spaceplane and fight the Cor—"

"John Dixter! Quiet!" Maigrey clapped her hand over his mouth. She cast a furtive glance back down at the shuttlecraft.

Dixter laughed, suddenly, and Maigrey laughed, and the

laughter—as it always does between lovers—drew them closer. But the laughter died quickly, too quickly, and it left them clinging together, but with an empty feeling, like lost children who hold each other out of fear.

"Why did you ask him that question, John?"

Maigrey's eyes were on the shuttlecraft.

"About how he knew the Corasians would strike this particular small section of the galaxy?"

"Yes."

"A question, first, for you, Maigrey. Did he tell me the truth when he answered it?"

"About the technology? Yes?"

"But not all the truth."

Maigrey clasped her hands over John's, held them tightly. "They're flinging him to the starving wolf pack that's on their heels."

"Why? He's the Republic's most skilled commander, a valued leader—"

"And one of the wolves. According to Robes, the most dangerous wolf of all."

John nodded, rubbing his cheek against hers. Her pale, fine hair caught in the stubble of his late-day growth of beard. "I guessed as much."

"What do you mean?"

Dixter appeared slightly embarrassed. "As usual, I seem to have walked into the right place at the wrong time. Have you ever heard of an Adonian named Snaga Ohme?"

"No, but don't look so surprised. My social life has been somewhat restricted lately. I don't get around like I used to."

"How can I describe Snaga Ohme? Like most Adonian males, he's incredibly handsome. He has three passions in his life—himself, rare jewels, and weapons. His collection of black fire diamonds is said to be the finest in the galaxy."

"The Royal Family's collection was the finest," Maigrey protested.

"He bought the Royal Family's collection."

"Bought!" Maigrey stared. "But . . . it was priceless!"

"Everything has its price. The new President needed warships, guns, missiles—"

"Ohme?"

"Yes, he's a genius when it comes to designing weapons. He demands and gets top gilder. One—one, mind you—of his combination palatial homes, warehouses, and firing ranges is

located on the planet Laskar. I've seen it. It's immense.
There're major metropolitan areas that are smaller in size than
his estate.

"Now, let me tell you, Maigrey, about this little altercation
in which we've been involved. You can't even call it a war. It
barely made headlines on the evening news on this planet. No
one else in the galaxy's ever heard of it. A bunch of miners are
sick of being shoved around by a bunch of goons. Marek is a
good man; he's not ambitious. He wanted his people treated
fairly, wanted control of his mines back.

"The goons call out the local militia, which is solidly mired
in the twentieth century—guns that fire bullets, some nuclear
missiles that they're all scared as hell to use, thank God, and
bombers that drop things that go boom in the night.

"*And* . . . one brand-new, never-been-used, ultramodern,
fully equipped, and very, very expensive prototype torpedo
launcher. Comes completely assembled with—as an added
bonus—a highly professional killer captain and a well-trained,
highly professional killer crew—all off-world."

"My God!"

Maigrey leaned back against the wall, rubbing her arms.
The evening wind was chill, and she had forgotten her cloak.
Dixter, hands thrust into his pockets, stared thoughtfully out
at the shuttlecraft.

"Yes, I thought that was rather peculiar. If it hadn't been for
Tusca's son, that launcher would have ended Marek's war
before it began. We couldn't have kept the uranium shipments
going out, and you know how touchy Sagan can be about
keeping his ships powered. But that's only the beginning. I
began getting reports that my soldiers were finding the most
remarkable weapons lying around the battlefields—weapons
so modern that most of the local boys couldn't figure out how
to use them and so they just ditched them."

"Somebody on this planet's scared."

"Of what? Of us? Mercenaries with a price on our heads? I
decided I better do a little sleuthing, find out who was behind
this and what he, she, or it was up to before something really
nasty happened. But about that time, it became obvious to
everyone that Marek was going to win. The oligarchy was in a
shambles—rioting in the streets, chaos, confusion—and when
I could clear away the rubble, it was too late. He'd packed up
and gone."

"Snaga Ohme?"

"Yes. The Adonian weapons dealer. He was here on this pile of rock; he'd been here for almost two years working on some sort of project that was so top-secret not even the people who worked for him knew what was going on. He used a uranium shipping company as a front—which put him in contact with *Phoenix.*"

Maigrey shook her head. "That would be natural—"

"So you would think. But contact was infrequent, transmitted in code, and as far as my people were able to determine, not one ounce of uranium was ever sent from this company to *Phoenix* or anywhere else that anyone could ever discover."

"So you've discovered the wolf's teeth," Maigrey murmured, glancing over her shoulder at the shuttlecraft.

"Let's theorize: Sagan's already got his own army and navy. He hires Snaga Ohme to provide him with weapons. He wins the support of a few of the other 'marshals' by offering to restore the true heir to his throne—"

"Would they support him?"

"Yes, I think so. Your old friend Olefsky would, for one."

"Bear Olefsky!" Maigrey grinned. "I didn't know he was still around. And I'm not certain whether he'd join with Sagan or knife him."

"He might not support Sagan, but what about Dion?" John Dixter suggested mildly.

Maigrey grew serious, thoughtful. "Yes, Bear would give his life for Dion if he were convinced the boy was genuine. So the Warlord has weapons. . . ."

"If Ohme hadn't panicked, if he'd sat tight and not blown his cover, I would never have discovered his operation. I'll bet Sagan could wring the Adonisn's handsome neck. So now I know the Warlord's secret. The question is, does he know I know?"

Maigrey nodded her head. "He knows. You're a threat, John, a dire threat. He must get rid of you. And I've led him right to you!"

"You? You didn't—"

"Yes, I did! It was my idea! Coming to you, asking for your help. You've got to get away! Escape him—"

John caught hold of her wrists, held her fast. "Very well," he said quietly. "I'll run. On one condition—that you come with me."

Maigrey stared at him. The hope that had dawned in her eyes at his astonishing agreement faded like the twilight at night's approach. She smiled wanly, looked down at her hands, twisting the handkerchief. "You always had the most subtle ways of letting me know I was being a fool. Why didn't you just slap me?"

"Because I'd much rather do this." Dixter took her in his arms and kissed her. "I thought you knew he was plotting something," he whispered when he could breathe again. His lips brushed against her hair. "When you sent me the message about the human impersonator."

"I *did* know," Maigrey said, her head drooping against his chest. "I just didn't know what. John, you're walking right into a trap!"

"At least I'll walk into it with my eyes open. We don't have any choice, Maigrey. We all hang together or we hang separately. War makes strange bedfellows—"

"What's this about bedfellows? Good thing I came along!" A grinning Tusk peered through the entryway in the wall. His face sobered. "Sorry, sir, but you told me to let you know when it was near time."

"Yes, thank you, Tusca."

"Please don't go!" Maigrey said, reaching out her hand to Tusk, who was about to discreetly remove himself.

"I'll leave you two alone to . . . uh . . . say good-bye, my lady," the mercenary said, looking and feeling awkward.

"We're not saying good-bye." Maigrey clasped her hands around John's arm. "It's too . . . final." She'd meant her words to be cheerful, lighthearted, but the circumstances of their last parting came back to her. Her voice faltered and she fell silent.

Down below them, the hatch of the shuttlecraft swung open. The Warlord appeared in the entryway, looked up to where they were standing in the garden. Maigrey read impatience in every line of the tall, armored form.

"I'll escort you back, my lady," the general said. He, too, had seen Sagan. Slowly, in no hurry, they walked out of the garden. "What was the decision of the officers, Tusk?"

"It's up to you, sir. Whatever you say."

Dixter nodded. His face was solemn and Maigrey, at his side, could not prevent a sigh. The general smiled down at her, squeezed her hand. "It'll be just like the old days."

"Yes," Maigrey answered and glanced back at the dead garden.

She turned away and the three of them entered the

colonnade. "Speaking of old days," she continued with forced cheerfulness, "I want to say that meeting you, Mendaharin Tusca, has been a true pleasure. Your father was one of my closest friends, though he was several years older than I was—nearer my brother's age, I believe. I remember the day you were born. He'd gone home to be with your mother. He sent us a vid transmission from the hospital. He was holding you up for us to see. Your mouth was wide open, you were wrinkled up like a prune, your head was covered with black fuzz, and you were screaming so we couldn't hear a word Tusca said. But we didn't need to."

Tusk walked along at her side, head bowed, his eyes on the ground.

"We knew how he felt by the expression on his face. He loved you very much. I wish he could see you today. He'd be so proud of you!"

The mercenary lifted his head. His black skin glistened with sweat. The dark brown eyes were shadowed, moody. "You think so?" He fingered the earring, as if it were irritating him. "I don't!"

Maigrey caught back her glib reply, paused to consider her words. "Dion told me something about your life, Tusca—"

"Tusk, my lady. Everyone calls me Tusk."

"Tusk. Your father was a brave man, an honorable man. He was a gallant warrior, a skilled pilot. He was proud and independent—perhaps too independent. If he had a fault, it was that he lacked tact. He never learned that if your way to what you want is barred, there are generally paths to be found around the obstacle. Your father"—Maigrey smiled ruefully— "put his head down and charged. More than once, he came back with a cracked skull and a bloodied brow.

"He fought with Sagan over battle plans and strategy, he fought with Platus over music. He and I fought over books." Her lips pursed. "He maintained Eldridge Cleaver was the greatest writer of the twentieth century! Eldridge Cleaver! Your father even fought the king himself, over his marriage outside the Blood Royal. Up there"—Maigrey glanced into the orange-clouded heavens—"I would guess he's probably fighting with God."

"That was dear old dad," Tusk said, kicking at a loose fragment of rock at his feet.

Maigrey stopped, laid her hand on his arm. "Tusk, don't you

understand? He loved us, all of us." Her eye went involuntarily to the space shuttle, to the figure in golden armor, flaming in the sun. "He gave his life, rather than betray the secret he had vowed to guard. But not before he had passed on his most valuable possession—that secret—to the person he loved and trusted most. His son."

Tusk kept his face averted.

"Thank you for all you've done for Dion, Tusk. Your service to your king is not ended, however. I name you a Guardian, Mendaharin Tusca. I wish I had a starjewel to present to you, but for the time being you'll have to make do with one in your heart." Maigrey held out her hand. "Welcome to our ranks. God be with you."

Tusk, dazed, allowed the woman to take his hand and shake it firmly. He couldn't match her strong grip; his bones and sinews and muscles were all tangled up and felt just the way the electrical wiring on his control panel looked.

Dixter and Maigrey walked on, leaving Tusk standing in the shadows of the colonnade, trying to cram his insides back where they belonged.

"What about Dion?" John Dixter asked.

He and Maigrey had come to the head of the stairs. The Warlord, impatience radiating from him, stood at the bottom.

Gathering up the folds of the blue dress in her hand so that she wouldn't trip over the hem, Maigrey began to slowly descend the stairs. Dixter kept fast hold of her, matching his pace to hers.

"You know who and what the boy is?" Maigrey asked.

"Yes," Dixter answered, his voice quiet, his eyes on the woman walking beside him, not on the figure blazing beneath them. "I saw him when he came back. More to the point, I saw him before he left."

"You know, then, what Dion wants. You can guess how he means to get it."

"If *it* doesn't get him first."

Maigrey put her hand over her twitching lips, but it didn't work. She couldn't help herself and began to laugh. The sound—incongruous in the stern, forbidding surroundings—echoed off the rocks. The mercenaries poured out onto the colonnade, peered over the fortress walls. Sagan's head snapped up, his eyes glaring at her disapprovingly from the depths of the helm. Even John Dixter looked mildly astonished and somewhat concerned, and Maigrey did her best to bring her self back under control.

"I'll leave with laughter between us," she said, starting to slip her hand out of John's grasp, but he held her tightly. His gaze went to the Warlord, who was approaching them.

"I've just received a report," Sagan said. "The enemy is preparing to move. Our time grows short. Have you reached a decision, 'General'?"

"I have," Dixter said, his expression and his voice cool and unperturbed. "We will join you. Allies under duress."

"Excellent. Captain Williams will stay behind to coordinate details. I will be in contact when you are on *Defiant*, 'General' Dixter. Oh, and by the way, you might be interested to know that our ship's doctor, Dr. Giesk, has developed a remedy for space sickness."

"Thank you, Lord Sagan," John Dixter said dryly.

The Warlord remained standing at the foot of the stairs, waiting. A gust of wind whipped his red cloak around him, the sun glinting off the threads of gold embroidery.

Stinging dust and her own hair blew in Maigrey's face, nearly blinding her. There was nothing more to say. This was only prolonging the pain. She started to go, but Dixter kept hold of her, turned her face to his. Reaching out his hand, he gently traced his fingers over the scar on her cheek.

"I've had nightmares about that night, Maigrey. I'd see you lying there, torn and bleeding—" His face blanched; he cleared his throat of a sudden huskiness. "I used to pray to God to drive that memory from my mind! He's answered my prayers, my lady. From now on, I'll see you smile, hear your laughter."

His handkerchief was still in her hand—wet, tear-stained, crumpled. Maigrey tucked it carefully back into Dixter's pocket over his heart. Resting her hand there, she kissed his cheek and, turning, left him.

Sagan, bowing, held out his arm.

"My lady?"

Maigrey laid her hand on his.

"My lord."

He led her back to the shuttlecraft. The mercenaries lined the walls of the fortress that could have halted any enemy except the enemy within. John Dixter stood on the stairs, watching. Maigrey did not look back.

The sun had set. The shuttlecraft had turned on its running

lights, they outshone the stars. In the hatchway stood Dion. The light streaming out behind him cast his shadow a vast distance, far longer than he was tall.

He's answered my prayers.

"God's answering *somebody's* prayers," Maigrey said, clinging tightly to Sagan's hand, night's rising wind threatening to blow her off balance. "I wish I knew whose!"

Chapter ··❦◯❦·· Seven

To war and arms I fly.
Richard Lovelace, "To Lucasta, Going to the Wars"

Tiny, puny, insignificant, the Warlord's fleet hung motionless in the vast darkness of space—a slender line of silken
cobwebs stretched out to stop a juggernaut. No one doubted
the enemy would endeavor to trundle over them. As Lord
Sagan was overheard to tell Admiral Aks, President Robes had
likely provided the Corasians with the fleet's coordinates. This
grim joke was passed around the mess room, the gymnasium,
and the lounges and became a favorite among the men. It was
a subtle compliment to their prowess, as the Warlord had
intended it to be. His crew knew now, to a man, who—after
the Corasians—would be their next enemy.

All was in readiness. The mercenaries—some five hundred
with their own planes and additional manpower available to
staff communications, computers, and fire and rescue units—
had arrived on board *Defiant*, where they had been cordially
welcomed by the energetic and intelligent Captain Williams.
The mercenaries were given their own quarters in their own
portion of the ship. They kept to themselves, the crew of
Defiant kept to themselves, and the alliance was, so far,
peaceful. General Dixter, sick as a dog, had locked himself in
his quarters.

The silken thread was stretched taut. Now there was
nothing to do but wait.

On board *Phoenix*, a woman clad in blue approached the
golden double doors that barred the entry to the Warlord's
private chambers. The captain of the centurions tensed; he
had been warned of the Starlady's (as she was now known
among the men) coming and knew what to do—or rather, what

not to do—but she made him nervous. It was much like being in the presence of the Warlord.

Accompanied by two guards who had been assigned to her on her return from Vangelis, Maigrey came to stand in front of the doors. Her gray eyes turned upon the captain.

"I will speak with Lord Sagan."

The captain went through the motions. "He's left orders not to be disturbed—"

"Tell him Lady Maigrey Morianna will speak with him on a subject of importance. I *will* speak to him," Maigrey emphasized. She had not raised her voice, she had not lost her calm and poised demeanor. And she left no doubt that she would speak with the Warlord.

The captain admitted defeat with a good grace. "My lord," he said into the commlink, "Lady Maigrey Morianna insists on being admitted into your presence."

Maigrey's foot began to tap on the deck; her breath came and went a little faster. This show was being performed solely for her benefit. If the Warlord had truly left orders not to be disturbed, the captain would not have broken them had Death himself demanded admittance.

"My orders stand, Captain," the Warlord's voice came over the commlink. "I am in conference. I will see no one."

Maigrey relaxed, faced the double doors, and concentrated. Her face was smooth and impassive; she didn't blink or move a muscle. The captain watched, his nervousness increasing. Her guards exchanged doubtful glances. A strong and slightly sweet smell of burning wiring pervaded the corridor. A wisp of smoke curled out from behind the control panel in the wall. With a grinding sound that set the teeth on edge, the double doors wrenched apart.

Maigrey had never touched them. Without a word, she stepped gracefully through them and walked into the Warlord's chambers.

The captain, recovering himself, sprang in after her.

"My lord! Forgive me, she—"

Lord Sagan, seated at a desk with Admiral Aks, was perusing a computer screen. The Warlord did not turn his head or look around.

"Very well, Captain, you are dismissed. Have a crew up here immediately to repair the door."

"Yes, my lord."

The captain retreated thankfully, glad to have come through the ordeal more or less unscathed. He had been warned what she might do and he had been told not to stop her. Looking at the damaged door, shaking his head in rueful awe, the captain wondered how in God's name he was going to explain this to maintenance.

The Warlord, continuing to read, heard in front of him a brief scuffling sound. The woman's guards were attempting to pin her arms; one would have his hand positioned at the back of her neck, ready to snap it if she so much as breathed the wrong way.

"You may relax, gentlemen," the Warlord said, turning a page. "If she wanted to, she could short-circuit your brain as she did the door and have you writhing on the floor at her feet. The lady intends me no harm. If I'm not mistaken, she is, in fact, here to beg."

The centurions released their hold and fell back a pace, neither being sorry to do so. The woman's skin was ashen and chill to the touch. As one said later, he felt as if he'd been holding on to a corpse.

Admiral Aks, sitting beside the Warlord, appeared extremely uncomfortable and even glanced involuntarily about the Warlord's chambers, hoping, perhaps, to find an exit that hadn't been marked.

"Perhaps I should leave, my lord—"

"No, Aks. This won't take long."

The admiral scooted his chair back into a convenient shadow.

Maigrey took a step forward, leaned her hands on the desk. The starjewel she wore around her neck sparkled at her breast. If the Warlord shifted his eyes, he must stare directly into the blindingly brilliant light.

"Very well, Sagan, I will beg!" Maigrey's hands clenched to fists. "Give me a plane. Let me fly."

The Warlord did not look at her. "No, my lady."

Maigrey reached out across the desk, grasped the man's hands, and fell upon her knees before him. Admiral Aks, watching, awed, saw light glistening on the woman's pale hair. Her gray eyes deepened to blue, a crimson flush stained the pale skin. The admiral was thankful from the bottom of his heart that he didn't have to answer, for—had she asked—he would have given her all he owned, his life and his soul in the bargain.

"My lord, I'll swear whatever oath you require of me! I'
take whatever vow you want me to take! You need me, Sagar
I was the best!"

This brought a reaction. The Warlord's eyebrow raised.

"One of the best," Maigrey amended, the color deepenin
in her cheeks.

She clung to his hands in supplication. The woman migh
thought a dazzled Admiral Aks, have been pleading for her li
instead of the opportunity to go out and die.

"Please, my lord!"

Sagan turned his head, shifted his eyes. They were cold an
hard and dark as endless space. "What oath would you tak
that you have not broken before? No, my lady, I cannot tru:
you."

He might well have shot her through the heart. The bloo
drained from her face; the scar was a livid streak across he
cheek. Her eyes dilated; her lips were white. Her fingers o
the Warlord's hands went limp, nerveless, and loosed the
hold, sliding slowly across the table. Her body sank backwarc
Aks was halfway on his feet, thinking that the woman wa
dying.

Maigrey remained on her knees, on the floor, her arms lim
at her sides, her head bowed.

"Guards." The Warlord made a gesture and the centurion
responded instantly, with alacrity, stepping up and saluting
fists over their hearts. "Escort the Lady Maigrey back to he
room. She is, from now on, confined to quarters."

The guards bent to take her arms and help her stand
Maigrey lifted her head, cast them each a glance that mad
them think twice about it, then rose slowly and haughtily t
her feet. She bestowed on the Warlord one swift look
promising defiance, sharp and cold and glistening as ice, the
turned and started to walk from the room.

"Your lives are forfeit, gentlemen, if the lady escapes,
Sagan added.

"Yes, my lord," both guards said, saluting.

Maigrey paused, and it seemed for a moment as if this las
shaft had been the one that drew life's blood. Her hea
drooped, her shoulders slumped. Pride alone lifted her chir
she seemed determined not to give her enemy the satisfactio
of watching her drop dead at his feet. Shaking back the pal
hair from her face, she squared her shoulders and walked ou

of the Warlord's chambers, through the broken door, with firm, unfaltering steps, never once glancing back.

Admiral Aks, finding the Warlord's stern and piercing gaze turned on him, shamefacedly dragged his chair up to the table and sat down.

"I thought the lady might have . . . been taken ill, my lord."

Sagan snorted and said nothing, resuming his reading.

"My lord." Aks found his gaze drawn to the door that was standing ajar. The captain had posted his own body in front of it. Maintenance crews, in their dark blue uniforms, could be seen swarming around it like ants whose hill had been knocked down. "Confined to quarters. Is that wise? The brig—"

"—could not hold her, Aks. But don't concern yourself. I've just bound her with chains of adamant: She'll never break them."

"My lord?"

"She would no more be responsible for the sacrifice of the lives of those two men than she would kill them with her own hands."

"Ah, I see, my lord. Very good, my lord."

Aks was supposed to be reading the same report Sagan was perusing—a report detailing everything known about the current strength of the enemy, garnered from the underground transmissions from Shelton's system. But the admiral slid about in his chair, fidgeting, until the Warlord, with an irritated sigh, looked at him.

"What is it, Aks? Spit it out and let's get it over with so that I can return to my work."

"My lord, Lady Maigrey is—or was—an extremely good pilot."

"One of the best, as she said. She should be; I trained her."

"Yes, my lord. And you have said yourself we need every skilled pilot. After all, you're allowing the young man to join a squadron. I was thinking that the lady might be useful—"

"And I should swallow my pride and allow her to come with us? Absolutely not, Aks. I will have enough trouble with the enemy in front of me. I don't want to have to worry about one behind."

"But surely, my lord, Lady Maigrey realizes how important you are to victory over the Corasians! She wouldn't dare risk harming you!"

"Yes, Aks, you're right. She wouldn't harm me. She would,

in fact, do all she could to protect me . . . *during* the battle."

The Warlord leaned back in his chair and rubbed his eyes,
fatigued from reading. His vision had always been perfect,
better than perfect. But now he noticed he had to hold
documents out away from him to bring the letters into focus.
He was past due for an eye examination; Giesk had been
nagging him about it. There were corrective drops that could
be used. Corrective drops!

The Warlord shut down the computer. "We made a good
team, she and I. A good team." He was silent, staring far
distant. The years of grim resolve, of vengeance and bitterness
erased their dark lines. His face smoothed, he looked almost
young.

The ship's bells rang, chiming the hour, and the present
charged in to banish the past. Sagan's expression hardened.
"It's *after* the battle, Aks, when the lady could prove an
infernal nuisance."

Light dawned. The admiral understood and nodded agreement. "You mean the orders concerning *Defiant*, my lord?"

"Yes, Aks. The orders concerning *Defiant*."

··◁▸ ▸··

In her quarters—the quarters that were suddenly small and
cramped as the secret holds in a smuggler's ship—Maigrey
paced restlessly back and forth, back and forth. She had
resolved to be calm, when the guards first brought her back.
She had resolved to sit down, eat her lunch, read Jane Austen,
relax, and listen to *Rigoletto*.

Lunch was splattered on the wall, Jane Austen was under
the bed, and Maigrey'd consigned Verdi to hell.

How dare Sagan say such a thing to me? *No oath you have
not broken!* How dare he! Twisting her fingers, she walked ten
steps from the head of the bed to the computer desk, ten steps
from the computer desk to the head of the bed. He can trust
me. He knows he can trust me! This was punishment, then.
The ultimate punishment. He can't kill me, but he'll wound
me again and again with—

The door to her chambers slid open. Maigrey whirled,
thinking it was Sagan, for he was the only one who ever dared
entered without announcing himself. Perhaps he'd changed
his mind. She'd sensed him wavering. . . .

It was one of the centurions, however, and he was dragging,
by the shoulders, the limp body of her other guard.

"If you could operate the control, my lady," the centurion said coolly, hauling his companion's feet inside, having some difficulty maneuvering in the confined space between the door and the bed. "Shut the door."

Maigrey, completely mystified, did as she was requested. The door slid shut.

"Is he sick? Did he pass out? Shall I call Dr. Giesk?"

"Don't call anyone, my lady. If you'd lift his feet, we could put him on the bed."

Maigrey took hold of the unconscious man's feet and helped to hoist him up onto the bed. Moving to look at him, she saw the bruise, forming at the base of the man's neck, just above the collarbone, and she turned to look at the guard.

"What's going on, centurion?"

"Thank you for trusting me, my lady."

"Trust, hell! As Sagan said, I could send you into a brain seizure before you could draw your next breath. I'm not the one in danger here. You are. What's going on?"

The centurion glanced at his unconscious companion. "Lord Sagan is just. He won't punish another for my crime."

"What crime?" Maigrey was growing exasperated.

"If you would look in your closet, my lady."

Maigrey took a step backward, moved out of the guard's path, and gestured. "You look."

The centurion, half-smiling, though his face was grave and serious, stepped in front of her and opened the closet door. Reaching inside, he brought out a flight suit, complete with squadron patches, and a helmet.

"You'll find the boots in there, too, my lady. I'm afraid they're probably going to be rather large. I got them as small as I could, but we don't have many men who wear your size."

Maigrey sat down, suddenly, and hoped the bed was beneath her.

"We were just given the report," the centurion continued. "The enemy has emerged from hyperspace. They're within instrument, though not visual, range. You have time, but you should hurry, my lady."

Seeing that Maigrey wasn't moving, the centurion laid the suit across the back of a chair, set the helmet on top of it, and turned to retrieve the boots and other gear. "I've arranged for you to be in Dion's squadron, my lady. I thought you would prefer that."

Maigrey's lips moved and, after a moment, coherent language came out. "What's your name, centurion?"

"I am called Marcus, my lady."

"Marcus, you heard your lord's command. You've signed your own death warrant. Why are you doing this for me?"

"Begging your ladyship's pardon"—Marcus glanced at her gravely—"but I'm not doing it for you. I'm doing this for my lord. You'll be able to help him out there, won't you, my lady."

"Yes," Maigrey answered, though it hadn't been a question. "Yes, assuredly."

"Many men will give their lives for my lord this day," Marcus said, with a peculiar smile. "I'm just doing it a little differently, that's all."

Drums sounded, the heart-stopping noise terrifying and exhilarating. Sagan didn't like sirens sounding the call to battle. He stationed drummers on every deck. The beat of the drum acted on modern man as it had acted on his ancient ancestors—it stirred the blood, quickened the pulse. The lights dimmed, power was being channeled to where it was needed most, all nonessential equipment would be shut down, including the galleys. It would be cold meals from now on, for those lucky enough to have time to eat.

"There's the signal, my lady. I'll leave you to dress."

Maigrey reached out, grasped hold of the helmet, and held it in hands that had no feeling in the fingers. She could hear the boom of blast doors slamming shut.

"I'm sorry I won't be able to take you to the flight deck, my lady. But I shouldn't be found away from my post."

"I know where it is, thank you," Maigrey murmured. "Level sixteen."

"Blue Squadron." Marcus, standing at the door, paused.

He wasn't a young man, Maigrey noted. He must have served Sagan long and well for many years. She saw herself, reflected in his clear brown eyes.

"Blue seems appropriate, doesn't it, my lady? Almost as if God Himself had chosen it."

Maigrey looked down at the blue velvet dress. "Yes," she said softly, "as if God Himself."

"Good flying, my lady." Marcus saluted.

"God be with you," she replied, more from force of habit than because she knew what she saying. But when she spoke, she saw the centurion bow his head as if to receive a benediction. The door opened, and he was gone.

The door slid shut. Except for the centurion on the bed who would be unconscious for a long, long time, Maigrey was alone. The drums beat, commanding haste. Fingers shaking, she swiftly stripped off the blue velvet dress. Looking at it long and hard, she rolled it into a ball and tossed it heedlessly into a corner of her room.

Whatever happened, she would never wear that dress again.

Blue Squadron, she repeated to herself, wriggling into the lightweight flight suit. She studied herself critically in the mirror. Fortunately, the suit was bulky and hid her shape. With the helmet covering her face and head, the commlink mechanizing her voice, no one would ever suspect.

"Blue Squadron," she repeated, her excitement mounting. Hurriedly she twisted the long, pale hair into a braid. "Well, it isn't Gold, but it'll do. Lord help us all! It'll do!"

Chapter ··❖◐❖·· Eight

And dream and dream that I am home again!
> James Elroy Flecker, "Brumana"

The din in the hangar deck was appalling, overwhelming. Huge winches, hauling the spaceplanes into position, rumbled, screeched, and whined. Bouts of hammering and the hissing of laserwelds were punctuations and accompaniments to shouted commands, shouted demands to repeat the commands, and fluent cursing in any number of languages. Droids squeaked and beeped and were in the right place at the wrong time and were kicked and cursed and sent away and ordered back and appeared to look on all this human confusion with a certain metallic smugness. Amid the confusion, some of the pilots stood in small knots, talking together while waiting for their planes; others stood by themselves, thinking last thoughts of someone far away. Some conferred with their crew chiefs. Others walked around the plane, inspecting it, going over it in minute detail, for when it came right down to it, for all the sophisticated technology, their lives might depend on a bolt staying bolted.

The pilots were tense, but it was a good tension laced with excitement and eagerness. After months of boring space travel, enlivened only by the occasional police action and endless maneuvers, anything—even the prospect of being blown to cosmic dust—was a welcome change. They tolerated the infernal noise level, yelling to be heard over it, putting on their helmets and speaking through their commlinks, or just shaking their heads in exasperation and walking off. One pilot, however, was having difficulty restraining herself from dancing.

Swathed in the bulky flight suit, her head encased in the helmet that she dared not remove, Maigrey was lost and confused, fearful that someone would discover who she was and whisk her back to Sagan, and she couldn't ever remember being happier. It was as if she heard, after years of banishment, the anthem of a beloved homeland. She was in such a flurry, she had to force herself to calm down and spent a few moments in silent prayer and meditation. It would never do for her to give herself away by inadvertently lowering the guard on her thoughts, allowing Sagan to discover her. Hopefully he would be too busy with his own numberless responsibilities to pay any attention to a woman he must assume was fuming safely in her own quarters.

Now, where was Blue Squadron?

It is a basic rule that if you're ever somewhere you're not supposed to be and you don't want to get caught being there, you must look like you belong. Walk purposefully and swiftly and always carry something in your hand. Picking up a stray clipboard a crew chief had left lying around, Maigrey tucked it under her arm and began shoving through the crowd, muttering imprecations at anyone who got in her way and darting swift glances left and right in search of her squadron. This was rapidly getting her nowhere, however. Blue Squadron was not to be seen, and time was running out.

"Hey," she demanded angrily, stopping to confront a flustered mechanic. "Did they relocate Blue Squadron?"

"Where the hell you been?" The mechanic glared at her. "Sure they relocated it. What did you expect? Bay Six." He gestured with a greasy thumb.

Nodding her thanks, Maigrey congratulated herself on her ploy and hurried to Bay Six. Ducking beneath the wing of a Scimitar, she stepped out into the open and nearly ran her helmet right into Sagan's broad shouldered back.

Maigrey retreated, hiding in the shadow of a winch, and leaned weakly against a girder until she was able to breathe again and convince her heart it belonged in her chest and not in her throat.

"It's what you get for being so smug," she said to herself, sweat rolling down her forehead, dribbling down her neck and into her suit. She didn't dare remove the helmet to wipe it away. "Of course, *that* was why they relocated Blue Squadron. Dion's flying in it. Marcus told you that, if you'd been paying attention. But now," she added, heart rate and blood pressure returning to near normal, "what the devil is Sagan doing here?"

A large crowd was gathered around the Warlord. It was easy to keep out of sight. Hovering on the fringes, Maigrey saw a flaming patch of red-gold and recognized Dion. And then she saw why Sagan was down here when, with the enemy in sight, he should have been ten other more important places. The serpent was bombarding Eve with yet another apple.

Maigrey drew in a deep breath of longing, let it out with a sigh that fogged up her helmet. She wasn't the only one. Every pilot standing around Bay Six was gazing with envy and desire at the glistening, sleekly shining, newly redesigned and modified Scimitar. Maigrey, in her studies, had come across this updated version in the files, but she had no idea the Warlord had built a prototype.

"I test flew it," she overheard one pilot say to another. "It's a beauty. Got more moves than a six-legged dancing girl."

"Why's the Warlord giving it to a kid?"

"Not *a* kid. *The* kid. That's the true heir. The one we're gonna set back on the throne." The men put their heads together, their voices dropping.

Damn, Maigrey thought, was everyone on this ship talking sedition? She edged her way closer to overhear.

"I'm glad I'm not in Blue Squadron. They're being sent out to babysit. The Warlord wants to let the kid get close enough to the fire to feel the heat but not get scorched."

The two walked away, continuing on to their own urgent duties. The crowd was dispersing, the Warlord hurrying off, probably heading for his own spaceplane. Maigrey had read about the Bloodspear, as he called it, and she longed to see it. It was a plane designed to function like the bloodsword, operating off the pilot's mental and physical impulses. The plane literally became a pilot's additional appendage, reacting directly to a thought instead of wasting time translating thought into motion. Sagan would be out there fighting, leading the battle, and—

"I'll be babysitting!" Maigrey sighed. Well, she was a Guardian, after all. Her hand stole to the starjewel she wore concealed beneath the flight suit. She had pledged her life to her king. She would do her duty. Perhaps this was why God had brought her here.

"Spoilsport," she muttered, and went off to find plane number six.

··◁■ ■▷··

"You the substitute for Captain Hefter?"

"Yeah." Maigrey nodded, going through the routine of checking out the aircraft. Blue Squadron, it turned out, was one of the last to take off. Surreptitiously she watched Dion climb into the cockpit, his face illuminated by excitement. She wished she could speak to him, but she didn't dare risk it. Eve and the serpent were getting far too chummy.

"What's the matter with the captain?" asked the crew chief.

"Mumps."

"Mumps? At his age?" The crew chief shook his head.

"He was swelled up so, he couldn't get his helmet on."

"That a fact? Hey, you're feelin' all right, ain't you, Capt'n— Capt'n— What's your name?"

"Penthesilea."

Maigrey hoped devoutly she hadn't come across a flight mechanic who was also heavily into the Trojan Wars. Sagan would recognize the name, but he was—please God—far away.

The man shrugged.

"I ain't even gonna try to pronounce that one, Capt'n. There something wrong with your voice?"

"Laryngitis," Maigrey said huskily. "Slight touch. I'll be fine. Things look good here. Guess I'll go aboard."

"Good flying, Capt'n." The crew chief touched his hat in respect. "What did you say that name was again?"

"Penthesilea."

"That's a strange one."

Shaking his head, the crew chief walked off to the front of the Scimitar to confer with one of his men.

Penthesilea. An Amazon queen who had brought her women to fight for Troy. Inside the plane, Maigrey relaxed into the pilot's seat, shut the hatch, sealed it, and began to believe she might actually pull this off. She'd never been inside a Scimitar before, but she'd spent her months on *Phoenix* preparing for just such a moment. She'd read every scrap of information, played through all the simulations. It wouldn't take her long at all to get accustomed to the feel of the plane in flight. Humming to herself the triumphal march from *Aida*, she activated the computer, introduced herself as Captain Penthesilea, and began running through the preflight checks.

Penthesilea. She was rather pleased with herself for using that name—her old code name. It had come glibly to her tongue; she hadn't thought, until the crew chief asked the question, what she would give as an alias. Everything on board checked out. There was nothing to do now but sit and wait for the command.

Penthesilea. The Amazon queen stands on the walls of Troy, taunting the Greek hero, Achilles, on the field of battle below. Her women shout for her to come down; she is in the line of fire. But Penthesilea has come to the siege of Troy for the honor and the glory, as has Achilles, and she scorns the pleas that she return to safety. Achilles draws his bow and fires at her, but even as he looses the arrow, he knows that he will slay the only woman he could ever love.

Funny, it had been years since she's thought about that old legend. Maigrey was suddenly extremely annoyed with herself that she'd thought of it now.

···◁■ ■▷···

Dion eased himself into the cockpit of the new Scimitar and looked around with delight.

"I wish Tusk could see this," he said before he thought, and he immediately felt a twinge, like a toothache, only this pain was in his conscience, not his molars.

"It's all Tusk's fault anyway," he muttered.

"Repeat the command, sir. That is not in my files. Repeat the command, sir."

"Sorry, computer. Just ignore it. It wasn't a command. I was talking to myself."

"Yes, sir. Will you be doing that often, sir?"

"No, computer. This was an accident. It slipped out. Now let's go through the preflight check."

"I've already done that, sir."

"Oh. And, uh, does everything . . . check out?"

"Of course, sir. What didn't, I fixed."

"What do you mean, what didn't, you fixed? What didn't? What did you fix?"

"I assure you, sir, the matter was trivial. You do not need to concern yourself. It is my duty to take care of such routine emergencies and keep you free from worry, sir."

Dion wondered just what a "routine emergency" might be

but decided not to ask. He felt somewhat intimidated by this cold, impersonal, and authoritative computer and decided he would ask the Warlord to have it reprogrammed. He'd prefer something with more personality, like XJ-27, which brought his mind back to Tusk again.

"What are we waiting for?" Dion demanded irritably.

"The signal to take off, sir. We're one of the last squadrons to leave, sir."

"Well . . . is there any way I can find out what's happening?" Dion had the feeling the war was going to end without him ever having been in it.

"Yes, sir. Visual on this monitor. Audio on this channel."

Dion looked and listened, but all he saw was a confusing blob of blips converging, dispersing, appearing, and disappearing. The audio was loud and equally confusing to him, though he supposed it must be making sense to somebody. He asked himself, suddenly, if he should really be going out there. It had all been exciting, like a game, when Lord Sagan took him to this shining new plane. Dion had seen the looks of envy on the faces of the other pilots, the carefully expressionless faces on the men of his squadron. He had exulted in his heady status, but now—listening to the tense, cool voices of men fighting for their very lives, fighting to keep a heinous enemy from their doorstep—Dion felt ashamed, inexperienced, and frightened.

"I don't belong here! This is crazy. Sure, I've flown before, but not as much as I led Sagan to believe. Why didn't I tell him the truth? Or maybe he knew the truth. He seems to know everything. Maybe this is a test. Another one of his goddam tests!"

"Sir, your pulse rate has climbed to an unacceptable level. Blood pressure and body temperature are both rising, sir. If you will look at the EKG monitor on your left—"

"I don't need to look at it! I wouldn't know what it meant, anyway! Damn it, when are we going to get out of here? Can't you cool it off in this cockpit?"

"My readings indicate that the temperature is quite comfortable for those of your species. And I must insist, sir, that you take steps to lower your pulse rate immediately. Otherwise I shall have to declare you unfit for duty."

"All right, all right."

Dion remembered Platus's training in meditation techniques. Leaning back, drawing in a breath, he let it out slowly through pursed lips, drew in another, and tried to send his fear out along with the impure air. That worked, to a certain extent. But what worked even better was the thought of what XJ would be saying right now to this fascist computer. Dion grinned and felt better.

"Tusk understands. It just caught him by surprise, me being a king and all. I guess he never really believed in it. I wish I could have stayed and talked to him back on Vangelis. We'd have worked everything out. But I had my duty to the Warlord. Tusk's a soldier. He understands. I'm sure he understands."

Was it your duty that kept you from visiting Tusk and Link and General Dixter and the others on *Defiant*? a part of him replied.

"I wanted to, I really did."

That was more true than he knew. Dion was lonely, desperately lonely on board *Phoenix*. Seeing Tusk had made his loneliness worse. He remembered with longing and regret the fun of being with Tusk and Link; of drinking stale beer in that hot, smelly cafe; of listening to the two try to outdo each other in tales of heroism; of watching them flirt—more or less successfully—with the local women. He remembered warmth, camaraderie, good-natured teasing about his flaming red hair.

"Are you doing it again, sir?"

"Doing what, computer?"

"Talking to yourself, sir?"

"Yes, and if you don't like it, you can short yourself out!"

"My internal security systems prevent me from carrying out that order, sir."

Outlaws. Deserters. A failed, broken-down general. Hardly suitable companions for the heir to the galactic empire. Sagan had never said so in those words, but by talking to Dion about how a prince should be "a fox to discover the snares and a lion to terrify the wolves," the young man understood that he was being raised a lion and the lion always travels alone.

He recalled another passage Sagan had quoted to him: "Because this is to be asserted in general of men, that they are ungrateful, fickle, false, cowards, covetous, and as long as you succeed they are yours entirely. . . ." An ancient writer on statecraft named Machiavelli had said that. Dion found it strange that Platus had never required the boy to read him.

Of course, you couldn't quite call Dixter fickle or false, or term Tusk a coward. Dion wasn't certain, therefore, that he quite accepted such a cynical view. Certainly Platus wouldn't have. But then, Platus had believed in man, not in God. Sagan believed in God. And himself.

Dion sighed. "I don't have faith in God, man, or myself!"

"We have received the signal to take off, sir. Please sit back and relax. I am programmed to handle everything. Is your seat belt properly fastened, sir? We cannot lift off unless your seat belt—"

"It's fastened, damn it! You're handling everything? Just what the hell do I get to do?" Dion shouted.

"Hell? Repeat the command, sir. That is not in my files. Repeat the command, sir."

Chapter ·◆○◆· Nine

A horrid front of dreadful length and dazzling arms . . .
John Milton, *Paradise Lost*

"General Dixter! You look terrible, sir, begging the general's pardon. Can I get you something?"

"Thank you, Rian. Bennett and the ship's surgeon between them have taken care of me."

"Nola's right, sir," Tusk added. "You should be in bed. There's nothing much going on now——"

"I'm shot full of stimulus. If I went back to bed I'd float about three meters off of it. I've been to the bridge, spoken to Captain Williams."

"Have you noticed that he smiles all the time?" Tusk demanded of no one in particular.

"He has lovely eyes and very nice teeth," Nola commented.

"What do his teeth have to do with anything? They're probably not his, anyway."

"Oh, nothing." Nola shrugged and grinned, crinkling the spray of freckles that spattered across her nose. "Except maybe that's why he smiles a lot. To show off his teeth."

"I know where I'd like to see his teeth." Tusk's fist clenched. "Comin' out the other side of his head. Jeez, Nola, why do you always have to——"

"That will do, Tusca," cut in Dixter, wiping his hand across his sweating face. He swayed where he stood. Bennett hurried solicitously to his side, but the general irritably waved his aide away and latched on to a control panel to steady himself. "I'm calling a meeting of all pilots and their crews, now."

"Here, sir?"

"Yes, here," Dixter said, smiling faintly. The knuckles on the hand holding on to the control panel were chalk white. "I doubt seriously if you could pry me loose."

386

The mercenaries on *Defiant* had been given access to two flight decks—Charlie and Delta. The decks were adjacent, but when the ship was cleared for action and the blast doors were in place, the decks were cut off from each other, the mercenary force split cleanly in two. Captain Williams had offered Dixter's people the use of berths aboard *Defiant*—there were extras available, since the usual contingent of fighter pilots had been transferred to other ships of the fleet. The general firmly and politely turned down the offer. He didn't like having his people spread out all over the ship, for one thing. He didn't like the fact that the doors to these berths could be sealed shut at the captain's command, for another. Dixter and his troops bivouacked on the hangar decks, much to the disgust of the *Defiant*'s flight crews.

Dixter *had* accepted Williams's offer of updated equipment and parts for his planes. The mercenaries either did the repairs and modifications themselves, or in cases where the equipment was unfamiliar, they breathed down the backs of the mechanics installing it. Tusk threw XJ into a state of near meltdown by dropping casual comments on the wonders of the new on-board computer systems the Warlord had developed and hinted broadly that he was considering having one installed. XJ spent nine-tenths of its time in its remote, prowling its perimeters, keeping a paranoid eye on the mechanics and zapping any who inadvertently came too near.

The humans and aliens of Dixter's Outlaws, as they came to call themselves, spent their time on board *Defiant* tinkering with their planes, cooking, gambling, squabbling among themselves or with the flight crews, and loving. Nola Rian had signed on as Tusk's gunner.

"You don't think I'm brave enough, do you?" Nola had said, with a toss of the short brown curls, when this subject first came under discussion.

"Of course I do. I've seen you in action, remember? It's just—"

"Then you don't think I can learn to operate the gun. This sophisticated equipment is too complicated for a girl from a backwater planet."

"Come off it, Nola! I could teach you to operate the gun. Nothing to it. It's just that it's going to be dangerous. It's not only the Corasians we're gonna have to watch, it's the Warlord, too. Dixter doesn't trust him. Neither do I. The Starlady warned us—"

"The Starlady? She's wonderful, isn't she, Tusk? So tall and slender and regal-looking, with hair like morning mist. If I were tall and slender would you take me with you?"

"Damn it, Nola, you come up with the weirdest notions. I don't want you tall and slender. I like you short and pudgy. Well, you know what I mean. Why do you do this to me? I don't want you along because I don't want anything to happen to you, you little fool!"

"Well, I feel the same way! I don't want you to go because I don't want anything to happen to you!"

"But it's my job, Nola—"

"And if you hired me, it'd be my job, too. And we'd be together. But, if you don't want me because I'm short and pudgy—"

"I never said that—"

"—other people happen to think differently. Link's already asked if I'd be interested in being his co-pilot."

"His co-pilot! That bastard doesn't have room for a co-pilot. His ego's so big it takes up the whole cockpit!"

Which, of course, settled everything. The only one left to convince had been XJ, who was totally opposed to having a female gunner until Tusk assured him that Nola was working for nothing, after which assurance the computer came up with all kinds of statistics proving that the female of the human species reacted better under stress than the male.

When the enemy was sighted, the alert was sounded, but *Defiant* was not yet on full alert status. The ship was hanging back, out of the forefront of the battle. There had been considerable activity around the *Defiant*'s hull, work crews swarming over it day and night, seeming to be trying desperately to affect repairs. There was nothing at all wrong with *Defiant*, but Sagan hoped the Corasians would think there was. Though he didn't expect them to remove the ship from their calculations altogether—the aliens were too intelligent for that old trick—the Warlord did hope that they would at least refigure the equation and come up with the wrong answer.

"As you know, for we've gone over the game plan, we're to sit out the first half," Dixter told his assembled Outlaws. "When the enemy's been knocked around pretty good and they've used up—hopefully—all their substitutes and their time-outs, then we go in."

"I don't like it, sir!" This was Colonel Glicka, the alien with the tentacles who'd been at the meeting. "I think it's a trap. The Warlord's going to leave us cooped up here to be slaughtered like pigs in a barrel."

"*Pigs* in a barrel?" Link said, nudging Nola, who giggled.

"It's the only way the translator knew how to translate the metaphor," Tusk snapped.

"Metaphor!" Link whistled. "Wow, this boy's been to college."

"Damn it, Link, I'm— Sorry, sir."

Tusk caught Dixter's stern eye and subsided, squatting back down on the desk and contenting himself with glowering at the handsome, grinning Link. Nola shook out her curls, glanced at Tusk from beneath a fringe of dark lashes, and giggled again.

"It's a classic battle plan, people. One used successfully by Philip of Macedon against the Greeks, more recently by Zachis Zelben against the off-worlders in System Qsub046. You hit the enemy with a solid front. They push and suddenly the front's middle begins to give and sag, drawing the enemy in deeper and deeper with a planned retreat. When the enemy's trapped in the center, you bring up your left and right flanks, send in reinforcements. I hope that translated all right? It's like catching a cat in a sack. We're the strings."

He glanced at the alien, who wiggled a tentacle but still looked unhappy. The mercenaries said nothing, but exchanged grim glances. They knew that the cat was, in reality, a tiger and they were trying to catch it in a very small bag.

"Understood? Any questions? Then, dismissed. Go to your planes and await my signal. Tusk, a word." The general motioned. Tusk loped forward.

"I'll take care of Nola," called out the irrepressible Link. "Don't hurry back."

"I'll wait for you, Tusk. Right here," Nola said.

Smiling at Tusk, she deliberately shrugged off Link's encircling arm.

Man, Tusk thought, a guy never knows where he stands. Maybe that was the attraction. After all, I don't really like short, pudgy women. . . .

"Yes, sir?"

The general relinquished his hold on the control panel and, glancing at the *Defiant*'s work crews, who were still busy around the planes, Dixter drew Tusk to one side.

"Tusk, I'll be relaying commands to you and the others from the bridge. Pass the word: Be careful going out *and* coming back. Got that?"

"Yes, sir. Do you really think he's going to try something, sir? The Warlord gave us a pardon, after all, and, I mean, whatever else Derek Sagan may be, he's known to be just and honorable. He keeps his word. I think we're worried about nothing."

Dixter glanced over the mercenary's shoulder and saw Nola, waiting for Tusk, her face cheerful and smiling. She and Tusk both knew about the Adonian, Snaga Ohme. The other mercenaries, if they didn't know the Adonian weapons dealer by now, knew about the torpedo launcher. They all know that something big was coming down.

"You're right, Tusk," the general said, forcing his aching facial muscles into a smile. He clapped the mercenary on the back. "It's the space sickness. Or maybe it's these stimulants. I'm jumping at my own shadow. But just let's be safe, okay? Don't take orders from anyone but me."

"Yes, sir. Anything else, sir?"

"No, go ahead. You've got someone waiting for you."

"Yes, sir. Thank you, sir." Tusk grinned, saluted, and hurried off.

Dixter watched the young man rejoin the young woman, saw their arms steal around each other, their heads lean together. He could almost hear Tusk's voice whispering, "The old man sure is jumpy!"

Tusk doesn't know—none of them know—that this is all my fault, Dixter reflected. Why the devil couldn't I have left well enough alone? But, no, I had to go snooping around. Ah, well, the general reminded himself. Perhaps it wouldn't have made any difference anyway. In Sagan's eyes, we had probably doomed ourselves simply by being on that planet.

"Sir." It was Bennett, hovering.

"Yes, Bennett?"

"Captain Williams's compliments, sir, and would you come to the bridge?"

Bennett's tone was approving. Captain Wililams had been extremely respectful and polite. The captain may have been the scion of a corrupt and rotting system of government, he may be hand in glove with the Warlord, which—as Bennett knew—his general considered tantamount to being hand in glove with the powers of darkness, but Captain Williams, at least, knew how to talk to a general.

"Bennett, did you ever notice that Captain Williams smiles a lot?" General Dixter asked, wending his way through the corridors of *Conquest*.

"Captain Williams has exceptionally fine teeth, sir."

So does a shark, John Dixter thought.

··◁■ ■▷··

Lord Sagan watched, from his white, spearheaded fighter, squadron after squadron lift in deadly grace from *Phoenix* and the other two ships of the line. Each fighter shot out in perfect formation, with the exception of one in the last squadron— Blue Squadron. The Warlord saw Dion's plane operating smoothly; he would have been vastly surprised otherwise. He had programmed the computer to do everything, including making certain the boy's nose was wiped.

It was another plane in the squadron that was behaving oddly—number six. When leaving the flight deck, it had gone into a forward roll, nearly crashing against *Phoenix*'s hull! The pilot's skillful handling had saved the plane, but Sagan was inserting a note into his computer to put that pilot on report. He stared at the Scimitar closely. There was definitely something odd about that plane! Something . . . familiar.

"My lord," came the communication. "All squadrons away. Red Squadron and Green have both engaged the enemy."

The Warlord shifted his attention to the battle being fought before his eyes. Other citizen generals would have remained on *Phoenix*, observing the battle on a gigantic lighted computer screen, seeing the planes as small blips, and issuing orders accordingly. Lord Sagan had tried such a command post once, after President Robes had assured him that a citizen general was far too valuable to his galaxy to risk losing him in battle. Sagan had ended by putting his fist through the screen and ordering his fighter.

If he had been Philip of Macedon, he would have been sitting on his horse atop a high ridge, watching the heave and surge of bodies below. As it was, his fighter was positioned high in space, his escorts hanging motionless at his side, watching the small sparks—the divine sparks, as Maigrey would have said—flare and flicker or flare and burst and die.

The dance, from his sealed-off and closed-up vantage point, was performed in eerie silence.

Would it make a difference, Sagan wondered briefly, if we heard the screams of the dying? Would wars end if we had to listen? He supposed not. Philip had certainly heard enough screams during his lifetime as a conqueror. And at the end, he'd heard his own.

Sagan shook his head. The Warlord's philosophic musings were cut short. The Corasian mothership was in sight.

The huge, black, ugly, missile-shaped vessel floated ponderously into view, visible only in that she was a blot against the stars. Corasians have no need for lights. They don't have eyes, can't see, and do not waste energy lighting a ship. The Corasians operated strictly by computer signal, computer command. It had been the computer which gave the aliens the means to conquer the stars.

"Mothership" was a term used in a literal sense. This terrible black egg would hatch a swarm of deadly offspring. Corasians are not creative. Creativity implies one mind thinking differently from another. The Corasians are a collective mind. Each entity thinks the same as every other. They are completely equal; there is no authority because there is no need for authority. All have the same goal, determined collectively in response to the collective need. If the goal is to build computers, the collective body builds computers. If the goal is to take over a planet, the collective body takes over a planet. If the goal is to kill, the collective body kills.

The Corasians, therefore, have never developed a battle strategy. Hordes rarely have need for one. They conquer by sheer force of numbers, by overrunning and beating down any opposition, by sending wave after wave of the collective body in to the attack until the enemy gives way out of sheer exhaustion. Sagan had planned his own strategy to react to this type of mindless assault. It should work. As far as Sagan could see, the overall design of the enemy ship itself hadn't changed in seventeen years and the flood of reports he received from his analysts aboard *Phoenix* indicated few modifications made to the vessel. Yet the Warlord had the feeling—call it the instinct of the warrior—that something was about to go wrong.

The enemy had waited seventeen years before attacking . . . for what?

For that.

Sagan's visual sighting and the instrument sightings aboard

Phoenix occurred almost simultaneously. He understood what was happening in an instant; the reports of his analysts merely confirmed his fears.

The Corasians weren't streaming out of the mothership in erratic mobs. They were flying out in disciplined order in groups, and in the center of each group of small black dots, which were the fighters, was a large black blob, which was, according to the computers on board *Phoenix*, a gigantic computer—a brain. The collective body had split and become innumerable collective bodies, and apparently each body had its own brain. Each body would be able to think for itself and act accordingly. Instead of commanding "Kill," the brain could command "Kill this way," or "Kill that way," which is, in warfare, the definition of strategy.

This is what they had been working on for years. It had taken a creative mind to design it—a mind the Corasians didn't possess, a mind like the one that belonged to a former university professor, Peter Robes.

The Warlord placed his palm on a control pad from which protruded five needles in a circular pattern. The needles inserted into the flesh in exactly the same manner as those of the bloodsword and with almost the same effect. Sagan could operate this plane by his brain's impulses. He drove the needles into his palm.

"By God, I'll live through this," Derek Sagan vowed, watching the Corasians spread out in organized groups, taking up formations, "just to have the satisfaction, Peter Robes, of making you wish I hadn't!"

Sagan felt the plane become another part of his physical body, another appendage like his hand or his foot. Unlike the bloodsword, the spaceplane had its own energy source and didn't completely sap the body's. Of course, it took a toll, just as performing any strenuous exertion takes a mental and a physical toll. Thus the need for discipline.

Having sworn his oath, the Warlord prayed to God to grant him the strength and the wisdom to live to fulfill it.

Sagan wasn't disappointed. The faith of the priest's son was rewarded. He had an idea.

"Computer," the Warlord said, his gaze fixed on the brains of the enemy. "Analyze and report on the following . . ."

Chapter ···❧◈❧··· Ten

Meanwhile war arose, and fields were fought in Heaven . . .
                    John Milton, *Paradise Lost*

One of the galaxy's most skilled pilots, a pilot whose exploits even then were legend, had just received a sharp reprimand from her squadron leader. Maigrey bit her lip and mumbled something into her commlink about a computer malfunction.

"Oh, shut up," she said crossly to the computer, which was indignantly denying such an accusation.

Who would have guessed the controls on the Scimitar would be so blasted sensitive? She had meant to go up, but not quite that far up—a move that had nearly caused her to crash into the belly of *Phoenix*. Her skill had saved her, but only barely. Maigrey's face beneath her helmet flushed hotly and she thanked God that Sagan hadn't been around to witness that little maneuver. At least now she knew better.

Once she was accustomed to flying it, she discovered that the short-range Scimitar handled quite well and she paid the Warlord a mental compliment that was not without a certain amount of pain. They had spent many pleasant hours, years ago, designing their own ideal spaceplanes. She recognized many of Sagan's old ideas and one or two of her own in this model.

That brought a sigh, and she quickly shifted her mind back from a shattered past to a dismal present. Maigrey glanced over at Dion's plane—Blue Four. He was flying perfectly, yet she had the distinct impression something was wrong with him. This impression didn't come from any power of the Blood Royal, it was simply there, a part of her. She wondered if she was beginning to experience maternal feelings.

"Blue Six." The squadron leader. "You're out of formation! Is something wrong?"

"No, sir, Squadron Leader. Sorry, sir. Just keyed up for action, sir."

"Stuck back in the rear, I doubt if we'll see much of that! Stay alert, Six."

Squadron Leader did not sound at all happy. Maigrey couldn't blame him. She was receiving reports that the enemy was in visual range, but you couldn't prove it by her. Babysitting. Glancing back at Dion's ship, Maigrey sighed again. She was a Guardian, after all. She had pledged her life to her king. She wished she could see what was going on!

Maigrey was about to instruct her computer to provide a visual of the enemy formation, realized she didn't need to. She saw the enemy, suddenly and clearly, through Sagan's eyes. She saw and she understood, just as did the Warlord, the change in Corasian tactics. His idea came to her clearly—their gravest danger could be their only hope. But it had to be proven, it had to be risked. Of course, he was going to attempt it alone. She recalled lines of the poet, John Milton.

> *Wherefore do I assume*
> *These royalties, . . .*
> *Refusing to accept as great a share*
> *Of hazard as of honour. . . .*

Proud as Lucifer, so the saying went. Maigrey looked again at Dion's plane, her soul writhing in an agony of indecision. There was something wrong, she knew it. The boy was too quiet, his computer—so far—had done all the talking. Maigrey was tempted to ask him to connect with the bloodsword. They could communicate that way, their thoughts revealed to each other. But she swallowed the words before they reached her lips. She didn't dare. That would reveal herself to everyone, and Sagan was quite capable of locking a tractor beam on her and having her dragged back to the ship.

I'm a Guardian. I should stay here and keep an eye on him, she thought. But then again, defending your king didn't necessarily mean tripping along at his heels, being prepared to fling your body in front of his. Sometimes it means being in the vanguard of his army. . . .

As Squadron Leader said, Dion certainly wasn't going to be in any danger back here. And he had the rest of the squadron to watch out for him, to babysit.

"Six! Where the devil do you think you're going? Get back in formation. That's an order. Six! Blue Six! I'm bringing you up on charges, Six! This is cowardice! Desertion in the face of the enemy!"

"You want your pound of flesh, Squadron Leader," Maigrey murmured, "you'll have to stand in line!"

··◄■ ■►··

Dion, sitting in his shining toy, had just realized what it meant to be a king—or perhaps "puppet king" would be a better choice of words. He was to be shut up in a prison—a prison that was wonderful and filled with marvels—and he was to be given everything he could ever want. He was to be *given* it. And he would take it and be happy or his prison would become a tomb, his jailer his executioner.

"Maigrey tried to tell me. I wouldn't listen, I wouldn't believe. I didn't want to believe! I wanted to think that he was truly doing for me what he claimed. I wanted to think he respected me. And this—this is what I get!"

"I do not understand your disparaging tone, sir," the computer said. "This spaceplane is equipped with the very latest in technology, much of it added within the last few days, as I was myself, and all designed to keep you safe and sound, sir. I might venture to state, sir, that you are far better protected here than you were in your mother's womb."

Dion began to laugh. "Having been born in a palace in the midst of a revolution, I'll grant you that one, computer. Hey, what's happening? Where's that guy going? Squadron Leader, Six is—"

"I will handle all communications between yourself and Squadron Leader, sir," the computer said, cutting Dion off in mid-report. "As for Six, pay no attention to it. The pilot appears to have gone berserk."

Dion tried turning the plane—a small experiment.

"I'm afraid I cannot allow you to make that maneuver, sir. That would be leaving formation, and we do not want to leave formation, do we, sir?"

Platus had been an acknowledged genius with computers. He'd passed much of his ability on to Dion. The young man sat back in the pilot's chair and pondered, staring grimly at the computer.

So then. Dion made up his mind. It was to be murder.

·◄■ ■►··

Sagan flew through "dark destruction." He did not travel, as Maigrey had assumed he would, alone, but took two of his men with him, sending another back to *Phoenix* with an urgent message for Admiral Aks—a message the Warlord wanted delivered in person, a message he didn't want intercepted by the enemy. The Warlord's target was one of the brains of the Corasian fleet. Analysis had confirmed what Sagan had surmised—knock out the brain and there was every possibility that the body would flop about aimlessly. Of course, they would still be faced with a horde, but the Warlord would far rather fight a mindless horde than an organized and disciplined army.

Unfortunately, reaching the brain would be like trying to reach the queen of a colony of fire ants. Sagan could count on getting stung, perhaps to death.

But the Warlord was not suicidal. Nor did he make the decision to attempt this himself out of misplaced heroics. Because of his unique mind-controlled spaceplane, he had the best chance to succeed. If this mission proved successful, he could then afford to change his strategy, perhaps send in the forces he was holding in reserve, their only goal to knock out the brains. But Sagan first had to determine if, as he had said once to Maigrey, "the sport was worth the candle."

Corasian fighters are small and compact. They do not need to accommodate the body of a pilot, because the plane is—literally—the pilot's body. Corasians have no survival instinct. When told to kill, they latch on to an enemy and hang on with mindless ferocity, attacking mercilessly until either the enemy dies or they do. Even when guided by the brains, the Corasians were slow to react and slow to maneuver. Sudden, unlooked-for moves rattled them completely. A pilot fighting the Corasians has the advantage of superior reaction time and creative mind but, over the long duration of a battle, these grow weak when fatigue and despair set in, when you seem to be battling the leaves of the trees of a never-ending forest.

Sagan rarely allowed himself to give way to fatigue and never to despair. His plane could react in the instant of a thought. Flying with him were two of the finest pilots in the galaxy. Yes, they had a chance. As a gambler, he wouldn't have laid any money on it, but they had a chance.

The Warlord waited until he saw one of the heavily armored, lumbering brains take up a fixed position in the center of the battle zone.

"There's the target," he instructed his wingmen. "We'll go down on top of it."

The Warlord's spearheaded plane dropped from the blackness. The wingmen were slower, having been caught off guard by his sudden descent.

"Close formation," Sagan snapped, and the wingmen pulled in tighter, their planes rocketing toward what continued to look like a small black patch cut out of starry space.

They swooped into the front lines, into the swirling melee of wheeling planes and crisscrossing tracer fire and exploding rockets. Three Corasian fighters, attracted by the technology of the Warlord's unusual spaceplane, attempted to entangle Sagan in what was known as a "web"—three interlocking tractor beams capable of paralyzing a small fighter, allowing the Corasians to drag it and its helpless pilot back to the mothership. Knowing what fate awaited him there, a pilot caught in a web would invariably either self-destruct or request his comrades to shoot him.

The Corasian spiders trying to catch this particular fly discovered too late they had made a mistake. Sagan vaporized them. The two wingmen soared behind their leader through three puffs of smoke and flame. The wingmen had not even fired.

Ignoring the battle, the Warlord held steadfastly to his goal and soon left the main assault behind. He was well past the front line of the fighting, deep among the enemy ranks. And as he suspected, the brain was capable of analyzing his attack. It had determined him to be a threat. A ring of fighters protectively encircling the brain leapt to the attack.

Sagan spared a glance at his computer. It was transmitting vast quantities of data on the enemy brains including three-dimensional renderings of the structure and the interior. The brain was shaped like a huge and ugly bell and contained banks of computers operated by Corasians in their robot bodies. Its central power source was located right in the center. There was little chance of hitting it, therefore, from the round top or the curved sides of the energy-shielded bell.

"The brain's weakness is at the bottom," the computer reported, confirming for Sagan what he saw on the screen. "A

large hatch located there"—visually enhanced on the screen—
"provides the only means of entrance and egress. That particular portion of the brain is not shielded." The computer
rotated the diagram. "An attack coming from directly beneath
the brain and centered on the hatch itself, which is the only
portion not shielded, has a chance of succeeding. The hatch is
approximately one meter in diameter."

"Defense systems?"

"Yes, sir. Gun emplacements around the hatch—"

"I see!" snapped the Warlord. "What kind of firepower
would it take to penetrate the shields?"

"Working." The computer hummed to itself for several tense
seconds, then returned, "The shields are extremely strong, sir.
Perhaps concentrated lascannon fire, sir, from *Phoenix*—"

"—would take out everything, including our own forces."

He could pull back his planes, turn to the big guns. But
Sagan had run those calculations both through the computer
and his own mind. If he pulled back the fighters, the Corasian
mothership would enter the game, moving up to pound the
Warlord's fleet. He would counterattack, of course, but . . .
massive and ugly, the Corasian mothership could absorb
unbelievable punishment. Sagan had calculated he must lose
two ships of the line immediately, without being able to inflict
anywhere close to corresponding damage on the enemy. After
that, it would be a matter of constant bombardment until
Phoenix either fell victim to a lucky shot or ran so low on
energy that life-support would fail. Those who had survived
the battle would die horribly of asphyxiation.

So all the Warlord had to do was blow up a hatch one meter
in diameter surrounded by guns.

"Computer, transmit all of that information by my private
code back to *Phoenix*. And add this: Fighters forming outer
defensive perimeter around the brain are converging on us,
leaving the brain unguarded. I judge there to be about twenty.
I suggest, therefore, that a feint made by one squadron would
draw off the defenders and allow another squadron to penetrate the unguarded perimeter and attack. This strategy may
work only the first few times it is attempted, for I submit that
the Corasian computers have undoubtedly developed the
ability to 'learn' from their mistakes."

The Warlord paused. There were still some few seconds
until he would join with the enemy.

"Computer, my personal log, uncoded and send a copy by 'accident,' to the main files. 'In the event of my death, this message is to be transmitted to the marshals, to the members of the Congress of the Commonwealth, and to the news media. I, Derek Sagan, accuse Peter Robes, President of the Republic, of being a traitor to the people. I submit that he 'leaked' technological secrets to the Corasians, that he knew of their preparations for war and did nothing to stop them, that he deliberately invited this attack on the galaxy.

"'What his motives might be, I can only venture to guess, but I further submit that a war causes people to rally around their leader and, in their fear, assign him whatever powers he wants. I have little doubt but that President Robes will demand virtual dictatorial power in order to deal with the threat. I further submit that the galaxy's greatest danger is not from without, but from within.'"

Within twenty-four hours, everyone on board *Phoenix* would have read that message. Sagan had little time for elation, however. Within twenty-four hours, unless he found some way to stop the enemy, everyone on board *Phoenix* would likely be dead.

The Corasians struck with fury, their intent now not to capture but to kill. The Scimitars rolled and twisted and dodged, always swinging back in to maintain battle formation, forming a wedge—the Warlord on the point—that pushed steadily toward the target. Then one wingman was gone, exploding in a ball of fire that took out two Corasians with him.

Sagan's screen showed him the enemy—small blips that dove down on him with all the finesse of a pack of wild dogs. Zigzagging in and out of the swarm, he kept up almost constant fire; they were jammed so closely together it was impossible not to hit something.

But it was like removing water from a bucket drop by drop. A sudden silence on his commlink let him know he'd lost his other wingman. He was closer to the target and getting closer all the time, and the number of the blips surrounding him had decreased markedly. There were only four left, two in front of him and two circling around behind him. But these four had him and there wasn't—Sagan realized with cold anger—a damn thing he could do about it.

The red light on his panel flashed its warning that the enemy had him in their sights. He was caught. It was maddening, frustrating that all his grand designs and plans should end in such ignominy. He feinted, dove, twisted. The enemy clung to him like evil hornets. At least he had the satisfaction of knowing he had chosen his own fate. Wellington's officers, protesting their general's refusal to seek safety during the battle of Waterloo, had pleaded with him.

"Sir, what are your orders for us if you are killed?"

"Follow my example," was the general's answer.

Follow my example.

Gritting his teeth, bracing himself for the blast that would reduce his body to specks of blood and fragments of charred bone and burned flesh, Sagan fired at the Corasians in front of him and commended his soul to God.

A powerful explosion rocked his ship. The Corasian blew apart in a blinding flash, but that alone couldn't account for the jolt he'd just taken. And Sagan's plane wasn't, according to his instruments readings, hit. He knocked out the second enemy diving down for its attack, and was preparing to turn his attention to the two behind him when he realized, looking at his screen, that there weren't two blips behind him. There was only one, and it, according to the data, was a friend.

Sort of.

My lord, came the voice in his mind.

Sagan blinked away a trickle of sweat running into his eyes. *My lady.*

··◁■ ■▷··

Blue Squadron was so far from the fighting that they could barely see what was going on. They heard, from the reports, that their planes were sustaining heavy casualties and it was difficult to tell if the current retreat was the one that had been planned or if it was truly a rout.

Squadron Leader spent his time filing a detailed report on the insane behavior of pilot number six. The others in the squadron maintained a grim, tense silence, knowing well why they were there, who was the cause of it, and resenting him bitterly.

Dion, meanwhile, toyed with the computer.

"Sir, I think you should know that I am aware of what you are attempting to do and I consider it my duty to tell you that you are wasting your time and mine. There is no possible way that you can get rid of me, sir. Nor do you really want to, sir, for if I go, then all functions of this spaceplane will cease to operate."

"Now, that's not quite true, computer," Dion said softly, continuing to work. "You see, you told me that you were a new modification, only been added a few days ago. I've come to the conclusion that you're like a virus that's been injected into the system. I think it's possible that I can remove you and the plane's original computer will be around to take over after you're gone. Hey, what are you doing?"

"I've sent a distress signal, sir, to Squadron Leader. Forgive me for saying so, sir, but you are obviously unhinged."

"Blue Four!" It was Squadron Leader, sounding angry and exasperated. "*Now* what's your problem?"

"I wish to report that—" the computer began.

Dion depressed a key, sat back, and waited.

"That . . ." The computer blinked frantically, trying to save itself. "Unfit—" it whispered, and died.

Everything went dark for a split second, but before Dion had time to panic or to consider that he might have made a terrifying error, all systems switched back on.

"Blue Four, what the hell—"

"Everything back to normal, sir," the computer reported, but Dion thought he noticed a subtle difference in the tone of the mechanical voice.

"Who are you?" he asked.

"Your computer, sir."

There was no doubt about it. Dion could hear it. Respect! Programmed, perhaps, but respect!

"Blue Four, respond! That's an order!"

"You'll obey my commands, computer?" Dion intended to make certain.

"That *is* my primary function, sir," the computer said, sounding slightly puzzled. "I trust I've given you no cause to doubt—"

"No! None! None at all," Dion hastened to reassure it. "Uh, this is Blue Four reporting, Squadron Leader. An electrical malfunction, but it's been repaired."

"What's happened to your computer, Blue Four? *It's* supposed to be responding."

"Knocked it right out, sir. But, as I said, it's all been repaired—"

"Blue Four! I'm ordering you to report back to *Phoenix*—"

"Computer, shut off the transmission."

"Shutting off, sir."

"Now"—Dion took the controls—"let's go find some action!"

··◀■ ■▶··

"Blue Four? Name of a name!" Squadron Leader swore savagely. "Has everybody in this squadron lost their fuckin' minds?"

"Blue Two to Squadron Leader. What's going on, sir? I just saw the kid head out—"

"The damn kid's shut down his computer and he's going off the devil knows where."

"Should we go after him, sir?"

"Hell, yes, we go after him! You heard the Warlord's orders. And you better hope," Squadron Leader muttered beneath his breath, his plane soaring to catch Dion's, "that if anything happens to that kid it happens to us first."

Chapter ·❦◯❦· Eleven

I could not love thee, Dear, so much . . .
    Richard Lovelace, "To Lucasta, Going to the Wars"

You owe me one, my lord.

I have no time for games, my lady.

I'm not playing games, my lord. I'm in deadly earnest, and if you think about it, you'll understand why.

The Scimitar and the spearheaded plane of the Warlord's spiraled upward, both noting that other enemy planes, having been alerted to the danger, were being called back from the front lines to deal with an annoyance in the rear.

Maigrey held her breath. Sagan's thoughts were dark and jagged-edged. He was facing defeat. The action he contemplated was risky, desperate; it would probably mean his death, an empty sacrifice. He would be robbed, even of his glory. Derek Sagan, defeated by the Corasians, a loser. History never deals kindly with losers.

"What are your orders . . . Commander?" Maigrey requested out loud.

His pain, his fear, his anger . . . his regret touched her. Long ago, when they had been close, very close, his pain had been her pain, her joy had been his joy. A tear slid down her cheek. Following the path of the scar, it seeped into the corner of her mouth.

"Just keep out of my way, lady. And stop sniveling!" His voice thundered in her headset.

Maigrey could see the target on her own computer screen, but she could see it more clearly in his mind. And how the devil did he expect her to blow her nose beneath her helmet? "Don't be a fool, Sagan. You can't take it alone. Let me go ahead of you and knock out the gun emplacements."

The Corasians were zooming in; Sagan was turning, preparing to make his run at the target.

"Go ahead . . . Gold Two."

Another tear, her eyes swam. Their old squadron, two of them left, was making its final run. The last flight of the Guardians. And no one would ever know. This was foolish, undisciplined. Swallowing her tears, indulging in one more sniff (she could almost hear him grit his teeth), Maigrey dove down on the enemy.

A Corasian fighter appeared on her left, visible both on her screen and out of the corner of her eye. She paid no attention to it, trusting to her partner. A briefly seen flash confirmed her faith.

"We're even, lady."

This was an old game of the squadron's. It had become a joke; they owed their lives to each other countless times over. And then one day the joke hadn't been funny.

Maigrey was beneath the bell (or on top of it, considering that there was neither up nor down out here). The enemy's guns had her in their sights and were swiveling around to bear.

"Beginning my run."

"I'm with you, my lady."

His voice was soft, hypnotic in her ears or in her mind or in both; she heard it yet she didn't hear it. A strange and awesome sensation crept over her. She was herself and she was him. He was himself and he was her. They were one and they were two—all barriers down, souls, minds flowing together. Light meeting darkness, creating a third force with a nature both terrible and beautiful.

It was her skill that flew the plane, his keen eye that found the target, his hand that fired, her hand that guided. Shells burst around her, but she was invincible. Nothing could harm her. She had the target in her sights but it seemed to her dazzled mind that the gun emplacements dissolved and vanished before the energy bolts from her guns ever struck it.

Swiftly she pulled out, away from the enemy. Sagan was right behind her, and she was with him, guiding his plane, waiting breathlessly until the precise moment to strike.

Two Corasians were diving down on Sagan. Maigrey couldn't consciously remember firing, but they blew apart, both of them, and it was as if they had done so at her express command. Sagan had seen them but paid no attention to them. It was not that he had confidence in his partner; he no longer had a partner. They were an entity. He continued his run, drawing closer and closer, and Maigrey wanted to scream from the tension, but she only breathed, "Now!" and he fired, or perhaps not.

Sagan's plane was blown backward by the force of the explosion that tore the hatch from the brain. The concussive blast nearly caused him to lose consciousness, but Maigrey was there to strengthen his limp hands and infuse her mind into his. He came to himself, regained control, and the two sped away. A second explosion—much larger than the first—tore the heart out of the brain.

Corasian fighters swarmed around them, but it was suddenly a swarm that had lost all guidance. Some of the enemy ground to a halt—waiting, perhaps, for instructions that would never come. Others continued the attack but with a mindless fanaticism that made them easy targets. Others appeared to have no idea where they were or why they were here and drifted about aimlessly. The solid fist had opened, and there was a chance, now, that Sagan and his forces could cut off the wriggling fingers.

But the Guardians had hit only one arm of the multi-limbed monster. The battle continued to rage; the planned retreat was going well. Rather too well.

Sagan needed to see, to think. He soared far out beyond the battle lines, Maigrey following him. Those few Corasians chasing them gave up and turned back, seeking other, slower, easier prey.

Maigrey said nothing. Absorbed completely in planning his new strategy, Sagan appeared to have forgotten her existence. She was just as glad. The strange and awful sensation, that "enhancement" or whatever it had been, was fading, draining from her like blood from a severed artery. She was suddenly shaking and exhausted and chilled to the bone. She couldn't breathe and nearly yanked off the smothering helmet.

"Aks! Did you see that?"

"We saw the explosion, my lord. And we're receiving the data you transmitted now. Congratulations, my—"

"Belay that nonsense! I'm shifting strategy. Stop the retreat! Strengthen the front lines, throw everything we've got at the enemy. Keep them busy, Aks!"

"Yes, my lord."

"Alert the reserves, including the mercenaries. Send them after the brain. I'm coming in."

"Yes, my lord."

The Warlord broke off the transmission. He glanced out his viewscreen at the Scimitar hovering at his wingtip, and his eyes narrowed.

"My lord." Maigrey's voice was calm and sounded strange, unrecognizable, even to her. "Final count: you owe me two. When you return to *Phoenix*, you will find one of your Honor Guards, a man named Marcus, has been placed under arrest and is awaiting execution for disobeying your orders. He's a good soldier. I ask that you set him free with a full and complete pardon."

"So that's how you managed to escape. I know this Marcus. He is, as you say, a good soldier and one I would hate to lose. Very well, my lady, I grant your request. And the other life I owe you?"

"My own. Let me go, Sagan. You've got the boy. I can't matter to you now."

"And where will you go, Lady Maigrey?"

"Back there. To the fighting. They need me. I'm a good pilot." There was no life in her voice, in her thoughts. There was, it seemed, no life left in her.

"Don't be a fool, my lady. Your plane's taken damage; you wouldn't last ten minutes." He paused, probing her mind. "But that's what you want, isn't it? You're afraid, my lady. You're scared. That was just a taste of what we could accomplish together, you and I! Of the power we could control! Just a taste. And you liked it, didn't you, my lady? You want more!"

She didn't respond. Everything was so still between them it seemed he could hear her breathe, hear the beating of her heart.

"This debt I owe you, Lady Maigrey, is like the genie's last wish. You shouldn't squander it."

"What do you mean, my lord?"

"I mean, my lady, that there are other lives in your keeping—lives besides your own. Lives that, perhaps, mean more to you than your own. And now, my lady, I have no time left to waste on you."

The Warlord's white, spearheaded plane sailed swift and true for *Phoenix*. He left her behind. The choice was hers.

Maigrey, after a moment's bitter struggle, cursed God and followed him.

··◁▷ ▷··

Dion found the action. And it wasn't exactly what he'd had in mind.

He was surrounded. There were so many of the enemy, coming at him from so many different directions, that he couldn't count them. He fired and fired until his hands ached from the physical strain of operating the guns. He stared at the target screen, trying desperately to align the blips in the little box as he'd been taught, but his eyes burned from fatigue, the box wobbled and seemed to expand and elongate in his blurred vision. The blips were in and out too fast. He couldn't react quickly enough. The ship took hit after hit and shivered and shook around him.

"Number four shield can't hold, sir," the computer reported in its stupid, mindless calm. "Number two is down. I'm effecting repairs—"

"Don't bother," Dion said through lips that had gone numb. He couldn't move his mouth, he couldn't move his hands, and he understood now the terrible meaning of the term "scared stiff."

He was going to die, horribly, awfully. Blown apart out here in the cold void.

"You got yourself into one hell of a mess, kid!"

Squadron Leader's exasperated voice rang in Dion's ears and he nearly wept in relief.

The enemy blips on his screen were joined by other blips, friendly blips, and the enemy blips began to disappear. Dion's courage returned, now that he wasn't alone. He began to return the fire.

"This is Blue Two. Enemy coming in, Squadron Leader."

"I see them. There's too many. Pull ba—"

The scream tore through Dion's head, seeming to rip out his brains—the high-pitched, gurgling wail of a man dying in slow agony. It was mercifully ended, cut short by a shattering explosion, but the screaming went on and on.

It was Dion. He was screaming and he couldn't make himself stop. Blue Two was saying something, yelling something, but it made no sense, and then Blue Two was gone. Debris slammed into Dion's ship, and he was rolling over and over, spiraling through the blackness.

"Take the helm, sir," the computer commanded.

Dion had quit screaming; he had no voice left. His throat

was raw. He tasted blood in his mouth. But the silent scream went on inside him. He stared at the panel in front of him, at the wildly flashing red alarm lights, at the stars outside the viewscreen that were revolving madly, and he was stable and it was the world beyond that was spinning out of control.

"Take the helm—"

"I can't," Dion whispered. His hands fell limply in his lap. He stared out the viewport. Nothing made sense. He had no idea what any of these myriad dials were telling him. The flashing lights were painful to his eyes and he squinched the lids tightly shut. "I don't know how."

"Shall I take over, then, sir?"

"Yes."

The word was inaudible. Shivering, Dion curled up in the pilot's chair, his knees to his chin, his arms dangling between his legs. He couldn't breathe for dry, heaving sobs.

The computer took command of the plane, brought it back under control. But it had no idea where to go.

Four Corasians, spotting it, had a place for it.

··◁▷ ◁▷··

"And that's it," General Dixter said, speaking from the bridge of *Defiant*, talking to his people in the hangar bays through a two-way vid hookup. "Our orders have been changed. We go after these 'brains,' as the Warlord calls them. You've seen the diagrams. You know how and where to hit them. I won't ask for questions because I couldn't answer them. You know as much as I do."

The mercenaries were silent, an ominous silence. Then. Link, stirring, voiced their opinion. "I don't like it, sir. It's a suicide run."

There were murmurs of assent.

"Each of you is an independent operator." Captain Williams cut in, appearing on the screen. "You are free to leave."

The contrast between the two generals was marked. Dixter's uniform was rumpled as usual. Tusk wondered how the general managed it. Uniforms that Bennett had pressed until the creases were so sharp they were practically lethal wilted the moment John Dixter put them on. He never buttoned the collar and would have neglected to put on his stars and medals (worn unofficially), but that Bennett insisted. By contrast, Captain Williams's black, red-trimmed uniform was immaculate, not a thread out of place. He stood stiff and rigid as if he expected the Warlord to call an inspection any moment. And the captain wasn't, Tusk noted, smiling.

"None of you mercenaries has to be here," Williams stated. "You can leave now—"

"—like the cowardly scum we are. Right, Captain?" Tusk demanded.

"The Warlord has conferred upon you a compliment. He has given you this assignment because you're—"

"—expendable," Link shouted.

Captain Williams regarded them with cold, grave contempt. "*Our* men are the ones currently expending their lives while you sit here safely on your—"

"That will do, people." Dixter came back on the screen, his face was flushed red. His people could hear the anger and embarrassment in his voice. The mercenaries exchanged covert glances, looking and feeling like small children who had been rude to a great-aunt. Most appeared ashamed; a few, however, remained sullen.

"Well, then, Captain," Nola sang out, shaking her curls and grinning—undaunted—at Williams, "I guess we better come to your rescue."

There was laughter and cheering.

"Yeah, we'll go out there and take care of 'em!" they shouted. "Don't worry, Capt'n Williams! We'll bring your babies home!"

The captain broke off the communication. The mercenaries were dispersing, hurrying to their planes. Tusk put his arm around Nola and hugged her tight.

"Thanks, Rian."

"You looked like a whipped pup. I had to say something. I think you're all half-scared of that man. But he puts his trousers on one leg at a time, same as you do," Nola teased.

"First his teeth, then his trousers. I think you just want to get into his trousers, that's what I think."

There was no cutting edge in Tusk's remark. It was half-hearted, dispirited. Nola, missing that spirit, crowded closer. "It's going to be easy, Tusk. Nothing to it. After all, the Warlord and the Starlady took out one of those things and there was only two of them. We'll have Link and all the others."

Tusk didn't tell her about the Blood Royal, about the phenomenal power. He didn't tell her about the Golden Squadron, about a group of pilots whose exploits were, to this day, legendary.

"Yeah," he said at last, with a light laugh. "It's gonna be simple. So simple that I think XJ can handle the guns. Look, Nola, I'm worried about the general. I don't like leavin' him here, alone, with that toothy bastard on the bridge. Why don't you go up there with him?"

"He's not alone. He's got Bennett—"

"Bennett!" Tusk snorted. "What help's he gonna be if something goes wrong? He might slice up a few men with the sharp crease on his pants leg—"

"Tusk, stop it. I'm going with you." Holding on to his arm, using it to pull herself up, Nola stood on tiptoe and planted a kiss on his ear. "Besides, XJ's got all the calculations worked out for the change in life-support with me aboard. You know how upset he'd get if he had to refigure all that again." ·

"Yeah," Tusk said, but he wasn't happy. He started heading for his plane.

Nola moved around to stand in front of the mercenary, blocking his way. "Tusk," she said, looking into the dark brown eyes, "you don't think I'm going to be a liability to you, do you? That's not the reason you're trying to get rid of me?"

Tusk reached out, put his hands on her arms. "Nola, I'll be honest. It's gonna be like Link said, a suicide run—"

"I know. And would you rather face death together or apart?"

Tusk paused a moment, thinking. When he spoke, he knew at last he meant it. "You give me . . . something, Nola. I don't know what. All I know is that when I'm with you I can do things I never thought I could do. If there's any way to beat this thing, it'll take us together to do it. And I guess if we gotta go out, we'll go out together."

"Tusk, you smooth-talker! Jeez, no wonder you never manage to hang on to women!" Link, coming up from behind deftly slid his arm around Nola's waist. "Stick with me, sweetheart. I'll show you the galaxy."

Nola gently, firmly pushed Link's arm away, entwined her hand in Tusk's. "I love you!" she whispered.

Tusk shook his head and sighed, softly.

Chapter ——— Twelve

. . . Loved I not Honor more.
Richard Lovelace, "To Lucasta, Going to the Wars"

"XJ, you infernal—!" Tusk ignored the ladder, swung down through the hatch, and dropped lightly onto the deck below. "XJ!" he shouted in a rage. "What did they do to my plane?"

The interior of the spaceplane was dark; the computer—conserving energy—had shut all systems down. It was unbearably hot and stuffy inside. Tusk beat on the bulkheads, stamped on the deck with his heavy combat boots.

Slowly, the lights flickered on, cool air began to circulate through the cabin. Nola, uncertain that she wanted to get involved in this domestic squabble, waited at the top of the open hatch, affecting to be deeply interested in watching Link, who was next to them, ready his spaceplane for takeoff.

"Ah," XJ said, "I see you've noticed the new paint job. We're regulation now!"

"Regulation if we were in the Galactic Democratic Republic Air Corps! Which we're not!" That was the gist of Tusk's sentence, after it had been filtered through the foul language. The pilot was frothing at the mouth. Nola began to hum loudly to herself.

"You even had them paint my goddam number back on, you—you misbegotten son of a vacuum tube—!"

"Vacuum tube!" The computer, shocked senseless, turned up its volume to the max. A high-pitched whine shrilled through the Scimitar. Tusk howled and clapped his hands over his ears.

"If this wasn't an emergency," XJ reverberated over the tooth-jarring sound, "I'd shut you down and let you roast!"

The altercation resounded throughout the hangar deck. People were turning to stare at them. Several began laughing.

412

Flushing deeply, her freckles completely disappearing, Nola slithered down the ladder into the Scimitar.

"—and"—XJ dealt a final, triumphant blow—"there was no charge for the paint!"

Tusk gabbled, his mouth working. His eyes were bloodshot; sweat beaded on the black skin. Nola quickly put her hand over his mouth.

"Tusk! Everyone's laughing at us!"

Her remonstrance was unnecessary. The mercenary seemed to have lost completely the power of coherent speech.

"It's all right, XJ!" Nola called out. "The shock threw him off, but Tusk's thought it over now and he thinks it was a . . . a brilliant move on your part. Here, he'll tell you himself. Tusk, say something." Tentatively, Nola moved her hand.

"No charge for the paint!" Tusk hissed through clenched teeth. Nola quickly muffled him.

"What was that?" XJ snapped suspiciously.

"He said, 'No charge for the paint!' He's ecstatic, really . . . overwhelmed. Words can't begin to express—"

"I could think of a few that could!" Tusk managed to snarl. Nola gripped his mouth tighter.

"—express his deep appreciation to you, XJ. He's speechless!" Nola gave Tusk a warning glance. "Aren't you?"

"Yeah!" Tusk muttered, breathing heavily. "Speechless."

"Well, if that's the way you really feel—" The computer, mollified, turned down the volume.

Tusk headed for the bridge, noticed Nola wasn't following. "Where you going?"

"Up in the bubble, where it's quiet." She grinned at him.

"Wait a minute, Rian." Tusk caught hold of her hand. "Take care of yourself."

"I'll be taking care of both our selves! Bye."

Placing her fingers on her lips, she kissed them, then transferred the kiss to him. Tusk was inclined to make the kiss much more interesting, but Nola wriggled out of his grasp. Laughing, she dashed up the ladder and was out the hatch before he could catch her. He could hear the bubble that covered the gun turret swing open, hear her settling into her seat.

Tusk, sighing again, slid down the ladder into the cockpit.

"I was going through my files," XJ-27 stated, "and I can't find where this Nola Rian of yours listed her next-of-kin. Could you ask—"

"Shut up!" Tusk yelled savagely, striking the computer a blow that split his knuckles. "Just shut up!" Sucking the blood from his hand, he began his preflight check.

"Sorry," XJ said.

It wasn't until later, when the signal was given and the mercenaries were finally spaceborne, that Tusk realized it was the first time he'd ever known the computer to apologize.

He took it as a bad sign.

··◁■ ■▷··

"Damn! Would you look at that! Makes me want to puke."

Link's voice echoed in Tusk's headset. The pilot peered through his viewport into the blackness. He could see plenty of things that made him want to throw up—planes exploding, the great dark hulk of the Corasian mothership moving ponderously closer—but nothing else out of the ordinary for a battle zone. "What? Where?"

"Right forty-five. That gorgeous spaceplane being hauled off by those bastards!"

Tusk saw, finally, and he whistled. "That Scimitar's a beauty, all right. Must be a prototype. I've never seen one like it."

"Let's take it away from them, Captain Tusca," came the synthesized voice of an alien, the number three man in the squadron.

"Negative. Get serious. First, we're under orders to hit those brain things, and second, how're you gonna take it away? Ask 'em real nice to let you have it? They'll let you have it, all right. Between the eyes."

The Corasians, noting they were under hostile surveillance, continued towing away their prize, but they had brought their guns to bear on the approaching mercenaries.

"There's only four of them," Nola pointed out from the gun turret, "and six of us."

"Red Squadron, keep back, outta range," Tusk ordered. "You're a good shot, Rian, but not that good. We'd take the Scimitar out, too!"

"That's an idea, Tusk! Aim for the Scimitar. Blow it up! That way they wouldn't get hold of it!"

"Negative, Link. The pilot might still be alive."

"If he is, he'll thank us!" Link's tone was grim.

"He should have a chance to put in his vote. XJ, see if you can raise that Scimitar."

"Sure thing. Hey, dude in the fancy plane—"

"Shit! You don't talk to one of the Warlord's pilots like that. Let me do it!" Tusk wrested the commlink from the computer. "Scimitar prototype. This is—" Swallowing hard, the pilot gave his old Air Corps number, now painted in shining red on the side of his plane. "I can see that you're in trouble." The mercenary paused, perplexed, wondering how to continue. *Would you like us to blow you up?* just didn't seem tactful. "Uh . . . is there anything we can do to help?"

"Tusk?" came a voice in his headset. "Is that you?"

"Dion?" Tusk gasped.

"Maybe it's a trick," Link warned.

"That's the kid," the computer said. "Voice analysis confirms."

"Dion! Are you hurt? How bad?"

"They died, Tusk. They all died. I heard them . . ."

"What's the matter with him? He sounds funny. XJ, run damage assessment on that plane. Kid, are you hurt?"

"Some superficial damage," the computer reported. "One shield's about gone, but nothing penetrated. The kid can't be injured too badly. Probably shaken up—"

"Sounds like he's in shock," Nola guessed.

"Sagan was right, Tusk." The boy's voice was empty, lethargic. "'Kings are made, not born.' I've let them down— Platus . . . your father. All those who died for me. I heard them die. And it was my fault."

"My God!" Link gave a low, ominous whistle.

"*We're* the ones who let you down, kid." Tusk was desperate, couldn't think of anything else to say. "Me. Dixter. The Warlord. The Starlady. All of us. It was too much, too soon. I'm a total bastard, kid. I'm sorry for the way I acted—"

"Tusk, we got company comin'. Comin' in, Mach five. Whatta we do?" Link's voice softened. "Give the word. I'll take care of it. One shot. He'll never know."

"No!" Tusk shouted harshly.

"I don't feel any better about it than you do, old friend, but think about what he'll face if he's still alive when those monsters get him aboard that ship."

Tusk knew. He knew better than Link, for Danha Tusca had fought the Corasians and he'd told his stories to his son. The mercenary swallowed and wiped sweat from his face. "XJ. Put me through to the Warlord."

"Oh, sure," the computer retorted. "And next I'll patch you through to the President. Who else would you like to talk to? The Secretary of Galactic Affairs? or the Treasury Depart—"

Tusk gnashed his teeth. "Listen to me, you—"

"Calmly," Nola hinted.

The mercenary snapped his mouth shut, drew a deep breath, and slowly let it out. "You know, XJ, I wouldn't have even asked that of another computer. But a computer who once raided Sagan's personal files, a computer who got me a free paint job, a computer who figured out that Dion was king— Well, I figure a computer like that could get hold of God Himself if it had to!"

"Oh, screw it!" XJ muttered. "Hang on a minute till I unravel their new codes—"

Tusk breathed a sigh, but he was too worried to feel elated at his victory. Another bad sign.

"Red Squadron, this is Squadron Leader. We've got a new objective. I've called for the Warlord. We're gonna keep track of the Scimitar till we hear from him. Kid, can you hear me? We're gonna stay with you—"

His words were interrupted by an explosion. A Corasian was diving straight for them. Tusk swerved and dodged, hearing overhead the whirring of motors, the hissing sound of Nola's lasguns firing at the enemy.

Over the commotion, Tusk listened anxiously for the boy's reply, but there was only silence.

··◄■ ■►··

Prior to his arrival on *Phoenix*, the Warlord had advised the crew that his spaceplane had sustained damage, as had that of his number two man. The deck was cleared for a crash landing, a wise precaution that proved unnecessary. Sagan brought his plane in and set it down without incident.

His number two man wasn't quite so fortunate. The Scimitar literally fell apart on landing, skidded across the hangar deck, and crashed into a girder. Rescue bots went into action, putting out fires, ripping off the hatch, preparing to extricate an injured pilot. The crew was amazed when the pilot climbed out of the cockpit unhurt, still more amazed when the pilot yanked off 'his' helmet and shook out a long braid of pale hair that fell limply down the back of the flight suit.

The flight crews immediately set to work repairing the

damage the planes had sustained, exclaiming over the amount and the extent, marveling that either one of the pilots had survived.

The two met in the corridor outside the hangar deck.

"A three-point landing, my lady, does not mean that you take out the deck, the bulkhead, and the overhead," was Sagan's first comment.

Maigrey's hair was damp with sweat and straggled over her face. Blood from a cut on her forehead trickled down into one eyebrow. Tears made tracks in the grime on her face. She didn't bother to glance at Sagan, but stared straight into a wall.

"Am I being sent back to my cell, my lord?"

"No, my lady. I can't afford to lose any more of my men. You'll come with me to the bridge where I can— Well, what is it, Aks?" The admiral rounded a corner. He must have been waiting to meet them. The Warlord halted, impatience expressed in every line of his body. "Have the mercenaries gone out? Are the 'brains' under attack?"

"Yes, my lord, but—"

"What, Aks? Don't stand there dithering!"

The admiral was staring at Maigrey, his eyes wide. "I—I was going to report, my lord, that the . . . uh . . . lady has escaped. . . ." His voice trailed away.

"Report noted." The Warlord resumed walking, nearly running the admiral down. Sagan's strides were long and rapid. Noting Maigrey lagging wearily behind, he caught hold of her by the arm to hurry her along. Angrily, she started to jerk her elbow free of his grasp when she suddenly gasped and came to a stop.

"What now, my lady?" Sagan snapped. He had nearly dragged the woman off her feet. She didn't seem to hear, but stumbled against him like one suddenly gone blind.

"Very bad news, my lord." Admiral Aks was hurrying to catch up. He licked his tongue over his lips as if he would like to sweeten bitter words. "The mercenary, Tusca, has been trying to reach you. It seems young Starfire broke away from the squadron and got himself into trouble—"

Sagan swore vilely, viciously—an unusual break in the man's iron discipline and one indication, to those who knew him well, of nerves stretched taut, of stress taking its toll on body and mind.

"The Corasians have him," Maigrey whispered, seeing in

her mind the four enemy fighters locking their tractor beams onto the unresisting Scimitar. Blinking, she came back from the awful vision to stare at Sagan. "It's that damn plane you gave him! That technological wonder! You might as well have given him to them!"

The Warlord said nothing.

Maigrey broke free of his grip. Backing a step away from him, she looked up into his face. He had removed his helmet, but he might well have kept it on. It seemed she looked into steel.

"Or maybe you *did* give him to them! That's it, isn't it, my lord? Dion isn't turning out to be the puppet you thought. He's got a mind of his own, a will of his own. *He* wants to be king!" Maigrey turned on her heel, started back down the corridor, back toward the hangar deck. "I'm going after him."

Sagan took a step to follow. She heard his footfall and whirled to face him. The bloodsword flared blue in her hands.

"So help me God, my lord—try to stop me and I'll kill you."

She was poised, calm, and resolute. There was no doubting her words. Sagan held perfectly still, his hands raised where she could see them.

"Admiral Aks." The Warlord turned his head slightly.

"My lord."

"The second Bloodspear is available?"

"It can be made so at once, my lord—"

"Good. Have it readied"—the Warlord spoke with grim irony—"for my lady."

"Yes, my lord!" Aks murmured.

"I'll be going out in mine. Aks, I'm leaving you in command. You have my orders."

"But, my lord! I was going to tell you! The mothership is moving up to—"

"Deal with it, Aks." The Warlord strode past Maigrey, who watched him warily, keeping on her guard. He paused, standing so near her that the heat from the weapon began to melt and blacken the fabric of his flight suit.

"My lady," he said coldly, "I'll meet you in hell!"

Turning, he continued walking down the corridor, heading back toward the hangar deck.

Maigrey straightened, shut down the blade, and replaced it in its scabbard. Wearily, she dragged the hair out of her face, wiped her hand across her eyes and forehead—smearing the blood and grime—and started to follow the Warlord.

The corridor suddenly slanted, the walls shook. Maigrey stumbled backward, Admiral Aks fell to his knees.

Phoenix was under attack.

··◁■ ■▷··

Tusk's squadron clung tenaciously to Dion's Scimitar. The Corasians kept the plane in tow, dragging it nearer and nearer the mothership. Wave after wave of enemy fighters dove at Red Squadron, trying to dislodge them from their position. Nola kept up a constant stream of fire; she could feel the heat from the lasgun through her gloves.

She'd been scared, at first; there were so many, it seemed hopeless. But now her fear was gone. She didn't feel anything. She was too tired. The situation wasn't hopeless to her anymore. It just simply wasn't real. It was all happening to someone else—to someone whose arm muscles were going limp from fatigue, whose hands ached from the strain, whose eyes hurt from the constant, blinding flares of exploding death. Nola, watching this person, felt a moment's brief pity for her.

Below, Tusk fought controls that jumped and bucked and threatened to tear his arms from their sockets. His flight suit was soaked with sweat; he would have traded a starjewel for a drink of cool water. Above him, the gun's firing was so constant that he didn't even hear it anymore, couldn't remember a time when he hadn't heard it. The nightmare flight went on and on. Corasians materialized out of the blackness, their planes forever coming at him. He couldn't see Red Squadron anymore—if it still existed. He dimly remembered hearing death screams, registered that it was someone he knew, but he couldn't think, couldn't care.

"Hang on, Tusk!" Link's voice, ragged with fatigue, was somehow still cocky. "It's just you and me now."

Time and again, the two pilots fought off attack, their only hope of staying alive resting with each other. Constant tracer fire lit the interior of the Scimitar bright as if they'd come up on a sun.

"My new paint job!" the computer mourned.

A Corasian popped up in front of them. Laser fire seared into the Scimitar. The plane rocked. Tusk was slammed violently against his restraining straps, nearly breaking his right shoulder.

"One more hit like that," XJ shouted, "and you can kiss that left shield good-bye!"

"Keep quiet a moment," Tusk ordered. He licked perspiration from his lips, wondering why his heart was beating painfully and his mouth felt as if he'd been chewing on his socks. "What's wrong? Something's wrong, XJ! I can hear it!"

"No, you can't," the computer said slowly. "It's the gun. It's quit firing. Shield's gone—"

"Nola!" Tusk fumbled at the restraining straps.

"Are you insane? Sit down, you maniac! That fighter's coming back around! I've got the guns under control. Rian's not dead. The bubble wasn't penetrated. I can register a heartbeat and she's breathing. If you want to keep her alive, you better pull yourself together!"

Tusk subsided, reluctantly, back into his seat. He stared out the viewport that was smeared with carbon scoring, making it practically impossible to see anything. "The kid! Where's the kid?"

"Lost him," XJ said quietly. "About fifteen minutes ago, during that last attack. There was nothing you could do."

The guns, manned by the computer, began firing. The Corasian dodged the tracer fire and dove in on them.

"Link!" Tusk shouted desperately.

"Got one of my own!" Link gasped. "I—"

There was a shattering explosion. The spaceplane rocked.

"Are we hit?" Tusk demanded.

"No," XJ said, its audio awed. "It was the enemy. They're both . . . gone."

"Tusca. Mendaharin Tusca," came a voice over the mercenary's headset.

Tusk was so relieved he nearly broke down and cried. But—recognizing the voice—he kept himself under strict control.

"Tusca here, sir."

"'My lord,' not 'sir'!" hissed the scandalized XJ.

Two planes came into partial view through his filthy viewport. Sleek and smooth, shaped like spearheads, they were glorious light in the midst of darkness, calm in the center of chaos, life-bringers to the dead. Tusk had to remind himself that it was Derek Sagan.

"The boy, sir." Tusk tasted defeat. "We lost him. I'm sorry."

"I can see him, Tusca," said a cool, feminine voice. "I have him in my mind."

"There's something wrong with him. I don't think he's hurt—at least not physically. He was talkin' real funny—"

"We're going after him," the Warlord said. "You needn't worry about him. You are to be commended for your bravery, Captain Tusca, you and . . . ?"

"Link, sir," came the mercenary's cocky reply.

"I note both planes have taken extensive damage. Captain Link will no doubt want to return to *Defiant*, but you, Tusca, might want to consider returning to *Phoenix*."

"Sir?" Tusk couldn't think. Exhaustion was seeping in, taking over his mind and body.

The Warlord's voice sounded exasperated. "The enemy brains have nearly been eliminated or their effectiveness reduced. It appears that we are on the verge of winning this battle. I'm offering you a commission, Mendaharin Tusca. In my personal command."

A low whistle came from the computer.

"Shut up!" Tusk ordered. "No—not you, sir. I was talking to my—my partner. Uh, thank you, sir—that is, my lord. It's not that I don't appreciate the honor, but I'm under General Dixter's command and . . . and I'm saying this real bad, but I guess I'll go back to *Defiant*—"

"Consider your decision well, young man." The Warlord's voice was grim, ominous. "My offer will not be repeated."

Tusk felt a chill grip his bowels, cramp his stomach.

"I understand, my lord. Thank you. But it wouldn't work out."

"You are much like your father, Tusca," Lady Maigrey said.

"Indeed he is," Lord Sagan added. "Danha Tusca suffered from a misguided sense of loyalty. Apparently it runs in the family."

"Thank the Creator. Farewell, Mendaharin Tusca. God be with you."

"Yeah. You, too, my lady," Tusk said.

The communication ended abruptly. The two gleaming white planes vanished, winking out of his line of sight. In a moment he could see them again, but they were distant and bright and cold as the other stars in the heavens.

"Link, we're heading back to *Defiant*." Tusk disentangled himself from his restraining harness. "Take over the controls, XJ. I'm going to check on Nola. Nothing fancy. That goes for you, too, Link! Just get us back in one piece."

"Nothing fancy for me, old friend. I'm played out. Say, Tusk. I gotta tell you. That was a pretty great thing you did, turning down the Warlord—"

"Great!" XJ was furious. "You can't eat 'great'! I say he's a big dope! You're a big dope, Men Da Ha Rin Tusca! We coulda made our fortunes! The Warlord would've given you a command of your own, probably made you a colonel. I could've had a new plane—like that one of the kid's—"

"Leave me alone, will you?" Tusk clambered up the ladder, snagging the emergency medkit on his way. "I'm worried about Nola."

"Oh, yeah? If you're so worried about her, why didn't you take Sagan up on his offer?" the computer demanded. "She could be getting class medical treatment now!"

"I wish I had!" Tusk stuck his head back through the hatch to shake his fist at the computer. "The Warlord purged all XJ-27 models!"

The word "purge" stuck in Tusk's throat. A chill crept up the back of his spine. Stupid. It's nothing. Someone standing on my grave. The mercenary shook himself out of it.

"I don't believe it!" XJ squeaked.

"Yep. Scrap heap. One of the mechanics aboard *Defiant* told me. Something about too much independent thinking."

Tusk pulled himself up into the bubble. Nola lay sprawled in the gunner's seat. Her flight suit was covered with blood. Splinters of metal filled the gun turret. A quick glance showed Tusk that the hit had torn a hole through the body of the spaceplane, not penetrating the bubble, but sending metal fragments whizzing around like thrown daggers.

Cutting away Nola's flight suit, Tusk sealed the wounds with plastiskin and managed to stop the bleeding, but he knew she suffered head injuries and there wasn't a damn thing he could do about that. He gave her a fix to alleviate shock. Cradling her in his arms, he sank down on the fragment-strewn floor of the gun turret and stared out the bubble.

The ranks of the enemy were obviously thinned, although numerous dogfights continued to rage. The mothership was launching a barrage of lascannon fire and torpedoes into the hull of *Phoenix*. Another cruiser was coming up to support her. *Defiant* had pulled back, out of the action. Tusk could see long lines of the mercenaries returning to the ship.

"I can't comprehend it!" XJ's audio was thin and tinny sounding. "The tragedy! My fellow computers. Purged! Maybe I'm the last survivor—"

"God, we can only hope so!" Tusk smoothed back the

blood-gummed curls from Nola's ashen face. "XJ, contact *Defiant*. Get in touch with Dixter."

Tusk could hear the computer raising the ship. He couldn't hear the response; something up in the turret had broken loose and was rattling loudly.

"Dixter's not available," XJ reported.

"Not available?" There was the chill again. "I don't like this. Are all our people going back?"

"Where the hell else they gonna go?" XJ demanded. "Half of 'em are shot up. The other half got barely enough fuel to make it that far. Besides, Dixter's on that ship—somewhere."

Tusk shifted Nola slightly. Easing his lasgun out of its holster, he examined it, made sure it was fully charged, and laid it across his knees.

"Let's be careful going in there, XJ. Real careful."

Chapter ·❦◦◦❦· Thirteen

Who shall tempt . . . the dark, unbottomed, infinite abyss?

John Milton, *Paradise Lost*

The white, spearheaded planes mingled with the debris of a wrecked brain. The battle had changed in nature and scope. The Corasian mothership, seeing defeat being snatched from the jaws of victory, had moved up to challenge *Phoenix*. The Warlord's ship was taking grueling punishment and was being forced to endure it without returning a shot, fearful of hitting its own planes.

Scimitars dove at the mothership, darting through withering fire to inflict what small amount of damage they could on the enemy's heavily shielded black hull. How the Corasian computers were analyzing this bizarre strategy was anyone's guess. Certainly it would be impossible for the "body" to comprehend that the Warlord was risking victory in order to protect the one.

Maigrey herself wondered at Sagan's motives. Knowing him as she did, she found it difficult to accept that he would throw away everything he'd worked so long and hard to achieve in order to rescue the boy. He must have some ulterior design, some stratagem in mind, but—aside from using the fighters as cover for their own assault on the enemy—Maigrey couldn't discern Sagan's plans. The exhilarating and frightening bond that had joined them when they fought the brain had been broken, cleaved in two.

Where they were going, in the dark night they were entering, they would have only each other. Sagan was furious at Maigrey. She was wary and suspicious of him. Their minds were shielded as heavily as their planes. Neither could penetrate the other; they communicated through mechanical means. Unless something changed, they were walking into certain death.

Maigrey knew it and wondered uneasily how she felt about it. She didn't trust herself. She had sought this final escape into oblivion for so long! And, she had to admit, she would rather die than experience that terrifying "joining" again. She also had to admit she would rather die because she longed for that joining with every fiber of her being.

With such power as the enhancement brought them, he and she could rule the universe and no one could stop them. Whenever she relived that moment, pleasurable pain, like liquid fire, burned in her veins, constricted her heart, and snatched at her breath. Her hands shook, her body trembled, and she longed to cry out that she was with him, they were one as they had been one so long ago. Only not even then, not in their youth, had they experienced power as they had known together in those flame-tinged moments of battle against the enemy.

Maturity. Age and the wisdom it brings. Definitive goals. Reality taking the place of airy and insubstantial dreams. Cold steel emerging from the ashes of youth's hot passions.

"What about the boy, my lady?"

Sagan had not spoken to her since they had left Tusca, and his voice jolted through her like electricity. Her spaceplane, guided by her mind, reacted, shivering like a leaf in a wind. Angry at herself, she latched on to discipline firmly, as a drowning man clings to a piece of wood.

"Dion won't respond to my attempts to raise him."

"Nor to mine."

"But I'm able to touch his mind through the ring. He can understand me, my lord."

"What's his mental state?"

"Not good. Frightened, guilt-ridden, overwhelmed by everything that's happened to him. Just what you might expect from someone captured and wounded by the enemy. And then, of course, there are the Corasians. . . ."

"Spare me your wit, lady."

"I count myself at fault, my lord. I forgot what it was to be young . . . if I ever really knew."

"Are you through wallowing?" Sagan demanded.

Maigrey couldn't help smiling, and felt better. "Yes, my lord."

"Good. Contact the boy and instruct him to connect with the bloodsword. He's not to use it, he's not to fight them. The Corasians will want to keep him alive; they'll need to know everything they can about his plane. Tell him to submit to them, but to keep his hand firmly attached to the sword. They won't be able to wrest it away."

No, the bloodsword could never be taken from a living person. It could be removed only from a corpse. Maigrey knew how Corasians "questioned" those they captured.

"We'll be able to keep in contact with him through the sword, even if he loses consciousness," Sagan continued. "I don't suppose that brother of yours taught the boy any techniques to withstand torture."

"I seriously doubt it."

"Then instruct the boy to use meditation, submerge his mind, sink beneath the pain. The bloodsword will aid him, but you don't need to tell him so."

"There's a danger in that, my lord. We might not get him back," Maigrey pointed out.

"That will be my problem."

"He may not listen to me."

"That problem, my lady, is yours."

···◁■ ■▷···

Dion sat in the pilot's seat, staring at the hull of the mothership looming closer, staring at the beak-nosed planes towing him nearer and nearer, staring at it all and seeing none of it. His gaze had turned inward and the dark horrors he saw in his own soul made those without pale by comparison.

Dion . . .

The voice came from the ring, his mother's ring that he wore around his neck. It seemed to him that the voice had been calling to him a long time, trying to penetrate despair's infinite shadow. He was sick of the voice. It irritated him, a pricking of pain that disturbed his comfortable numbness. Dion reached up his hand, slowly and lethargically wrapping cold fingers around the ring of flame, ready to jerk it off, snap the chain, throw it from him.

Dion, we're here. We're with you. The Guardians, we're here to protect our king.

"King!" Dion laughed. "King of cowards! King of fools!" His hand closed over the ring. "I failed the test. I know it now. You just didn't want to tell me."

No, you haven't failed. Not yet.

"Not yet? I suppose you're going to say this is another one! Another test to pass! What this time? Courage? I've flunked that. Maybe stamina, fortitude? See how much pain I can endure? I've flunked that, too. I've had enough."

All your life you will be tested, Dion. Some you'll pass, some you'll fail. You'll learn from both. If you have the courage to keep fighting, put your hand on the hilt of the bloodsword. Don't resist your captors. You can't win against them. Submit to them. It will be terrible for you, but center your mind on us and we will come to you.

Dion blinked; cognizance returned. The black hull of the mothership filled the viewport. The spiders were bringing him to their queen. Her huge gaping maw opened wide to suck him inside, suck him dry. It was dark inside—horribly, unbelievably dark. Fear crackled through him; the will to live had returned, and with it debilitating panic.

God, I'm such a coward!

Your hand on the sword! came the urgent voice in his mind. *Your hand on the sword.*

The plane was moving more rapidly now, or perhaps movement just seemed swifter because of the nearness of the mothership. Dion thought for a moment he couldn't obey the voice. The right hand that grasped the necklace was paralyzed. But fear proved friend as well as foe. Adrenaline loosened his fingers, moved his shaking hand to the sword. He withdrew the hilt from the scabbard. The plane's interior lights shone on the five sharp needles protruding from the side of the hand-grip. The darkness outside the plane grew thicker and denser. The needles gleamed.

The lady's words sounded good, but he didn't believe them. She was only offering him an excuse. He had only to drop the sword and he would die—die a hero.

Angrily, tears welling up in his eyes, Dion jabbed the needles into the palm of his hand. The pain was intense, the virus streamed into his bloodstream, and he cried out, but he held on to the sword tightly.

The maw absorbed him and boomed shut behind him, and all the lights in the universe went out.

··◁■ ■▷··

"He's done it, my lord," Maigrey said wearily. "He's taken the bloodsword."

"Yes, I can sense him now. His mental attitude isn't good."

"No, he's too young to know that sometimes it takes more courage to live than to die."

"A lesson I hope you've taken to heart, my lady."

"I'm going in there *for him*, my lord."

"But you're going in there *with me*, my lady."

"I'll be right at your side, my lord, you may be certain of that."

"I hope so, for your sake, my lady. I wouldn't trust you anywhere else . . . say at my back, for instance. Start your run."

Maigrey's plane rocketed out from behind the brain, soaring upward with such ferocious speed that she didn't pay any attention to where she was going and two Scimitars had to scramble to get out of her way. She attacked the Corasian mothership wildly, blindly, not remembering that this was a feint. She needed to vent her rage, wanted most desperately to destroy something. She was only sorry she couldn't do it with her bare hands.

Explosions bursting around her plane literally knocked sense back into her. Her plane rocked and bucked and began to spin. Instinct screamed to her to bring it back under control. Maigrey yanked the needles from her hand, fearing she wouldn't have the discipline to remain attached to the plane. The computer automatically took over, and Maigrey had to force herself to shut down all systems, including the plane's life-support, and rely solely on those in her helmet and flight suit. For a terrifying few moments, she spun wildly. The other fighters had been warned to watch for the maneuver and to keep clear, but it seemed to Maigrey that she must careen either into one of them or the enemy.

The dead ship routine. They'd used it before, but never against Corasians. Maigrey couldn't stand it. Her hand hovered over the controls; she was within a centimeter of snatching them up and inserting the needles into her flesh. A bone-jarring thud and then a jolt. The spin stopped, nearly jarring the teeth out of her head.

Glancing to her left, fearful to move too much, Maigrey saw Sagan's plane tumbling wildly through space and saw it, too, come to an abrupt and sudden stop as an enemy tractor beam locked on to it. Slowly, like her plane, Sagan's was being dragged inside the mothership. Maigrey started to breathe a sigh, but caught herself. She didn't dare make even that much noise. The Corasians had opened the city gates and were wheeling in the wooden horse. Hiding inside, she had to be very, very quiet.

Closing her eyes, Maigrey banished fear, banished anger, banished love. She centered herself and then she pulled herself from her body and walked into her mind and took all visible, outward signs of life with her.

Chapter ··◆━○━◆·· Fourteen

Character is what you are in the dark.
            Earl Mac Rauch, *Buckaroo Banzai*

Blazing flame and hideous night. The creatures plucked at Dion with steel pincers, gouged and tore his flesh, and herded him before them like a sheep to the slaughterhouse. Their horrid bodies burned inside plastic shells—that fire was the only light and he'd rather be struck blind than look at it any longer. He stumbled through a corridor and down another, some part of his mind registering where he was going, where he'd been, acting on old instinct, acting according to how Platus had taught him. He held on to the bloodsword tightly.

Synthesized voices questioned him: *Tell us how the plane operates. Tell us this, tell us that!*

He couldn't. He wasn't being heroic. He didn't know. His mind had shut down. He couldn't have told them how a dry-cell battery operated.

Claws gripped him, lifted him, and he was lying on a steel table in a small room, lit only by the fire of their bodies.

Tell us, yes? Now, you tell us!

Clamps closed over his wrist and ankles. A whirring, buzzing sound went off near his right ear. He twisted his head to see, fear churning inside him. His captor's pincerlike hand had been removed. In its place was a razor-edged round saw blade. Dion couldn't cry out. He grasped the bloodsword tightly, but it wasn't going to matter.

The saw blade zinged, lowered, and cut off his arm.

··◆━ ━◆··

A thin filament of consciousness attached Maigrey to reality. She felt the spaceplane settle and was aware of noise, aware that sensor probes were investigating the plane, confirming—no doubt—the presence of a human corpse. Slowly, she brought herself back to life, steadily increasing her heartbeats per minute, agonizing in silence at the tingling pain of blood resuming its flow. These were the tense moments, the moments when you were helpless. If the sensors were still on, still registering, the enemy would know they'd been tricked, know that what seemed dead was really very much alive.

Maigrey opened her eyes, looked—without moving her head, without moving a muscle—out the viewport. She could see the red-orangish glow given off by the Corasians trundling about, the flaming molten mass of body and mind encased in clear plastisteel robots. Impulse energy operated the hands that had taken their civilization from crawling across the ground to blazing paths among the stars.

Corasians are not particularly frightening to look at unless you've seen the robot body suddenly open wide, the burning molten mass slide out and go in search of food. Maigrey had seen it; she'd seen the Corasians devour trees, plants, humans, anything with life energy. She counted six of them in this area, surrounding her plane, and she shuddered.

Moving slowly, with excessive caution and in absolute silence, Maigrey inserted the needles that were the plane's controls back into her palm. The spaceplane—all parts of it—were now a part of her, an extension of herself. The Corasians apparently suspected nothing.

The last time she'd flown the dead plane routine had been, what—eighteen years ago? During the so-called Battle of the Celestial Throne. A well-meaning scientist had programmed several million droids on his particular planet to have only one object—that of making human life forms absolutely happy. The droids attempted to do just that, but had eventually come to the unfortunate conclusion that the only truly happy human was a dead human. Even then the frustrated droids weren't certain humans were happy, but at least they didn't appear to have any more complaints. The droids set out to bring happiness to the galaxy.

Maigrey picked up two disrupter grenades in her left hand and, fumbling at them awkwardly, managed to align the switches so that she could operate each with a flick of her thumb. She paused a moment to concentrate her mental processes and to hope, briefly, that somewhere on this godforsaken ship Derek Sagan was doing the same thing. Maigrey couldn't spare the time or the mental discipline needed to try to link up with him.

Swift as her thought, the hatch whirred open. Maigrey flicked on the grenades, bobbed up out of the hatch, tossed the grenades, and dove back down, closing the hatch behind her. Two near simultaneous explosions rocked the plane and pelted it with plastisteel debris and blobs of molten, flaming Corasian.

Maigrey opened her eyes and raised her head. Another grenade was in her hand, but she didn't need it, apparently. Everything had gone dark.

"An understatement," Maigrey muttered, shaken.

It was a darkness unlike any she had ever before encountered, a darkness that had no memory of light, could not even imagine light. The darkness blotted out sight, seemed capable of blotting out existence. Maigrey's hands groped for the reassurance of the control panel of the plane. She wouldn't have been much surprised if it had been swallowed up.

She found the switch for the interior lights and flipped them on, but they made her feel horribly exposed. Hastily, she made her instrument readings, then shut off the lights again. The atmosphere was safe to breathe. Corasians, in their robot bodies, could exist anywhere under any conditions. On board their ship, they didn't need oxygen-rich air, but their human-copied computers and other instruments—as well as their prisoners—did.

She removed the controls from her hand, feeling a reluctance to detach herself from the protection of the spaceplane. It was this damn darkness. It was unnerving. But she couldn't stay here forever. Those explosions were bound to have set off alarms. Hurriedly she removed her helmet and wriggled out of the bulky flight suit.

Beneath it, she wore a black, lightweight body armor that fit almost skin tight. It would not stop a direct laser hit; that wasn't necessary. The shielding capability of the bloodsword provided that. The armor offered protection against flying debris and projectile weapons, however, and it allowed her freedom of movement—something Maigrey had the distinct feeling she was going to need.

On her breast sparkled the Star of the Guardians.

The light of the starjewel always gleamed more brightly when in complete darkness. It glistened radiantly now, with a dazzling blue-white brilliance. Maigrey closed her hand over it, starting to hide it away beneath the body armor. But she found the light comforting. The enemy was bound to discover her with or without a beacon.

Her fingers lingered on the starjewel, and Sagan's voice came to her mind.

My lady?

Maigrey closed her eyes, weak with a relief she was extremely careful to keep hidden. Adrenaline, apparently, had reestablished the link between them.

My lord!

Where are you?

God only knows. No, I take that back. He probably doesn't. I can't see a damn thing now, but before the lights went out it looked as if I was in some sort of salvage hangar—where they bring planes to scavenge.

I'm in the same type of place. I have the impression I'm near you, my lady. Can you sense Dion?

Yes. I can sense him and you, my lord. You seem to be nearer to me than he is. The boy's some distance away and . . . and he's in terrible pain, Sagan. They're torturing him.

The quicker we move, the quicker we'll reach him. For the time being, we must concentrate on each other. Our thoughts link us and will guide us together.

Like iron to a magnet, Maigrey thought.

Set your plane's controls to self-destruct in thirty minutes if you don't return to give the shutdown command.

So, that's your strategy. That's how you plan to destroy the mothership and us, too, if we don't succeed. Maigrey rigged the computer. Sagan's thoughts came to her. "Mark five, four, three, two, one." She repeated the countdown and on "one" set the computer's clock to read 1800, ticking downward. Her inner clock in her brain registered and began ticking along with the computer.

1799. 1798.

Before leaving, Maigrey inserted the needles of the bloodsword into her right palm. In her left, she could either carry a lasgun or a grenade. She'd never been that good a shot with her left hand, and so opted for the grenade. Pulling herself up out of the hatch, she dropped down over the side and landed heavily on the deck below.

The darkness was a living, breathing entity. It wrapped

around her, smothered her. It had weight and form, and she involuntarily stooped and ducked her head, though she knew perfectly well that she was standing in a vast, wide-open hangar. The starjewel shone brightly but did not illuminate. She activated the bloodsword. Guided by its pulsating light, she made her way through the wreckage.

Cables, like snakes, wrapped around her ankles or dangled from the overhead. Sharp bits of twisted metal jutted up out of the wrecked deck. She moved as quickly as she could by the sword's dim light, not daring to cause it to shine brighter for fear of expending too much of her own energy. Consequently she stumbled and tripped and once stepped in a sticky substance that clung to her boot.

"Dead Corasian!" Maigrey almost gagged and, with a final lunge, reached a doorway.

Here she halted to catch her breath, shake her hair out of her face, and reconnoiter.

A long, wide corridor with smooth decks designed to accommodate the wheeled robots stretched off to her right and to her left. Sagan was to her left, she sensed, and moving toward her. Dion was somewhere to her left and straight ahead, within the heart of the ship.

The corridor was empty, and Maigrey was puzzled. She had expected Corasians to be whizzing to the hangar deck to investigate the explosion. But then she considered. No, why would they? To them it must seem nothing more than a malfunction of one of the dead planes they'd salvaged. As for loss of life, a few cells of the massive body had simply winked out. The enemy had other, more urgent problems—such as the attacking fighters, the bombardment of *Phoenix*, and the torturing of captured pilots.

Dion was still linked to the bloodsword. Through it, Maigrey shared his pain and fear and suffering. It was dreadful, and it took all of her discipline to shove it into a corner of her being and firmly ignore it. Risking a little more light so that she could see where she was going, she began moving rapidly, warily, down the corridor.

Nothing blocked her way; the deck remained level, the corridor bent around at a slight angle. She was moving nearer and nearer Sagan; she could feel, in fact, his mounting impatience for her to reach him. The corridor took a sharp turn to the right. She followed it and nearly collided with two Corasians emerging from a doorway.

Maigrey had the advantage. Although taken by surprise at the enemy's sudden appearance, she had been expecting trouble and was prepared to fight. The Corasians were caught with their wheels locked, as the saying goes.

The bloodsword slashed a blue streak and a robot head went hurtling through the air, struck a wall, and blew up. Maigrey's return stroke cleaved the plastisteel body of the second Corasian, but not, apparently, before it had found time to sound the alarm. Klaxons dinned in her ears. She could sense Sagan fuming.

You're wasting time, my lady!

What the hell was I supposed to do?

The first Corasian had toppled over. Still alive, it was unable to operate its body and was rolling helplessly about like an overturned turtle. The second, however, had broken free of its split case and was oozing out of the plastisteel. Its orange, fiery mass moved at alarming speed, slithering across the deck for her feet.

Maigrey slashed at it with her sword and was astounded to see it keep coming. If anything, it flamed more strongly!

"Sagan!" she gasped, stumbling backward.

Change the polarity! Negative energy! Switch to the shield!

Of course. She should have thought of that. But then it'd been seventeen years and she'd never actually fought one of these creatures face to face.

Maigrey activated the sword's shielding beam and, at its touch, the Corasian blackened and hissed and began to smoke.

To your left, my lady! Sagan instructed. *I've found a corridor that leads to the boy! Swiftly!*

Maigrey dashed down the passageway and saw, suddenly, to her right, another corridor opening into hers. It was lit by orange light reflecting off the metal walls—an orange light that was growing rapidly brighter. She could hear the whirring and clicking of robot bodies. To reach Sagan, Maigrey would have to pass the opening of the corridor. She would be an easy target, with no hope of cover.

I see them, my lady. Come to me.

Side by side. I'll be with you. Trust.

There was no time, no choice. She caught her breath and lunged forward, running headlong down the corridor, straight toward the approaching enemy. Flicking on the grenade, she hurled it into the corridor as she sped past. The shattering explosion nearly blew her off her feet. She was thrown up against a bulkhead. Pushing herself away from it, shaken but unhurt, she saw, out of the corner of her eye, that she had killed some but not all. The orange light was still hideously bright. The robots fired. Flaming bolts flared around her. A flash of pain tore through the flesh of her left arm.

The iron to the magnet.

A strong hand caught hold of her and pulled her close within the circle of a protecting arm. Sagan raised his sword, the shield activated, deflecting the blasts. Maigrey pressed her body against his, giving him room to maneuver the sword, careful to deactivate her own. Sagan's arm tightened around her almost convulsively. In a moment, they would have to fight. He would release her and she would take up her position at his side. But for this brief instant they were once again each other's best comfort, each other's best hope.

Maigrey could hear his heart beating in his chest, feel the lean hard muscles of his thighs taut against her, the bone and sinew and muscle of his encircling arm. And the enhancement came back, enveloping them, surging through them, bursting around them like a glittering shower of stars.

Well, she thought shakily, so it hadn't been adrenaline that had linked them after all.

"Across the corridor!" he ordered, somewhat breathlessly, and almost shoved her away from him.

Maigrey acted on the split-second of his thought and was ready. Her bloodsword flared to life. Sagan leapt forward, charging the enemies, and Maigrey was at his side. She never touched one, she swore it, but a concussive blast shattered the plastisteel robot bodies bearing down on them and suddenly the corridor was silent and intensely, blindingly dark.

Maigrey caught a sobbing breath and waited impatiently for her eyes to adjust, although she knew it wouldn't make any difference. It would still be just as dark. A flash of pain that wasn't her own made her flinch.

"Dion!" she whispered. "We're . . . losing him!"

Sagan caught her by the elbow. "This way. Down the corridor. I found it . . ." He, too, was short of breath. ". . . before you brought the . . . army down us."

Another passageway opened up to their right and Maigrey felt, like a cool wind blowing against her cheek, a sense of the boy emanating from it.

But, behind them, the darkness was growing steadily brighter.

·─◁▪ ▪▷─·

They ran for it. Maigrey's legs ached, her breath burned in her throat and tore through her lungs. The mystical power, it seemed, enhanced the mind but not the body, and there was only so much strength the mind could lend to muscles that had been doing their duty for forty-plus years and seemed to think they deserved better than this.

The knowledge that they were nearing Dion and her own determination not to let Sagan know she was in any way weak spurred Maigrey to keep up with the Warlord nearly step for step. If she noted that he was running slower than he used to or heard him begin to labor for breath himself, she was too scared, too exhausted to register the fact.

"Stop!" Sagan came to a halt so suddenly that Maigrey stumbled into him. He steadied her, his arm around her waist. "Listen, I hear him."

Maigrey leaned against the Warlord, straining to hear above the pounding of blood in her ears. It wasn't a cry, but it might have been a silent scream. She wasn't certain whether she heard it in her head or in her heart.

"There!" She pointed down the corridor to a half-open door on their right. "That room."

"The one with the bright orange glow," Sagan said.

The light behind them was growing brighter, now that they had stopped, and she could hear, too, the whirring of wheels.

"Can you see him, my lady?"

Maigrey closed her eyes, trying to calm her fear and excitement enough to concentrate. The vision came to her almost immediately, however. She'd forgotten about the enhancement.

"He's lying on a steel table, like a surgical table. There are four . . . no . . . seven Corasians in the room with him. Two at the foot of the table, two on his left, one on his right, and two at the head. His feet are toward the door."

"Four will have their backs to us." Sagan reached to his belt, detached a lasgun, and handed it to her. "Aim high. I hope to God the boy won't sit up."

"I don't think he can," Maigrey murmured. She glanced at the gun and shook her head. "I'm not a very good shot, you know."

Sagan looked down at her. She could see the starjewel glitter in his eyes that were darker than the darkness. "I don't think it will matter," he said, and she felt the power heave and surge and tremble between them.

Maigrey reached for the gun. Their hands touched. A burning sensation shot through her arm, hurting her worse than the Corasian laser. She snatched back her hand.

"And don't forget to change the polarization," Sagan admonished.

"I wasn't going to!" Maigrey snapped, trying to convince herself that she was telling the truth, though she knew she was so keyed up and strung out that she would never have remembered. Hurriedly, hands shaking, she reset the gun and gripped it tightly.

Back pressed against the wall, hoping to escape immediate observation if one of the enemy happened to stick its sensors out the door, she eased forward. Sagan was by her side, a grenade in his left hand. Maigrey saw that he wore several attached to his belt and she cursed herself for not remembering to do the same.

After all, it'd been seventeen years!

Reaching the door, she paused, drew a deep breath, then lunged into the room. A quick glance showed her the boy still lying on the table. She raised the gun and fired four times in rapid succession, aiming high and in the general direction of those she was supposed to take out. Plastisteel exploded. Maigrey had a vague impression of a blast in the corridor behind her.

The four Corasians were no longer standing around the table; two were lying dead at her feet, a third was helpless, and a fourth was crawling out of its shell. Maigrey fired twice more and ran into the room.

Sagan plunged after her, the two never speaking but reacting to each other's thoughts, moving together in a chaotic dance to a music only they could hear.

Maigrey fired at the two standing at Dion's head. Sagan's sword whistled. He cut down the one standing on the far side of the steel table. Another Corasian that Maigrey hadn't seen emerged suddenly from behind some sort of diabolical machine.

Left! his thought came to her.

She turned, set her foot on a piece of something, and lost her balance. Her shot went wide. The Corasian aimed for her, point-blank. Sagan lunged at it, caught hold of the robotic body in his hands, lifted it, and hurled it against the machine. Fire spurted, electricity crackled, smoke spewed out.

And, for the moment, they were safe.

1040 and ticking.

Chapter ·◦◦○◦◦· Fifteen

Bone of my bone, and flesh of my flesh.

Genesis 2:23

Maigrey ran for the boy. Sagan returned to guard the doorway.

Metal clamps secured Dion's hands and feet. Maigrey sliced through them with her sword, casting Dion worried glances as she worked. The bloodsword's blade burned with an eerie luminescence, giving the boy's pallid face a whitish blue cast, turning the red-golden hair purple. A black stream of blood trickled from Dion's mouth, but, Maigrey determined swiftly, it didn't come from any internal injury. In the extremity of his pain, he'd bitten through his tongue. She could find no other wounds on his body.

Mental torture. The Corasians had developed it into an art form. After all, if the mind thinks its body's limbs are being hacked off, what's the difference if they're not? Don't want to damage tomorrow night's dinner; let's keep the meat intact, the juices flowing.

Maigrey laid her hand on Dion's forehead. The boy shivered at her touch and tossed his head, crying out frantically.

"Dion!" she said, trying to be gentle, yet conscious of the fact that the orange glow in the corridor was growing steadily brighter. "Dion, it's Lady Maigrey. Hush, there, it's all right."

"You sound like his nursemaid! Get him on his feet!" Sagan growled. He tossed a grenade. A flare of white light, an explosion, and the orange glow dimmed again.

"Dion!" Maigrey pleaded. Putting her arms beneath his shoulders, she raised the young man to a sitting position. He shook his head groggily and groaned in pain. "Dion"— Maigrey's voice grew stern—"you're all right. It's in your mind. There's nothing wrong with you."

Dion's eyes flew open, looked swiftly, wildly, at his right arm. He appeared puzzled, then stared at her. Maigrey saw the terror in his eyes and her heart ached for him, but he was going to be a lot more terrified if they didn't get out of here.

"Dion—" she began.

Sagan shoved her roughly aside. "Guard the door," he commanded, thrusting a grenade into her hand. "That's the last one."

Maigrey ran to the door and peered out. The corridor was dark in one direction; an orange glow, like a setting sun or a raging fire, lit the other. The Corasians were being cautious, waiting. They could have stormed the room, but why bother? The "meat" would be forced to come to them eventually. It occurred to her, too, that there probably weren't many of the enemy left on board. They would be forced to ration both supplies and energy this far from their home base, and so undoubtedly operated with the barest number of crew possible. Not that this mattered a lot. It only took one to kill you.

Maigrey glanced back over her shoulder, saw Sagan grab Dion by the collar of his flight suit, drag him from the table, and force him to stand. The boy's legs collapsed and he crumpled to the deck in a heap.

"Get up, boy. You look just like that Guardian of yours—Platus—groveling at my feet!"

Dion was awake, alert, the blue eyes glittering in the sword's light as brightly as the starjewel. Slowly, hand on the steel table, he pulled himself to his feet. His eyes never left Sagan's.

"Platus didn't grovel!" Dion's voice was thick; he spit blood. "I saw him. He faced you—"

"The Starfires, then. The blood of your father runs in your veins, runs piss-yellow!" Sagan laid his hand on the boy's shoulder.

"Why did you come for me, then?" Dion cried.

"Because I need a warm, living body with red hair and the Starfire eyes and genes and chromosomes. Whether or not that body has a backbone isn't my concern."

The Warlord gave Dion a shove that sent the boy stumbling across the deck toward the door. Maigrey caught him as he reeled into her. She saw tears in his eyes.

"Snap out of it!" Maigrey gave him a shake.

900 and still counting.

Maigrey took hold of one of Dion's arms; Sagan had the

other. Together, they guided the boy down the corridor. Dion walked like a blind man, uncaring, letting them take him where they would. "You didn't have to be that rough on him, my lord."

"I suppose I could have wakened him with a kiss, my lady, but at the moment it didn't occur to me. Here they come. Get behind us, boy!"

Dion's head snapped up. "I can fight," he said, and raised his bloodsword.

The Warlord heard the dullness in the tone and cast the young man a keen, speculative glance. "Good," was his only comment.

The orange glow burst upon them, fiery bolts whizzed around them. Maigrey hurled the last grenade. They flattened themselves against a wall, braced for the explosion, and when it came, jumped forward and dashed down the corridor before the debris had settled.

Dion moved in time with them, the bloodsword connecting their minds, playing its mystical music. The three slashed at anything that still glowed or moved. But that had been their last grenade. The exhilaration of the shared power could support the spirit but not the flesh.

The light of Maigrey's bloodsword was growing dim. She was losing energy. Sagan's sword, too, wasn't flaring as brightly. The breath whistled through his clenched teeth, and he winced when he swung the blade and paused to massage his shoulder. Dion fought numbly, the look on his face the look of one who walks in his sleep.

We're finished, thought Maigrey. We can't survive another onslaught. The darkness will close over us, enfold us, peaceful, restful. . . .

Darkness. Maigrey looked around. She was in darkness. They were standing in the corridor that led to the hangar decks, to their planes, to escape, and it was dark.

"Shut down the swords," came Sagan's command, and Maigrey reacted a split-second before he spoke. "Conserve your energy."

The light of the bloodswords gone, the starjewel gleamed brilliantly. Seeing Sagan's stern gaze fixed on it, Maigrey tucked the Star of the Guardians away beneath her body armor. The darkness around them was now complete and absolute.

"This is weird," Maigrey whispered. She thought, all in all, she preferred the enemy.

"How did you leave your plane, my lady?"

"As you ordered me, my lord. It'll blow in"—she was too distracted to calculate—"however many seconds we have left."

"779. What about your plane, boy? Where's the Scimitar?"

"I don't know. I can't remember," Dion said dispiritedly.

Maigrey heard the sound of a blow, not a gentle one.

Dion staggered back against her and she caught him and shoved him upright. Taut and tense, unnerved by the smothering darkness and the seconds beating faster than her heart, she was tempted to slap him herself.

"You have to!" Sagan said, his breathing labored. "You told me once that Platus taught you to take note of your surroundings. It was apparently the only worthwhile thing he ever did teach you. You'd better make use of it!"

Dion was silent. Maigrey, standing near him, could feel his body tremble.

"Down this corridor. Second hangar we'll come to on our right."

They activated the swords for light and protection and began to move stealthily down the passageway, Maigrey taking the front, Dion in the middle, Sagan walking behind, guarding the rear. Maigrey glided warily past each doorway, prepared to see it flung open; ready for the sudden attack.

Nothing. 598.

"This is it," called Dion.

They flattened themselves against the wall. Sagan motioned and Maigrey cautiously, sword at the ready, slid to the entryway and twisted her head around to peer inside. Cool air flowed from it, lifting her hair, drying the sweat on her scalp and temples.

"The plane's there. The hangar's empty. No sign of the enemy."

500.

"Then let's get the hell outta here," Dion said, scowling. He started forward.

Maigrey heard a click, the sound coming from somewhere near her ankle.

That was why there were no Corasians in sight.

She hurled herself at the boy and knocked him backward as far as she could carry him. Maigrey landed on top of Dion and

felt a heavy weight smash down across her. A strong hand
pressed her head down flat, covered her face and eyes.

A sheet of flame shot out into the corridor. The intense heat
seared the lungs; noxious fumes poisoned the air.

"Run!" Sagan grunted.

Twisting to his feet, he dragged Maigrey up and propelled
her forward. Shaken from the fall and dizzy from the fumes,
she pressed her hand over her nose and mouth and staggered
into the hangar. The air in here was cool, and she gasped for
breath. The bomb had burst outward, avoiding damage to the
coveted spaceplane.

439.

Sagan helped Dion into the hangar.

"Go on ahead," he commanded the stunned boy, "and get
the plane started."

Dion nodded wordlessly and ran past Maigrey, heading for
the Scimitar. She looked him over as he went by her. He
seemed unhurt, but she noted that he was rubbing the back of
his head with his hand.

I hit him pretty hard, she reflected ruefully.

Maigrey glanced out the hangar. The orange glow could be
dimly seen reflecting off the steel walls of the corridor—the
Corasians coming to see the results of their booby trap. Sagan
was searching for the controls to shut the doors. Sword ready,
Maigrey took her place by his side.

350.

Sagan found the controls. Copied from the human ships the
Corasians had scavenged, the mechanism was familiar and
easy to operate. The doors rumbled shut and the Warlord
slashed at the controls with his sword, effectively putting them
out of commission.

Maigrey sighed, and shut off the bloodsword. The darkness
that enveloped her now was welcome—cool shade to one
sweltering in blazing sun. Strength ebbed from her body,
every muscle ached, and it was going to take an effort to make
it to the plane. She should feel elated, but she didn't. She was
drained. Unable to see in the darkness, she tripped and fell
headlong over something unknown. Sagan caught hold of her
arm, supported her, steadied her.

His grip was strong, almost painful.

"Thank you, my lord. I'm all right now," she said, keeping
careful control of her voice. "You can let go of me."

Instead of releasing her, his hand tightened. He drew her

close, drew her to warmth and strength, a fast-beating heart and deep, quick breathing.

Maigrey hesitated, knowing that this was a seduction not of the body but of the soul. She saw in his mind what he wanted from her, what he wanted her to give him. She saw clearly what he could give to her.

A galaxy, with its billions of people, all looking to her in adoration, hailing her their queen.

Maigrey struggled, not against him, but against herself. His lips brushed the scar on her cheek; his chin, unshaven, was rough against her skin.

To rule was wrong, it wasn't her right; she hadn't been born to it.

That didn't mean she didn't deserve it. That didn't mean she couldn't take it.

Maigrey clasped her arms around the Warlord's body, pressing close to him, almost as though she would crawl inside him, become part of his flesh and blood and bone.

Sagan's mouth crushed against hers, drawing out her breath, her life.

300.

Something sharp was piercing her flesh—the edges of the starjewel. Drawing back from Sagan to catch her breath, she reached to break the chain around her neck, snatch off the necklace. Her hand closed over it.

A brilliant white light flared around her, nearly blinding her.

"I might have known," said a young and bitter voice.

The lights of the spaceplane illuminated the hangar with a harsh, artificial radiance that threw everything into sharp relief—white and black, seen and unseen, visible and lost in darkness. Maigrey freed herself from Sagan's embrace and twisted around. The Warlord let her go, but kept his hand on her shoulder, kept her near.

Dion stood in front of them, his arms crossed across his chest, his blue eyes wide and rimmed with white, his face pale and bloodless.

"Guardians! Old comrades! Pah!" The boy spit blood. "You were lovers!"

230 seconds.

Their lives were ticking away and they stood immobile.

225 seconds.

"I told you to start up the plane, boy," Derek Sagan said.

"Don't call me 'boy'!" Dion flashed. "My name is Starfire,

Dion Starfire!" He threw back his head proudly; the mane of
red-golden hair glistened in the shining light. "And I am your
king!"

His words echoed in the silent hangar. Maigrey clasped the
starjewel tightly, welcoming the scourge, the sharp points
pressing into her flesh. She stepped away from Sagan. His
hand lingered on her shoulder an instant. Maigrey tensed, her
body stiffened, and he let her go. Glancing at him, she saw his
lip curled in a sneer. His shadowed gaze was fixed on Dion.

"King? You're a whelp, a pup, and you'll do what I tell you
to do." The Warlord strode forward. "We have barely enough
time to escape. You may have cost us our lives, boy—"

Dion's bloodsword flared. The young man stepped in front
of the Warlord, blocking his path.

189 seconds.

Sagan activated his sword. He wasn't going to kill, Maigrey
knew. He was going to maim. A royal heir missing an arm or
a leg, his eyes slashed to eternal darkness, would be useful to
him still.

The Warlord raised his sword. Dion moved clumsily to
block the blow. Maigrey, forgotten, slid her sword noiselessly
back into its scabbard. Clenching her fists together, concen-
trating all the enhanced strength of mind and body, she lunged
forward and clubbed Sagan on the back of the neck, right
above the shoulder.

At the last moment, he was aware of her and tried to swing
around to defend himself, but she had the advantage. The
blow felled him; he sprawled unconscious at Maigrey's feet.

"You should have never let me get behind you, my lord."
Maigrey glanced up at Dion, who was staring at her, open-
mouthed.

"He'll be all right. We don't have much time. Help me carry
him to the plane."

"We could . . . leave him." Dion was white to the lips.

"We'd never get back onto *Phoenix* without him," Maigrey
returned.

100.

Between them, they dragged the Warlord to the plane and
pushed and shoved and hoisted him on board.

"You take the controls," Maigrey ordered.

Dion nodded and hastily sat down in the pilot's seat. The
Scimitar's cockpit was cramped and crowded with three of
them. Maigrey stretched Sagan out on the deck; she was too

tired to try to lift him into a seat. Hastily, she sat down in the co-pilot's chair next to Dion.

75 seconds.

The plane's engines roared.

"We can't get out!" Dion cried hoarsely. He pointed. "The hangar bay door's shut!"

70 seconds.

"It'll open. Automatically, when the plane's engines switch on. A safety precaution. That's how they're designed."

That's how *we* design them, Maigrey said to herself. That didn't mean the Corasians designed them that way. Or maybe they've had time to realize their booby trap didn't work. Maybe they've sealed us inside the hangar. . . .

65 seconds.

The plane lifted with a slamming blast from behind, the thrust of the engines propelling them forward. Slowly the steel doors shivered and began to open, then stopped. The Corasians, realizing their prize was slipping away, had shut them down.

"You can do it," Maigrey said, her hand closing over Dion's. "The opening's wide enough. Fly through the crack."

53 seconds.

If it wobbles, if he can't hold it steady, we'll crash.

Hold it . . . hold it . . .

The plane scraped through the opening, metal screeching, and then they were frantically clawing into open space. Traveling this fast this soon after starting up the engines was extremely dangerous—the computer was reminding them loudly of this fact in no uncertain terms. But it would be extremely dangerous not to. Maigrey glanced back, behind them.

2.

An explosion—a single explosion—tore apart the Corasian mothership. For one plane to blow up, it had done an incredible amount of damage. Maigrey waited for the second explosion, but it didn't come. Then she understood. She and Sagan had matched each other to the nth second. Their planes had blown up simultaneously.

Maigrey began to shake. It seemed her body was going to fall apart. Once again the flesh and sinew and muscles of his arms were around her, holding her close; his lips brushed against the scar on her cheek. Tears burned her eyes, seeped beneath the closed lids.

A sound came from behind her. Maigrey turned, fearfully, her hand on her bloodsword.

The Warlord was sitting up, rubbing the back of his neck. Glancing up at her, he said irritably, "For God's sake, my lady, stop sniveling!"

Chapter ❦⚬❦ Sixteen

The ceremony of innocence is drowned.
   William Butler Yeats, "The Second Coming"

"I'll take the controls."

His great height bent in the small spaceplane, the Warlord came up behind the pilot's chair.

Dion glanced at Maigrey.

"I'll take the controls," Sagan repeated, "or we'll stay out here in space and rot."

Maigrey shrugged. She was tired, very tired and thirsty, and she didn't care anymore. Dion rose. He and Sagan shifted positions, squeezing past each other in the cramped space, the Warlord sliding into the pilot's seat. Grimacing in pain, he reached to massage his aching neck and shoulder muscles.

"As I remember, you killed a man like that once, my lady."

"As I remember, my lord, I did so because he was about to kill you."

The Warlord said nothing; the memory she'd summoned like a specter from the grave was a disturbing one to him, bringing with it vivid images of magenta robes and dark lightning. He looked behind her, saw Dion slump over in his seat. Beneath the grime of battle, the young man's skin was pale. Sagan saw a tremor convulse the boy's body. The Warlord was expert in forms of torture. He had watched other men suffer it and he had endured his share, as had Lady Maigrey, once, long ago, when they'd been captured by the mind-seizers. That was when she had killed the man who had been about to . . .

Sagan shook his head in angry dispersal of the thought, and almost immediately regretted the move. A flash of hot pain shot through his neck. He glanced at Maigrey. Her eyes were closed; she might have been asleep. Sagan's hands and part of his brain concentrated on flying the spaceplane, another part sorted thoughts.

Dion was growing to look increasingly like a Starfire. His lips didn't tighten, they tended to pout. He brooded, lived too much in the mind. Dion's father—the crown prince—had been, in Sagan's estimation, a fop, an affected dandy, a pseudointellectual. Starfire had managed to marry one of the most beautiful and spirited women in the galaxy, but Sagan didn't give him credit for that—the wedding had been arranged, as was usual with the Blood Royal. Admittedly, from what Sagan's heard, Starfire had died bravely, fighting overwhelming odds, trying to save his wife and newborn son.

The Warlord's fist clenched over the controls. To this day, seventeen years later, their deaths still galled him. He hadn't meant that tragedy to happen. It *shouldn't* have happened, as Robes realized soon after, when the Guardians had managed to escape with the boy. The President would have been much better advised to have followed Sagan's suggestion—keep the Royal Family alive, use them for propaganda purposes, allow them to sink into the mire of parties and dinner balls given by elderly and infirm duchesses.

But Robes hadn't listened to Sagan's advice. And now Sagan had a good idea of who had made the decision to kill the king. This Other—as the Warlord was wont to think of him, preferring not to give him a name—had taken control of the minds of the mob. He had driven them to murder and to mayhem. The king and crown prince had been made martyrs, the vanished heir a subject of romantic speculation and fomenting royalist revolt.

The Other. The Warlord's clenched fist trembled. His arm ached with the tension and he forced himself to end this dark and unnerving train of thought. He glanced, out of the corner of his eye, at Maigrey. His thoughts had not been well guarded. She might have read them, discovered his weakness, his one real fear.

The lady leaned back in her chair, her eyes open now and staring out into space. Her face was covered with soot and black ash, her tears had made tracks through the grime—a mockery of the scar on her skin. Who had she been crying for—herself . . . or for him?

The pale hair, damp with sweat, had come undone from its braid; it clung to her forehead and hung limply, lifelessly around her shoulders. He remembered—with a deep, wrenching pain—the fine strands of hair tangled in his fingers. The pain was lust, desire, but not necessarily for a brief moment of sexual gratification. The enhancement of their mental powers, of his own powers, magnified by hers— that was his true desire. He must find a way to make that happen . . . permanently.

The Star of the Guardians, untouched by blood or the soot of battle, rested lightly on her breast. It rose and fell with her even breathing, sparkling brilliantly in the dim lights of the plane's interior. Maigrey's thoughts, he sensed, were turned inward, on herself, wrestling with her own fears—or her own desires.

The Star of the Guardians.

Sagan cast a final glance back at the boy. He'd succeeded in one goal, at least. He'd broken Dion's spirit. The Warlord had now, if he wanted, a limp doll, a spineless puppet that would dance at his bidding.

I should be pleased. Derek Sagan cursed himself. What damning weakness within him always shriveled the sweet fruit of victory every time he brought it to his mouth?

··◁▪ ▪▷··

It was bitterly cold in the plane. Maigrey, shivering, missing her flight suit, huddled into the seat for warmth. She should have been watching Sagan, should have been probing, touching his mind, trying to discover and forestall whatever might be his next design. But she didn't dare come near him. She felt his lips on her cheek, more painful than when he'd inflicted that first wound. She banished the feeling, banished the pain and tried to banish the memory of the power, the knowledge that—for a moment—they'd been invincible.

Maigrey shifted to look back at Dion. His head drooped. He was shaking so, it seemed as if he must crumble into pieces. For a moment he'd been king. Now he was . . . ordinary. Maigrey turned away in dull despair. It was hopeless. Why keep fighting?

Her gaze shifted to the viewport and she saw, reflected back to her, shining brighter against the blackness than a real sun, the light of the starjewel. White, glistening, pure.

Only the dead are without hope.

Maybe, she thought. But they have other benefits.

Sighing, Maigrey crossed her arms and tucked her hands beneath them for warmth.

"The enemy," Sagan said.

Maigrey jumped, and refocused her gaze. The Corasian fighters had ceased their attack. Confused, lacking direction, they drifted aimlessly—easy targets for the Warlord's men. It was only a matter now of picking them off.

"It seems you have won, my lord," Maigrey said.

"Try not to let your elation overwhelm you, my lady."

The Warlord turned to face her, his eyes fixed on her, drawing her eyes to his, and she shuddered, for all within him was dark and empty and, like a black hole, seemed to suck her inside.

You should have left me to die, my lady. He spoke those words to her mind. The next, he spoke aloud. "Computer, transmit this message to *Defiant*: Lord Derek Sagan to Captain Michael Williams. Battle won. You may proceed with the extermination of the mercenaries as planned. Take no prisoners."

"What?"

Perhaps nothing else would have jolted Dion to life. The young man was on his feet, gripping the back of the Warlord's chair with white-knuckled hands.

"You can't! You promised! You gave them a pardon!"

"So I did, boy. They'll face their God—if they have one— free of sin."

"They trusted you! I"—the boy's voice rattled in his throat— "*I* trusted you!"

"That's your misfortune and theirs. Computer! Where's the verification of the transmission?"

"Do something, Lady Maigrey!" Dion turned to her, his blue eyes glittering, hard and piercing. "Stop him!"

Maigrey did not look at the boy. Her face was empty of expression, devoid of warmth, of life. But her arms uncrossed, her hand moved slowly and stealthily to the bloodsword.

"Transmission failed, sir," the computer reported.

"Check for damage!"

"Checking, sir."

"And try to raise *Phoenix!*"

Fuming, Sagan ran his hand rapidly over the control panel, his attention focused on the dials, activating, shutting down, reactivating, and once giving something a sharp rap with his thumb and forefinger.

Maigrey's hand closed over the hilt of the bloodsword,

driving the needles into her flesh. She waited, hoping Dion would take the hint.

"No damage, sir."

"Then transmit!" Sagan snarled.

What was the boy waiting for? Maigrey wondered impatiently. Did he expect her to rise up and attack, start a fight to the death in this small, cramped space? They'd all end up dead, and while that might solve her problems, it certainly wouldn't do much for Dion's.

"Verify transmission of message to *Defiant*."

"Transmission failed, sir. Damage recheck negative—"

Maybe it was her imagination, but Maigrey thought the computer was beginning to sound panicked. She gripped the sword tightly, keeping it hidden by her thigh, and concentrated her thoughts on Dion. To her relief, she heard a rustle of fabric behind her and the very slight gasp of pain when the boy closed his sore palm over the needles.

Maigrey spoke to him silently, through the bloodsword, keeping her thoughts carefully shielded from Sagan.

Dion, can you understand me?

Yes! He was nervous, excited, angry, and hurt. His emotions were a jumble and tangling up his thoughts.

Calm yourself, Dion. Sagan can't get his order through. There's still a chance to warn Dixter. Count backward. Do something to clear your mind. Don't take a deep breath, though; Sagan would hear you.

Ten. Seven. Six . . . six . . . fourthreetwoone. There. I'm all right.

Well, Maigrey thought, it will have to do.

When we reach Phoenix, *steal a plane and fly to* Defiant *and—*

Steal . . . How?

You have clearance. You can go anywhere. You know the codes; they'll let you fly out without saying a word.

Fear. Terrible, debilitating fear flowed from the boy like a cold and sickening wave. Whatever had happened to Dion in that spaceplane out there must have been horrible.

You go, Lady Maigrey. I . . . I can't fly, ever again. I'll help you—

Maigrey understood. She pitied the boy. And she hardened her heart against him. It had to be done. This plan might not save the mercenaries. But it could save her king.

*No, Dion. I must stay behind. Sagan will try to stop you.
And I'm the only one who can stop him.*

"Computer!" The Warlord's harsh voice. "Activate emergency landing distress code, since we can do nothing else."

Phoenix loomed large in the viewport. They would be landing in minutes. Maigrey released her hand from the bloodsword. Sagan's attention might return to them at any moment, but it wasn't that danger which caused her to break the connection. She didn't want to cajole or urge Dion or force him. That wouldn't help. He had to decide to take this risk on his own. He would never do it to save himself; he was thinking too little of himself right now. But a threat to others, to people he loved, might impel him to act. The urge to protect and defend. It was in his blood—the Blood Royal.

Or it had been, once.

"Emergency distress signal sent, sir."

A docking bay door yawned wide to receive them. Maigrey could see a flurry of activity inside. They wouldn't know the nature of the emergency and there'd be medics and crash squads and fire details. Chaos. Confusion. And *Phoenix* had undergone heavy shelling, had doubtless sustained serious damage. The Warlord's full attention would be claimed the moment he set foot on deck.

No, it wouldn't.

Maigrey closed her eyes.

I'll have to kill him this time.

Chapter ·❦✺❦· Seventeen

The end is where we start from.
T. S. Eliot, "Little Gidding"

Emergency personnel in their ungainly, protective suits swarmed over the plane when it was safely down. The Warlord lifted the top hatch, and men peered into the cockpit. Their faces, dimly seen through the panels of the huge helmets they wore, registered extreme astonishment at the sight of their Warlord seated in the prototype Scimitar.

"Get that thing out of my face!" Sagan snarled, shoving aside a man waving a radiation detector at him. The Warlord rose from his seat, obviously glad to stretch to his full height.

"Admiral Aks!" A lieutenant was shouting into a commlink. "Lord Sagan's arrived safely, sir! Yes, sir. Docking bay sixteen. Yes, sir. I'll relay the message, sir."

The emergency crews were scattering, disappearing to attend to some other pressing duty. Red lights were flashing, Maigrey could hear the distant sound of drums.

The lieutenant's head popped up in the viewport. "My lord, Admiral Aks requests your presence on the bridge. As quickly as possible, my lord."

Sagan released the side hatch and started to exit. "I'm on my way. First, send this message to *Defiant*—"

The harsh sound of weeping interrupted him. Maigrey turned, the Warlord glanced around. Dion was bent double, head buried in his arms, sobbing. His body shook; he could scarcely draw a breath.

Disgust darkened Sagan's face. His lips twisted in a sneer. "He seems to have inherited your weakness for tears, my lady. Lieutenant, send for Dr. Giesk."

"I'll stay here with him until help comes," Maigrey offered. She tasted despair like gall in her mouth.

455

The Warlord paused and looked at her, intently, steadily, and Maigrey could have sworn, in that instant, that he knew everything. If so, he must be triumphant, she thought and couldn't help but avert her gaze, biting her lip to keep from screaming in frustration.

He turned without a word. When she was able to risk looking after him, she saw him striding across the hangar deck.

"Is he gone?" came a clear, cool voice.

Astonished, Maigrey whirled around. Dion lifted himself up out of his seat. There wasn't a trace of a tear on his face.

"You're all right?" Maigrey gasped.

"No, but I notice that doesn't seem to stop anybody around here." Dion drew a deep breath. "I'll fly this plane to *Defiant*."

"My God, child, I'm glad you're . . . you're not ordinary!" It was all she could think of to say. "You'll have to leave quickly, while there's no one in the hangar. Give John my . . . my love"—Dixter would understand, he always understood—"and godspeed, young man!" She added fervently. "Godspeed!"

Dion caught hold of her. "Come with me! Give John Dixter your love yourself! We've tricked the Warlord. We'll be away from here before he knows we're gone!"

Maigrey recalled the look Sagan'd given her before he left. "He'll know," she said.

"Lady, please—"

"You have your duty, Your Majesty, and I have mine. Yours is to your people. Mine is to you."

Dion's blue eyes flared beneath the flaming hair, the reddish brows creased, the underlip thrust out. He was a Starfire, and they were accustomed to having everything they wanted. He was afraid, too. The fear must twist inside him. He didn't want to go by himself.

"Our duty isn't easy sometimes, Dion, but it must be done. It's what we were born to do." Maigrey clasped his hand and held it fast. "You won't be alone, Dion."

The struggle was brief and bitter. When it ended, the boy's lips had tightened into a straight, dark line.

"I'll be alone. I'll always be alone. It's what I was born to." Dion released her hand. "God be with *you*, at least, Guardian. If that's what you want."

Maigrey backed away.

Dion sealed shut the hatch and did not look at her again. Through the viewscreen she could see him—face set and rigid, the blue eyes a sheet of ice, jaw hard and clenched. The red-golden hair burned like living flame.

Dion was a Starfire, and they were kings.

Acknowledgments

I would like to thank my excellent friend and science adviser, Gary Pack, for his creation of the bloodsword and the really horrible and terrifying new weapon featured in the next book.

I would like to thank Janet Pack for moral support, even if she didn't know who wrote "I love my truck"!

I would like to thank Patrick Price and his mother, Camille Chasteen, for their translation of the French language in this text and John Hefter for the translation of the Latin.

I would like to thank my wonderful friend and co-author (on most everything except this), Tracy Hickman, for his overall help and inspiration.

DARKSWORD ADVENTURES
by Margaret Weis & Tracy Hickman

In the enchanted realm of Thimhallan, magic is life, and the fate of the world rests in the hands of the one who wields the powerful, magic-absorbing Darksword . . .

Now the Darksword saga comes to life in this all-new fantasy role-playing game that takes you to a time when Magicians and Technologists battled to rule the world. A companion volume for gamers and nongamers alike, DARKSWORD ADVENTURES is an indispensable Who's Who guide to the world of Darksword that no fan of the bestselling trilogy will want to be without. Here is the full, never-before-told history of Trimhallan, the secret texts of its priestly caste and expanded character backgrounds of Joram, Saryon, Bishop Vanya, King Garald, the Duuk-tsarith and much more.

Including a full set of rules and guidelines for play, this single volume contains everything you need to join the adventure. Let the quest for the Darksword begin!

0 553 17681 1

ROSE OF THE PROPHET III
THE PROPHET OF AKHRAN
by Margaret Weis & Tracy Hickman

From the authors of the bestselling *Darksword Trilogy*.

Since time began, twenty Gods have ruled all the universe. Though each God possessed different abilities, each was all-powerful within his realm. Now one of the Gods has upset the balance of power . . .

As the Great War of the Gods rages, it seems as though the terrible Quar, God of Reality, Greed and Law, will emerge the victor. Even the immortals have abandoned their mortal masters to join in the battle above.

Trapped without their immortal servants on the shore of the Kurdin Sea, Khardan, Zohra, and the wizard Mathew must cross the vast desert known as the Sun's Anvil – a feat no man has ever performed.

Like the legendary Rose of the Prophet, the nomads struggle to survive the journey. If they succeed, they will face more than combat with the enemy, for the Amir's hardened warriors are led by Achmed, the fiercest of men . . . and Khardan's brother.

THE PROPHET OF AKHRAN

Volume 3 in the wondrous trilogy of forbidden romance, betrayal, and magic.
ROSE OF THE PROPHET

0 553 40177 7

ON MY WAY TO PARADISE
by Dave Wolverton

Here is a powerful first novel, at once disturbing and compelling – the chronicle of one man's odyssey of self-discovery within a world at war.

In a world of ever-worsening crisis, Angelo Osic is an anomaly: a man who cares about others. One day he aids a stranger . . . and calls down disaster, for the woman called Tamara is also a woman on the run, the only human with the knowledge that will save Earth from the artificial intelligences plotting to overthrow it.

Fleeing the assassins who seek him now as well as Tamara, Angelo seizes the only escape route available: to sign on as a mercenary with the Japanese Motoki Corporation in its genocidal war against the barbarian Yabajin. Jacked into training machines that simulate warfare, Angelo "dies" a hundred times . . . and is resurrected to fight again. In a world of death, he dreams only of life – and the freedom to love once more.

Vivid and passionate, *On My Way to Paradise* is a major accomplishment by an award-winning writer. It is a story not easily to be forgotten.

0 553 27610 7

THE POSTMAN
by David Brin

"TO ALL CITIZENS: Let it be known by all now living within the legal boundaries of the United States of America that the people and fundamental institutions of the nation survive. A provisional government is vigorously moving to restore law, public safety and liberty once more to this beloved land . . ."

In a few years from now, a handful of men and women struggle to survive in the dark days after a devastating war, battling disease and hunger, fear and brutality.

Gordon Krantz is one such man, an itinerant story-teller. One night, he borrows the jacket and bag of a long-dead postal worker to protect himself from the cold. In the next village he visits, he finds the old uniform still has power as a symbol of hope, for the return of an age now gone.

Unwilling to disillusion the villagers, Gordon accepts their letters to loved ones who may or may not still live, and in doing so creates his greatest tale, of an America on the road to recovery. His deception takes on a reality of its own, as others come to join him, supported by the strength of a vision he himself only half-believed.

'It is a powerful novel; a perfect example of a good story told with emotional honesty and depth, resonant with myth'
FANTASY REVIEW

0 553 17193 3

THE UPLIFT WAR
by David Brin

David Brin's epic *Startide Rising* swept the Nebula, Hugo and Locus Awards. Now this master storyteller returns us to this extraordinary, wonder-filled world. Drawing on the startling events of *Startide*, he tells a tale of courage, survival and discovery.

As galactic armadas clash in quest of the ancient fleet of the Progenitors, a brutal alien race seizes the dying planet of Garth. The various Uplifted inhabitants of Garth must battle their overlords or face ultimate extinction. At stake is the existence of Terran society and Earth, and the fate of the entire Five Galaxies. Sweeping, brilliantly crafted, inventive and dramatic, *The Uplift War* is an unforgettable story of adventure and wonder from the pen of one of today's science fiction greats.

0 553 17452 5

A SELECTION OF SCIENCE FICTION AND FANTASY TITLES AVAILABLE FROM BANTAM BOOKS

THE PRICES SHOWN BELOW WERE CORRECT AT THE TIME OF GOING TO PRESS. HOWEVER TRANSWORLD PUBLISHERS RESERVE THE RIGHT TO SHOW NEW RETAIL PRICES ON COVERS WHICH MAY DIFFER FROM THOSE PREVIOUSLY ADVERTISED IN THE TEXT OR ELSEWHERE.

☐	17193 3	THE POSTMAN	David Brin	£3.50
☐	17452 5	UPLIFT WAR	David Brin	£3.99
☐	17351 0	THE STAINLESS STEEL RAT GETS DRAFTED	Harry Harrison	£2.99
☐	17352 9	THE STAINLESS STEEL RAT'S REVENGE	Harry Harrison	£2.99
☐	17396 0	STAINLESS STEEL RAT SAVES THE WORLD	Harry Harrison	£2.50
☐	17154 2	DAMIANO	R. A. MacAvoy	£2.99
☐	17155 0	DAMIANO'S LUTE	R. A. MacAvoy	£2.50
☐	23205 3	TEA WITH BLACK DRAGON	R. A. MacAvoy	£1.95
☐	17532 7	DESOLATION ROAD (60)	Ian McDonald	£3.99
☐	40044 4	OUT ON BLUE SIX (50) (B)	Ian McDonald	£4.99
☐	17681 1	DARKSWORD ADVENTURES	Margaret Weis & Tracy Hickman	£3.99
☐	17586 6	FORGING THE DARKSWORD	Margaret Weis & Tracy Hickman	£3.99
☐	17535 1	DOOM OF THE DARKSWORD	Margaret Weis & Tracy Hickman	£3.50
☐	17536 X	TRIUMPH OF THE DARKSWORD	Margaret Weis & Tracy Hickman	£3.50
☐	40265 X	DEATHGATE CYCLE 1: DRAGON WING	Margaret Weis & Tracy Hickman	£4.99
☐	02015 4	DEATHGATE CYCLE 2: ELVEN STAR	Margaret Weis & Tracy Hickman	£12.99
☐	17684 6	ROSE OF THE PROPHET 1: THE WILL OF THE WANDERER	Margaret Weis & Tracy Hickman	£3.99
☐	40045 2	ROSE OF THE PROPHET 2: THE PALADIN OF THE NIGHT	Margaret Weis & Tracy Hickman	£3.99
☐	40177 7	ROSE OF THE PROPHET 3: THE PROPHET OF AKHRAN	Margaret Weis & Tracy Hickman	£4.50
☐	27610 7	ON MY WAY TO PARADISE	Dave Halverton	£3.99

All Corgi/Bantam Books are available at your bookshop or newsagent, or can be ordered from the following address:

Corgi/Bantam Books,
Cash Sales Department,
P.O. Box 11, Falmouth, Cornwall TR10 9EN

Please send a cheque or postal order (not currency) and allow 80p for postage and packing for the first book plus 20p for each additional book ordered up to a maximum charge of £2.00 in UK.

B.F.P.O. customers please allow 80p for the first book and 20p for each additional book.

Overseas customers, including Eire, please allow £1.50 for postage and packing for the first book, £1.00 for the second book, and 30p for each subsequent title ordered.